C000108494

NATHAN AND ALEX

A. M. CRIDLAND

www.mariuspublishing.co.uk

PRINTED IN THE UK

NATHAN AND ALEX

MARIUS PUBLISHING

Originally published in Great Britain by Marius publishing

Printing history: Marius publishing edition printed 2012

ISBN: 978-0-9573324-0-9

Address for Marius publishing can be found at:
www.mariuspublishing.co.uk

For everyone that
knows true love.

Acknowledgements

To Caz, Laura, Ed and Gaelle, you are four of the best friends a person could have, thank you for your unerring championing and constant support.

To my parents, James and Harry, Auntie Maglit and the rest of the family who upped sticks and shoved off to Australia, a huge thank you for always being supportive and proud of my achievements. Thank you too, to Jose and Simon for all the coffees and chats, and for being two of the most positive people I know.

To Doctor Spring for making me laugh so hard my cheeks hurt through our consultations, and to the John Radcliffe Hospital in Oxford, for putting me back together. To Bill for being a gentleman, and to Jimmy, Paul, Polis and Karen, your support and guidance has been invaluable.

And to everybody that reads my book, I hope it brings you joy and I wish you the very best.

Chapter one.

Nathan sat in class that afternoon for the hundredth time wanting desperately to stop thinking about Alex, the most popular jock in school, who had no self esteem issues and was also liked by everyone because he was just so damn nice. Nathan hadn't ever thought he was gay but since this term had begun again and they'd all grown up a bit, all he could think about was how deliciously shiny and brown and soft Alex's hair looked, his skin was so clear and in the locker room he'd noticed his arms and taut abs and had had to make himself look away fast.

What the hell was happening to him ? He knew he must always have seemed like a loser to Alex but he still couldn't change how he felt. Every now and again he could feel him look in his direction, he probably wasn't actually looking directly at him he decided but he deliberately didn't look back. Every time it happened, the most awful thing was that Nathan felt himself blush so he'd developed a strategy of both hiding his face with his right hand and grimacing as he did so, as if in pain, so if Alex saw the colour of his cheeks he would think he had a sports injury or something. At last the bell went to end the lesson and everyone headed off for lunch, Nathan felt himself calming down as the lunch chaos ensued but suddenly he realised that almost everyone had gone except a couple of drifters fumbling through their bags and they departed almost at once, and then it was just him, and horror of horrors, Alex !

He felt his breathing quicken at once and tried to look interested in his text book as if he was just looking something up. Oh no ! He saw Alex get up and move toward him. This was no good, very soon he would be actually right by his side. Concentrate on the book, concentrate on the book he thought until... "Hi," Alex stood beside his desk, medium height, slim, and utterly beautiful in every respect. Nathan could barely breath, he daren't look up. "Look, I know we haven't chatted much recently Nathan and I hope you don't mind me asking, but you seemed to be in some kind of pain in that lesson, is everything alright ? Are you ok ?" Nathan nodded but then he had to look at Alex's perfect face and he couldn't help but blush. "That's really nice of you," he husked, it's just my ankle, I think I sprained it in rugby yesterday." "Well it must be pretty sore, you didn't look well all lesson. Do you want me to take a look ? I'm doing first aid and it could help both of us." Nathan felt breathless, my God, Alex could actually be touching him soon. "No!" He jumped up and grabbed his books, "No, that's so kind but no, I'm ok." He tried to sound normal and didn't at all.

5

Alex frowned.

"Nathan ? I thought we were friends, have I upset you or something ?" "No!" Nathan tried to smile and then bolted from the room. For the rest of the week he actively avoided Alex but it seemed only to spur him on to keep seeking Nathan out. He couldn't understand it, he knew he'd been almost rude to him. Two more weeks went by and this funny dance continued between them, then a day came that would change everything. In Art, the class were left entirely alone at the end of the lesson to clear up and Nathan was the last one as usual, he liked to be thorough and it was the last lesson of the day, most people therefore sprinted for the hills instantly but Nathan liked this extra time to be organised and sometimes finish a project with a bit more style than most.

On this particular Thursday night however, he was about to pack up his last bits when he started to think about Alex again and managed to catch his hand in the heavy supply door, he knew he'd cut it immediately but it was more the pain to the bony outside that sent him reeling. "Fuck !" He swore through clenched teeth of pain and doubled over hugging the injured hand. After a minute of initial agony he gingerly raised it and looked, there was a small superficial cut but more than that there was going to be a huge painful bruise as the whole area was purple and deep red. He didn't know what to do and thought some cold water might help but as soon as his hand was under the tap it hurt like hell and he yelped. From behind him someone said, "hey ? Are you ok ? Hey, Nathan, it's you ! Oh my God what have you done ?" It was Alex, he let his books and sports bag drop onto the nearest table, he looked shocked. "Let me see?" He asked with worried eyes and this time Nathan was glad to be in real pain as he thought it might make him less red. He let Alex carefully take his hand and have a look, he examined it and then asked Nathan to sit down while he got the first aid kit.

" How did you do it ?" He asked as he stood beside him and unclipped the first aid box. He started to rifle amongst sterile wipes and bandages. " I closed it in the supply door, duh eh ?" Nathan genuinely shook his head at his own stupidity. Alex laughed and looked fondly at him in a way that he didn't quite recognise but made his heart flip over. "Do you mind if I bandage you ?" Alex asked. "No, if you think it needs it," Nathan replied and actually felt totally at ease for a moment. "I do," Alex got out some bandages and bits and pieces. He ripped the packet open on a sterile wipe and said, "this might sting a little." He gently applied the wipe to the wound and Nathan nearly leapt off his seat. It took all his strength to just clench his eyes shut and restrict his language to "Jesus !" Alex looked anxiously at him, "ooh, sorry, sorry...I know, these things sting like buggery." "You're telling me !" Said Nathan and blew out a deep breath. Alex eyed him carefully again and proceeded with bandaging his hand. When it was done he cleared everything up and then said, "Are you going to the bus ? I'll walk with you." Nathan smiled, luckily his hand really did hurt so his face flushed a lot less than usual.

The two boys walked to the stop and boarded the bus together, they shared the first ten minutes of the ride before Alex got off and to his utter surprise, Nathan found that he did actually seem interested in him. As Alex talked Nathan couldn't help hoping that he could like him in a different kind of way and when it came to his stop it was difficult to hold back. For a second he almost leaned in and kissed Alex but managed to hide his desire and seemed kinda lacklustre in his goodbye. Alex was already heading to the stairs to make his exit but he frowned and looked back, "Nathan, have I...I mean, did I just do something then that you didn't like ? You seem a bit funny with me ?" Nathan blushed for all he was worth, there was no hiding it, "No!" He shrieked, "no Alex, you never do anything wrong to me, it's just, erm.." the bus was about to go, " look, ring me later yes, tell me then. Don't forget." Alex said and pelted down the stairs just in time. Nathan peered forward out of the window and was more than surprised to see Alex standing in the rain looking up at him as the bus departed. He blanched, what did that mean ?

That night he was quiet at supper and though it was nice chatting with his sister and brother and watching telly, having a great talk with his parents about a holiday this year and stuff, he was very glad to be undressed and comfortable in his dark blue jersey pj bums by ten o'clock and reading in bed. He liked hearing the others still bustling about in the house as he read. When his eyes got tired he leant his head back on the pillow and held his hand up to admire Alex's handy work, it was very neat. He started to yawn and switched out the light, slowly he drifted off to sleep. An hour passed and he became aware of a noise having woken him. He raised his head to listen and realised that someone was throwing pebbles at his window. His heart quickened as he stumbled to the glass and peered out. He was stunned at first to see Alex standing below in a grey hoodie and jeans. "Hi," Alex stage whispered as he swung the window open. "Can I come up ?" Nathan glanced at the clock and then back at Alex, was this really happening ? "Ok, how ?" He ventured back. "I'm a good climber," said Alex and began to ascend the trellis to the flat roof above the laundry room below, then he shinned up the rest of the trellis to Nathan's room. Nathan helped him in and Alex pulled the window to but didn't shut it, he breathed hard for a minute from the climb. He grinned at Nathan who looked dumbfounded. He was utterly terrified, what if Alex found out what he felt for him ? He gulped and lay back down on his bed. Alex stood still for a moment and just looked at him, then he slowly walked over and sat on the edge of the bed.

"What are you doing here ?" Asked Nathan, " I mean, not that it's not nice, it really is but...what do you want ?" Alex rubbed a finger over his own lips, thoughtful for a moment, he gulped a little nervously and then looking Nathan straight in the eye in the moonlight he said, "Put your head back down on the pillow." Nathan's heart began to race but he did it anyway. With his eyes never leaving Nathan's face, Alex climbed onto the bed properly, lying right next to him. He propped himself up on his elbow and scanned Nathan's face. " Close your eyes for me," he whispered. Nathan could hardly breath, he looked up anxiously and licked his lips. "Go on," Alex smiled and ran a finger softly down his cheek. Nathan thought he might pass out but slowly closed his eyes anyway, breathing hard. He lay still and waited for whatever was to come next, and then Alex's lips touched his.

He groaned beneath Alex who moaned back and licked between his lips, Nathan opened his mouth to accept Alex's tongue and let him suck at his lips and moan while he sank his tongue over and over again into Nathan's hot throat. Eventually he pulled away and looked down at him, he kept one hand on his cheek, stroking him lovingly. Nathan gazed in ecstatic joy and wonder up at him. "Oh my God," he whispered. Alex grinned and kissed his lips lightly again. "Where did that come from ?" Nathan breathed. "I've liked you for so long Nathan, so so long." Alex whispered, gazing adoringly at him. Nathan couldn't quite take it in. "you have ?" "Yes," said Alex and swept his gaze down the bed over the rest of Nathan's body. "You are so toned and beautiful, look at you." He ran his hand across Nathan's skin, sweeping it over his taut chest and abs and swirling it down over his tummy button, just above the waist of his pjs. Nathan gasped and lifted his hips up. "You like that eh?" Alex husked naughtily. Nathan was so turned on, he had never had an erection like it. Alex swirled his hand above his pjs still and Nathan screwed his eyes up. "Oh God," he groaned.

"Would you take these off and let me touch you ?" Alex whispered. Nathan thought he would explode immediately, this was unreal. He gulped and opened his eyes, "yes," he whispered back. Alex bent and kissed him again, his tongue deep, deep inside Nathan's mouth. When he pulled away he said, "I don't want to scare you," he stroked Nathan's face gently and lovingly, "but if you take them off, I want to lie on your bed and have you slide into my mouth, will you ?" Nathan covered his face with his hands, he could hardly believe this. A few seconds passed and he uncovered his eyes, he was almost panting but he nodded slowly and reached down to push them off.

Alex stroked his face and did not look down at his nakedness. He kissed him deeply, deeply again and then rolled underneath him. He shifted down the bed a bit and pulled Nathan's hips toward himself. Nathan was so hard, he gasped as Alex manoeuvred him into position and then as he lowered himself down and Alex gently pulled on his hips he began to pant. Suddenly he was in Alex's mouth and the pleasure was like nothing he'd ever known before. Automatically he plunged his hips up and down, spearing himself into Alex and groaning as loudly as he dared so as not to wake his parents. Alex sucked him like the most delicious thing he'd ever tasted and after just a minute or two Nathan knew he was about to come, his whole body tensed with ecstasy and he thrust his cock deep into Alex's willing jaws, it was so so good, with four more thrusts he burst into Alex's throat and exploded inside him. He jerked and gasped as Alex licked every drop of him up. When he'd stopped thrusting, Alex moved out from underneath and disappeared into the bathroom. He came back quickly smelling minty fresh and with a lovely happy look on his face. He took off his top and climbed into bed beside Nathan. He touched his cheek and kissed his lips. Nathan stared at him in wonder, barely able to speak.

"You're not offended are you?" Alex breathed. "Offended ?" Nathan looked mystified, "you just gave me the greatest pleasure of my life." Alex beamed and caressed his cheek. "Can I stay in your bed until 5.30am if we set your alarm and then I'll run home and change and meet you at school ?" He asked. "I'd love that," Nathan smiled. "Good," Alex clicked off the light and snuggled down beside him. He kissed him on the forehead and sighed contentedly. Nathan shook his head. "What is it ?" Alex whispered. "I just can't believe this," Nathan husked in the darkness.

Alex made the duvet crackle as he moved to a more comfy cuddle position, "believe it," he whispered. Then he propped himself up on his elbows and looked down at him. "Can you see me in the moonlight?" "Just." "That's good enough," he whispered and started to smooth his finger along Nathan's cheeks again. "This isn't about one night for me Nathan, I've liked you for a long long time," he looked away, " but if I'm honest, I'd say that I've been in love with you for most of that too." Nathan gawped, wide eyed. "You love me ?.... but I, erm.....oh my God!" He whispered. Alex nodded and smiled at him. "Is that ok?" Nathan nodded very very slowly and stared at him. Eventually he gulped and exhaled heavily, "it's more than ok with me Alex." "Good," Alex beamed and lay his head down. "Maybe one day quite soon I'll be able to hear you say you love me too. Night night Nathan, sleep well." They snuggled into each other and Nathan's heart took a long time to take in what had happened and slow down, it was so utterly wonderful. In total happiness he drifted off to sleep.

The alarm went off as planned at 5.30am, Nathan was glad he'd moved it so close to their heads so that it didn't wake the house up. They both yawned and stretched, the bed was so invitingly warm. Alex pressed his face back into the pillow for a moment, "oh I don't want to go," he moaned. Nathan smiled, "I know it's cold this time in the morning." "No I don't want to leave you," he whispered. Nathan snorted a little laugh. Alex propped himself up on his elbow, "can I ask you something ?" "Yes of course."

"Why did you seem so off with me over the last few weeks, did I piss you off ?" Nathan shook his head, "no, when I came back to school this term I... erm...," he squirmed, "well I just couldn't stop thinking about you and I didn't want you to see because I had no idea you felt the same way and I was scared." Alex closed his eyes, he was blushing now in the dim summer sunrise. He reached over and touched Nathan's cheek, "that's so great Nathan," he blinked and his face was very serious. They stared at each other. "Would you like to do something this weekend with me?" Nathan smiled and nodded. The alarm sounded again and Alex groaned, "oh no, why do the good things take ten seconds to flash by and everything else 12 years !" He pushed his face into the pillow as Nathan laughed a deep throaty laugh. Alex looked up at him, "right, I'm going to have to go, ugh, what a thought." He leant closer and kissed him gently on the lips, then pulled away and looked with gentle eyes at him. "I'll see you at school." Nathan climbed out of bed with him, " Wait, don't go down the trellis, it's harder in the morning, don't ask me why, we'll sneak to the front door, c'mon."

They dressed quietly, Nathan pulled a long sleeved T over his head. "Your room's so cool by the way," Alex looked around at all the posters and drawings. "That's my favourite bit," he pointed to a Lord of the Rings trilogy poster on Nathan's old stable style cupboard door, with a fine pencil drawing of a dog above it." "The poster or the dog?" "The dog," said Alex, "that is a seriously nice drawing." "Thanks,"Nathan blushed, "you drew that ?" Alex's mouth gaped, he was stunned. "Yeah, c'mon" Nathan brushed it aside, looking at his watch. Alex went over to the picture. He stared in awe, "wow, you are so talented." Nathan joined him at the picture and took it in again as if it was the first time he'd seen it. He liked the way he'd managed to get the throat and muzzle so lifelike and felt proud all of a sudden. "You did a really good job," Alex breathed. Nathan jumped as an arm slipped around his waist, his heart beat faster still as Alex drew him closer. He only stopped gently pulling him when he was close enough to kiss and then he turned and pushed his lips onto Nathan's. Nathan felt as if his heart would pound through his ribs. When Alex pulled back slowly he noted Nathan's closed eyes and rapid breathing. He felt elated that he could get him into such a heady state. He looked him up and down, he was so trim and so sweet natured, there surely couldn't be a nicer guy around.

Nathan's eyes fluttered open and he gazed back at Alex. Alex blinked at him and loved everything he saw, even the stitching on his dark blue T looked perfect up close because he wore it. Alex smiled at himself noticing such a daft thing. Nathan smiled back at him. "Are you going to be ok walking home ?" Alex nodded and pulled him close to kiss again. "I wish we were 27 not 17, it's frustrating sometimes isn't it ?" "It doesn't seem to stop you actually," Nathan whispered. Alex laughed and his eyes shone. "I love you," he kissed Nathan's still astonished mouth and turned to pick his top up off the floor. "You're gonna get so cold like that," Nathan frowned. "No I'll be fine, I'll run and I've got happy thoughts to keep me going," he grinned. Nathan blushed and bit his lip, "come on, this way." He headed to his bedroom door and they snuk out onto the landing. They shimmied down the banister and tip toed over squeaky stair treads but made it to the front door undetected, giggling in a whisper. As Nathan unlocked the three locks Alex muttered, "blimey, worse than Hogwarts !" Nathan shushed him and giggled again. Alex stepped out on to the doorstep and turned to face him. He shivered and pulled up his hoodie.

In the fresh morning light his eyes shone, he hugged himself for warmth and then surprised Nathan even more, as if anything could. He looked down right sad to go and suddenly slipped his hands around his waist and underneath his T. making him gasp as the cold air hit him. Alex pressed his head into Nathan's abs and then kissed them gently. He looked up into his eyes, "I'll see you at school, I'll be thinking about you all day and about last night and what we did. See you in a bit." He stood on one tiptoe and reached up to slide another kiss onto Nathan's lips, he looked serious for a moment and then jogged off down the road, he turned twice on the gravel and waved and Nathan didn't shut the door until he could hear that he was far away.

He leant against the front door breathing slow, long heavy breaths to try and slow his hammering heart. He had never ever felt so alive and thrilled in his life. No one in the house stirred yet, it was ten past six, he pottered to the kitchen and put the kettle on, if anyone caught him up he'd just say he couldn't sleep any longer. He made himself a strong coffee and leant against the counter top sipping it, trying not to burn his tongue, he'd need that later, he smirked to himself and his stomach knotted up with butterflies, what a wonderful thought. He put the cup under the tap and added some cold water, then he crept back upstairs and slipped into his room. He reset his alarm for 7am and closed his eyes.

The next thing Nathan knew, his Mum was shaking him, "come on darling,

gosh you're a big sleepy head today. Get showered, breakfast's on the table."
She left, taking his laundry basket with her. Nathan rubbed his eyes, frantic for
a moment, had it been a dream ? He leapt up and looked around the room with
his heart hammering, then he caught sight of his dog drawing and beamed, it
was all true. With that he grabbed his deodorant, fresh boxers and sprinted for
the bathroom. As he washed himself it seemed sacrilege to wash away Alex's
licking tongue and hot mouth from his body, he could have stayed dirty all day
just to be reminded of him.

Thinking like that didn't help speed up the shower, he turned on a quick
blast of icy water to sort himself out and gasping from the cold, jumped out
and towelled off with great speed. Once in his room with the towel around his
waist he looked at himself in the mirror, his short hair spiked upward naturally
as it dried and he was undoubtedly lean and honed, in fact his body really was
pretty fine. He frowned, he never looked at himself like this, why not ? He knew
some of the girls thought he was good looking but he didn't take it to heart. In
the locker room he was teased by the other boys, "look at you, chiselled gut.."
then they'd try and goad him when he didn't react but anything they did just
provoked a rolled eye reaction. Nathan lived in his own bubble of not quite
believing in himself and yet being downright comfortable with who he was
when other people just accepted him.

Today he grabbed his school uniform and wished he could wear his own
stuff. There was nothing he could do to vamp up this look, but then nor could
anyone else he shrugged to himself. As he slipped the school blazer over his
shoulders he added a dab of aftershave and for once pulled out the L'Oreal for
men moisturiser he'd been given at Christmas, he rubbed a little on his forehead
and hands, it felt and smelled much better than he'd expected and when he
looked again at the finished picture in the mirror, he was shocked at how nice he
looked. He grabbed his coat and school bag, swimming trunks from the airing
cupboard and zipped downstairs into the kitchen.

He plonked his school stuff in the corner as usual and grabbed a slice of
toast that bobbed out of the toaster, reached across the table for the apricot jam
and poured himself a coffee. It was only as he started to butter his toast that he
realised his whole family were staring at him. He paused with his knife above
the jam, "what, what is it ?" His family just stared still, his parents looked at
each other.

"You look really excited," said his sister, "yes awaker," said his brother.
"More awake darling," corrected their mother. Jack rolled his eyes, "I'm
fourteen mother, I do know that, I was just teasing !" Nathan took a huge bite
out of his toast and sipped his coffee, his stomach filled with butterflies as he

thought about Alex having been in the house only a couple of hours before and now he was going to see him again very soon.

"Right you lot, finish this up so that Dad can drop you to school," Nathan's Mum poured orange juice into everyone's glasses. As they drained the last drop Jack giggled, "ooh look, he's left his toast, he must be in love," "he's blushing so it's definite," his sister joined in. Nathan narrowed his eyes and glared at them, "alright, that's enough of that, teeth, loo, books etc.., go now !" His Mum scolded and chivvied them all out of the kitchen.

On the way to school Nathan could hardly hold his breathless excitement back and as they drew up to the usually chaotic gate he waved goodbye to his Dad and walked as slowly as he could up the wide pebbled driveway to the sprawling gothic mansion that was school.

It was a wonderful, marvellously sunny day and he watched his siblings wander off to their year while he walked almost right up to the stone steps at the front door and then, he saw him. Alex was standing to the left of the steps, looking straight at him. He smiled a slightly self conscious gulping smile when he saw him. It took only a minute or so for Nathan to cross the ground toward him. He drew up breathless and excited. They stared into each others eyes and then Alex reached out for one of Nathan's hands, holding it he gently rubbed his fingers over the palm. Nathan groaned and Alex pulled him close to kiss his lips, he was almost panting when they pulled apart and Alex loved the look on his face. "I wish I could take you home right now and show you what I feel for you," Nathan gasped and shut his eyes, "don't, don't say things like that to me here," "why not," Alex stroked his face. "Because I can't go in yet now !"

Alex's heart leapt, he felt beside himself to be able to have that effect on him. " Really? Why's that," he teased. Nathan looked down, desperately shy at his state for a moment. "Hey," Alex raised his chin gently with one finger and looked him in the eyes, "I love you," he said with total seriousness and then he cupped Nathan's face in his palms and drew him close, kissing him with all the passion that he felt. They crushed their bodies together and moaned in ecstasy. When at last they pulled away the bell for class had rung but they stood holding hands gazing at each other. Alex stroked Nathan's face, his thumb caressing and loving as it swept softly over his skin. Nathan exhaled a purr of pleasure and an unquieted longing groan. Alex breathed out shakily, " Oh when you make those noises," he husked, "God I want to be with you." He kissed Nathan's hot lips with a great gentleness. "C'mon," he tugged at his hand, "Let's go in." They walked up the steps together and walked into class at the same time. Everyone stared as neither were usually late, but no one worked out the truth just yet.

The day was a wonderful blur of excitement, some of Nathan's friends thought him extra happy today but everyone seemed to have fab days and crap ones so they thought nothing of it. At lunch Nathan tried to sit with his usual small posse of middle of the class friends but Alex brought himself and his lunch tray over immediately and the popular boy crowd flocked to his side. They ended up with the most amazing mix of people who had never thought of sitting together in their lives but suddenly it just worked and by the end of lunch three of Nathan's friends had try outs for rugby and swimming fixed up, two for choir and he himself was asked to be part of the most talented artists drawing afternoons every Thursday as they needed more pictures to sell at the end of year exhibition.

All through lunch Nathan and Alex talked as excitedly as everyone else getting to know new people, and were able therefore to cast heartfelt glances in each others directions with everyone still none the wiser. It made both their hearts flip over and their stomachs fill with butterflies, Nathan could tell when Alex was having a 'butterfly' reaction and vice versa, it meant neither of them finished or even barely started his food, but no one noticed. As they stowed the lunch trays to be cleaned for tomorrow, and Nathan upended almost his entire lunch into the bin, Alex stood right behind him for a split second, "eat, damn you, eat, I'm not having my boyfriend fade away," he whispered. Nathan laughed a low throaty sound as quietly as possible. "Oh God that laugh !" Breathed Alex with longing and glided past him to the middle of the group, he looked back once as he reached for an apple on the way out of the dining room and the look in his eyes took Nathan's breath away.

As the day drew to a close, it had been a busy one and Nathan was glad that Saturday and the chance of a lie in loomed. He was trying out for a local swimming crew outside of school on Sunday but Saturday was a definite lie in. The guys were heading for a pizza and a movie on Saturday night, Paul, Simon and Sam his three best friends made up the group. He wondered when he and Alex were next going to get a chance to be alone together, he didn't expect Alex to drop everything for him at a moments notice but he also knew that if he didn't see him all weekend he would miss him like crazy. His stomach started up again at that and he drew in a deep shaky breath. "What are you thinking about ?" Alex was beside him. Nathan jumped a mile and blanched, "blimey, don't do that !" Alex grinned, "sorry, I really gave you a shock then didn't I?" Nathan smiled, his colour coming back at once, "yes you did, and I'm not telling you what I'm thinking about." "Why, was it me?" Alex beamed and then laughed. "No!" Said Nathan looking away and then looking back he shook his head laughing too, "what are you like !" Alex grinned and looked down at the ground. Nathan watched his handsome profile, God he was good looking.

"Hey, I don't know what you have planned but shall we do something over the weekend ?" He asked, Nathan was elated.

"Sure, what were you thinking ?" "Saturday night, my parents are going away all weekend, if you wanted to come over, I love cooking, we could just eat something, dvd it...that kind of thing ?" Suggested Alex. Nathan nodded, "that sounds wonderful but, I'm so sorry I'm not free then." "Oh, ok, well.... what about Sunday, brunch at mine ? I've gotta show off my cooking skills and impress you somehow." Nathan smiled, his heart was thrumming against his ribs. "That sounds great."

They walked out of school and down toward the driveway, cars were pulling up left right and centre and suddenly Nathan wished that he walked more often to school, he made a mental note to start doing it asap. As they got closer to the gathered parents Alex sighed and slung his bag over his shoulder, "I wish I could kiss you in front of my Dad but he doesn't know yet so I'll call you later instead, ok ?" He looked searchingly into Nathan's eyes, "don't worry, mine don't know either." Alex nodded, "I'll be thinking about you all the way home, call you later, bye." He said the last word with regret and sloped off to meet his father with a tender glance over his shoulder. Nathan felt like a million dollars, his insides turned over again, it was damn good to be alive. His Mum picked him up, the others had gone home a half hour before and so he could spend five minutes of older sibling alone time with her, they usually had lots to talk about and loved this time together. His mum turned the car around and they slipped out onto the road, Nathan tried not to look like he was looking but he just caught the tail end view of Alex's dads white range rover as it disappeared. His mum looked over at him and he snapped his view back to the other window. She was no fool. She smiled to herself knowingly but she was going to be careful if she wanted her son's confidence, there was a special someone and she knew it. "So, how was school my love ?" She beamed, "it was one of the best day's at school I've ever had," blurted Nathan before he could stop himself and then reddened and looked away. They were nearly home already so not much time to talk as the Friday traffic seemed to have disappeared this week, "I won't ask any more but if you want to invite him over for dinner some time then do." Nathan's heart almost stopped, he gawped at his Mother who had turned the car away from the house to do a round the block drive, "What ?" She didn't say anything, just let her knowledge of him sink in. "I..." Nathan couldn't speak and the extra bit of journey had bought them seconds not minutes. As his mum pulled the car to a stop at home she turned, put her hand on his wrist and looking him in the eyes she smiled calmly and said, "I'm your mother Nathan, who you love as in how happy you are is far more important to me than if it's a man or a woman and

I've known for quite some time, perhaps more than you that it wouldn't be a girl.

We're another generation darling, we're not shocked in the same way any more. I will just say please stay safe, never put your health second and come and talk to me or dad if it all goes wrong, which I'm sure it won't." She smiled again kindly and Nathan had tears in his eyes, "Dad's ok with it...is he ?" She nodded, "yes darling, don't worry. Come on, let's go in and have some supper, you look starving." Nathan choked back a sob, he threw his arms around his mum and clung on. "Thank you," he husked against her shoulder. She hugged him back and patted the back of his head gently, "it's all going to be ok darling, sshh." She soothed. A few more minutes passed and Nathan wiped his eyes as his mum disengaged herself from the hug and reached into the back seat for two shopping bags.

Nathan took them off her and they walked up into the house. Once inside there was the usual chaos with the twins arguing over the remote and their dad trying to get dinner started in the kitchen while every now and again shouting, "I said NOW you two !" The twins groaned together eventually and stomped into the kitchen to set the table. Nathan laughed at the scene, he always found his family comical, especially his brother and sister, his dad came into the corridor to retrieve his glasses from his coat pocket and saw Nathan wipe his eyes as he was hanging up his jacket and school bag. He frowned and paused for a second, "everything alright son ?" Nathan cleared his throat and suddenly found his bag fascinating, he was still emotional from his mother admitting that they both accepted him for who he was but he didn't want his dad to see him cry now. "Er, yup, yup,...just REALLY tired," he mumbled into the depths of the bag and pretended to be thrilled at finding his german text book, "great there it is." He pulled it out and flicked to a random page, pretending it was just what he'd been searching for. "Aha, it's meringue...!" He said vaguely. His father shook his head smiling at being a teenager and headed back to the kitchen wondering if he'd seemed as random at that age.

Dinner that night was a fun affair, Nathan's earlier great spirits hadn't diminished after being held and kissed by Alex all day. As they finished their meal the family were laughing and joking and the twins seemed to be worse than usual in their high jinks. "Too much sugar !" Nathan shook his head as they tore off around the kitchen table waving each others books, ipods, school scarves, anything they could get their hands on to wind each other up. Nathan got up to stack the dishwasher and his parents made their way into the living room to start the friday night dvd, a family tradition. He took a huge bar of dairy milk out of the fridge and threw a bag of popcorn kernals into a massive lidded pan. He sponged off the table mats and left them to dry just as the phone leapt to life. Whoever was closest in his house grabbed the calls. "Me !" He shouted to the living room and said "hello ?"

"That's a nice cheerful voice," breathed Alex. Nathan's heart rate shot through the ceiling and he grinned into the phone laughing happily. "Hi," he said. Alex yawned, " God I'm so sorry, I'm a bit tired." They both laughed nervously, shyly. "So, did you have a nice big dinner after our ridiculous lunch attempt today ?" He asked. "Yes, we've just finished it right now and I'm almost completely stuffed," Nathan replied. "Almost ? That doesn't sound good enough, go and have something else immediately," Alex commanded. Nathan laughed again and the pop corn started jumping around in its pan in the background. "That's a funny sound?" Alex queried. "Popcorn," Nathan answered, we're about to have a family movie and popcorn sess. Usual Friday night for us." Alex gasped, "that's such a cool idea!" Just then Nathan's mum called him as they were starting the movie. "Bugger," he said, "I've got to go, I'm really sorry." "Don't be, it was really nice talking to you at all. But before you go, are we on for Sunday ?" Nathan smiled, removing the pan from the hob and taking the lid off to throw in some sugar. "Yes we are," he replied. "Good," Alex breathed. "Look I'll let you go, have a great time with your family and I'll text you before bed. See you at 12 on Sunday. Sweet dreams Nathan." Nathan's hands were starting to tremble, "you too, night." Was all he could manage and then Alex was gone. He blew out a trembling breath as he decanted the popcorn into a massive bowl, God, a whole few hours with just him and Alex on Sunday, anything could happen and he prayed that it would.

Saturday morning in bed was heaven for Nathan, any time to daydream about Alex was beyond wonderful. He was warm and snuggled in a heap of duvet at first drifting in and out of sleep, eventually the clock struck midday and he lay, fully awake and filled with lovely thoughts. He lay back in bed and looked up at his posters and drawings on the ceiling then across at the one that Alex had admired the other day. Alex. He closed his eyes and imagined his lips coming toward him, their delicious warmness and Alex's hot tongue. He ran a hand under the duvet and touched his chest and abs, Alex didn't lie, he was toned. He ran his hand up and down his body and found himself moaning gently aloud. Breathlessly he slipped his boxers off and took his rock hard penis in his hand. Smoothly he worked his stroking fingers up and down around his shaft, "Alex," he groaned and imagined Alex naked above him, ready to touch him and make him orgasm over and over again.

It was such a heady gorgeous thought, his heart banged against his ribs, he thrust himself faster and faster through his own fingers and suddenly he came, bursting and gasping against the duvet. After a few minutes he came back down to earth, got up and showered and dressed and joined the family but after lunch he was fidgety and over excited and went up to his room to get the latest Rick Riordan to finish reading. His phone vibrated on his desktop, picking it up he read : "Less than a day til I have you in my arms, Alex." He put the phone down, amazed and grinning, rested his forehead on the desk's cool surface and then texted back, "I'm counting the hours." Immediately Alex put: "Only the hours ? What's wrong with the minutes, seconds, milliseconds....x !" Nathan put the phone down and laughed out loud. He fell back on the bed and grinned up at the ceiling again. He sighed, would this be the view he had tomorrow lunchtime ? He gasped and chewed his lip, he was getting turned on again. He unpopped the fly of his jeans and slipped them past his hips, repeated his earlier performance and enjoyed every single moment. He came easily and gasping lay his hips back trying to calm down as fast as possible. He felt over excited and completely terrified about tomorrow, what if he couldn't control himself and came on Alex within two thrusts, what if Alex just wanted to talk and kiss a little and he himself sat there getting beyond turned on. As he thought of it he got so het up he had to play again and this time he imagined the feel of every part of Alex's body, he imagined making him groan and explode and the two of them in bed actually making love to each other.

It was so incredible that he wanted to cry out as he came again and he had to drag the pillow to his mouth to stop himself being heard. He lay there for some time afterward thinking through every possibility of tomorrow. He looked at the clock and saw that it was only 5, an hour and a half til he met the guys, and suddenly he didn't want to go. He knew he'd love seeing his friends but it seemed like just another thing in the way, blocking up time til he saw Alex. He knew it was stupid but he couldn't not feel like that, tonight he was just so worked up he couldn't think straight and didn't want to either. He rolled off the bed and slipped out of his clothes, wrapped a towel around his waist and headed for the shower. As the water ran down his face and body, he tried to think about what movie to watch tonight and while he mulled that over he realised two things, one, he really wanted to have an exhibition of his drawings and make some money out of it, and two, he shook as the knowledge crept over him, he was completely and utterly in love with Alex.

Nathan had an unexpectedly fabulous time with the guys that night, they ribbed him for being preoccupied and he felt totally at home in their company. There was a skirmish before the movie started much pop corn wastage and other stupidity. The movie was great, 'The Kings Speech,' Colin Firth was fabulous they all agreed, but Geoffrey Rush stole the show. When he got home Nathan quickly googled Lionel Logue and sat up reading about him for a bit. His family all headed off to bed at midnight and he was left alone with his thoughts. He looked at the clock as he undressed, what time should he set the alarm for in order to shower, dress and head over to Alex's for twelve ? He closed his eyes, sick with nerves and climbed into bed. With the light out Nathan wondered if he would fall asleep at all. He turned over and squashed the duvet all around his slim frame, it was so cosy. He imagined sleeping the night, the whole night legitimately with Alex, his heart thrummed and he groaned. Slowly, slowly he drifted off to sleep that night, his stomach full of butterflies and in the early morning he awoke knowing his life was going to change forever that day. He got up and wretched, his fingers trembled almost uncontrollably and he had to sit on the bathroom floor with a cold cloth pressed to his head. Twenty minutes passed and he slithered back to bed shaking.

When he next woke up it was like a different day, Nathan slid his legs out into a long stretch and felt very warm and fuzzy. In the background he could hear his mothers muffled voice calling his name loudly then she followed this with "it's almost ten o'clock, I'd get up if you have things to do today." Nathan lay still, then it hit him. He leapt from the bed and stood panting, confused, frightened. He looked at his clock, she wasn't wrong, so he charged into the bathroom. It was one of the best showers of his life for calming properties, he washed every single micropore of his body at least a thousand times, used his sisters conditioner to make his hair extra shiny and brushed and flossed his teeth with incredible care and attention.

Half an hour later he stood in his room with towel dried shiny dark hair, his face freshly shaved and moisturised, dark blue jeans on and a white t-shirt peeping out from under his dark blue long sleeved Abercrombie top. He slipped on his favourite dark denim Converse and stood back to admire himself and for once he admitted that there was actually more than enough to admire. Nathan hadn't a mean arrogant bone in his body, what he did possess was a great British ability to put himself down at the slightest thing so liking what he saw and admitting it to himself was a more than welcome change. He sprayed on a light dab of aftershave, just enough to combat any extra nerve induced sweating but not enough to knock out a room. It was now 20 past eleven, Alex lived five minutes away on the bus because of the three closely spaced stops and about the same on foot. He swung his dark brown original bikers leather jacket on and pushed his shades into his hair. He gulped and checked in the mirror again, apart from the terrified expression on his face he felt a million dollars.

He picked up his wallet in case they wanted to order in any food and pulled his phone out of his pocket. Quickly he dialled the swim team number and spoke to the coach, he told him that he was coming down with a very sore throat and the last thing he wanted was to infect the other swimmers. Immediately coach Swan changed his try out to Thursday morning, 7am, Nathan leapt for joy. He snapped the phone shut as relief ran through him like wildfire. He hadn't told anyone where he was going today but at nearly 18 years old his parents usually trusted his judgement, he just hoped he didn't get too many questions now. He glanced at his watch and saw 12 minutes to, perfect timing.

Downstairs Nathan's sister and brother were watching the gadget section on Something For The Weekend, their Dad had gone out for the Sunday papers and Nathan's Mum sat at the breakfast table with one place still laid for him as she clamped an ironing press shut on a shirt. "Erm, I'm going over to a friends for the day Mum, is that ok ?" She looked up and did a bit of a double take. "Wow, you look very nice darling." Then she took in the gulping expression and Nathan's red cheeks. She put down the shirt, "where are you going ? Sit down and have some food first." "Mum," Nathan groaned and looked a bit anxious. He glanced at his watch, 9 minutes to. "I've got to go Mum, it's a friend from school, you can reach my mobile at any time you know that, PLEASE trust me for now though." "Darling, your dad will want a name so tell me that and when you're likely to be home and you can go."

Nathan felt annoyed and breathless but he composed himself as the minutes were ticking away. "Ok, it's Alex, Alex Nesbitt-Hall, he lives in Doverhouse Road, number 12, a lovely Georgian mansion rather than a house, pool and everything." His mum made an 'ooh, how swish' kind of face and Nathan rolled his eyes, "is that ok Mum, please, look I don't want to be rude and he did say 12." His Mum smiled, she loved her son very much and knew he'd be sensible. "Go on, off you go and have a lovely time, what time are you back?" "About 8pm I think," Nathan tucked his hair back using the kettle as a makeshift mirror. "Ok darling, have fun," she said, getting back to her ironing and he was released.

He stepped out of the front door and felt a colder than anticipated chill in the air but he didn't care. He ran the first 100 metres to give himself a bit of a head start and then realised that being five minutes late wouldn't hurt either of them. He rounded the corner and headed off down the hill, it was a beautiful view from this part of the street and Nathan thought how lucky Alex was to have a house so well situated. He imagined waking up after a night of love in that house and taking in the view over breakfast and the nerves took solid hold again. He slowed his pace to a calmer walk, he didn't want to arrive sweaty and as he passed the bus stop where Alex had got off the other night he felt his stomach knot up again. He tried to control his breathing and slowed his walk even more but it didn't help things, he was outside Alex's.

Even the front door of the white stucco fronted house was beautiful with roses climbing up the columns on either side. Nathan turned on the doorstep to look behind him, maybe the view would steady his nerves. It didn't, it was as breathtaking as the way he felt about Alex. He faced the door and pressed the bell, his mouth had gone dry. He heard Alex's last few steps before the door opened, then it was swung wide and they stared at one another. Alex looked incredible in a white shirt with a white T poking out at the throat, dark blue jeans, Abercombie socks and his sunglasses on his head too. His hair and eyes looked so dark and shiny, he glowed with health. He gulped and then grinned widely at Nathan. "Come in," he breathed and shut the door behind them.

Nathan stepped into the open plan front room and was knocked back by the stripped floor boards, white furniture and mind blowing view from the huge bay windows. He gazed around for a moment, partly because he was so terrified at not knowing how to handle Alex. "Wow," he breathed. "I agree," husked Alex, staring at him. Nathan blushed profusely and turned his head away. He looked back and watched Alex walk toward him. "Here, give me your jacket," he took it from him and hung it up, then he turned back toward Nathan, taking in his athletic frame so well presented in his jeans and blue top. They stood looking at one another for a moment and then Alex crossed the floor almost at a run, "I can't stop thinking about you..." he gasped and clutched Nathan in his arms, locking his lips down onto him.

Nathan felt so light headed, he couldn't believe Alex felt so strongly about him. He kissed him back with all his might. His whole body felt tingly, adrenalin pumped hard around his veins. Alex groaned and Nathan panted hard whenever their lips moved apart. Alex reached down and pulled at the hem of Nathan's top, his T underneath came with it as Alex slipped it over his head and threw it to one side. Nathan gasped as Alex touched his chest, feeling his honed abs and washboard stomach. "Christ your body's incredible," he husked and Nathan moaned in reply. They kissed on, clutching at each others heads and bodies to keep one another close. Nathan pulled at Alex's clothes and Alex helped out by tearing them off himself. Nathan pushed him away for a moment to get a good look at him, naked from the waist up, he was beyond divine. Alex went to clutch Nathan to him again but Nathan had been breathing so erratically that he was genuinely afraid he might pass out. He gasped extra loud and pushed his hand up against Alex's chest, then he leant his head forward, resting it just above his hand.

Alex's head was in a spin too but not as bad as Nathan's. He looked down and put a hand on the back of Nathan's head. As soon as he did that he stopped to listen carefully and realised that Nathan could really be in trouble. He felt a horrible dread and fell to his knees to look up at his face. "Nathan, Nathan...my God, can you breath ?" Nathan nodded and managed, "just,..give..me, a second here."Alex stayed stock still on his knees looking up at him as he puffed and tried to get his breath. Another minute passed and Nathan lifted his head, he rubbed his forehead looking very white. "I feel pretty stupid," he said shakily. "No, you musn't," Alex was tight lipped with fear. Nathan looked down into his eyes, "I'm ok, I just...hyperventilated," he gave Alex a half smile. "Please, will you just come and sit on that sofa, get your breathing back, for me..?" Alex knew Nathan would be embarrassed.

Nathan looked at him with already a little colour coming back to his cheeks and nodded, "ok." Alex slid his arm underneath his and stood up carefully. Nathan felt sure he would be alright when standing up but he was wrong. His head suddenly felt very, very wobbly and dizzy indeed. He was upright for half a second before he felt really terrible. He staggered against Alex and groaned, "Oh my God the room's spinning." Alex's heart turned over in the most horrible way, he was terrified. "Ok, you're ok, I've got you," he said, trying to stay calm. "Come on," he carefully but firmly manoeuvred Nathan toward the sofa, he had to grip on tightly to his body to keep him straight up. He lowered him into the seat and quickly fetched his top so that he wouldn't get cold. Then he sat looking at him anxiously, holding his wrist. Nathan leaned his head back against the sofa and closed his eyes. Alex moved his fingers round to take his pulse. It was absolutely racing.

"Ok, I'm getting you a glass of water, don't move." Alex ran into the kitchen and with shaking hands he ran a full glass for him. He was back crouching at Nathan's knee and handed him the drink. Nathan took a long sip and leaned his head back. He kept sipping the water for the next few minutes and as his breathing slowed, Alex felt for his pulse again. To his utter relief it was well down. He leant his forehead against the sofa arm and breathed out a huge sigh of relief. He looked up at Nathan who was now watching him. Alex moved to sit beside him and brought his legs up onto the sofa. "How are you feeling?" He asked. Nathan stared into his eyes and began to blush, "idiotic," he replied. Alex reached out and stroked his face very gently, "I'm not having you say that about my boyfriend."

Nathan grinned immediately and the crisis was over. Alex took the glass from him and put it on the table. "So, if I kiss you again are you going to be alright ?" He teased. "Arrogant arse !" Nathan giggled. "Alex threw his head back and roared with laughter. They laughed together, relieved that all was ok and so happy at having the rest of the day to enjoy each other. As Nathan looked at Alex he blinked, Alex saw his lovely long lashes and the dark blue of his eyes underneath. It made his chest pound. He leaned close and put his lips to Nathan's, gently starting up again. He let his tongue slip between his lips and brought his hand up to caress his face and body while he kissed him. He pulled away and looked at Nathan, he was breathing hard again but it was ok.

Their excitement was palpable and Alex stood up and slipped Nathan's top off over his head and arms again then very gently he pushed him to lie on the sofa. He clambered onto his waist, straddling him on the wide soft seat and lowered his body so that their chests met. With acute care and love he touched and caressed Nathan, kissing his face and body, stroking his skin. As he moved up him a little and their nipples grazed each others, both gasped and Nathan began to pant again, he was so in love and so turned on. Alex looked down at him and brushed his fringe back from his forehead. "I hope you're truly alright now," he whispered. Nathan nodded, "I'm fine, I was just embarrassed at possibly passing out in front of the man I love on our first proper date."

Alex's head snapped up, "what did you say ?" Nathan looked into his eyes feeling a little alarmed for a second and only managed"Erm...," Alex breathed heavily, excitedly. "Did you just say...that you love me ?" Nathan reddened severely, "yes I did." Alex's mouth fell open. "I'm gob smacked," he breathed. " I know you like me and I know you know that I am in love with you but ...I just didn't know I would hear you say that yet." His voice went all crackly and his eyes became watery and red. "Oh my God Nathan." He kissed Nathan's lips as if they were the most precious thing in the world and caressed his face so tenderly. "I am in love with you Alex, so in love." Nathan whispered shakily into Alex's ear. Alex buried his face into his chest and a small sob caught him by surprise, he turned his face away leaning up a bit and pushed at both his eyes with his fingers. Nathan was beside himself with elation, he didn't know Alex could be so in love with him, it was beyond his wildest dreams. Alex looked back at last and shaking his head while his fingers caressed and loved Nathan's handsome face, he breathed, "I think you just made my life."

Chapter Two.

They lay there, gazing into each other's faces and taking in what had just happened, it was incredible. Alex's stomach began to growl noisily, he grinned sheepishly, "I guess we're having brunch next then," Nathan nodded and reached his lips up, he gave him one gentle long kiss, just their lips touching. He pulled away and opened his eyes slowly, then Alex did the same and looked deeply into Nathan's eyes making his stomach flip over. He pushed himself up and climbed off the sofa, stretching out his hands for Nathan to take, "c'mon, let's get you some eggs and bacon, feed you up."

Nathan beamed, "that sounds lovely." In truth it did, but he'd started to feel a bit ill and something told him his fainting spell hadn't been nerves after all. He tried not to worry but he'd be damn pissed off if he was getting sick now.

Alex was already in the kitchen clattering pans about whilst struggling into his tops again. He opened the fridge and rumbled around in it for all the stuff he'd need. Nathan perched on a stool at the kitchen counter and watched his love getting creative. They flicked on some music in the background and started to banter with each other again. It was lovely, a magical afternoon. Alex was a fast and decisive cook, he seemed totally at ease in the kitchen and kept looking up at Nathan, his beautiful bright eyes shining with happiness. Nathan was starting to feel very upset, he was definitely sickening for something now. He didn't know how to tell Alex yet as he seemed so happy and to cut short their perfect day was inconceivable. He propped his head up on one fist as Alex talked, and tried not to concentrate on the aching moving up his spine and through his hips. He tried to look well but he could feel himself paling by the minute.

He sipped coke as Alex talked, hoping that would stop his stomach from throwing up anything he might eat. It was a pleasure watching him so happily busy and he felt so incredibly blessed to have such a wonderful man. As Alex dished up, Nathan realised that he hadn't actually spoken for the last fifteen minutes at all. "Bon appetite," smiled a starving Alex and began to fork up scrambled egg and crispy bacon. Nathan knew it looked good but he couldn't think of the taste at all, his body wasn't up to thinking about food any more. Thank God he'd moved the try out. As Alex still burbled happily Nathan tried the eggs. He ate a small forkful but it felt like a hundred weight of food and he groaned slightly putting his fork down. Alex didn't notice at first as he was on cloud nine and having a whale of a time. Nathan's body was hurting more and more, he felt sicker by the second and he had to keep repeating, "don't throw up, don't throw up," to himself to stay calm. As Alex chattered on and had nearly finished his plate, Nathan couldn't pretend any more.

He let his fork slide into the middle of his food and dropped his head down slowly to rest it on the counter. He turned his face toward Alex and shut his eyes. Alex burbled on for another few seconds and then looked at him, not sure at first of what he was doing, but then he saw the untouched food and noticed how pale Nathan had got. His movements were also slow and careful now as if each hurt him. Alex pushed his plate out of the way and Nathan's. "Hey, Nathan ?" Nathan opened his eyes very slowly and Alex suddenly realised that he looked very ill. "Oh no, Nathan, Nathan my love, what is it?" He asked worriedly. "Are you ill ?" He reached his hand over to touch his forehead. He winced and withdrew it, "Oh God, you're really hot. That explains your fainting. How bad do you feel ?" Nathan groaned gently, "not so good," he husked.

Alex felt his head and cheek again, both hot and clammy. "Come on, come and lie on the most comfortable sofa ever and I'll dose you up with something." He stood up. Nathan raised his head very carefully and steadied himself before he stood up, he felt as if he could puke at any time and the thought appalled him. He rested his head in his hands, swaying in his seat. "There's every chance that I might be sick in your house very shortly," he breathed. "I don't care," said Alex.

"I don't want you to be ill but don't give a second thought to throwing up or anything else, it happens to everyone, no embarrassment needed." He soothed. Nathan groaned, his stomach was about to make its first ejection. "Oh god, I'm sorry Alex, I'm about to be as sick as a dog." Alex moved over to him and kissed the back of his head. "I'm so sorry for you but I told you, you have nothing to worry about, I've seen it all before." Nathan felt his whole body tense, an unreal feeling of pain and numbness over came him and all he could think was how quickly he could make it to the kitchen sink. He didn't have time to think, in the next breath he felt himself heave and sprinted for it. He made it and hurled his guts up in one forceful ejection. He half lay against the sink edge, gasping and hating that acrid taste in his mouth. His stomach felt better but not quite enough and he knew that one more expulsion was on its way up. He heard Alex come up behind him and then he threw up again. It was so hard that his eyes watered and his throat stung. He coughed and dangled over the edge gasping for a moment. No more came up and he gingerly lifted his head. He felt so weak and reached for the taps to wash his face and rinse out the sink. Alex stood behind him and turned them on for him, he was trying not to embarrass Nathan but wanted to be there for him too.

He'd fought every sinew in his body not to rush over and support him while he threw up but he knew he would have hated it. Nathan gripped the edge of the Victorian square sink with trembling, dripping hands. He hung his head out of sheer illness and exhaustion. He wanted to move away and sit or lie down but he dared not let go in case he fell. Alex was watching him like a hawk and realised what was wrong. He put his arms around Nathan's back and chest, "come on, don't worry about it, use me." He whispered. Nathan tried to protest a bit but his legs were so wobbly. He let go of the sink and only just caught hold of Alex in time who grabbed him around the waist. "It's ok, it's ok." he comforted and walked him slowly to the biggest sofa, the extra comfy luxuriant pull out.

He lay Nathan down on his side and reached into a near by wicker chest for a soft red and orange blanket which he threw over him. Nathan's eyes were closed and his teeth chattered. Alex lifted his head gently and put a soft cushion underneath. He sat down on the floor near his head and took one of his hands, the fingers were freezing and almost lifeless. He looked down at them and rubbed them gently. Nathan opened his eyes and found his. He shook his head with regret, "Alex I just don't know what to say, I really don't." Alex began to stroke his neck and behind his ear soothingly, he looked into Nathan's eyes. "You didn't do this on purpose ." He kissed his hand, "don't be so hard on yourself. I don't mind, I still have you here don't I ! I just wish you were ok, it's horrible you being ill." Nathan gave him a wan smile, "I love you," he whispered. Alex bit his lip, he wanted them both to be saying that as they licked each other's bodies from head to toe and made each other shudder and come and cry out in ecstasy. "Oh God," he groaned. Nathan gave a deep deep sigh, "I know exactly what you're thinking," he breathed in a deflated tone, me too." Alex laughed a little 'oh well,' kind of laugh and held his hand. "You know, now we have each other I don't mean to let go, so frustrating as it is not to be able to have you gasping in my arms for all the right reasons, I know it will come to that in a few days time." Nathan managed a bigger smile at this and blinked his lovely big blue eyes at Alex, "in your arms....what a wonderful thought." He closed them again and Alex's stomach rolled over with happiness.

Shortly afterward Nathan fell asleep and Alex snapped on the dvd he'd slotted in for them to watch together. He lounged back against the edge of the sofa while Nathan slept, every now and again he checked on him and though they weren't having the euphoric day of fun that he he'd hoped for, it had started out in exactly that way and made him breathless to recall it and to think on next time, but just having Nathan beside him, even in his sickened state was beyond wonderful.

The dvd finished and Alex was hungry. He didn't want to eat anything too strongly scented and make Nathan throw up again so he decided to pop some corn. He put the pan on and cleared up the brunch things. He glanced over at him and wondered what time he was supposed to be home. It was 3.30pm so he supposed they must have quite a lot of time left yet. He shook his mound of popcorn into a huge bowl and sat at the kitchen consul to read. He got bored after ten minutes though and picked up a magazine about cars. He flicked through it but he couldn't concentrate.

He sighed deeply and looked over at Nathan again, all he wanted was to be able to cuddle up with him in bed, making love and talking about one another. He felt a bit sad at not being able to all of a sudden and decided that as soon as he was awake he would climb onto the pullout behind him and shift him into his embrace and then if he had to sleep some more at least they would be together. He got up and started to select a couple more dvds that might see them through the evening as it seemed unlikely Nathan would be up for anything else. As he knelt in front of the dvd towers to chose a couple of good ones, Nathan woke up.

He lay still as soon as he realised where he was and took a few minutes to test his stomach. He looked around the room taking in it's beautiful furnishings and the incredible view from his sofa. He propped himself up on one elbow and smiled when he saw Alex sitting on the floor looking at dvds. He looked so handsome. He watched him slide the boxes out, flip over to the back and either add them to a small pile on the floor or reject them. His arm got tired so he reached for another cushion on the floor and added it underneath his head. He watched Alex with great pleasure. After a while he needed to stretch his legs and arms and extended himself all the way across the sofa. It felt good. His stomach growled loudly and he let out a big yawn as he snuggled back into a ball under the blanket. Alex turned around and looked into his eyes, "Hey, you're awake !" He beamed and scrambled up off the floor. He crossed the room in bare feet and Nathan's heart beat faster as he watched his tall frame saunter toward him.

He dropped easily to his knees in front of him, and put out a hand to touch his cheek. They both grinned. Alex blushed a bit and chewed his lip. "This is going to sound a bit silly as I know you were only asleep, but I missed you." Nathan's heart leapt, "Did you?" He smiled. Alex stroked his cheek and kissed his lips very gently, "yes I did." Nathan grinned and blushed heavily, "don't, you're going to get my stomach going all over again." Alex stroked his forehead. "How is that sensitive area doing ?"

Nathan breathed in a long deep breath, "I think it feels a lot better, keep your fingers crossed." "I will," smiled Alex keeping his stroking hand going.

Nathan shut his eyes, it was bliss. "That's so lovely." "Good," Alex whispered. Nathan's stomach growled loudly. " Do you want some food ?" Alex asked. "I do but I'm not sure what I can eat, I don't know if that was it or if I'm going to relapse." Alex nodded and looked thoughtful. "Toast ? Popcorn ? Something dry like that's probably good ?" Nathan nodded, "ok, either's fine with me." Alex jumped up and headed to his huge bowl of popcorn, it was fresh enough to try on an upset stomach.

He brought the bowl over and Nathan sat up gingerly. He flopped his head into his hands to rub his face and then moved around to sit on the sofa properly. Alex crawled up beside him and they both dipped into the popcorn. Nathan chewed thoughtfully, this time food actually tasted like something, not the horrible cardboardy unreal flavour from lunchtime. He tried a bit more and actually enjoyed it.

Alex munched handfuls at a time and said through one of them, "ghloof ?" Nathan looked at his hamster cheeks and laughed, "yes you twit, it's going down ok thanks." Alex nodded and stuffed a bit more in. Nathan helped himself to a few more handfuls and then started as Alex kissed him unexpectedly on the neck. "Sorry, didn't mean to make you jump." He grinned, but then frowned, "Nate are you feeling alright ?" Nathan's smile disappeared and he sighed, "ok I don't feel great again actually." Alex put a hand on his head, "I can't really tell if you're hot anymore which must mean that you're not too bad. "Ugh," Nathan groaned and put his head in his hands. He sighed, "I thought I was getting better." Alex stroked his neck, "I'm so sorry for you, what can I do to make you more comfortable ?" Nathan lifted his head, "I think I'd like to lie down." "Do you want to lie here ?" Alex patted his lap. Nathan crawled forward and sank down on his side, he laid his head gently onto Alex's lap and let out a small groan. Alex pulled the blanket back up around him and moved the popcorn to the arm of the sofa. He put both hands on the side of Nathan's head and stroked his hair and cheek. Nathan shut his eyes, "if you could metaphorically do that to my tummy please." Alex smiled, "if I could I would. How's it doing ?"

"It's battling with me, I'm winning at the moment."

"Baby," Alex soothed, "I wish I could make it better. Would you like some peptobismal ? Milk of Magnesia ?" "I think both of those would make me hurl immediately," said Nathan. "But if you have some more coke it might help." "Ok, let me squeeze out of here, I'll get the remote and our phones too, you can call your Mum if you like, maybe you should stay here tonight ?" Nathan lifted his head, "no no, don't you move, I'll slide out gently." Alex moved carefully out from under him but Nathan sat up anyway. He watched Alex walk into the kitchen and wished he would feel better soon. Alex came back quickly with two glasses, a big bottle of coke and the remote and both phones sticking out of his pockets. He deposited everything on the little table next to the sofa and looked at Nathan. "Are you ok ?" He frowned anxiously as Nathan swayed going quite green. He shut his eyes for a second, "just tell me where your downstairs bathroom is please." Alex pointed to behind the kitchen.

Looking completely done in, Nathan struggled to his feet. He stood with his head hanging down a bit and then looked toward the loo, "play something nice and loud on tv for me would you, I'll be back in a second." He made his way unsteadily to the bathroom. Alex sat down feeling helpless and tried to think if anything would help. He did as Nathan asked and turned up the tv. Then he had an idea and grabbing his phone, he went outside to the doorstep to make a call. Two minutes later he was back inside and Nathan appeared at the bathroom door. He shut it behind him and leant against the door frame. They looked at each other. Alex stepped toward him a little and stopped, holding up his phone. "My mum says it's cool if you want to stay tonight ? She also said there's not much to be done about you being ill for now except maybe go to the doctor tomorrow if you're worse." Nathan nodded gently and stood up from the frame, he walked forward a short way and came to rest at the kitchen consul. He leant both arms and his head down onto it and sighed. Alex came up beside him and put a hand on his shoulder. "How're you doing ?" He asked. Nathan sighed again and lifted himself up. "I feel pretty shit actually." He replied and suddenly grabbed forward at the consul, clutching it with white knuckles. His eyes were wide and confused looking for a moment. He swayed badly. Alex grabbed hold of him. "Thanks. Christ I feel dizzy."

Alex held him up feeling incredibly anxious. He watched Nathan's eyes start to roll back in his head and felt him stagger backward. "Nathan !" He screamed just as Nathan's knees gave way and he buckled almost all the way to the floor, but for Alex holding him. Alex slid him fully down, cradling him in his arms. He was barely conscious. "Nathan, Nathan, NATHAN !" He screamed. Nathan groaned and opened his eyes a bit, looking up at him. He licked his lips, "sorry about all this drama," he whispered. Alex shook his head, "no, don't be sorry, but you are scaring the hell out of me now, do you want me to get the doctor?" Nathan shook his head.

"Nate, please, I'm really worried about you." Nathan's hand came up and hooked over Alex's wrist. "It isn't anything to be scared about, ok ? I'm just really dehydrated or something." Alex didn't look convinced. "I don't like it. That may be true but I don't like it. If it happens one more time or you don't look so good to me I'm calling the doctor out. Agreed ?" Nathan gave him a wan smile. "Agreed nurse." Alex wanted to smile but his heart was thumping with fear. "Sofa?" Nathan suggested. Alex shook his head, "I'm afraid to move you, you didn't see yourself just then." Nathan sighed sounding a little stronger. "I just came over very dizzy, it's almost passed now, come on, please, I'll be better with my head resting on you again if you don't mind." "Of course I don't mind," Alex watched him very carefully, his eyes were certainly looking a bit brighter again. "Are you sure you want to get up now ?"

Nathan nodded, "I am not spending the first day in your house lying on the kitchen floor, it doesn't make a good story for our grand kids." Alex's jaw dropped open, "What ?" He gasped and laughed at the same time.

"Don't pretend you haven't done just the same as me over the last twenty four hours and haven't seen a life together flash by in all it's detail and glory," Nathan smiled. Alex looked even more shocked and couldn't speak for a moment. When his voice came back to him he just said, "how did you know ?" "Because when it's right it's just right isn't it." Nathan reached a hand up and caressed Alex's cheek. Alex had to look away or spill the tears that were forming in his eyes. He cleared his throat and blew out a deep breath, then he looked down at him again, "bastard.." he breathed. Nathan smiled lovingly back at him. "Help me up?" he asked.

Alex slid his arm fully around his ribcage and pulled him up holding his hand. He braced him when they finally stood and Nathan looked a bit wobbly. "Ok?" Alex asked. "Ok enough to make it to the sofa I think," he replied. They moved slowly together and he did feel dizzy but not as bad as before. They got onto the sofa and he lay himself down again across Alex's lap. Alex was about to start the dvd when he said, "Look, I love you being here but I don't want you to be in trouble or your anxious folks to turn up later while I'm trying to sneak a look at you naked while you sleep." Nathan's lips went up at the corners. "just call them and tell them you're staying here ok?"

He passed Nathan the phone. "Ok, but I'm not sitting up and brace yourself," he replied. "Brace myself for what ?" "My mum !"

Alex laughed, "Why is she a worrier?" Nathan dialled, "just wait," he breathed, gingerly sitting up after all and leaning against the sofa back. "Mum, yeah hi it's me, I...Mum, I've got to tell you something, er....yes that's great about the twins...Mum I did ring you for a reason, Mum...., Mum, Mum, MUM !" Alex was starting to laugh quite hard in the background. Nathan rolled his eyes looking a bit sickly. He held the phone away from his ear and Alex could hear his mother gabbling away in the background. He gripped his sides he laughed so hard.

Nathan listened again and then held it away again, Alex doubled forward and wiped at his eyes. At last Nathan held the phone back to his ear and then just switched it off and dropped it onto the blanket. Alex looked perplexed, "what are you doing ?" "wait," mumbled Nathan just as the phone sprang to life. "Hi Mum," he said sounding a bit bored. "No I rang you to tell you that I'm staying here at Alex's tonight. Yes I know it's a school day tomorrow and my uniform's at home but the truth is I can't go to school because I've got some stomach bug thing and I've been throwing up all day." He paused, listening, "no I'm ok, mum, I really am, don't worry. Yes they are away but Alex has been really nice looking after me and he said if I get worse he'll call the doctor, he's worse than you !" He smiled then and listened again, "ok, yes I will. Love you too. Bye." He dropped the phone and leant his head back with closed eyes. "She does sound like she cares though," Alex commented. Nathan looked at him, "she does care, she just gets so excited if you phone her for some reason, she's perfectly rational on a one to one but can't stop yabbling if you phone."

Alex sniggered, "she's ok with you staying though right?" Nathan nodded, "and she's glad you're worse than her and said if you do call the doctor please call her too." Alex nodded, "will do. Now come on you, if this is all the cuddling I'm getting out of you this weekend then bring it on." He patted his knees. Nathan smiled and crawled back across his lap. He laid his head down with a sigh, "bring on the movie." He breathed as Alex pressed play.

He slid in and out of sleeping as they watched, Alex stroking his neck and hair. At one point he shifted round to face Alex's tummy and Alex loved that he got to look down and see the face of the man he loved so close to him. He'd been dreaming about Nathan for a long time but struggling with admitting it. He knew they were incredibly lucky to have found each other and that if he played his cards right he could have him for life. He stroked his sleeping love's cheek as the credits rolled on the second movie. If only Nathan were well his happiness would be complete.

He realised he must have fallen asleep when he woke up with a stiff back and looked down expecting to see Nathan but he wasn't there. He shot up immediately, all senses blaring all of a sudden. "Nathan?" He called and looked around the room. There was a lamp on in the corner and a chink of light coming from under the bathroom door. Alex ran to it, not caring about being noisy. The door was ajar and he pushed it fully open in great trepidation. There, curled up on the floor with his head on a towel was Nathan. He looked up at Alex through slits for eyes, he was pale and had both arms crossed over his stomach. "My sweet!"Alex dropped to his knees.

"This is really crappy I'm sorry you have to put up with it," Nathan breathed. Alex hung his head and closed his eyes. "Don't even begin to think like that, this is crappiest for you for God's sake. "Ugh," Nathan groaned and hugged his stomach tighter. Alex pulled a fresh towel from the shelf propping it under his own head and lay down too. He put his arms around Nathan very gently, "try and sleep," he whispered and kissed his forehead.

He next awoke with a start and couldn't understand why the room felt so light, then he remembered where he was and felt his arms rise up and down with Nathan's breathing. Carefully he extricated himself and went out into the kitchen. It was light outside but not full daylight. He rubbed his eyes and looked at the clock, 6.15am. He looked back at Nathan sleeping peacefully and ran upstairs for a shower and to change for school. He sprinted back down fifteen minutes later, he'd been afraid to leave him for too long, but when he checked again, Nathan was still asleep, so he busied himself in the kitchen making coffee and toast and flicked the tv on in the background.

As he watched the news he wondered what was going to happen with Nathan all day? He supposed he would have to go home and be looked after by his Mum. He breathed in a big shaky breath, it was daft but he didn't want to let him go, not now, not when it had been so wonderful having him there as if they lived together. Alex breathed into his hands, why did it feel so natural to have Nathan here ? He didn't want to come home to an empty house or one with just his family, he loved them but he'd found his love. As he looked at him, the force of his feelings was so strong that Alex had to fight back tears. He shook a little and then tried to get a grip on himself, if this was what he wanted, to always have the man he loved in his life, then he would just make damn sure he got him for good. "I'm going to look after you so well," he whispered and smiled at the thought, he picked up the phone and looked at Nathan again, "I really do love you."

Nathan's Mum answered, so Alex put on his most polite and calm voice possible, he told her that Nathan still wasn't good and she offered to come and pick him up in the car. She also would brook no refusal when offering Alex a lift to school at the same time, he was very embarrassed but grateful too, grateful to be spending more time with Nathan. He cleared up the breakfast things and went back into the bathroom, he kissed Nathan's cheek very gently. His eyes flicked open, he looked lithe and beautiful and Alex could have cried just from looking at him. "Hello handsome," he whispered. "Are you looking in a mirror?" Nathan husked. Alex roared with laughter. "Sense of humour still intact," he beamed. Nathan gave a light smile and pushed himself up onto his palms. He groaned looking at the floor and then took in Alex's dress. "Oh blimey, school !" He breathed.

"You're not going are you ?" Alex looked stunned. Nathan gave him a don't be daft look. "Oh thank God for that. I hope you don't mind but I called your mum and said you were too ill still so she's picking you up and...," he blushed a bit, "and what?" asked Nathan. Alex grimaced as he said it, "she's insisting on driving me to school!" Nathan looked up at him and despite himself, giggled. Alex blushed again, "yes, laugh away...! Anyway, how are you feeling now ?" He stroked Nathan's cheek. "Well, apart from a bit foolish for doing this on our first date, I still don't feel so good. I'm so nauseous," he groaned again and rubbed his stomach.

Alex kept stroking him, "if you say you feel bad about this one more time I'm gonna have to brain you with something heavy, you do know that don't you !" Nathan giggled and lay back on the floor. Alex looked at his watch, "she said 8am, it's twenty to, can I do anything for you?" Nathan looked at him, "a cup of tea feels like a good idea." "I'm on it," said Alex, heading back into the kitchen. He put the kettle on and rumaged about for a new box of teabags. As he finished making it, he felt Nathan moving about behind him and turned to see him lower himself gingerly onto a kitchen stool.

"Hey what do you think you're doing?" He asked. Nathan gave a wan smile and took the offered mug, "well my mum's not lifting me up off the floor, that's for sure." He sipped his tea and then shivered, "bbbrrrr." "Do yo want to borrow a hoodie ? You look really cold," Alex suggested. Nathan nodded and Alex sprinted off to get it. He came back with a mock Abercrombie and Fitch, it was Nathan's favourite in because it said "Apple crumble and fish," instead. He slipped it on and added his jacket over the top. Holding the mug in both hands he felt a little better and he and Alex managed a few minutes of normal banter before his mum arrived. As soon as the doorbell rang Alex looked at Nathan, "I love you," he whispered and went to open the door.

Nathan's Mum looked shocked and sympathetic when she saw her son, "darling!" She came straight over to him putting her hand on his head. "Can you walk to the car?" She asked as Nathan looked mortified, "Mum I'm not dying, it's just enteritis, we've all had it before as you well know." His mum looked to Alex and back to her son again, she quickly caught on, this handsome seventeen year old was, she was sure, the cause of Nathan's recent euphoria. "Yes, yes, you're right darling, - I just can't help being a mum," she beamed, "now can you get to the car yourself ?" She saw the look on his face, "ah yes, ok, well I'll just go and get in, see you both out there," she smiled and left them to it.

Alex grinned and Nathan shook his head, he stood up and walked uncomfortably toward the door, Alex locked up behind them both, "she just cares," he whispered. Nathan nodded, "yup." They got to the car and he paused looking white and sick, he held onto the roof edge for a moment and blew out a deep breath. "You alright ?" Alex frowned. "I will be soon, hopefully," Nathan managed a weak smile but gave Alex his eyes for a moment, "I love you too," he whispered. Alex's lips creased into an immense smile, "you've just given me butterflies again," he grinned and they slid into the back seat.

As soon as the car started to move Nathan felt hideous, he groaned so loudly that his mum and Alex both shot him a look of concern. Alex didn't like the look of him at all, "Mrs H, I don't mind if you drop Nathan home first, I mean I can walk anyway ?" He shrugged. Nathan's mum glanced at her pale sick child and said, "thanks Alex, we'll just drop him off but then I insist on taking you to school, after you've been so kind it's the least I can do." Alex blushed, "ok, thanks." He said. They headed into Nathan's driveway and he opened the door immediately, Alex was sure he was about to throw up again, he caught his eyes and gave him a look that said everything. Nathan did the same. As he leapt out Alex stuffed a small folded up piece of paper into his jacket pocket, "for later, get well." Was all he said before they pulled out of the drive and Nathan stumbled to a bush, throwing up nothing but bile, falling to his knees with streaming eyes.

It took him ten minutes of panting on his hands and knees before he felt well enough to stand up again, he got inside the house, hanging onto walls and furniture all the while and pulled a bottle of coke and dry crackers from the kitchen cupboard as he passed through. He kicked off his converse the moment he was alone in his room and pulled the curtains across. He threw his jacket on the bed, it had his phone in and the note from Alex, he couldn't forget that. Then he crawled under the covers and lay still shivering while the bed warmed up and within a minute he was fast asleep.

Mrs Henderson checked on her son as soon as she was home. She left him sleeping peacefully, hoping the rest would knock the virus on the head and busied herself around the house, it took all morning to put three loads of washing on, dust, iron, hoover and order the groceries from Ocado. After another check on her sleeping son and a light lunch she settled down for an afternoon of writing, her short stories had started to sell very well recently and her publisher wanted another two by the end of the month. Soon she was lost in her imagination as her fingers sped over the keys and Nathan slept, recovering above.

Alex was lucky that school had always been a breeze for him and today was no exception in many respects. He wasn't fabulous at everything, but he was good and tried bloody hard. He was first to hand in his homework and with a smile. He was fast on the sports field and very focused and he enjoyed being part of a team. This day therefore had a lot going for it, as did every Monday but he had never felt so lost and alone in his life. He knew he was popular, the other kids laughed and joked with him and invited him to parties as usual. People complimented him on his clothes, asked him where he was going on holiday, reminded him of practise nights for all his sports and club events. It was all good and he felt just as blessed as usual, but for one thing, one big huge almighty thing, Nathan wasn't there.

It seemed impossible to concentrate in the first lesson with Nathan's empty desk not six feet away from him. He kept glancing over and the hole left by his not being there hurt. He did his best to join in but he was so popular and so busy at school all the time that people expected him to be the same today. He joined in but his heart wasn't in it, he was so worried about Nathan. By lunchtime he hadn't had a chance to send him a text all day so he ran into the loos and quickly sent "I hope you're feeling better, it's just so odd without you. Nathan I miss you. xx"

He put on a brave face at lunch but kept running a hand over his pocket to see if it was vibrating. He hated hockey practise that day because it took him an extra hour longer than usual to finish school and he had to leave his phone unattended all the while, by which time he was frantic about Nathan. He hadn't heard a thing from him all day. He prayed it was because he was simply getting better.

Having taken himself to bed at just after 8am that morning, Nathan had hoped he would be much better by the end of the day but he had still been so sick. His poor stomach now hurt much more from the strained muscles as he'd retched all day, there was nothing left inside him. His temperature raged and his mum had called the doctor just before 3. There were many other people in the district with a similar bout of gastric upset he'd said and knowing Nathan to be young and strong he had had to leave him til the end of rounds and so he still writhed in pain in bed, sweating and groaning and unable to do anything. Just as Alex was leaving school with his heart in his mouth with worry, Nathan's mum was on the phone to the doctor again, she hated seeing him in such a state, he couldn't keep anything down at all and was in danger of serious dehydration.

Alex changed and packed up his things in double quick time. Normally he would have walked with a group of lads from hockey, talking and laughing all the way home but not today. He ran out of the changing room without an explanation, he knew everyone would ask him tomorrow, but they would also know that it must be something serious for him not to say goodbye. He ran all the way home and sprinted into his room, throwing his clothes at the laundry bin, he didn't care where they went. He leapt into the shower and was out again in minutes.

As Alex ran through his shower and changing like lightning, the doctor had finally arrived at Nathan's. He quickly confirmed that he did have the same bug as everyone else but he was quite concerned about his dehydration. A hospital bed and drip was mentioned as a possibility if things didn't improve by the following afternoon but he gave him an anti nausea injection and a prescription to settle his stomach and kill off the aches and pains. Nathan's mum helped reposition him more comfortably sitting up in bed afterward and was relieved when he asked her for a little bit of food. She disappeared downstairs to find something suitable and he leant back against his headboard with his eyes closed. He felt rough but apart from that, the worst thing was that he missed Alex so damn much. He pulled the duvet and blankets higher up around him and looked up at his drawings. God he felt miserable. Then the doorbell went. Nathan looked toward his half open bedroom door, determined to hear who it was. His heart quickened and he hoped with all his might that it would be Alex.

"Er, hello, - I'm sorry to disturb you Mrs Henderson, but how's Nathan," came the voice from below and Nathan beamed from ear to ear and felt himself redden considerably. "Go on up," he heard his mother say and his stomach filled with instant butterflies. He'd managed to shower and brush his teeth with some embarrassing help from his mum but what if he looked horrendous ? He gulped as he waited nervously but then, the bedroom door opened gingerly and Alex stepped into view.

He looked so good it took Nathan's breath away and stirred his groin. He paled this time with shock, was this really the boy who was in love with him, he was so bloody handsome. Alex jumped a bit too when he saw him, he looked so utterly beautiful, worryingly pale but beautiful all the same. "Is it ok if I come in ?" He asked, suddenly nervous. "Of course," Nathan groaned and Alex literally ran to his side. They clutched each other in the tightest embrace, Alex's heart thrummed against his ribs so hard, he'd missed Nathan so badly. They pulled apart a little and gazed into each other's eyes. "God I missed you !" They both said in unison and then laughed.

Alex leant forward and pressed his lips to Nathan's, he kissed him gently, tenderly, licking between his lips, sliding his tongue against Nathan's, making him gasp. He pulled away a little, "I wanted to do that to you all day," he whispered. Nathan squeezed his eyes shut for a moment. He let out a trembling breath, "don't turn me on like that with my mum downstairs, Christ !" He put a hand over his groin. Alex smiled and interlaced his fingers with his right hand, "sorry," he grinned. Nathan lay back against the headboard and sighed, he felt really rough. "How are you doing ?" Alex asked, stroking his cheek. Nathan looked at him, "I must be getting there but I wish it would bloody hurry up and go !" He'd gone even whiter than before. "Talk to me," he asked as he shuffled back down in the bed. "What happened today ?" He breathed, turning his beautiful eyes back onto Alex's again.

Alex helped pull the blankets up around him, "well, it was a mad Monday as usual," he started, "everyone wanted to know if you were ok so I said not really." He looked at the floor for a moment and sighed. Nathan reached his hand out from under the covers and interlocked their fingers again. Alex smiled at him, "biology was tough, we're getting into some complicated stuff and hockey never seemed so long in my life !" He rolled his eyes and shook his head. Nathan smirked slightly, "you love hockey," he commented. "Yeah well, there's something I love even more than that now and it wasn't anywhere to be seen today." Nathan laughed a joy filled giggle, it did his heart good hearing him talk like that. Alex raised his head and looked down at Nathan who looked up into his eyes, blinking at him through long eye lashes. "We have got to have a whole weekend to ourselves, just you and me when you're better." Nathan squeezed his hand, "I can't wait," he breathed. Alex looked at his watch, "shit, I've got to go home now. God I hate this, we've just found each other and we have to keep being separated." He looked at Nathan and his heart did a backflip of pain, as one big tear slid down his cheek and plopped onto the pillows.

Alex dropped to his knees and stroked him with both hands, "don't, please don't.." he trembled and kissed his forehead all over. Nathan coughed and a sob escaped him. Alex held his head in his arms feeling like his heart would break. "I just feel so rough and I've spent today feeling as crap as you at being parted. We're supposed to have one first amazing experience together and then this happens to me and I see less of you than if we hadn't got together," he sobbed again; - "and now I'm being a total woos for fuck's sake." "Ssh, you're not a woos, or if you are it makes me the biggest pansy on the planet, I've been worse than this all bloody day," Alex replied. He felt Nathan jerk with a laugh not a sob and looked into his eyes.

"We are going to have the most awesome time, the first weekend that you're well we're going to spend every minute together and I'm gonna have every inch of that amazing body all to myself, you're hardly going to be able to walk after I've finished with you and that's just using my tongue !" Nathan laughed out loud and brushed roughly at his eyes. "I'm ok, really," he squeezed Alex's hand, "I know you have to go, don't worry." Alex shook his head, "I'm gonna be fucking worried all the time until you are better. It hurts to leave you Nathan." He kissed him long and deep and bit back a tear himself. "I'll be back after supper if you'll have me," he breathed from the doorway. "It'll make my night," Nathan smiled.

Alex roared through his supper that night, basically inhaling it not chewing, and drummed his fingers on the table while everyone else ate at a snail's pace. His mum got a bit pissed off with him for bolting it down and looking irritable for the rest of the meal, she tried to get him to talk about his day but he was unusually sullen. She was so surprised at his behaviour that she let him excuse himself and head over to Nathan's but as he threw his jacket on she met him at the door. "Alex, are you alright ? I know you said Nathan's ill but I didn't know that you two were so close ? Why the sudden rush to be there for him so much ?" Alex reddened and tried to disguise it by fidgeting around and looking anguished about the time, which wasn't hard. "Mum please, he's expecting me ! We've just become really close friends, he's an amazing guy, you should get to know him more."

His mother looked non plussed for a second, her son had never said that another boy was an 'amazing guy,' but she trusted Alex's judgement, so far it had rarely let him down. "Well give him our best and say hello to Mrs Henderson ok ? Ask her if I can help at all ?" Alex smiled and pecked his mum on the cheek, one thing that could always be said about her was that when the chips were down she knew how to back off and let him make his own way or to barrel in with unmitigated support, whichever was needed at the time. "Don't change mum," he smiled again and ran out of the door. His mum felt incredible pride in Alex as she walked back to the rest of her brood, she was proud of her entire family and felt very happy as she dished up the pudding.

Alex pelted up the street toward Nathan's with his heart pounding, the worst thing earlier had been seeing him cry in sheer pain and frustration, it broke his heart.

Upstairs in his room Nathan had been snuggled deeply among the bedclothes since Alex left. He'd managed quarter of a digestive biscuit and five sips of coke, so far all had stayed down, it was an improvement but he felt light headed and completely hacked off with the whole thing. He was sick of not feeling like his usual self and being unable to do anything at all with Alex was beyond upsetting. He shifted to get more comfortable, his back was stiff from retching and lying in bed but at least the fever pains had gone now. He glanced up at the clock and saw 7.15pm, he knew Alex's family ate at 6.30pm because of his younger sister so it meant he would be round soon. Suddenly he shouted for his mum, he didn't sound urgent or upset but she was concerned anyway and appeared straight away.

"Yes darling ?" "Mum, Alex said he would come round after supper and sit and talk to me for a bit, can I have some privacy with him please, I mean door shut talking just him and me for twenty minutes, I've really missed him." His mum smiled, "yes darling, of course you can, thank you for still asking, I know it's only four months til your birthday." She leant down and kissed him, tucking the blankets in around him. "Thanks Mum," he breathed and she slipped out of his bedroom door, closing it behind her.

He must have fallen asleep straight away, as Nathan never heard Alex knock and let himself into the room, instead he just felt the most reassuring presence behind him as Alex climbed on to the bed and put both arms around him. He kissed Nathan's cheek and held him close. Nathan pushed himself backward into his arms and groaned. "Alex, my Alex," he whispered. "Yes I am your Alex, always," Alex replied, squeezing him lovingly, "always, always yours Nathan," he husked and Nathan's lips went up at the corners and his hand felt backwards until their fingers entwined.

In the morning Nathan woke up feeling different, he was a lot better in himself, a little hot and quite tired but definitely nothing like as sick as before. He tested out how his mouth tasted today and found the horrible metallic taste of the last few days had gone. He rotated his head and found it moved without hurting his neck for a change. Yet he still sighed, he felt in a bad mood. He rolled over, fully onto his back and wondered why he felt pissed off, but as he glanced at the clock and then up at the ceiling, taking in his drawings and the same familiar posters as usual, he realised that it was 9.15am and that he was missing another day of school, but worse than that, the horrifying realisation crept over him that last night he had had Alex cuddled up behind him and that was the last thing he remembered.

He covered his face with both hands, "shit !" He whispered, realising that he must have fallen asleep in his arms and been totally unaware of him leaving. He felt cold, how could he have let him leave without a kiss goodnight. He looked sorrowfully up at the ceiling again but then a wonderful thought hit him and he sat up and began to frantically search for his phone. He found it almost immediately and with trembling fingers searched for new messages and missed calls. His heart thumped wildly as he scanned the phone. He beamed and kissed the screen, there from last night, were two messages from Alex and again this morning, another one. He scrolled to last nights messages and read the first one:

"My darling Nathan," it said, "I tip toed out of your room leaving you to sleep, it was more than hard to do. Get well soon, love, Alex. xx" He scrolled to the next message at 9.45pm. "I hope you're still asleep and getting better but I miss you so much Nathan, I miss you so much." Nathan reddened and beaming, clutched the phone to his chest. He scrolled to this mornings message, it said : "Morning my beloved, how are you ? If I don't hear anything by first break I'll ring you but don't worry if you're still sleeping. I love you and miss you badly, school is so strange when you're not here."

Nathan kissed the phone and grinned madly, just as he did so it buzzed against him. He scrolled to the new message, it was from Alex again. "Hello my lovely Nathan, are you awake yet ? Your Alex. x" Nathan grinned like mad and typed back, "Yes my lovely Alex, I am awake and I miss you too, your Nathan, x." He pressed send and immediately his phone began to buzz again, "thank God, thank God. Oh Nathan, I WISH I was with you, I can't tell you how much." Nathan beamed and texted back, "Me too, so much. In the mean time I'm going to go and find some breakfast and see how that goes down." Alex immediately texted, "are you better ? That's fantastic news !" Nathan replied, "cross your fingers, I don't feel completely right yet but I am hungry." Alex was even faster than before, "Nathan please, please don't go down those stairs if you feel dizzy." Nathan smiled at Alex's love for him, he didn't know what to say, it felt so good to be cared for. ! "I'll be careful I promise," he sent back.

"I love you," Alex typed, "I love you so much. Mr Sheen's staring straight at me so I'll pretend to concentrate for a while but my God Nathan I wish I were with you. Take care, until I can text you again, Alex."

Nathan snapped the phone shut and lay back against his pillows, suddenly he was crying. He missed Alex so much and he really didn't feel completely well yet. He dashed the tears from his eyes in annoyance but they wouldn't stop so he let himself cry it out. Without warning, a new wave of exhaustion overcame him and soon he fell into a deep deep sleep.

Three hours later he woke up, drowsy and disorientated for a moment, he turned over in the warm bed and then smiled to himself as he remembered Alex's lovely messages. His stomach suddenly growled loudly and he decided to wrap himself in his thickest fleece and a blanket and make his way down stairs for some cereal. He stood up and realised that for the first time in days he didn't feel at all sick or dizzy, just a bit woozy headed. He picked up his mobile and slipped it safely into his pocket then headed toward the kitchen.

There was a note from his mum saying she'd gone to the supermarket but would be quick and he was to ring if he woke up and felt awful. He put the note down and pulled out the Alpen. He spooned it into a dish trying to get as much of the sugary dusty bit into his portion as possible and scooping out most of the raisins and big chunks of almond into the bin. He made himself a cup of tea and sat at the kitchen consul to eat.

It felt so good being up again, slowly he chewed and sipped, flicking through a magazine on the counter. He finished his bowl and the tea and went to make himself another. Sun began to stream in across the worktop and he padded to the tall windows which overlooked their garden. It may not be as impressive as Alex's house but theirs wasn't bad at all he decided. He slipped on his trainers, left by the back door, wrapped the blanket tightly around himself and stepped out into the sunshine. It felt good. As he wandered around the garden Nathan felt the warmth of the sun on him and began to smile, he sipped his second cup of tea and then making sure he wasn't overlooked, jumped around like a fool for a second, he really felt so much better. His grin didn't diminish as he spent the next twenty minutes ambling about in the sunshine, he turned his face up to it, absorbing its rays, "colour me, shaft that white sickly look big time sun !" He giggled upward and went to sit on the garden bench.

No sooner had he sat down than a small orange rocket leapt onto his knee, he jumped for a millisecond before he realised that it was Toffee, their ginger mog. She purred loudly and wiped her head against him over and over again as if she hadn't seen him for weeks. "Sweet puss," he soothed, running her tail through his fingers and tickling under her jaw and the back of her head. She purred even louder still and her mouth seemed to tip up so far at each edge he could have sworn she was wearing a big cheery smile. He snorted a little laugh at the thought, "you're grateful that I'm better too eh ?" Toffee did her best silent open mouthed meow, the one that meant "love me, I'm so neglected !" He laughed and stroked her back, lying back against the bench and let her and the sun heal him.

At school for a second day without Nathan Alex was feeling very low. Everyone had asked him why he bolted out of the gate the day before without a backward glance, they weren't pissed off, just worried and now his mood made it even worse. He couldn't answer them, he felt so desolate, there was a need in him to get a day with him and Nathan just committing their feelings to each other which was so strong it was all encompassing. He'd never felt anything like it before. He felt physically sick at school and used that as his answer for everything, it wasn't a lie. At lunch he was summoned to the nurses office. She sat him down and put her hand on his forehead, "I don't think you've got a temperature but you don't seem well Alexander. I'm sending you home." Sister Westcott frowned at the schools best student.

Alex was so shocked, he rarely ever missed a day at school and now this ? "Erm, no, I'm ok,....I just..." he didn't know how to answer her. She raised her eyebrows and signed his sick note. "Go on," she said, shaking her head. "It's a rare thing when one of my pupils doesn't want to go home I have to say but that just tells me even more that you are not well sunshine." She smiled kindly and handed him the note. He blanched and got up slowly, suddenly he really was tired. "Do you know what, I do need some sleep, I don't know why but I'm completely shattered...I..," he couldn't finish his sentence and without warning tears streamed down his cheeks in a hot torrent.

"There now !" She comforted and took him into her arms, he sobbed against her, suddenly loudly and with force, a great racking sob and then another. She sat him back down and let him put his face in his hands and cry. A few minutes passed and he sat up, red faced, embarrassed and exhausted. Sister Westcott shook her head and squeezed his shoulder. "Now just sit there and relax for a minute, alright ?" She comforted. Alex shook his head, "I'm so embarrassed," he sniffed and dabbed his eyes. "No need," she replied, "I think you've taken on a bit too much recently and you're exhausted. We all know you work very hard." Alex smiled in spite of himself, "thanks," he sniffed again. "Right, get this down you and then I'm driving you home." She handed him a sweet cup of tea and a plate with some bourbon biscuits on it, Alex tried to protest at it all but she was having none of it. He bowed to her gentle but firm pressure and ate and drank.

When he'd finished she rang through to his form room and explained what was happening before marching him out to the car park. It was nice to be taken care of for a change, Alex mused as he sat back in the car for the five minute journey home. He was still worried about Nathan and missing him beyond measure but he also knew that getting sick himself would only delay the day that they could finally be together properly. His stomach flipped over at that thought and he inhaled sharply. Sister Westcott cast him a quick glance of concern but knew she'd done the right thing for him as they turned into his driveway. He looked done in as they got out of the car.

She walked him to the door and Alex was incredibly embarrassed when his worried mum opened it with a look of utter consternation. She listened to what had happened to him at school and thanked the nurse profusely. Then followed an embarrassing ten minutes while his mother fussed over him more than she ever had done in her life and Alex dissolved into tears again. She sat him down and put her hand on his arm but was terrified to find him shaking bodily. "Alex, Alex darling, this isn't like you ?" She gasped and held onto his arm firmly. He dropped his face into his hands and sobbed. She came and put her arms completely around him and soothed him wordlessly for a few minutes. At last he breathed more normally but the tears still came. His mother sat and looked closely at him, raising his chin with her finger tips.

"My son, whatever this is that's got you in such a state, I want you to tell me now. There isn't anything that you can tell me that's going to make me love you less or not want to help out," she said firmly. Alex looked into her honest eyes and wasn't afraid of her but he didn't want her disappointment or her judgement, he just wanted to tell her who he loved and have that accepted.

He drew in a deep breath, it was the hardest thing he'd ever had to go through and he knew he was much luckier than most, they were a close supportive family but he was more scared than he'd realised now that it came to the crunch.

"I love someone Mum." His mother looked astonished, it hadn't occurred to her. "Wow ! I didn't see that one coming !" She said in a genuinely surprised voice. Then she smiled, "but that's good Alex ?" He nodded, "it is good Mum," a huge smile crossed his face and his eyes shone in a way that she had never seen before, "it's not just good in fact," he looked elated, "it's the most bloody brilliant thing of my entire life." He beamed and his mother grinned at his infectious happiness. She shrugged, "well then what's wrong my love ?" He shook his head and looked down at the floor for a moment, he blew out a deep breath. "Alex ?" Her voice quavered, was he going to tell her he'd got a girl pregnant ?

"Mum," he looked her solidly in the eyes, "I've been so worried for the last few days because Nathan's been so ill," she frowned, what did this have to do with him ? Alex continued, "the thing is, I've been so worried about him that I didn't look at the broader picture and wonder why I was feeling so jittery too. I am very very worried, I want to go round there as soon as possible and check on him but more than that Mum, I want to tell you that I completely and utterly love Nathan beyond anything else in the world." His mother looked stunned for a minute and didn't speak.

They sat there in silence. All the colour drained out of Alex's face, he'd never seen his mum look like that, for a moment he wondered if she would hit him and then immediately knew that was stupid. Another minute of silence passed. "Mum ?" He tried tentatively. His mum looked away for a moment and then she looked back at him breathing hard. "What do you mean ?" She asked quietly. Alex's heart hammered hard against his ribs, he was genuinely scared. "I mean that I'm completely in love with Nathan Henderson and I want to be with him always."

Chapter Three.

He visibly shook as his mother took one more look at him and then suddenly snatched him into her arms, crying for all she was worth. They stayed that way for some time and Alex just thanked God that his father didn't come home early. She rocked him as she cried but then at last, as he wriggled, more emotionally uncomfortable than physically, she pulled away and slid the counter top tissue box closer. Grabbing a handful she dabbed at her eyes and then shook her head. "Oh Alex," she sounded terrible, cleared her throat and sat herself up properly in a more dignified grown up way in her seat. She reached for his hand, "my darling, are you sure ?" Her eyes searched his and he nodded gravely, "I have never known anything more certainly in my life."

She smiled through slightly mascara tinged eyes and cleared her throat again. " Well my darling, I must apologise for sobbing but I'm your mum and I had no idea at all !" Alex looked dumbfounded, "you didn't ?" She shook her head, "no, not a clue ! I didn't mean to behave badly though and I'm sorry if I've upset you." Alex beamed, "Mum !" He squealed with wet eyes and hugged her. He was accepted. He sat down again and they laughed a small connected mother son nervous laugh, she did accept him but her mind was full of worry and horror images.

They weren't a bury their heads in the sand kind of family and she wanted to get things out in the open, for him as much as her. "I need to ask you some questions," she breathed. Alex nodded, "ok." "Have you...erm....." she raised her eyebrows at him. "Have I slept with him yet ?" He filled in her sentence and she shrugged and nodded in a sorry for asking kind of way. He breathed in deeply, "no, but I want to very soon. It's not so much about the actual sex but I love him Mum." She whimpered slightly and then shook herself. She cleared her throat again, "I understand." She breathed in a deep shaky breath. "My main concern is your health...I..," Alex held up a hand, "Mum, whoever I slept with, man or woman, I would never go near them without a condom."

His mum looked taken aback for a second at his maturity. She shook her head and seemed to mentally right herself entirely, she sniffed and threw her used tissues in the bin. "I don't know what to say darling ! Except, I love you, if you change your mind or you have any problems come and talk to me." He nodded and they hugged again, "love you too mum." He husked against her shoulder.

After this revelation, Alex needed some alone time, the earlier exhaustion from the day had transmuted into a more low level tiredness, as if he'd had too many late nights. He slipped on his jacket, hugged his refreshed faced mum and ambled off up the road. Before he knew it he was outside Nathan's. He looked up at the beautiful house and smiled, hoping that he was so much better. He took out his phone but looked down at it and knew he was too emotional to speak to him right now.

He stood on the pavement and realised that he was now 'out,' to his family. It made him shake a little. Breathing in a deep breath and walking up the hill to the park, he sat down and pulled his feet up onto the bench, resting his chin on his knees and taking in everything over the last few days.

Back at Nathan's, after his wonderful hour or so in the garden, he'd taken himself back upstairs to bed. He knew the cardinal sin was to get up and run around too soon feeling fabulous before you dipped down badly again. He'd closed the curtains, taken a big slug of coke and before he'd even read half a page of Riordan he was asleep. Now as he woke again, totally unaware of the time, he stretched and blinked in the dim evening light peeping through his curtains. He lay there for a moment and knew he was well and truly on the mend but he felt unsettled, unnerved, and what Alex said about wanting and needing to spend some time, just the two of them together very soon felt so desperately true.

He felt an actual ache inside his ribs as if Alex were ten thousand miles away not just a mile or less down the hill. He gulped and glanced at his clock, it was 6pm. He rolled over in bed and swung his legs out to the side, standing up had no adverse affect on him at all, and in spite of missing Alex he smiled at the realisation that he was well enough to be able to meet him and to do anything with him now. They would be able to be together, he gulped, that meant touching and loving, kissing and letting himself be entirely naked and.... he couldn't go on with the thought, it was too terrifyingly real, wonderful and nerve racking. He hoped he would measure up to what Alex wanted and needed and that he would love everything they did as much as he expected to.

He gulped again and stripped to the waist, disappearing into the bathroom for a long hot shower and emerged feeling warm and cozy and as if his fresh clothes enveloped him in Alex's love. He felt quite drifty and out of it, lost in thought as he tiptoed down the stairs. "Well," smiled his mum, "you do look better." Nathan blushed and it was good to see some colour come back to his cheeks. He sat at the kitchen consul and chatted to her while she finished making dinner. Everyone was pleased to see him up and around again and after dinner they decided to do an additional dvd night with him choosing the movie. He picked a comedy and went to the fridge to fetch the next massive bar of chocolate.

When they sat down to watch the film, the twins came and snuggled up to either side of him. Jack not so much at 14, but he sat as close to a snuggle as brotherly comfort dictated, but his sister had no problem cuddling her big bro. She squeezed him around the waist as the starting credits rolled, "I'm glad you're better Nathan," she smiled. He kissed the top of her head, "thanks sis." "Ooh, you are a bit ribby though, can you eat loads of that chocolate please and put some flab back on ?" Nathan made a face, "ok I will try but I got that out for you guys tonight, I'm not sure I fancy that kind of thing just yet." She squeezed him again, "I'm just glad you're ok." Nathan beamed and they settled down to the film.

After Alex's walk and a rather subdued supper with his family they too decided to sit down and watch a movie. At first his heart wasn't in it at all, he knew things were better out in the open and he wasn't ashamed of himself but Nathan being ill and then his attack of nervous exhaustion and consequent 'coming out,' had taken it out of him. He felt low and depleted and just really wanted to be alone and re-charge. His little sister picked the movie and thankfully she chose Avatar. After the first two minutes Alex had stopped spinning his mobile, wondering if Nathan was worried not to get a text yet tonight from him, and he became totally absorbed in the film. Half way through he began to dip into his dads massive bowl of sugary popcorn and the old cheerful Alex started to come back. He munched loudly and joined in when they all commented on some amazingly done bit or another.

The 'Tree of Tranquility' had him practically weeping for Nathan, he missed him so much, but just at that moment Alex felt his phone vibrate in his lap and snatched it up in the dark, three little words made his heart leap and a tear stream down his anxious cheek. "I love you," Nathan had written. "You've got my heart in your hands," Alex replied. "We're watching Avatar and I wish you were here." Nathan bit back a tear of his own, "don't, it's so tempting just to sprint down the road and climb into your lap." Alex grinned at that and texted, "does that mean what I think it means...?" He held his breath, then it came, the news he'd longed to hear, "wanna walk me to school tomorrow ?" Nathan typed. Alex read the message and before he could even think about what he was doing he hallelujahed and punched the air. His family all looked at him for two seconds and then went straight back to the film rolling their eyes.

He grinned from ear to ear as he typed, "come to mine for breakfast ?" "I'll be there, 7.50am," was the reply. Alex hugged himself with glee. "Then whatever else you may have had planned I'm telling you now, I'm having you here all weekend. My parents are taking my sister to an ice skating thing in Birmingham overnight on Friday so you can come here then if you want and stay all day Saturday." Nathan's grin almost reached his ears. He trembled as he replied, "It's a date. Be gentle with me..." Alex closed his eyes as all sorts of wonderful possibilities crossed his mind. He texted back, "you're getting the longest kiss ever in the morning, and I can't wait."

Nathan shook as he read the message and could barely type back, "I'm shaking and laughing at the same time, do you think that's a good sign ? See you in the morning. xx" Alex felt his own heart rate speed up as he read the lovely message. He sent a kiss back and put his phone aside. His mum was watching him which made him jump. She'd be leaving just as Nathan arrived and his Dad would have gone already. She smiled knowingly at him which made him avert his gaze immediately and go back to watching the film. His pulse raced when he thought about tomorrow morning, which he did for the remainder of the evening.

As Avatar finished Alex's family all made a swift move toward bed, it was late for a school night but worth it for such a great movie. Alex's stomach filled with butterflies as he got into bed knowing that he would be kissing Nathan in a few hours time. He turned over and imagined Nathan's lips on his, he groaned and stretched his hand down inside his shorts, he had to do something about his state, he stretched his head back on the pillows and gasped with delight as he imagined Nathan's hands and lips on his body. It didn't take long for him to come as he thought about Nathan's mouth kissing his and then moving down his body, closing his lips around him. The first time with Nathan it was going to take him only about three bucks of his hips and he would explode, he knew, he trembled at the thought and hoped it wouldn't seem bad or too quick. He snuggled into the pillows and whispered, "Nathan..." then he was asleep.

The following morning, Nathan woke up at the alarm and sat up rubbing his eyes. His mum knocked, bringing a cup of tea, she was fully dressed and looked as if she'd been up for ages. "You do look so much better, how do you feel ?" She smiled. He smiled back and then paled instantly when he caught sight of the time again and realised that he had forty five minutes until he would be kissing Alex. His mum put the tea down and passed him a fresh towel. "Are you sure you're alright, you just went awfully white ?" Nathan nodded and flipped back the duvet. "I just thought of something about school," - it wasn't a total lie. "Alright darling but don't be heroic, if you do feel ill, please come home again or just ring and I'll come and get you, ok ?"

He nodded, "I will. Er..Mum, I'm going over to Alex's for breakfast, I hope you don't mind ?" She stopped for a minute and looked at him, "Oh, ok, well make sure you eat something. In fact text me when you get to school so that I know you're alright will you ?" Nathan smiled at her protectiveness and pecked her on the cheek. "I will, I promise." He skipped into the shower, racing through it and out again in a flash. He rumpled his hair dry and dabbed a tiny bit of aftershave behind his ears, nothing too obvious. Finishing his tea he collected his school books and deposited them in his rucksack. He took one quick check in the mirror as he pulled on his coat and shouldered his bag.

He had to admit, since he'd taken a bit more care and started to appreciate his looks, he looked really good. He smiled and gulped hoping that Alex would think so. He looked down at his abs, he'd definitely lost some weight over the last few days, maybe a bit too much but time would sort that out. He wished he wasn't so pale too, quite a lot of colour had come back to him but his cheeks could be brighter. He licked his lips and drew in a deep breath, twenty to, he had to go. The butterflies started up in his stomach with serious intent and it was hard to draw in a decent breath as he kissed everyone goodbye, but then he was walking, walking, not feeling sick and hearing his own heart thrum in his ears as each step drew him closer to having his arms locked around Alex and Alex's tongue licking hotly inside his mouth. He quickened his pace and as he turned the next corner he knew he was only a few minutes from that kiss.

Outside the beautiful white stucco house, Nathan forced himself to take a deep breath, he was so excited and nervous. Inside, Alex made himself do the same and checked his appearance in the mirror, he ran a hand through his soft dark hair. It felt so nice to his fingertips, he could only hope that Nathan might be running his hands through it soon and making him groan with passion. He blanched white in the mirror as excitement gripped his stomach, and then the doorbell went.

Nathan stood with his knees virtually knocking on the doorstep, the door swung open and he caught his breath, Alex was utterly devastating as usual, such a handsome face, lightly tanned. His dark hair shone with health and his eyes lit up when he saw Nathan.

"I've missed you so much," he gasped and reached for Nathan's hand. He took his school bag and coat from him, dropping them both on the floor and slid his hands inside his blazer, his mouth was on Nathan's immediately. Nathan let out a gutteral groan of pleasure as Alex held him and sank his tongue deeply inside his mouth. Alex felt breathless, "God, oh God Nathan," he gasped between kisses. Their lips felt electrified against each other, Nathan's heart tried to break through his ribs once more and when at last they pulled apart Alex just couldn't let go.

He pulled Nathan to the sofa and pushed him down onto his back then he unbuttoned his shirt to reveal his taut body once more. Nathan panted as he watched Alex admire him with such pleasure. Alex bent to lick his chest and nipples and it was difficult for Nathan not to explode immediately all over him. He went very red and pained looking. "Am I hurting you ?" Alex asked looking anxious. "Far from it," gasped Nathan making Alex grin from ear to ear. "Sorry, I just needed to feel your skin at least once before this weekend and if I get you totally naked now I'm not going to stop." Nathan squeezed his eyes shut with longing and gasped. Alex looked down at his body and back at his face again, "I'm glad you're better," he whispered. "I was so damn worried Nathan." Nathan gazed up at his gorgeous eyes and felt so loved. Alex bent to kiss him, gently holding his hands down onto the sofa as if holding him captive. It was the most delicious, sensual kiss. When he drew away he looked down at him again, "you've lost so much weight, don't get too thin, it makes me worry about you."He kissed him once more. Nathan felt Alex's tongue sliding against his and his head spun with both excitement and amazement that he was at last in the arms of the man he loved so much. He kissed him back as if nothing could sustain him more in the world. Alex pulled away from him eventually, breathing very hard. "God, your kisses," he groaned.

Nathan's eyes were looking a bit foggy and unfocused. Alex slid a finger down the edge of his cheek, "hey, are you alright ?" Nathan nodded, he could barely speak. "You're just turning me on so much..." he looked pained. Alex grinned and took a naughty look down toward his groin making Nathan blush vividly. He could see how excited and worked up he was, hard as iron with anticipation. Alex looked back up toward his face and kissed him again, then he breathed, " I could do something about that for you if you like ? We've got a little bit of time...." he bent and kissed Nathan's nipples.

Nathan jerked and gasped beneath him, he couldn't believe what Alex was offering to do, right here on his parents sofa, half an hour or so before school. He screwed his eyes shut and just moaned "Alex..." Alex looked at him and made a decision, he moved his hand but not his body and unzipped Nathan's fly, watching him all the while. Nathan's breathing was hard, accelerated, he moaned and whispered, "oh God, oh God."Alex moved deftly, carefully, each movement purposeful. He freed Nathan's cock easily from his clothes and moved down to take him in his mouth. Nathan was in heaven, his head flung back, his body arched already in ecstasy as Alex's fingers lightly touched him. Alex positioned his tongue at the base of him and licked all the way up. "I'm gonna come in three strokes if you do that to me," Nathan rasped.

"Good," said Alex, meaning it. As long as it pleasured him, he didn't mind how fast or slow things went. He closed his lips around Nathan's iron shaft and as he sucked he realised just how excited he'd got him, Nathan cried out loudly almost immediately and within five strokes he came, bursting into Alex's throat, bucking his hips and thrusting himself hard into his mouth. Alex gently covered him up again afterward, leaving him for a second he went to flick the kettle on and took a big sip of his already poured coffee. He returned to Nathan, still in a state of undress and watched him steady his breathing and open his eyes again. He knelt beside him so as to give room to rebuckle himself and stroked his face lovingly. Nathan gazed up at him with red cheeks, "is that what you meant by breakfast ?" Alex nodded and laughed, Nathan blushed. "But what about you ? That's the second time for me without taking care of you ?" He looked concerned. Alex kept the stroking finger on his cheek. "I did that before you got here, twice," he smiled, with his cheeks colouring a bit. Nathan gasped and then laughed, "well I only did it last night, that must be why I couldn't control myself."

They grinned at each other feeling sexy, shy, incredible and breathlessly excited by one another. "So would you like me to do that to you...?" Nathan asked. To his great surprise Alex went incredibly red and looked away, he looked back shyly at last and nodded. "I'd love you to do that to me," he whispered, "but when you do I'm going to be noisy and....," he looked so shy, "what ?" Nathan was worried, "well, Nathan it's you, you doing it to me. I've loved you for so long, I might get...well, emotional." He looked him in the eyes, concern at his confession written all over his face. Nathan smiled and said, "and if you do get emotional, what makes you think I won't too ? The day you actually have me naked, in your bed, I'm gonna be more nervous and scared than you by far."

Alex looked at him with surprised eyes, "you feel that way too ?" Nathan nodded, "it's you Alex, this scares the shit out of me, but I also can't wait." Relief spread across Alex's face, "is that why you said 'be gentle with me?'" Nathan nodded, "you might be better than me !" Alex shook his head, "there is no better than you Nathan." They gazed at each other, silent for a second with flaming cheeks, excitement at the coming weekend pulsing around their veins. "Would you like me to do 'that,' to you this weekend ?" Nathan asked. Alex blushed and drew in a deep breath. "Yes I would." Nathan smiled a shy smile back and his cheeks burned again. "Would you like to do other stuff this weekend ?" He asked. Alex gazed deeply into his eyes and nodded very slowly. "I'd like to do everything with you," he breathed. Nathan blushed. "Me too."

Alex crossed his arms on the edge of the sofa and half hid his red face in them, but their eyes never left each other. They sat, taking in the fact that this weekend would be as special to both of them. They let out shaking breaths, trembling at the thought in nerves and elation.

At last Nathan's stomach growled and they laughed. "Have we got time for breakfast ?" He asked. "Yes," said Alex and pulled him upright. He rebuckled himself properly with one hand while Alex pulled him close and kissed his mouth very tenderly. They drew apart, eyes combing each other's beautiful faces, "I love you very much," Alex whispered as he swept his thumbs over Nathan's cheeks. "I love you too"Nathan whispered, and kissed his lips with utter gentleness. Alex took him by the hand and lead him into the kitchen for some food.

They ate with the tv on in the background, gulping somewhat at the time, "crap!" Said Alex as he poured Nathan's coffee. Nathan saw the time and stood up, about to shrug on his blazer. "Oh no you don't !" Alex grabbed him by the wrist, "you're not going anywhere without food. I can barely see you when you turn sideways right now anyway." Nathan blushed and giggled, sitting down again, "ok but it's gotta be quite fast." Alex pulled two waffles out of the toaster and jumped around for a second as they were so hot on his hands, before flinging them on to a plate, blowing at and shaking his fingers. "Yowser ! Ok, here you go, waffles and ice cream for breakfast." He scooped a portion on top of each waffle and sat down to eat. "Very american but fun eh ?" Nathan reached for his hand, which was freely given, "thanks for doing this." He blushed again. Alex looked up at him and his cheeks reddened a bit too. He gulped and looked seriously at Nathan. Nathan frowned as he forked up the waffle, "what are you thinking ?"

Alex sighed, "I've got you, I...don't want to lose you." He looked down at his plate and seemed a bit sad for a second. "Why on earth would you think about losing me?" Nathan looked taken aback. Alex looked him in the eyes, "because I love you so much." Nathan slid off his stool and encirled Alex in his arms, Alex wrapped himself entirely around Nathan and kissed his neck, he crushed his body in against him as hard as he could. "I'm not going anywhere, I promise," Nathan breathed. Alex squeezed him longingly and looking up into his eyes said "I'm so glad." He glanced over at Nathan's plate and then his watch, "Ok, you've got one minute 38 seconds to clear that plate and then we're out the door !" Nathan sat immediately and wolfed down his waffle, Alex did the same as they both drained their mugs with alacrity.

The walk to school had never felt so good, leaving the house with Nathan at his side felt beyond wonderful to Alex. They laughed and joked and messed around the whole way and kept pushing each other up against walls and bushes for a kiss. When they reached the school gates they were almost late and Nathan was inclined to run to class, he tried to detach his hand from Alex's to sprint up the pebbled driveway but Alex held on, "no don't, let me walk hand in hand with you today." He smiled over at Nathan who looked even better than before, it made him catch his breath. Nathan gently squeezed his hand, he loved it when

Alex asked things like that, he smiled back at him, "your hand feels so good in mine." Alex grinned, and they walked hand in hand to the classroom door.

They were late,- just, Mr Martin their form teacher knew they'd both been ill, in fact the whole staff had been very worried. Nathan never seemed to get ill so his stomach bug had made them all overreact a bit, and Alex, being the entire school's top pupil had shocked them all with his semi breakdown a couple of days back. There was a general whispering and shifting about from the rest of their classmates as they took their seats.

"Alright, alright everyone settle down," Mr Martin called out. "Welcome back you two. Are you feeling better Nathan ?" Nathan nodded, reddening a little as everyone stared at him. A couple of people slapped him on the back to say 'glad you're ok.' "And what about you Mr Nesbitt-Hall, are you better ?" Alex nodded and caught the puzzled look on Nathan's face in his periphery, uh oh ! He reddened a bit and Mr Martin continued, "stay behind after class and we'll go through your timetable, you may be taking on too much." "Yes sir," said Alex sheepishly, he daren't look at Nathan. He knew he'd be grilled later but then he smiled to himself, it was worth it to have someone who loved him so much.

His stomach turned over as he looked across to his hockey friends who were all trying to attract his attention, they wanted to talk to him at lunch, desperate to keep him on the team. Alex was desperate for something else, to tell everyone how in love he was and to celebrate that, but he was bloody nervous too.

He whispered yes to the hockey group, just 'yes I'm still in, don't panic, I'm not cutting the team,' so that he wouldn't have to have a long talk with them at lunch. He wanted to sit with Nathan, holding his hand under the table, eating and maybe revealing their relationship to some key friends.

They split off into different groups just before lunch as Nathan's drawing skills took him into an art class Alex could never hope to join. Instead he did an extra revision hour for their upcoming exams. As the bell went for lunch he couldn't wait to see Nathan again, what the hell was it that made time apart from him so hard ? Nerves at not being absolutely convinced that he had him yet he decided, that and the fact that however great the rest of his life was, being with Nathan was the icing on the cake, nothing gave him greater happiness.

As he sat down at his usual table in the dining hall, Nathan strode into the room on his long lean legs. He was talking to a friend from his art lesson and laughed a throaty laugh that made his eyes light up. They picked up their trays and made their way over to the tables, as they neared the usual three or four, Nathan looked up and met Alex's eyes, the look in his own said it all. He bit his lip and squeezed his eyes shut for a moment, when he looked up Alex was still staring at him with that heart stopping delicious look on his face. Nathan's friend waved at someone across the room, he slid his tray down next to Nathan's and then patted him on the shoulder, "back in two mate, Alistair's still got my cds," and he was off.

Nathan straddled the bench and sat down, no one else was at the table yet, although two other trays of untouched food showed that a couple of Alex's friends had got distracted too. He looked up as he slid his knife and fork off the tray. "Hi," Alex beamed and Nathan's grin spread from ear to ear, he blushed. Alex giggled and looked around him for a second, "hey, move your tray round here would you so that you can sit next to me ?" Nathan slid round straight away and then looked directly into Alex's eyes from just a few inches apart.

Alex slipped his hand caressingly around his knee. Nathan closed his eyes and let out a shaky breath. "God not here, don't give me an erection here at school," he gasped. Alex stroked him even more languorously and laughed out loud. "Sorry," he grinned, meaning it but full of excitement at just sitting together. He shook his head, not moving his eyes from Nathan's, "what is it that I just can't seem to get enough of you ?" His gaze combing his face. Nathan smiled back with his beautiful shiny eyes, " I feel exactly the same way," he replied and then groaned and jerked for a second as Alex squeezed where he was stroking.

He coughed out a strangled breath and looked Alex in the eyes, "two things are going to happen here, one, I'm not going to eat any lunch at this rate, and two, you're very likely to....," he blushed, "to what ?" Alex looked mystified. "Make me come any second now, just by doing that if you keep bloody going !" Alex grinned, "sorry." He lessened the stroking until his hand simply stayed on Nathan's leg. "But I am going to do that all weekend," he said. "What ?" Nathan asked. "Make you come and come and come." He breathed excitedly. Nathan's eyes flew wide and he reddened wildly before covering his face with both hands. Other people were coming back to the table now. They were half way across the room, Alex looked up sharply and back at Nathan. "Do you mind if people know ?" He suddenly asked. Nathan looked up as the others re-joined them and turning back to Alex he slowly shook his head, "no, I don't. I don't mind at all." Alex let out a deep breath. "Good," he smiled and the look that passed between them made them both want to abandon school and run home together immediately.

"So," Rupert, Nathan's art class friend started chatting. He shovelled food into his mouth as if it were the first time he'd eaten and talked at the same time. He ate so much but he was built like a whippet. Other people came and stocked up the rest of the table and all of a sudden Nathan and Alex both had to talk to everyone, but both of them refused every time someone tried to make them come and 'see,' this or that or meet whoever it was they thought was worth meeting and maybe doing something after school with. They stayed put for most of lunch and talked and talked, laughed with everyone and talked some more.

As most people got up to leave, Alex took his tray to the stowing shelf and whacked it in there. He brushed his hands together and turned around to walk back to the table, nearly bumping into Tony who was in his top level french group, "shit, sorry !" He gasped. "Don't worry, I'd love it if you spilt something down the front of this to be honest," he looked down at his thread bear uniform, "is it true we can wear what we want when exams start ?" Alex nodded as they walked back to the table, "yeah, sure is." He smiled. Tony walked with him, starting to chat about the holidays, cars, girls, etc..., most of it was quite interesting except the penultimate bit, but Alex was desperate to have his last ten minutes of lunch alone with Nathan He wanted to grab him and have him up behind a bush somewhere, his hands stroking inside his shirt, while kissing his beautiful mouth with all his might. They sat down opposite Nathan who was talking to Rupert and another blonde boy. Alex and Nathan glanced at each other with butterflies again.

"Alex you'll go won't you ?" Rupert suddenly piped up. "Where to ?" Asked Alex, half listening while he looked at his watch. "You'll come with a group of us this friday to 'Swordfish,' won't you ?" "What's that ?" He asked. Rupert looked taken aback, "only the coolest new place in town Alex ! Blimey, I would have thought you'd have heard of it."

Alex shrugged. "Anyway, I just said to these guys why don't we all go on Friday, loads of hot girls there apparently and you know what you're like to hot girls, bees round a honey pot springs to mind !! He he !" He laughed. Nathan was staring intently at Alex who gave him a reassuring little look and turned his attention full onto Rupert, "no mate, not interested, I'm all loved up actually." Everyone who hadn't yet drifted outside for the last five minutes and was within earshot started listening. Rupert's face was a picture, "you what ?"

Alex nodded, "yep, I'm not on the market anymore, I've met the love of my life." Nathan reddened and Alex wondered if he'd overstepped the mark, he knew how shy he could be. He mouthed a quick sorry to him but Nathan shook his head and though red cheeked he smiled back. So did Alex. "WHO ?" Rupert's eyes were saucers, "who the hell is she ?" He asked agog. Nathan nodded gently. "Him," Alex pointed, "Nathan James Henderson." No one spoke for a moment. There were other gay guys around it was just no one had ever believed that Alex was one of them. Rupert didn't know what to say.

He turned sheepishly to look at Nathan who looked quite confidently back at him. His stomach felt in knots, he was a fairly loud but nice guy and he felt as if he'd just forced them 'out,' at school. "Erm...," was all he could say after that. Alex shook his head and stood up as the bell went, "don't worry Rupe," he grinned. "You coming Nathan?" Nathan's smile reached from ear to ear, "yep." He beamed and walked out of the dining hall with Alex. When they got into the corridor both felt their hearts smashing against their ribs with joy. "We're out!" Alex grinned, "we sure are!" Nathan laughed. Alex grabbed his hand, "I know we're gonna be late, but come on," he ran with him to the front door, they tore down the steps and into the nook underneath where Alex took him in his arms and kissed him longingly, sliding his tongue deeply inside his mouth making him groan.

"Oh God," Nathan pulled away and gazed at him, "I seem to be a really bad influence on you at the moment." Alex put a hand on either side of him and shook his head, "no, I just love how you make me feel." Nathan scanned his face, "my lovely Alex," he breathed. "I'm so tempted just to bunk off the rest of school today and let you take me home and do what you said earlier...." he blushed. Alex gasped, shutting his eyes. He pulled Nathan into his arms and held him close. "I can't wait to do that to you, I can't wait." He whispered. Nathan shut his eyes and let the glorious feelings flood over him. He didn't care that they were now well and truly late, he just looked forward to being like this with Alex all day in 48 hours time. "School's cruel," Alex husked, rubbing his cheek gently against Nathan's. "It bloody is," Nathan breathed back. They moved around each other's bodies to kiss again and Alex gently tugged at his shirt to untuck it, Nathan groaned. Alex tugged the shirt out all the way and gently traced his fingers over Nathan's washboard stomach making his skin shudder with excitement.

Nathan crushed his groin up against Alex and moaned tilting his head back against the stone behind him. Alex undid all the buttons on his shirt and slid it aside, then he was touching Nathan's naked chest and abs, swirling his fingers about on his smooth gorgeous skin. Nathan was breathing very hard. Alex slid his hand into his trousers, taking hold of him. Nathan cried out as quietly as he could make it and clutched Alex's hand. As he panted he looked him in the eyes, "you..really...will...make me....come right now Alex, Christ," he pulled gently at Alex's hand and he withdrew it carefully. "Sorry," Alex breathed and looked pained, "I don't mean to push things." He looked worried.

Nathan smiled at him, still trying to calm his breathing, "you don't push things, I know what you're feeling because I feel it too." He pecked him on the lips, "fuck I feel horny now though." Alex pulled him into his arms, "oh you do eh ?"

Nathan laughed as he struggled to do up his shirt and tuck it in again, "stop it," he giggled, wanting nothing of the sort but knowing they only had two and a half hours to go until they could sneak off on the way home from school and kiss the face off each other. He stopped and looked at Alex, thinking, that wasn't enough for them anymore though and they both knew it. It wasn't just about the sex, even though the thought of touching each other's bodies was fantastic beyond belief, they had an all consuming need just to have each other, to be, to taste, to touch, to love and to do everything to one another. Nathan couldn't imagine how he'd existed for so long without knowing there could be this with him.

Alex looked at him, smoothing a piece of hair back from his forehead, "what were you thinking ?" Nathan breathed in deeply, comfortably, "I was thinking that I need to be with you, we need this." Alex nodded, understanding exactly. "We do," he smiled with a look that could have lit the moon. They breathed in together, slowly, deeply, just staring. "I suppose we should go in," Alex whispered at last. "We're going to be in big shit !" Nathan nodded. Alex frowned, "Wait !" He said with a gasp, "is this double English ?" Nathan frowned, "yes, it is." "Brilliant," Alex beamed, we won't be in any shit at all !"

"How so?" Nathan slid his blazer back around his shoulders as they walked up the steps. "Well, you know how Mr Mc Cloud really likes me ?" Nathan smiled, it was common knowledge that Mr Mc Cloud's favourite English student was Alex because he spent the longest on his essays and never got less than a 36 out of 40, "yes," he agreed. "Well I had a bit of a bad day last week, I'll tell you about it later, but Mr McCloud's top marks average is still the best, but if I'd missed today's essay hand in he would have lost out to Mr Stone. He needs us ! We barge in looking a bit harassed and say 'I'm SO sorry Mr Mc Cloud, we both forgot our essays so ran home to get them, and we're home free !" Nathan laughed as quietly as he could, they were at the door, "I think it's a master plan," he grinned. "I love you," Alex whispered and they went in.

It was a master plan, and, having sounded so down hearted about being late and both presenting their essays immediately to back up their plan, Nathan and Alex were asked to stay after class where Mr Mc Cloud thanked them both profusely.

Friday morning came and as usual Nathan packed his rucksack for school, homework went in last so that it was easiest to get to. He looked at the small pile of clothes neatly folded on the end of his bed, he had his things laid out for tonight already. He closed his eyes for a moment, he was so nervous ! He pulled his wash bag out of the cupboard and checked its contents again. When his hand touched the new pack of condoms he trembled slightly, this was a big step, he was actually quite scared. Not scared that Alex would hurt him or that it wouldn't feel good, just afraid of the unknown.

He finished getting ready and joined the others for breakfast, his mum knew he was spending the night at Alex's but it hadn't occurred to her what he might be planning. Toast was eaten on the run that morning, not only in Nathan's house, Alex's nervous heart hammered so much that he could barely keep still either. His parents and sister kissed him goodbye and said "see you on Sunday," which made him flip around at the door and question them, he didn't normally get things wrong, but he had this time, they would be away all weekend. On the walk to school it made him even more nervous and when Nathan walked silently up beside him it made him jump a mile.

"Sorry !" Nathan blushed at his reaction as Alex blanched and then happily slid his fingers into his palm, "Hello," he said with a big smile and though many people walked around them he gently kissed Nathan's lips. They grinned at each other. "I've just found out my family are away, ALL weekend," he explained. "Oh," said Nathan and then looked at him again, "OH....I see....." He bit his lip shyly and Alex thanked God that they were both as nervous and jumpy today.

As they'd done it so overtly, no one seemed to have noticed the boys kiss on the way into school, but as the first lesson ended and they all sat there catching up before the next teacher arrived, Jake Reader, a bit of a cock at the best of times, turned to Alex, "So," he jerked his head at him looking smug and said loudly enough for everyone to hear, "Alex Nesbitt-Hall, I hear a little rumour about you ?" Alex turned in his seat and looked Jake square in the eyes, "oh yeah ?" "Yeah," Jake continued, "I hear you're all loved up ?" Alex smiled and nodded, "yup, that's right." A few people looked surprised but no one shocked. "And," Jake went on, "that it's a BLOKE !" There were a few astonished gasps at that and a few, "No, don't be stupid !" Comments from the back of the room. Alex sat up a bit taller, "no, it's not 'A' bloke Jake, it's the best bloke in the whole world and he's sitting right next to you. Try not to piss him off, he's your wing man in rugby."

And with that Alex shot Nathan an almost imperceptibly fast wink, turned all the way around in his seat and faced the front just as Mr Dix walked in and shushed them. There was a slightly astonished air in the room for about 30 seconds and then everyone had to get on with their work. The lesson ended as usual and no one made any daft comments, the rest of the class just talked about what they had planned for the weekend as they walked out, many people stopping to talk to Alex as usual. It just wasn't a big thing for them, gay, straight, who minded these days ? Not 17 year olds that was for sure. Jake exited without another word.

Nathan came over to Alex's desk, there were only a few people milling about in the room now. Alex grinned at his sweet expression and kissed his lips quickly. Nathan jumped slightly and then blushed happily. "I love it when you blush," Alex whispered which made Nathan do it even more. He rolled his eyes, "Oh my God ! Stop saying that, you only make it worse !"

"I know," grinned Alex. They walked out of the room together and down the corridor, "Are you going to keep kissing me all over school now ?" Nathan asked. "Probably," Alex looked at him and laughed. Nathan hid his face in the pile of books he carried. "Oh blimey," he groaned, making Alex chuckle a low throaty laugh. "Don't do that for a start," Nathan whispered.

"Why, does it turn you on ?" Alex pulled him around the waist and gave him a little squeeze which made him shriek, it felt bloody nice. "Alex !" Nathan pushed him away as they got to the door of their next class, "bugger off !" "Do you mean that ?" Alex pretended to look hurt. Nathan put his hand around the back of Alex's head and kissed him full on the mouth, suddenly they were sliding their tongues in and out of each other's mouths. They broke apart quickly, breathlessly turned on, "what the fuck do you think ?" He breathed. Alex leant his forehead against Nathan's for a second, " I love you so much." "Every time you say that you get my heart racing," Nathan breathed and Alex could see his chest moving rapidly up and down, he so badly wanted to touch him. "I'm going to do so many wonderful things to you tonight," he husked, Nathan drew in a trembling breath, "Alex," he whispered, kissing his lips again and headed into the classroom. Alex followed with wobbly legs, he glanced at his watch, only about seven hours to go.

There seemed to be so many classes for the rest of the day but they were wonderful, each one seemed like a specific lead up to the most incredible evening of their lives. Eventually the school day ended and everyone packed up to go home. Nathan's heart was in his mouth as he stowed stuff into his locker and turned the key. He made his way out to the front steps, the sun shone brightly on him. He turned his face up to it and felt the gorgeous warmth. He jumped a bit as a hand slid into his but then a great smile creased his face and he lowered it to look at Alex, now holding his hand. Alex's heart hammered with such intensity and excitement. They gazed at each other. He looked at his watch, "it's four o'clock, why don't you come round at 7pm. Just enough time for some r and r, a shower and change and then.....'us!'" He said.

Nathan looked at his own watch and grinned at Alex. He nodded and felt his tummy fill with excitement and terror, he gulped, tonight was it. He breathed out with difficulty."Yes, 7 o'clock," he whispered. Alex shut his eyes and stiffened like it was both an instant relief to have it confirmed and just as terrifying as Nathan thought too. He opened his eyes again, "see you later," he whispered, stroking Nathan's cheek once more and was gone.

Nathan shut his eyes and steadied himself, at this rate they'd both drop to the floor in a dead faint before anything could happen. He gulped again and made his way slowly, slowly down the steps, he had his outfit picked out, he needed a long hot bath and a quick chill, then he would be with Alex. He put both hands over his nose and mouth as he walked, as if to stop himself hyperventilating. The day was beautiful, he was deeply in love and loved, he just wanted to take it all in.

He soaked in the bath for a long time, lying his head back against the tub and made himself come twice. He was tempted to go for a third and forth time but didn't want to run out of steam later. He got out and lay in a warm huddled haze of butterflies and pleasure on his bed for an hour, dipping in and out of sleep. He'd got over the bug but still got tired, he'd need a few more good sleeps to get fully back to normal but tonight he didn't care if they stayed up all night. He fell asleep again and woke up with a start, confusion reigned for a second and then he leapt off the bed, was he late ? His heart hammered as he scrabbled for his clock, 6.30pm, phew ! He calmed a little but then gulped to himself, he was still half naked and time was marching on. He checked his over night stuff in his rucksack, it was all sorted, he zipped it up and got dressed.

A few minutes later he looked at himself in the mirror, he actually looked amazing. He turned all around to check but the mirror didn't lie. He wore a white t-shirt and dark blue jeans with washed denim thighs. Over the top he'd put a dark blue black and red checked lumberjack shirt, open at the neck and a pair of dark blue converse on his feet. He slid his biker jacket over the top, sunglasses in his hair and slung his rucksack over his shoulders. He'd moisturised after shaving very carefully and smelt of Hermes 'Orange,' it suited him perfectly. He licked his lips and smiled at his own reflection, he was scared but more excited about tonight than he'd ever been before in his life.

As he walked into the kitchen his mum looked up and gasped, he looked breathtaking. She put down what she'd been reading while this evenings chilli cooked in the background, and stood up. "Wow, look at my son !" She breathed.

Nathan blushed, this was for Alex, he didn't really want anyone else's views and he felt as if his mum would know exactly what was going to happen tonight. She wasn't stupid, but she was kind, and she saw the look on her son's face and understood completely. She hugged him briefly, "be safe my love and have a great weekend. Stay in touch." Nathan coloured even more deeply but looked back over his shoulder as he left, she cared and he hoped he wouldn't be sobbing on her shoulder at any point, "thanks Mum," he croaked, emotional for a moment and scared. She smiled and gave the chilli a stir. Nathan shut the door behind him, a light breeze ruffled at his short hair, he struck out on the short walk to Alex's, glancing at his watch, ten to, his stomach leapt with nerves as his legs carried him onward.

Alex felt breathless, he had everything ready, food, some great dvds, clean sheets....he blanched and clung on to the kitchen work top at that thought, he shook his head, he could handle everything usually but tonight felt so different, he was truly scared. He looked around the open plan kitchen and living room, there really was nothing else to do. He took a slug of his coke and up ended a pan of fresh popcorn into a huge bowl, sprinkling liberal amounts of sugar on top. He stuck the pan in the dishwasher just as the doorbell went, his insides turned to jelly, Christ, where was his confidence, he knew he wanted to be with Nathan but he shook like a leaf. He needn't have worried.

He pulled open the front door and gasped, Nathan looked so beautiful. "You're breathtaking," he said but then guffawed with laughter, Nathan looked as terrified as he did. Nathan grinned, understanding and it broke the ice, they slammed the front door and threw their arms around each other in a bear hug, "oh God I love you," Nathan breathed against his cheek. Alex found his lips and kissed him with a great longing. He swirled his tongue about and licked Nathan's mouth, loving every fibre of him.

They pulled apart a little, arms still locked around each other's waists. Alex gazed into Nathan's eyes and began to unpop the poppers on his shirt, Nathan drew in a trembling breath, Alex unpopped the last one quickly and slid his hands in and around Nathan's naked waist, under his T, feeling his smooth skin beneath his fingertips. Nathan shuddered. Alex moved his hand gently upward and found Nathan's hard nipples, he brushed each with his thumb, making him groan, such a throaty sound. He put his hand against Nathan's chest, feeling his heart pound beneath it and looked him deeply in the eyes. He kissed him again and unbuttoned his own shirt. Nathan pulled off his T and Alex tossed his shirt to one side, they stood, breathing hard looking at each other's sculpted bodies. Nathan put his hand on Alex's chest, Alex inhaled shakily and shut his eyes.

Nathan watched him, he moved his hand and grazed his fingers across Alex's nipples, Alex yelped with longing and opened his eyes, staring deeply into Nathan's. He pulled him to him and held him against his own chest, panting with desire, he sank his tongue inside his mouth and groaned as he held him. When they pulled apart Nathan looked drunk, his lips bee stung and glistening in the light, Alex gulped, his chest rose and fell rapidly with excitement and nerves,

"I want to take you upstairs," he whispered. "You don't have to though...," he added anxiously. Nathan shut his eyes and they leant their foreheads together. A minute passed before he spoke,"I want to," he said, "I want to be with you," and looked deep into Alex's eyes.

Alex nodded very slowly, he looked down as he reached for Nathan's hand. They turned toward the stairs and climbed them slowly and carefully, taking their time until they reached the bedroom quietly and slid noiselessly onto the bed where they resumed kissing and tenderly stroking one another's faces. Alex picked up a remote and flicked on some music. He looked down at Nathan, half naked beneath him and couldn't believe his luck, "I love you so much," he breathed, Nathan stroked his chest, it felt so smooth and warm. "I'm scared Alex," he suddenly said. Alex loved him so deeply, he kept his stroking hand on the side of his face, "I would never hurt you Nathan, don't be scared, I promise to stop if you don't like anything."

Nathan nodded and reached his lips up to him, they kissed longingly, Nathan couldn't help but push his hips upward. Alex pulled at his belt, unhooking it and sliding it from from its loops, he threw it to the floor. His fingers deftly undid the buttons on Nathan's fly. Nathan slid Alex's belt from his jeans and unzipped him. They groaned and crushed against each other. Nathan shut his eyes as Alex bent down and slid his clothes from him and undressed himself. He breathed hard, knowing he was harder than he'd ever been before and standing up like a tent pole, Alex was seeing all of that. His heart thrummed hard as Alex returned to the bed, sliding down on top of him, as each part of his body touched Nathan's skin it was like electricity shooting through him at a million miles an hour, he gasped at every touch and trembled with excitement, it was exquisite.

Nathan opened his eyes as Alex gently pushed his hands back against the bed, interlocking their fingers. His face was gentle, kind and nervous too, "Nathan," he breathed and squeezed Nathan's hands a little, "my Nathan," he gently kissed him, Nathan's heart felt like it might explode, he was so excited, so ready, "Alex," he breathed, "Alex, make love to me," Alex's face got whiter and he bit his lip, catching his breath. "Turn over," he whispered. Nathan rolled onto his front, it was difficult because his stiffness pressed into the bed. He heard Alex click a bottle open and lube himself liberally, 'oh my God, oh my God,' he thought silently and then Alex's arms were lightly down on his as he lowered his hips and Nathan felt the most urgent pressing into his most intimate place.

There was a difficult moment, he was tense, it might not work....and then, Alex was there, gliding, gliding in and out of him. It took them both by surprise, Alex threw back his head at the most incredible pleasure and Nathan pushed his hips upward to receive him. He pressed his head into the bed and groaned a hard sexual noise he didn't even know he possessed. It only spurred Alex on deeper, "oh yes," he gasped, "yes." Nathan was gasping into the bed now, Alex rode him quicker, swifter strokes, it pressed Nathan down into the mattress, a surprisingly good feeling as it rubbed his cock on the top of the duvet and gave him double pleasure. For a moment all he could think about was this, this two facet pleasure that his body was discovering, he didn't remember it was Alex doing it to him for a moment, he just gave himself entirely over to the feelings erupting within him.

He groaned and rubbed himself hard on the bed, the grinding cock in his backside was hard and wet and like nothing he'd imagined, it massaged the most erotic part of him, he was away, caught up in his building orgasm, grunting and gasping and suddenly Alex moved faster, groaning and holding his hips, he rode him and rode him, Nathan started to buck up against him as he came close to orgasm, he plunged at the bed as Alex plunged at him, he was there, nearly there, every ounce of energy slammed his body into the bed, oh my God this was a big one, he burst onto the bed with a ferocious noise of agony and ecstasy, clasping his hands around the edge of the mattress, Alex rammed at him, seeing his boyfriend in the throws of such abandonment sent him into sexual ecstasy, he grabbed at Nathan's buttocks and in three more strokes as he gasped for his life, he blew inside him, gasping for air as if he could barely find any, he thrust a few more times as his ecstasy slowly subsided. Little after shocks ran through him making him judder and catch his breath. Nathan was down on the bed, panting and red faced, lying in his own dampness. He gasped to catch some air, his head and body spinning from the experience. A few more seconds passed and Alex withdrew himself, he pulled back and sat on his haunches gasping and looking at Nathan, breathless before him.

As another minute passed Alex thought it only polite to wash before he cuddled Nathan, he disappeared to the bathroom and turned the shower on himself as fast as he could. When he soaped himself his penis still tingled from the excitement and pounding, water ran down his hair and face and he couldn't believe what he'd just done, it would take a while to sink in, though he knew it was real.

Nathan turned over on the bed and did his best to clean up the damp patch, he picked up his shorts and jeans and headed for the next nearest bathroom of three, he too turned the shower on himself and washed carefully around the newly discovered area. He didn't hurt exactly but it had been an unusual stretch which his body would need to get used to. Alex had taken incredible care to ease into him and not bruise him, as he thought about that, Nathan was stunned to feel himself rise and harden again. He stroked his shaft and jumped a bit at his own touch, he was on fire to any contact, every nerve ending awake and ready. He showered for a little longer thinking about Alex being in love with him. He knew they were young but he saw this lasting forever, in his minds eye this was it, he could see every part of his future with him.

Their form teacher had said a very pertinent and intriguing thing at the end of last term. He said, "kids, life is as simple or as complicated as you want. See your life and its goals and they will come true." It had helped comfort and guide Nathan more than the man knew, being a natural worrier, it had been like a simple key offered to unlock all his fears and it had allowed him to let go of many and focus on what he did want instead, and what he really wanted was a creative life and Alex. Just two simple things. As he towelled off he was amazed at himself, could it be that simple ? Think about what you want and with some work you'll get it ? He smiled at his reflection and marvelled a little bit at his body again, it really did look good. Just then there was a tentative knock on the door, "Nathan ?Are you ok in there ?" Alex sounded really worried. Nathan had already slipped into the legs of his jeans, he popped the fly shut and opened the door, rubbing his hair with the towel.

Alex watched as the bathroom door swung open and he stood in the steamy room, jeaned, beautiful and smiling at him. He smiled a hugely relieved grin and stepped forward, wrapping his arms around Nathan's neck. "Thank God you're alright" he breathed against his soft damp hair. Nathan squeezed his waist in return, "of course I am," he whispered. Alex found his mouth and kissed it gently. He pulled back to look him in the eyes, "I didn't hurt you did I ?" Nathan shook his head, "no you didn't." Alex stroked his face, "thank God," he breathed. Nathan looked down at Alex's towel wrapped hips and back up at his eyes again, thinking about what they'd just done.

"Bit of a milestone," he smiled. Alex breathed out an amazed breath, "it was incredible. I've never had sex before but I know that was incredible." Nathan blushed as he looked back at him and Alex folded him into his arms again. "You, are incredible," he breathed, holding Nathan, wrapping him tightly in his arms. Nathan rested his head on Alex's shoulder and closed his eyes. He was in seventh heaven. They stayed that way for many minutes, loving the feel of each other, hearts thrumming with love. Alex's tummy growled and they both snorted a little laugh, "I think we need some food," he stated, beginning to pull away. Nathan lifted his head and stepped back a little to follow him downstairs, but the room was so hot after his roasting shower and his head so light from excitement that he felt a strange energy sapping burst of dizziness.

He stumbled as it felt as if his ears were completely tightly blocked for a moment in the same way a plane makes you feel during take off. The room lurched hard, he had no balance for a moment, he didn't feel sick or bad just absolutely dizzy and off kilter. He stumbled again, it all happened in a split second. Alex didn't see the first stumble but he heard it and as his head whipped around he saw the second one and the way Nathan flayled to get a grip on the door frame for support. He dived at him, catching his body around the waist. He held him tightly and felt like he might faint himself. He couldn't let go for a moment as he was so frightened, but it was good as it allowed Nathan a little time to recover. "I'm ok, I'm ok," he said calmly, "it's going now," and it was true, his ears were unpopped, painfully in this case but he didn't need to say so, and his balance was fast returning.

He tried to push Alex's arms away gently but he was terrified, Nathan's push was insistent so Alex relented just a little, still holding him but a few inches away so that they could look at each other. "What, the hell, was that ?" He trembled as he looked at Nathan with alarmed eyes. "That was nothing more than a hot room, not enough food and far from enough sleep since I've been ill, I'm fine, honestly."

Alex shook his head, "you are not fine, and you are so going to the doctor tomorrow." Nathan rolled his eyes, "no I AM fine Alex, really I am, I don't need a doctor." Alex still looked utterly terrified, he shook his head. "I don't know what to say ! This dizzy fainting thing really scares me Nate." Nathan shrugged, "honestly Alex, I'm really ok." Alex still held him and didn't look convinced. "So are you ok to get dressed now ?" He asked. Nathan dropped a little kiss on his lips and smiled, "I love that you care, I am ok and yes I can get dressed. Look, put some clothes on too and let's have a massive dinner then you won't be worried about me anymore, ok ?" Nathan squeezed past him to go and pick up his clothes from the floor. He wasn't keen on prolonging this bit of their weekend.

Alex stood in the bathroom doorway for a moment, he was sick with worry about him. One way or the other he was going to make sure he saw a doctor. He walked down the corridor and watched as Nathan bent to pick up his T, no dizziness left now, he didn't lie, but Alex was still frightened. He shook himself and calmed down, it probably was just sapped energy from the bug, why hadn't he just put it down to that ? He wondered. But he was in love with Nathan and that gave him permission to worry he smiled to himself and followed him into the room to hurry into his clothes.

By the time they were dressed, Nathan's stomach growled loudly too. They laughed and headed into the kitchen. Alex pulled out a stool and pushed Nathan onto it, "I KNOW you're fine but just humour me and sit down will you ?"

Nathan looked pretty hacked off. Alex put down the wooden spoon he'd just plucked from the utensil pot, "look I'm allowed to worry, I'm sorry I don't mean to piss you off though." He put his hands on either side of his face and kissed his lips gently. Nathan breathed out a contented breath and let his tongue play along Alex's lips. Alex opened his mouth and let Nathan's tongue in, it sank deeply into him. He started to groan and wrap his arms around Nathan, he let one hand wander down and lift the edge of his shirt, feeling his gloriously warm smooth body underneath.

Nathan let out a guttural murmur and said " Christ !" Alex's hand played further up under his shirt until he found his nipples again and then he was teasing them, swirling his fingers around and over them, rubbing each tip with his fingertips, making them swollen and erect. "God !" Nathan groaned and covered his groin with one of his hands. Alex pulled away and took in his flushed face and covered groin, he was just about to suggest they move to the sofa when Nathan's stomach protested loudly, Alex smiled, "food first I guess," he backed away over to the saucepans and cupboards and started getting out what he needed.

Nathan looked completely wanton and sexual, his hair was all over the place, his face blushing red and his hand still covered his groin. Alex looked at him and his heart turned over, he was such a wonderful guy. He stared at Alex, "food first ?" He said tentatively, one eyebrow raised, and then he grinned and ran his hands through his hair, aware that it was looking a bit wild. "Food FIRST," he repeated. Alex laughed with his back to him and started preparing their home made macaroni, cauliflower cheese.

He poured milk butter and flour into a pan and started to stir it while another pan full of water simmered to boiling point with cauliflower and macaroni in it. He salt and peppered his sauce and took a block of cheese out of the fridge. He passed it to Nathan with a huge ergonomically designed grater. Nathan began to grate and nibbled a bit of cheese out of the collecting tray at the bottom, it was deeply tangy cheddar, "God that's yummy," he said with a mouthful. "It's supposed to be for the macaroni," Alex grinned, he walked over and dropped a kiss onto his lips. He walked back to the macaroni and gave it a stir around, some was sticking to the bottom.

Nathan sighed and stretched, he rubbed his neck and shook his head, a naughty smile played across his lips. "What's that for ?" Alex asked, leaning across the counter. Nathan flushed and looked a bit shy, "oh, that's just me thinking about what we did earlier..." he said coyly. He looked up and saw Alex's eyes shining with delight and his cheeks flushing a little too. He drew in a deep breath, "I know," he grinned. He walked back over and stood right in front of him looking down, then he bent his body and kissed him full on the mouth again, there was no mistaking what that kiss said. Nathan's groin leapt to life, he groaned longingly.

Alex pulled away with a wicked smile and went back to stirring the sauce, Nathan moaned and put his head on his hands, "you evil tormenter!" He husked. Alex laughed a happy throaty laugh and Nathan tried to think of something else. He got up and walked over to the big sofa, throwing himself backwards onto it he shut his eyes and covered his face with his arms. His body was singing with longing, he so wanted Alex to touch him again. He lay there for a minute or two, hearing him clank around a bit with the pans in the background. He sighed, relaxing but frustrated and tried not to imagine Alex's tongue around him. He squeezed his eyes together for a moment as he thought about it. His arms slumped behind his head, resting on the sofa arm as he tried and failed repeatedly to stop his imaginings. Just as he was starting to get some success at it, the sofa moved as Alex clambered on.

Nathan's lips turned up at the corners but he didn't move or open his eyes. Alex bent over him on all fours around his body and kissed him lightly on the lips, Nathan breathed out a longing sigh and opened his eyes, Alex was topless and looking down at him with such a look, Nathan's tummy filled with butterflies, - 'here we go again,' he thought. Alex stroked his cheek with the tips of his fingers as if he'd never felt anything so lovely. He looked as if he couldn't find the words. He helped Nathan pull off his shirt and T and gently lowered his body so that their chests touched again. "Alex," Nathan breathed and opened his mouth as Alex slid his lips back onto him. Alex kissed him as if he were imparting part of his soul, Nathan's heart thumped. He groaned against Alex's lips and pulled away, rubbing his cheek against him, he started to pant, nothing mattered now except him and their bodies together. He felt for Alex's belt, it hit the floor in a second. He unzipped him, Alex started to groan and puff above him, his eyes shut slowly as Nathan reached into his loosened jeans.

Alex caught his breath, he was swollen to bursting and Nathan's firm caressing fingertips were amazing on his skin. He gasped and prayed that he would close his hand around his shaft. He needn't have worried, he let out an animal like cry as Nathan began to move his hand up and down. He opened his eyes a slit and saw Nathan's face, concentrated only on giving him pleasure. "I won't be long," Alex gasped through contorted lips, "I don't care," Nathan whispered back, "as long as you come all over me, I don't care how fast you go," Alex let out a cry of surrender as Nathan spoke and with two more thrusts he exploded onto his chest. He grunted and his body jerked as his orgasm peaked and the after shocks took hold. Nathan didn't take his hand away until Alex stopped gasping and writhing, little tremors of ecstasy ran through his penis as he slid it gently back and forth still. At last he stopped, gasping and squeezing his eyes shut, he got off Nathan and sat unbuckled on the floor, leaning up against the sofa edge. Nathan reached for his t-shirt and cleaned himself up, it wasn't like that was going to stay on for much more of the day if they had their way. Alex turned, leaning against the sofa and gazed up at him. "Oh my God," he breathed with a big smile.

Nathan grinned back at him, playing with the light hairs on his arms, "I aim to please." Alex's eyes shone with happiness, he grinned and ran a hand over his groin making himself jump a little. "Nope, still wouldn't fit back in there yet." He said, looking down at his fly. Nathan roared with laughter, thrilled to be able to please him. Alex laid his head against the edge of the sofa and let Nathan move his fingers to stroke his hair. After a minute he looked directly at Nathan's groin and then raised an eyebrow at him. Nathan grinned sheepishly and said, "what ?" "How are we feeling ?" Alex nodded toward the tumescent bulge. Nathan leant his head far back against the sofa arm and squirmed.

Alex put his hand on his thigh, as high up as he could without actually touching his groin. Nathan sucked in air sharply, Alex watched his face for a moment, his eyes were shut and he gulped. Alex turned his eyes back to Nathan's lap, he reached over and carefully slid off his belt, curling it around one hand before he dropped it gently to the floor. He unpopped the first button, Nathan's breathing got heavier, Alex unpopped the rest. Nathan's hand came up to press against his eyes for a moment. Alex pushed his jeans down a little and slipped his Calvin Klein's with them, revealing the smoothest hardest cock, it looked fabulous. As the cool air hit his skin Nathan gasped and tensed with anticipation.

Alex slid his fingers into Nathan's free hand, draped over the side of the sofa, he squeezed gently and Nathan squeezed back. His chest rose and fell rapidly now and Alex slid his clothes even further to reveal more flesh. He knelt up to see the whole view fully, Nathan's head, eyes shut, was pushed back hard into the sofa arm, Alex couldn't wait to make him shudder and explode. He retracted his hand from Nathan's fingers and wrapped both together around his cock as he lowered his mouth to encircle the tumescent tip. Nathan coughed a huge groan of caught breath, arching his back and gasping as Alex began to move his mouth on him. He sank his lips up and down, up and down Nathan's hardness, stroking at his balls and perineum with deft fingers. He'd never done it before, it just seemed right. "Oh fuck, oh fuck," Nathan gasped as Alex sucked him, he thrust his hips upward. Alex's lips and the amount of suction he supplied were beyond heavenly. He put both hands to his face, gasping into his palms. Alex moved his lips to just the top of Nathan's shaft and that was it, the intense pleasure was so enormous he couldn't hold back. He thrust violently upward, gasping and clutching at the sofa, "I'm gonna come," he shrieked and burst hot liquid deeply into Alex's throat.

Alex swallowed and kept his lips there, gently massaging Nathan through the inevitable after waves of pleasure. They came and Nathan gasped and shuddered beneath him. When he had stopped thrusting, Alex withdrew his mouth and licking his lips, looked down at him breathing hard. Nathan opened his eyes, looking up at Alex's smiling face, he blushed comprehensively. Alex put his arms on either side of Nathan's body, he bent and kissed his lips very gently. "I love you." Nathan's beautiful face split into a huge happy grin and he wrapped his arms around him. They held each other tight. "I really, really love you," Alex breathed against his ear. Nathan squeezed him harder and breathed back, "me too Alex, me too."

Chapter Four.

Alex pulled away and looked down at Nathan again, "I was so worried we wouldn't get to this when you were ill, when you kept getting faint it really scared me." Nathan nodded, "I know, but I am ok now I promise." "You'd better bloody be, get dizzy once more and you're going straight to casualty or the doctor, which ever's closer at the time." Nathan laughed and shook his head, "no I'm not." "You frigging bloody well are !" Alex glared at him. Nathan giggled more. "Hmm, well just hope we never have to test that one out."

Alex smiled and got up. He pulled his tops on and re-belted himself. It was getting a little chilly all of a sudden. Nathan frowned at his scrumpled up t-shirt, "I think I'm gonna get cold in just a shirt, let me grab my hoody from my bag." He moved across the room, popping his fly closed at the same time. "Borrow mine," Alex pointed at his Apple crumble one on top of a pile of freshly ironed laundry. "Thanks," Nathan pulled it over his head, the soft fleecey inside felt gorgeous against his skin. Alex was back in the kitchen, "er, I don't think we'll be eating macaroni for supper, this looks pretty grim now, how about bacon sandwiches instead ?" "Yum !" Nathan licked his lips. He helped Alex clear away the congealed bechemel sauce and jellified macaroni, stacked the dishwasher with him, amid many little lip to lip moments and the odd cuddle as they kept passing one another.

When the kitchen was clean, two plates sat waiting for the sarnies and the bacon sizzled under the grill, the boys sat down at the kitchen stools and decided what to watch after dinner. It was already past 10 as they started to eat, Nathan's stomach protested loudly, "ok we have to get some more food into you after this, what else do you fancy ?" Alex asked before taking another huge bite. "You ?" Nathan suggested and bit into his sandwich too. Alex's stuffed cheeks turned red and he coughed as if he was going to choke on his mouthful, his eyes shone with laughter as he tried to chew down and swallow the bite as fast as possible, when he'd just about accomplished the feat he started laughing out loud and had to go and grab a fresh glass of water. He sat down again and shook his head at Nathan, "come here," he smiled, leaning toward him. He kissed his mouth with delicious stroking tongue movements. It made Nathan groan. Alex put his hand a little way up inside Nathan's top, feeling his supple waist, Nathan gasped at the feel of his fingers. He closed his eyes and pressed his forehead into Alex's shoulder. Alex cupped his head and loved the feel of the silky short hair at the base of his skull, he smelt so good too, shampoo, aftershave and a smell of.....what was it ? Alex wondered, just Nathan's skin he decided, healthy, soft, lush skin. He breathed in against Nathan's head as his hand gently stroked across his tummy and up around his ribs. He did it so softly that it had a gorgeously soporific affect on Nathan. He felt his eyes becoming heavy, as if he wanted to curl up in Alex's arms on the sofa in the dark, a dvd playing softly in the background as they snuggled up to each other.

He let out a relaxed sigh, "you like that do you ?" Alex breathed against his hair, Nathan looked up with groggy eyes, "it's amazing." Alex smiled at him and pecked him lightly on the lips, "you fancy curling up together in front of that dvd then ?" He asked, stroking Nathan's face, " I would love that, had just the same thought." Nathan replied.

"Go on, set it up will you while I clear up. Won't take me a sec, then I'm bringing loads more nibbles over and we're troughing them down, I'm not having you go hungry." Nathan nodded, "good plan." He walked sleepily over to the dvd tower and started to look for their choice of earlier, it was hiding from him and took a moment or two to find, by which time Alex was locking the front door and closing the curtains.

He ambled over shortly afterwards, with an armful of edible goodies and dropped them on the carpet in front of the sofa. They both reached for some cushions and soon had a snug mini nest going with crisps, chocolate, bags of peanut m and ms etc..., all scattered about them. They munched as the movie started, Alex flicked off the lights and they could only see each other by the glare from the screen. Every now and then Alex would gaze at Nathan and feel so happy to have him in his life. He watched his profile as he reached for a crisp and thought how God damn handsome he was. Sometimes Nathan would feel Alex looking at him and look up shyly for a moment, each time this happened Alex would instinctively crawl forward and place a little kiss on his lips.

Just as they came to the midway point this happened again, Alex crawled across the few inches or so between them and watched this time as Nathan rolled onto his back on the carpet and found himself looking up at Alex who hovered above him on his hands and knees. He looked down at him with so much love and desire. Nathan breathed a very contented yet excited breath and smiled with all his love up at Alex. "You give me the most amazing butterflies when you look at me like that....," he whispered. Alex smiled with utter happiness and reached down to caress his face, " every time I look at you I can't believe you're here." He shook his head, " I told you, I've loved you for a long time. Climbing up to your window that night was something I'd dreamt about for so long." Nathan's mouth fell open in surprise, "but....? I..." he didn't know what to say. Alex straddled his body and sat across his hips, then he frowned, "I'm not hurting your back like this am I ?" "No," Nathan answered and reached for one of his hands to caress while they talked. Their fingers interlocked as Alex looked thoughtful, "do you know, I even..." he broke away looking a little unsure. Nathan rested his other arm under his head, "you even what ?" He looked intrigued and happy so Alex continued.

"I came to your house on two other nights, the first time I threw a stone at your window and you didn't appear, I lost my nerve after three more throws and legged it. The other time, I just looked around to see if I could work out how to climb up and then I knew I had to take a chance." He looked a bit worried. Nathan squeezed his hand, "I'm so glad you did. I'd been so scared that you'd see how much I liked you for the whole of last term and I had no idea you felt the same. It's pretty much a miracle that you do." They both gave a little snort of relief. Alex sighed and looked down at the hand he was playing with. "That night," he breathed and gazed deeply into Nathan's eyes, "that incredible night when you let me in through your window. My day went through so many ups and downs that day. I was so glad to talk to you and you seemed strangely keen to chat but awkward too as if I'd done something."

Nathan groaned and tried to retract his hand to cover his eyes. "No no, don't, it's ok," Alex assured him. " But you were off with me and I didn't get it, I really thought we were friends and before I fell in love with you I wanted to get to know you more anyway, so when you hurt your hand and I was walking past the tech room, I was so glad to be able to help you." He looked at the floor for a moment with a slightly guilty smile, " I didn't like you being hurt but I must say it was nice to have an excuse to touch you." Nathan laughed. Alex gave him a mega watt smile, "ah but then, then then then....that lovely night. After you sending me such confusing signals, letting me bandage you, lovely chats on the bus and then 'boom,' it was like you switched off as I left the bus." He shook his head. I got home and I just couldn't concentrate on anything, all I could think about was you so I knew that that night I would have to come to your room and try and find out once and for all if there was any hope at all." He shook his head, " God my heart was in my mouth." He turned his eyes fully back onto Nathan's and squeezed his hand gently, "when you let me take you in my mouth," he squeezed his eyes shut for a second, "Oh God Nathan," you made all my dreams come true that night, but, - am I being too literal ?" Nathan shook his head, "Alex," he breathed and shut his eyes. He gulped, the emotions welling up could crash out of him like a torrent very soon if he wasn't careful.

Alex saw the momentary crease in his brow and stroked his face feeling anguished, "hey, hey my sweetness, have I gone too far ?" He questioned. This only heightened Nathan's emotional buzz, it wasn't too far just intensely amazing and wonderful and he didn't know how to express that in words all of a sudden, all he could do was gulp and try not to let it all flood out of him in a gushing sob. He squeezed his eyes shut as tight as possible, "no, no you haven't gone too far. Just give me a second here," he crossed one of his arms over his face annoyed that he felt so much like sobbing. It was no good, he needed more pressure, only both hands pressed over his face would stop the sobs he knew it, he pulled them both free and clamped his palms over his eyes.

Alex looked on with a horrible feeling in his stomach, my God, was he blowing it ? "I..., Nathan....I'm...I.." he didn't know what to say. Nathan struggled out from under him, giving a sudden burst of force when Alex didn't want to move. He was up on his feet in a second, he walked over to the kitchen consul and pressed at his eyes. Alex was white, "Please," he asked, following Nathan across the room, "please tell me what I did to upset you ?"

He came up behind him and put his hands on his shoulders gently. Nathan turned around, his eyes were moist. "You didn't do anything to upset me." Alex looked confused, "Please I can tell some thing's wrong, what did I do ?" Nathan drew in a deep breath and biting his lip he looked into Alex's eyes, "it's just that you make me feel incredible and suddenly having my wildest dreams realised makes me more emotional than I thought possible." He looked embarrassed, "I hope you can cope with that...?" Alex grinned and shook his head, "really, that was what was happening to you ?" Nathan nodded shyly, "big girl's blouse aren't I ?"

Alex looked watery eyed and smiled deeply at him, "no, you're wonderful, completely wonderful." He kissed his lips, cupping his face. "You're so wonderful," he groaned and pulled Nathan's top off, making him gasp, he undid his jeans and slid his hand inside, quickly finding his smooth hard cock. He wrapped his hand fully around it and began to pull up and down. Nathan rolled his head back and caught his breath. "Oh Alex," he breathed in an anguished voice. The pleasure was so intense. Alex stopped for a second and pulled his own top off, unzipping his jeans and then returning his hands to Nathan's cock and the back of his head as he pulled his mouth close again to devour him entirely with his loving.

He brought Nathan so quickly to the point just before orgasm as he was so in tune with him. He kissed him with electric passion and moved his hands with absolute confidence, caressing him as he'd never been before. Nathan thrashed his body as his orgasm took hold, and pressed his mouth on to Alex's with complete abandon, he never wanted this moment to stop. He cried out as he came and Alex moved his sticky hand to his side, clutching his body as if stopping him from going. He pulled at his jeans, they were immediately on the floor and then his own. In another second they stood naked and pressed bodily against each other, kissing, wet, hard, groaning in ecstasy.

Slowly Alex turned Nathan around, Nathan's heart rammed against his ribs. Alex slicked himself and eased inside. Nathan gripped the kitchen counter and gasped a ragged breath with his eyes shut. He couldn't believe the man he loved was doing this to him again. Alex's hands gripped him around the hips, Nathan arched back against him and heard both of them groan, he leant his head right back against Alex and felt his lips brush his ear. It was exquisite as Alex inched in and out of him and they writhed against each other. Alex's pumping became faster and his breathing more gasping and short, Nathan bowed his head as he pushed himself against his beloved.

Alex seemed to harden further still, taking Nathan to a level of excitement he had never previously known, he bucked against him and groaned out , 'fuck me Alex, fuck me,' through clenched teeth. "Oh baby," Alex husked back and ground himself into him. Nathan's knuckles were white, his veins bulging under his skin as blood pounded around his body. Alex cried out, thrust with one almighty surge, and exploded inside him. Nathan gasped and shuddered, his knees felt weak. He leant back against a panting Alex who wrapped him up in his arms. They gasped against each other, wet, sweaty and utterly ecstatic. "I can feel your grin," Alex whispered beside Nathan's ear.

Nathan grinned some more and Alex did a throaty little laugh of happiness. Nathan slowly turned to face him and Alex locked his arms around him again. They kissed with lingering tenderness, loving the feeling of each other's hearts banging with adrenalin against their chests. Alex pushed his hand gently through Nathan's damp hair, watching his face, closed eyes, lovely lips, so much beauty. He kissed him gently and pulled away again. Nathan opened his eyes and gazed back at him. "I love you," he whispered, barely an inch from Alex's lips.

They kissed and looked at each other, wordlessly. Nathan breathed in a long deep breath and blinked slowly, nothing bad could ever happen while he felt like this. He felt strong, muscular, beautiful and confident beyond anything. He was entirely happy and it shone from him. Alex smiled and nodded, "it's a good feeling this isn't it ?" Nathan blushed, "you know what I'm feeling ?" "Yes, because you make me feel just as good inside." Nathan shook his head and Alex slipped his arms around him, kissing his neck and then reached for his hands, "do you want a shower ?"

Nathan nodded, "I'll meet you up there," he beamed and pulled his shorts on, disappearing to the loo. Alex looked down at himself, he looked so normal, his body was the same, it didn't smell funny or different, it was like it had been the day before.

He frowned and edged over to a nearby mirror, turning sideways in it. In fact, if he really thought about it, he actually looked better than ever, what did that mean ? He grinned at his reflection and grabbing all their clothes from the floor, ran upstairs. He dimmed the lights in the bathroom and stepped into the full force of the water. It was so warm and welcoming, his body tingled with satisfaction and sheer joy, now all that was missing was Nathan. He turned his face up to the water, exposing his soft features to the harsh pressure. The door clicked and a second later Nathan stepped into the bath. Alex's heart filled with excitement, he jumped a little at Nathan's cold skin as he folded his arms around him and stepped under the water too. They stood together, so warmed by the shower, deeply in love and wrapped tightly in each others arms. "I don't want this to ever end," Alex breathed back against Nathan's chest. "It won't, Nathan husked. "It will always be this good."

Alex let out a tremulous breath as Nathan squeezed him tighter still. "I know," he breathed and then said aloud, "Marry me."

Nathan jolted against him and a little nervous laugh shot out of him. Alex held onto his arms, still wrapped firmly around him, breathing hard. He waited. "What ?"

"I said, Marry me." He repeated.

Nathan's head spun, he couldn't speak. Within the space of three weeks, he had got everything that he wanted in the world and he was still only 17. Anything else from here on in would be pure 'gravy.' He realised he was trembling, despite the water, and he hadn't answered yet. Alex turned around to face him and folded his arms around him. "I meant it," he said, looking deadly serious, his eyes locked onto Nathan's.

Nathan's stomach flipped over with disbelief, he could barely breath or speak. He wanted to say 'it can't be true,' but he knew it was and it was the most marvellous feeling in the world. He didn't know how to be this happy. He looked back at Alex with an expression that said everything and then he managed just one word.

"Yes," he said in wonderment, and Alex broke down in a sob, his face completely red with emotion as they clutched each other. "Hold me, just hold me for God's sake," he begged into Nathan's chest. Nathan re-wrapped his arms around him, trembling hard he held him until his legs gave way and he had to sit. Alex grabbed at him, afraid he was fainting again, but as they touched the bath they were still locked together, breathing hard but fine.

He lifted his head and looked at Nathan's slim, beautiful face, "you're really going to marry me ?" Nathan nodded, his smile split into a huge grin, "yes I am." They snatched each other up again and stayed curled into one another's warm wet bodies, alive, happy and utterly sated. It was half an hour before either wanted to move and then Alex kissed Nathan's lips and pulled him upright. "I'm so happy," he said, reaching to turn the water off.

"I will never be happier in my life than now," Nathan returned and Alex's jaw dropped. He pulled in a shaky breath and drew Nathan to him. "I don't know what to say, I can't put into words how incredible this is. I love you more than anything in the world Nathan." "I can't wait to marry you Alex," Nathan gasped as Alex's arms tightened around him like a vice. He held him like that for a moment and though Nathan could barely breath, it meant everything to him. It was Alex saying 'never doubt me,' and Nathan knew he never would.

The bathroom was so filled with steam that neither felt cold as they dis-entwined and Alex stepped out and passed Nathan a huge chocolate brown fluffy towel. The air fizzed between them, full of their known future, certain in its outcome. Nathan watched Alex as they rubbed themselves dry, Alex tucked his towel around his waist as Nathan rubbed his hair once more and did the same. "I'm 18 in three weeks time you know," he let the end of his sentence go up like a question. Alex nodded, " and I'm 18 in 6, I know what you're thinking and I agree. Let's tell our parents then.

Shall we look into jobs and where we want to live ?" He asked. Nathan grinned, his stomach flipped over, this was really happening. "Yes, and I want to pick a honeymoon destination. When do you want to get married ?" Alex applied his deodorant and passed it to Nathan, "October the 10th," he replied without missing a beat. Nathan looked up at him with shining eyes, "really ?" Alex came toward him for a kiss, "yes," he pulled back again, "We'll never forget the date, 10.10. if it were last year we could have had the whole three in a row but we can't very well do November 11th just to line up this year can we." Nathan jumped up and down on the spot for a moment and covered his face with his hands. He breathed hard into them until Alex stepped forward and gently pulled them away.

He wrapped him in his arms and held the back of his head. Minutes passed until he kissed Nathan's lips and looked at him with such soft loving eyes. "I can't believe you're mine," he smiled. "I am," Nathan whispered, blinking his lovely long eyelashes at him. Alex opened the door and as the cold air hit they ran into his bedroom to dress, fast. When they were finished Nathan heard Alex laugh loudly, he looked up, "NOOO, oh for God's sake, we can't do this !" He looked down at his dark blue hoodie and across at Alex's grey and orange stripey one. Both Abercrombie. "Oh come on," Alex laughed, "it's only you and I seeing us. I'm bloody starving." Nathan chuckled and shrugged, "yeah, I guess so. Come on, let's get some food."

They tore off downstairs and decided on a chinese, Alex grabbed the local menu from the kitchen drawer and they sat on the floor in front of the tv.

Nathan slumped comfortably onto his elbow and scanned the menu, he was so hungry. He decided on Chicken in black bean sauce, egg fried rice and mini prawn toasts to start. Alex looked at him, "that's it ? With the serious ravaging you're getting over the rest of this weekend you need to keep your strength up you know ?" Nathan rolled onto his back in fits of laughter. Alex snatched the menu out of his hand and tossed it over his shoulder. He hovered over Nathan on all fours, "what are you laughing about, I'm serious !" He said with a giggle.

Nathan rolled about, his cheeks hurt from laughing. His stomach growled loudly, "shut up, I'm talking !" Alex said to it. Nathan clutched his sides which made Alex laugh even more, he tried to lift his head to look up at him but seeing Alex's cheeks all bunched up and red too only got him more, "stop, stop..." he pleaded. Alex snorted and roared with laughter, Nathan's stomach growled again and tears ran down his cheeks. Alex sat back on his heals and clutched his ribs. An extra loud rumble from Nathan's hollow tummy brought Alex back to earth, this was so much fun he couldn't have him all weak and fainting again. He wiped his eyes on his sleeves and grabbed the phone.

Nathan giggled gently in the back ground as Alex dialled so he tried not to look at him. It wasn't long before they had their order in and Alex dropped the phone on the carpet. He turned to look at Nathan, now leaning with his back up against the sofa and smiling at him. He looked beautiful, tired and elated. Alex shuffled over and sat beside him. They leant their heads against each other. It was silent apart from the ticking of the kitchen clock, leather effect but £2 from Primark, Alex's Mum never stopped reminding them.

The curtains were open and they could see the town in the distance, moonlight bouncing off everything in between. "You really are bloody lucky to live here," Nathan breathed, "that view." Alex nodded against his head. "I know, and now I've got you, I must be the luckiest boy alive." Nathan grinned, "next to me that is." He felt Alex curl his hand around his, lacing their fingers together again. This would definitely suit him for good.

Later, after the boys had devoured their Chinese and stuffed down every last crumb of the snacks, they slumped across each other on the floor, Nathan ended up more draped over Alex who was supported by about six cushions. They flicked on a dvd and lay curled about each other as the story unfolded. Neither stayed awake for long. An hour into it and Alex woke in a little pain, his neck was stiff. He looked down and saw Nathan fully asleep and utterly beautiful. He reached out and stroked carefully behind his ear. It was enough, Nathan stirred and groggily looked up at him. He blinked and stretched. "What's going on ?"

He croaked. Alex smiled and said softly, "sorry to wake you my love, shall we go and sleep in my bed ?"

Nathan nodded, still half asleep. He looked so lovely all foggy headed and sleepy. Alex switched the tv off, there was enough moonlight from the open curtains to see where they were going, and led him by the hand up to his room. He closed the door behind them and flung the duvet back, Nathan got in and shut his eyes, he shivered a little despite his clothes. Alex laughed softly at him, too sleepy to undress, who cared. He slid in behind him and pulled the duvet back around them both. "Sleep well," he whispered. "You too," Nathan mumbled and they were out like a light into a deep, contented sleep.

Nathan dreamt that night, he saw Alex waiting at a hilltop alter for him, in a white suit, his dark hair dazzling in the sun. That was the only thing he dreamt and it was the most peace filled refreshing sleep of his life. When he woke up he wasn't sure of anything for a moment, had everything just been a dream ? The duvet crinkled as he moved his leg gently, immediately he felt Alex's warmth behind him, his face broke into a grin as he remembered everything from yesterday and butterflies started up in his stomach. He bit his lip and inhaled a sharp breath, he was getting married !

He screwed his eyes up tightly and lay his arms gently on top of Alex's which were wrapped around him. He really was getting married. He let out a little giggle and Alex stirred behind him. He hugged his arms in tightly and yawned, coming to a little, he released his arms, opening his eyes. As Nathan pushed back against his body to show he was awake, Alex realised he had been squashing him and released his hold, "sorry, was I holding you too tightly ?" He croaked. Nathan laughed, "I could take it." Alex grinned behind him and kissed the back of his head. Nathan rolled onto his back, turning his head so that they could see each other. Alex looked groggily at him, his face half hidden by the pillow.

"Lean your lips this way so that I can kiss you good morning properly," he husked. Nathan's beautiful face split into a huge grin. He stretched his neck up across and kissed Alex's lips gently. "Oh no you don't !" Alex lifted his head, one eyebrow raised and moved across on his elbows, staring down at him. "That, was not, a good morning kiss now lay one on me properly big boy." Nathan's stomach tied up in excited knots, he laughed out loud and licked his lips as Alex slowly lowered his mouth down on top of his. He licked Nathan's mouth open, tasting his delicious tongue, and carefully manoeuvred his body down so that their chests pressed together. He held either side of his face, stroking his cheeks with his thumbs. It blew Nathan's mind, he groaned softly, his head spinning with sheer pleasure. Alex pulled away and looked down at him. "Morning," he whispered, running his thumbs over his warm moist lips. Why did everything that Alex did like that feel so luscious, Nathan shuddered beneath him and slowly lifted his gaze to fix on him. Alex's expression spoke of so much love that Nathan let our a shuddering breath and blinked hard. Alex's lips went up at the corners, " I don't know what you're thinking but I love it when you do that," he smiled.

Nathan blushed and blinked slowly again, "I'm thinking of you and how awesome you make me feel." Alex gasped and bending his head down kissed Nathan with so much passion. When they drew apart Nathan found it hard to breath.

"Sorry, I've been crushing you again haven't I ?" Alex whispered, shifting off him. Nathan turned on his side to face him, "hold me." He said. Alex pulled him into his arms and wrapped him tightly there. "Are you ok ?" He checked. Nathan nodded in his arms and Alex relaxed. They lay snuggled under the duvet for a long time, half asleep, half awake and totally in love.

At last when it seemed as if the sun was desperate to break through Alex's curtains he disentangled himself enough to pull one aside slightly and peer out, but he had to squint and look away as it was so bright. He let the curtain drop back but the light had stirred Nathan who sat up slowly and rubbed his face. The duvet dropped down to his waist revealing his slender body and sculpted abs. Alex drew in an awed breath, he sank back onto the bed and kissed him again. Nathan rubbed his eye with the palm of his hand, his hair was sticking up everywhere and he still looked sleep drunk and pink cheeked. Alex loved it. He slid onto his side and laughed at Nathan who grinned groggily back.

"What are you laughing at me now for ?"
Alex shook his head. "You just look so knackered, but lovely."

"Thanks," said Nathan in a "I don't think," kind of way. Alex grinned and rolled his face into the bed and then jolted upright as Nathan got his own back by pinching his side between two fingers. Alex was fiendishly ticklish. "No!" He screamed. "Fucking cheeky git, knackered am I...." Nathan grabbed him again with both hands this time and tickled mercilessly. Alex thrashed about screaming and going redder and redder, "no, no Nathan no, please stop," he coughed and giggled. Nathan stopped, pushed him onto his back and bent to kiss his stomach.

He did it so tenderly that Alex groaned and shut his eyes, hoping it was the beginning of a tongue and hand session. It wasn't. Nathan was up and stepping into jogging bums and Alex's Abercrombie top from yesterday. "That's what you get, for saying I'm knackered." He leant across Alex, kissed his lips and grinned at him. Alex jumped up immediately, making a grab for him, he wasn't going to be teased and let him get away with it, he was up for some serious loving this morning.

Nathan leapt out of the way, laughing with all his might. "Get, that, pretty arse, over, here." Alex shrieked as he sprinted after him. Nathan pelted out of the door and down the corridor, then the stairs, two at a time. He screamed as he rounded the kitchen consul, realising how close Alex was, he was a bloody fast runner. He turned on another burst of speed but it wasn't fast enough, as he launched himself to jump lengthways over the massive sofa, Alex caught him by the hood and yanked him back, they crashed down together on top of the sofa, not hurt but hurting for a moment or two from clashed limbs. They lay panting and laughing, looking up at the ceiling in a tangle with each other's bodies.

Alex squirmed underneath Nathan who laughed aloud and moved his hand, he found Alex's tummy easily, giving it a little grope making him howl with ticklishness again, "no no, no more, please," he begged, breathless with laughter. Quick as a flash, Nathan rolled over him and pinned his wrists to the sofa, smiling down at him he pecked him on the lips and said, "you're such a bloody fast runner ?" Alex laughed and nodded, "see, you'll never get away from me now...!" He exclaimed. Nathan's expression went all soft above him and he let go of Alex's wrists. "I'll never want to," he said gently.

Alex took in his mood and sat up, "good, me neither." He husked and pressed his mouth onto his. They wrapped their arms about each other and hugged tightly, Nathan laid his cheek on Alex's shoulder and felt his beloved stroke his head and the nape of his neck, it was a wonderful feeling. He shut his eyes and exhaled a long gentle breath. Alex loved holding him, nothing gave him greater pleasure. He sighed too and closed his eyes. After a while he said, "we just end up like this all the time don't we, it's wonderful."

Nathan lifted his head and gazed at Alex with foggy eyes, "I've never known anything like it." Alex pushed his hair back from his forehead, "Come and have some breakfast," he smiled and took Nathan's hand to walk him into the kitchen. While their bread toasted and bacon grilled, Alex tore upstairs for some clothes, cold as he had been in just his boxers. A short while later they sat facing each other, cross legged on two kitchen stools, eating bacon sandwiches and blueberry and maple syrup pancakes which Nathan had never had before but they were delicious. Alex leant forward and kissed him on the mouth. Nathan kept his eyes closed for a moment afterwards. When he opened them Alex was gazing at him lovingly.

Nathan sighed, smiling, and forked up more pancake. He slid the plate onto the kitchen consul and groaned putting his head in his hands. "Are you ok ?"

Alex frowned at him. "I'm so tired," came the muffled reply. Alex chewed down his mouthful and got off his stool, "do you want to lie down ? You can go back to bed if you want ?" He suggested, coming forward and stroking the back of his neck. It felt good, Nathan leant his head in against Alex's hip. "All of the above sounds marvellous," he groaned. Alex laughed gently and reached for his hand.

They made their way back upstairs and as soon as they got to Alex's bedroom Nathan crawled back into his bed and pulled the duvet over him. He looked absolutely shattered. Alex's heart went out to him, he still wasn't completely over his illness, a week or two more of long sleeps and much loving, Alex decided, and he would be totally fit again. He slid in beside him and whispered, "turn your back to me, I'll put my arms around you." Nathan's brow creased and he opened his fuzzy eyes, "no, I want to face you." He frowned. Alex grinned at him and brushed his mouth with his lips, "I love you so much," he breathed and manoeuvred himself around Nathan who pressed his body in against him. "I love you more," he whispered looking up into Alex's eyes, "not possible," Alex whispered back and kissed his gentle mouth before laying his head on the pillow.

Some time later, Alex was surprised to wake up and realise that he had fallen asleep, he really hadn't expected to. He stretched and opened his eyes and saw a fully awake refreshed looking Nathan reading, sitting up with the book resting on his knees. Alex ran a finger down his arm and Nathan smiled down at him, blushing beautifully. "Hello sleepy." He grinned, his eyes sparkling. Alex's stomach filled with butterflies. Nathan was so incredibly pleasing on the eye. "Hello yourself, are you feeling less shattered ?" He asked, sitting up against the headboard and rubbing the sleep out of his face. Nathan nodded, "yes thanks, so much better. I hate being so tired but it will go." "As long as you're ok, that's all that matters." They kissed each others lips with utter tenderness, Alex thumbing Nathan's cheek as usual, making him groan gently. There was no sex this time, just gentle touching, their mouths imparting what their minds and hearts felt, soul to soul. When they drew apart they sat a few inches from each other, breathing shallow, gentle breaths. "I've no idea of the time," Alex suddenly said. "It's four o'clock," Nathan replied.

"Four ! - Already !" Alex looked stunned, "blimey, time sure flies when you're having fun." Nathan laughed and ran a hand through his hair. They were both dressed still and pushed back the duvet as it was getting hot. "What shall we do now ?" Alex arched a questioning eyebrow. "Erm, I don't know," said Nathan and then, "Well it's gorgeously sunny, how about we go down to Flatsmore lake and feed the ducks, veg on the bank in the sun, that kind of thing then there's an open air movie night there at 7pm ?" Alex's face lit up, "that's a fab idea, let's do it. I'm starving again though, fancy cramming some food in a rucksack to take with us ?"

"Definitely," Nathan nodded as they got up. A shower and some stroking and kissing later, the boys followed each other down stairs and stuffed as much of the fridge and larder into two rucksacks as possible. As they set off for Flatsmore Lake, the sun was so strong and the sky so blue above it felt amazing to be alive. Nathan looked extra gorgeous in his Ray bans, it made Alex's heart race to look at him. He couldn't separate anything that they'd done into 'preferred,' elements at all. Holding, kissing, talking, sex, sleeping and eating together, all of it was wonderful, but better than that, there was no fear.

Although he knew he was unusually young to be so sure that he'd found the right guy, Alex also knew what his parents and their friends always said, when you find the right person you just know, and it was true. He trusted Nathan in every single respect and not a moment of worry crossed his mind about him. He was only afraid for Nathan's health and prayed that he would never be truly unhappy or hurt in his life, he looked over at him again and wanted nothing more than to protect him from all possible harm. Nathan smiled at him just then and it fuelled his butterflies. October the 10th couldn't come soon enough.

They found a sunny spot right in front of the lake opposite the big screen on the other side. There was a post not too far away from them with some pretty nifty looking speakers hanging from it. "Aha, for tonight eh ?" Alex looked up at them. Nathan spread a brilliantly useful picnic rug over the grass, it was huge and folded up to almost nothing with a couple of velcro carry straps around it. They took all the freshest food from the ruck sacks and laid it out on the rug, kicked off their shoes and socks and lay back to graze. The sun beat down and felt so wonderful on Nathan's face.

There were a few bangs and drillings from across the lake as the technicians sorted out the last parts of erecting a big outdoor screen. This worked in Nathan's favour as all the ducks, coots and geese headed over toward he and Alex seeking peace but also recognising both food and a soft touch, their favourite combination. He crawled forward clutching a big white roll and sat on his haunches in front of the waters edge. A Canada goose nosed toward him, its black beak outstretched, scared but hungry. He tore off a small piece of bread and stretched toward the goose, it snapped up the bread without snapping his fingers. Two white ducks and a mallard crept up the bank quacking loudly. Nathan laughed and threw them some bread. Four more ducks flew in and skittered across the water with their legs outstretched, creating a lot of wash before they came to rest on its surface and paddled across to join the throng.

Alex watched contentedly as he grazed from their picnic. He loved that Nathan was so at ease, there were several geese, a pair of black swans with dark orange bills and an assortment of other foul with the odd pigeon thrown in for good measure. They were all gently stalking Nathan but not aggressive toward him in their hunger, just toward each other as competition. When the roll was evenly dispensed between as many of them as he could possibly reach Nathan held up his hands and shook his head, "all gone guys, no more," he shrugged and clapped his hands together to prove it. That drove most of the posse away but a few brave stragglers made it up the bank and hung around the edge of the picnic rug for a few minutes until someone else further down started throwing bread into the lake and all at once they were alone again.

Nathan took off his t-shirt and rolled it up under his head as he lay back against the rug. A light breeze ruffled his hair and he sighed, "this is the life." Alex stretched back too and closed his eyes against the sun. "I know," he breathed and felt for Nathan's hand. He could almost feel his smile broaden as they closed their fingers around each others. It was bliss lying there together with a lovely evening to come. This weekend was living up to and beyond anything that either had anticipated.

They lay in utter bliss for a few more minutes until grass muffled footsteps came toward them and stopped abruptly. "Ugh, fags !" They heard. Nathan's heartbeat quickened, he didn't want trouble. There was more. "Fucking homos, - holding hands, yug !" They heard again. Alex opened his eyes, sun glassed but still shielding his eyes from the sun with his hand, he squinted backwards and saw four boys he instantly recognised from school. He let go of Nathan's hand and stood up, shirtless and bronzed he looked pretty awesome. He pushed his sunglasses back on his head and raised an eyebrow at the wanker from school who'd taunted them before.

"Can I help you ?" He said sarcastically as if he was utterly bored already. Jake Reader from their class looked him up and down as if he were the most disgusting thing he'd ever seen. "YOU !" He spat, "that's the correct nominative, well done," Alex looked even more bored, "your English is improving Jake." Jake reddened. "Fuck you, you can't insult me, you're a knob jockey, homo little queer !" Jake continued, although most of his posse wished he hadn't, it had made them groan inwardly when Alex stood up and they immediately identified the most popular boy in school and now the look on his face had them really worried. Alex seemed to grow by a few inches as he stepped toward Jake by only a pace and looked him right in the eyes.

Aware that there were some families around he lowered his voice a little and then said in a cold hard tone, "You really are a bit of a cunt Jake aren't you.

Firstly you can't insult a person on your own, you either need a full classroom behind you or a few of your tethered cronies. Apart from that you have nothing and I do mean nothing going on in your life that's of the slightest interest to anyone otherwise you wouldn't have sought me out and jealously made fun of my relationship." Jake's lips moved like a goldfish, he tried to mouth 'jealous, ' indignantly, but Alex took another step toward him with eyes like steel. "I've seen the way you look at me, and Nathan come to that. He's beautiful isn't he ? But Jake I'm sorry to tell you, I did get there first and I'm not giving him up for anyone so take this little day trip back to the playground where it belongs or I promise you we'll 'talk,' again and this time on my terms."

He stood barely three inches from Jake's flushed face, thirty seconds of silence later and Alex smiled, clouted Jake roughly on the shoulder and said, "good, glad we got that sorted." He stretched his lean sculpted body upwards, enjoying the feel of the sun on his skin and feeling moderately sleepy, slid his sunglasses down over his eyes again and climbed back onto the picnic rug where he rubbed Nathan's smooth upper arm a little, "you ok ?" Nathan smiled and nodded. Alex's eyes were only just visible through his sunglasses but they shone with love. Nathan trembled a little and Alex saw, he frowned. "Nath ? Are you ok ? Not frightened of that prick are you ?"

Nathan reddened and covered his face, "ssh !" He hissed. Alex looked behind him and shrugged, "why ? He's not here anymore." Nathan couldn't believe it. He propped himself up on his elbows and followed Alex's gaze, it was true, in all of a few seconds, Jake and his twattish band had disappeared completely. Nathan flipped his sunglasses into his hair, he was astonished and gawped at the space where the boys had been. He stared back at Alex, "how the fuck did you do that ?" Alex grinned a delighted grin and laughed throatily. "He's just a boring tosser, they never stick around once they look like a dick to their backup gang. They'll be off buying porn and picking on someone half Jake's size to make him feel 'manly.'" He concluded. Nathan shook his head and stared at Alex again, "yes but they just disappeared totally like something out of 'The Fog !'"

Alex laughed and pointed to the left side of the lake, "actually I expect they're off down there, it's the quickest way to look out of sight as there's a hidden path amongst the edge of the bushes. It literally takes about three seconds from here to the beginning of it so you can just disappear." He shrugged and looked toward their picnic basket, "hmm, now then, what else can I eat apart from you that will taste really good I wonder ?" He bent over the food and loved to hear Nathan cover his blushing face with both hands and start to laugh in that sexy gasping way of his when he was embarrassed and thrilled at the same time. He felt him quiver as he laughed and pressed his knee up against his thigh, "oh you just wait til I get you home, you just wait my darling," he husked and leaned back on his haunches with an apple in his hand. He gazed down at Nathan who shielded his eyes against the sun to look back at him. Alex put a hand on either side of his chest and leant over him. "I love you so much," he whispered and gently kissed his lips. Nathan groaned, loving the feel of Alex's lips against his. " Oh Alex," he moaned in unmistakable longing.

Alex found it hard to breath, "don't, don't groan like that here, please my love. I can't keep away from you when you do that and I'm only wearing shorts." He blew out a deep shaky breath and Nathan gave a low thrilled chuckle. Both boys turned over onto their stomachs quickly and Alex whispered again, "just wait, I mean it, just wait til I have you in my arms later." Nathan laughed his throaty laugh again. "Nathan." Alex groaned once more and pressed his face into the ground.

A sudden blast from the nearby speaker made them both jump. "Shit !" Alex sat bolt upright. Nathan sat up too and looked at him, "jumpy ?" He smirked. Alex shook his head, his lips in a tight line of mock disapproval, "if you weren't so bloody beautiful I'd kick the crap out of you about now !" He growled. Nathan's heart leapt with excitement and pleasure, he laughed heartily and found it harder to stop when every time he looked up Alex was glaring at him moodily. He rolled back on the blanket grinning and laughing, Alex beamed down at him, "right, get your clothes off, punishment time."

Nathan clasped his sides as a tear streamed from his eye, "no, no...please.." he gasped as he rolled about. Alex looked down at him as if he were about to devour him when the tannoy leapt to life again and a voice rambled on about bollocksing health and safety blah blah for a bit until at last a half hour of music before the movie was announced. The half hour flew by, mainly because Alex and Nathan seemed to forget that there were any other people around them as they laughed and kissed and wrestled one another over and over. But at last the movie was about to start just as the sun was setting, the boys pulled on their hoodies and moved round to curl into each other, comfortable enough to watch and loosely folded enough to reach each others arms and faces, never letting off softly stroking one another, just to say 'I'm here and I love you.' It was the best night.

It got dark and a little breeze blew up then died away, the movie was good, gripping, the park filled with people and the night above with stars. As the film drew to a close Nathan stretched across Alex who yawned languidly. People were beginning to drift lazily away. Just as they turned to face each other to discuss what to do for the rest of the night, a small torn piece of lined paper fluttered to the ground between them. They looked from it to each other and then sharply all around but whoever had thrown it had run for their life, leaving just one word for the boys and 7 little words from himself. The piece of paper was only two inches square, Alex picked it up, it read : "Shelter" and then underneath, ' Because Jake's a tosser and I'm sorry.'

They frowned at each other. Nathan reached for it and took it from Alex, "that's all it says ?" He re read the paper. "Shelter ?" He looked up. "Don't ask me ?" Alex shrugged, "but I think we found what to do next tonight, we're googling 'Shelter,' it has to mean something with that as a name because he wrote it with a capital and in inverted commas too." Nathan gasped, "so he did !" Alex laughed and rolled his eyes, "come on Watson, - super sleuth." "Fuck off," Nathan punched him on the arm grinning, and they packed everything away, heading for home.

This weekend just seemed to get better and better, if it could. Back at Alex's they were in such good spirits they mucked about and fell all over each other on the floor, tickling and laughing so hard it hurt. Alex ended up panting really hard on top of Nathan and as he looked down at his grinning red face he felt so elated to see him so happy. Nathan stared back up at him with shining eyes, he blinked a long slow blink showing off his extraordinarily beautiful long lashes and deep blue eyes. Alex stroked his cheek with the back of his fingers. "You're so beautiful," he breathed. Nathan blushed, "Alex..."

"You are you know," Alex continued and smoothed his hand down his cheek once more. Nathan looked him intently in the eyes, "thanks," he drew in a deep breath looking serious and laced his fingers into Alex's beside his cheek. They shared a gentle kiss, and then jumped as someone hammered on the front door. "Christ !" Alex yelped and leapt to his feet, leaving Nathan guffawing on the floor, he propped his chin on his hands to see who it was. Alex peered through the peep hole and then looked back at Nathan shrugging, "who is it ?" He asked gruffly, there was no reply. He didn't unlock the door, instead running round to the bay window and leaning his head on the pane to look around to the door. He shrugged again, "weird, oh well, whoever it was has definitely gone, that's for sure." Nathan got up and walked behind him to the front door, putting a hand on his shoulder as he unlocked it, "careful Alex," he warned.

There wasn't anybody around outside, just a flat brown cardboard box on the top step marked 'Alex.' Nathan leaned over his shoulder frowning. "What the hell ?" They locked up and tangled themselves around each other on the sofa, Nathan leaning back against Alex, his legs around him. Alex started to wrestle the box open, holding it where Nathan could see it at the same time. With one strong rip the end tore open and a dvd came flying out, narrowly missing hitting

Nathan in the eye, he ducked just in time. "Ooh sorry sorry !" Alex sounded concerned. Nathan just laughed, "it's fine, don't worry. What's the dvd ?" Alex stretched to reach where it had fallen and gasped. "I don't believe it !" "What ?" Nathan sat up and looked at him. Alex turned the dvd over and read, " 'Shelter', one of the best gay surfer love movies ever made....!"

There was a stunned silence. "Is that Jake's ex cronie again do you think ? I mean it has to be doesn't it ? Which means...OH MY GOD !" His eyes flew wide, Alex nodded at him, "yup, it sure does, ex-cronie is one of us too." He shook his head, "good for him. This must be his own copy of this, shall we watch it ?" Nathan hesitated, took the box and looked it over before he nodded. "I've a good feeling about it actually, why the hell not." Alex headed back into the kitchen for more snacks and drinks. He turned the lights down as he came back and plonked all the goodies down. He crunched a pringle as he curled himself back around Nathan's body. The dvd was breathtaking. Nathan shook his head half way through and said quietly, "I never knew this existed ?" "Neither did I," Alex replied, "it's incredible."

The moment came when Zach, the younger surfer realised he loved his friend Shaun and his internal struggle ended by him rushing over to his friends house and them kissing each other all the way upstairs to bed where they made love for the first time. It was an incredibly passionate scene and as Zach drove home the next morning the orange glow of sunrise filling his car, he smiled and beat his fist gently on the steering wheel as a broad grin spread across his face. Both boys didn't know what to say, it was like watching themselves, exactly. A little further along Alex gasped, in a tender bedroom scene, Zach and Shaun were discussing a future together, facing each other on the pillows when Shaun reached out and swept the back of his fingers gently down Zach's cheek and said "you're so beautiful." Zach grinned and punched Shaun away gently, embarrassed and laughing he said "shut up." Shaun scolded him, smiling he advised, "..learn to take a compliment," Zach looked at him with so much tenderness and love in return, reaching out he stroked Shaun's face too and whispered, "thanks."

Alex pressed pause. They were both silent. So many things circled around in Nathan's mind, it felt like them ! It really felt like them, a very different background and location but them all the same. Alex squeezed his arms tightly around his waist, he kissed his ear and ran his fingers down his cheek again. "Oh baby, I can't believe that scene can you. I...I...." he wasn't sure how to express what he was feeling. "I'm just blown away Nate." Nathan looked down at Alex's strong arms around him and laid his on top of them, feeling his lusciously warm skin. "Alex," he breathed, leaning back against him, "this is

our movie." "I know," Alex husked and kissed his ear, "shall we watch the rest
?"

Nathan nodded and they watched Zach's disillusioned, selfish sister drive him
to the brink of despair with guilt about being gay and not supporting her and
her son enough. They watched as he imploded inside, not knowing how to put
himself first or even if he should. It looked as if all hope were lost as he snapped
at Shaun and pushed him away. They sobbed together and clutched each other
tightly. "It just has to work out, it just has to.." Nathan croaked. "Sssh baby, it
will," Alex replied and pulled him closer. The ending was lovely, Zach came
back to Shaun, revealing how much of himself he'd previously sacrificed for
his sister and nephew and that he didn't want to anymore. He wanted to be with
Shaun, live with him and love him and his eyes were moist as he admitted how
wrong he'd been and that he wanted his help.

It was freely given, "anything," said Shaun and the two moved in together,
raising Zach's little nephew into the bargain. The music was haunting and
painful at times but also beautiful.

As the movie finished Alex got up to put lots of their empty snack rubbish
in the bin and bring over a big jug of water. In reality he was shaking so much
at the thought of anything ever happening to split he and Nathan up that he just
needed to re-group alone for a moment. He bent his head to the kitchen work
top, feeling its coldness ease him and then rose up, pressing his fingertips into
his eye sockets. He breathed out a heavy long breath and filled up the water.

He was about to carry it back through the almost dark kitchen when he heard
a small sob and turned around. In the light of the living room he could see
Nathan, he was roughly brushing a few tears aside with his sleeves pulled over
his hands, he looked about twelve. Alex's heart was in his mouth, it was good
to know they both felt the same but what the hell would he do if he fucked it
up with him ? He put the jug down for a moment and squeezed his eyes shut,
the thought was too terrible. He looked up out of the darkness of the kitchen
again and watched Nathan clamber to his feet and go to lean on the window as
he gathered his thoughts.

His movements were fluid and easy, he had the most beautiful body and Alex
could watch him run, swim, surf or just plain muck about all day long. He drew
in a calming breath, pulled himself up tall and walked back into the dimly lit
living room.

Nathan turned around slowly looking at the carpet and then slower still, back
up to Alex's eyes as he walked over to join him at the window. "That film.."
he breathed in awe. Alex nodded, "I know," he reached up to cup Nathan's
cheek and suddenly he felt like Shaun and was terribly frightened that Nathan

might get scared and leave one day. He folded him into his arms, "Oh Nate, never leave me, never leave me please.." He husked, lying his head against his shoulder. "I won't, I really won't I promise." Nathan whispered back and they stood holding each other, never wanting time to move on or any possible hurt to ever come their way.

They pulled away to face each other. "What do you want now my Nathan ?" Alex breathed, stroking his hair. "Such a long sleep in your bed and to do this all again tomorrow," Nathan whispered. He looked tired and red around the eyes but still so lovely. Alex squeezed his hand, "c'mon then, I can't think of anything better," he smiled and lead Nathan by the hand back upstairs and into his arms once more.

Chapter Five.

Sunday morning was bright and warm, as Nathan stirred in Alex's arms he felt utterly blissful and realised that he could smell fresh coffee and warm pastries, his stomach reacted, gurgling loudly, hungrily. He grinned to himself and felt Alex's arms tighten around him. "Mmm, we need to get you some breakfast handsome." Alex breathed, sliding around his body until he straddled him over the top of the duvet. Nathan looked groggily up at him but then his eyes widened, "you're dressed already ?" He said in surprise, appreciatively surveying his jeans and dark blue top. Alex beamed and nodded, "who do you think nipped out for all these and warmed everything up for your breakfast ?"

Nathan turned his head to a stack of Sunday papers on the bed and laughed out loud, Alex grinned down at him, "see, I'm just showing you what a good husband I can be already." He leant forward and tickled Nathan's sides making his face crease up, "stop it, stop it....no no..." he screamed through his laughter. Alex giggled too and finally stopped. "Ok, ok..." he smiled and bent forward over him to find his lips. He pressed his mouth down onto him and groaned as their tongues slid together. Nathan's hands came up to cup the back of his head, they were warm and caressing. Alex felt himself becoming totally lost to the sensation. When eventually they pulled away, his head felt like cotton wool. He looked foggily down at Nathan who gazed upwards, still caressing him. Alex shook his head, "how did I get so lucky ? God I love you."

Nathan's stomach filled with butterflies, he gently touched the base of Alex's throat and ran his fingers up his neck to his cheekbones. He blinked a long slow blink as he drew in a deep breath, "me too," he husked, "me too." Alex kissed him very softly and looked down into his beautiful blue eyes again. "Come and have some breakfast ?" Nathan nodded and they rolled into each other's arms for one more cuddle and kiss, holding each other again before they got up.

Nathan was cross legged on the sofa, the papers strewn across the carpet. Alex, back in the kitchen, put a fresh pot of coffee on and brought a plate of warmed pastries over to the coffee table. He handed Nathan a glass of orange juice and felt his stomach flip over with love. He looked so cute sitting there in his grey raglan hoodie with black sleeves, faded black jeans and no socks. He had no idea just how gorgeous he was. He felt Alex stare at him and grinned blushing slightly before looking up. The look Alex gave him made his heart thump. "What is it ?" He asked shyly, going red. Alex shook his head, "nothing. I just love looking at you." He beamed as Nathan's smile seemed to light the room with happiness. Alex stepped forward and dropped a kiss just where his dark hair touched the edge of his temples. It was electrifying. Nathan's eyes stayed shut as he drew away and went back to fetch the coffee.

He looked up as Alex put down the refreshed pot. Their eyes met and held for a moment, there was no need to speak, Nathan felt part of him. Sitting there in that moment, simply looking he knew he was entirely meant for Alex and Alex for him. They were each others right arm and utterly certain in that knowledge. Neither wanted to look away but scalding coffee on skin wasn't a good option so Alex turned back to pour out the cups and handed one to Nathan, then he shuffled down amongst the papers on the floor, set his coffee far enough away so as not to be a risk, and then suddenly rolled about in them all like a mad dog.

Nathan almost seared the inside of his mouth, he had to spit back the mouthful he'd just taken as he watched him, then set his cup down and laughed for England. It was hysterical. Alex stopped rolling and breathing hard covered his face with his hands and laughed louder than Nathan had ever heard him before.

"You stupid loon, what are you doing ?" Nathan roared with laughter. Alex dropped his hands behind his head and grinned back at him. "I don't even know, I just felt in a really silly mood all of a sudden !" He giggled and sat up with his hair all over the place and his t-shirt twisted and almost off one shoulder. It very nicely revealed a taut strip of his delicious tummy and Nathan loved him all the more.

"You idiot !" He grinned, shaking his head. Alex laughed again and then rubbed his eyes and face, ran his hands through his hair and righted his t-shirt, in those five to six seconds he completely transformed himself from handsome twit into heart stopping Adonis, Nathan wondered how he did it. Alex lifted his hips to pull out some of the papers and rolled over onto his tummy, flipping over the first page.

"Hey, hand me that mag would you ?" Nathan nodded over at a supplement on the floor and Alex passed it to him. They relaxed with their coffees for a few minutes whilst they read and then Alex said, " I never got why people did this until now," he let out a contented sigh, "it really is a nice thing to do." He looked over at Nathan who nodded, "it really is." He shut the magazine and looked thoughtful though. "Hmm," he frowned. "What ? What is it ?" Alex sipped his coffee as he asked.

"Well what shall we do after this ?"

Alex's brow furrowed,, "hmm, good question." He looked thoughtful and then sat up with a hugely enthusiastic look on his face. "I know, yes ! This is brilliant, I know you'll like it. Let's go riding !" Nathan looked stunned, "wow

! I wouldn't have thought of it, I'd love to but Alex it's Sunday, they won't be open." Alex nodded, "they are. To make ends meet they have to now, all the extra health and safety bollocks has come into play and they've upped their fees enormously as well as opening on Sundays."

"Will they have space ?" Nathan asked hopefully. "Only one way to find out," Alex jumped up and grabbed the landline, the stables were on speed dial as his sister always went.

He got through quickly and asked if they had two spaces left. He made a crossed fingers sign at Nathan as the girl went to check. "One o'clock ?" Alex looked over to Nathan to check that would work with him and they both turned to check the current time. Nathan nodded a yes, it was 10.30 plenty of time, and plenty of time after an hours ride for one more sess with Alex before his parents got home he mused. Alex seemed to be thinking exactly the same as he looked into his eyes.

He turned his attention back to the call and pulled out his credit card. He paid in full for the ride and hung up. Watching Nathan's face as he crossed back over to the paper strewn floor, he tilted his head to one side and shrugged in a 'come on,' kind of gesture at his expression.

"Look, when we do this next time you pay for what we pick to do at a moments notice then, ok ?" Nathan's face softened slowly and he nodded, " well ok, but I'm not being a kept man, you know that." Alex dropped himself onto the sofa and stroked his forearm. "I know," he said comfortably and the kiss that followed turned into their tops coming off and a fever pitch of excitement.

Alex nuzzled at Nathan's nipples making him groan aloud and then Suddenly Nathan was in his mouth, thrusting his hips up and gasping, stretching his arms back behind his thrown back head. He came with such force it hurt, his whole pelvis and groin felt pulled a little. "Ow...ow.." he whispered as Alex's swirling tongue finished him off. Alex licked his lips and looked up with concern. "Ow ? Did I hurt you ?" Nathan, blowing hard, shook his head. "No, nothing like, I think I just pulled every muscle down there with pleasure." Alex frowned, "you sure ?" Nathan nodded, his cheeks pulled up into a glowing smile which made Alex's heart leap. "Good," he grinned and thumbed his cheek.

"Now you," Nathan breathed and pushed Alex back to the carpet across the papers where he tugged his jeans and boxers off, sinking his mouth straight down onto his rock hardness. It made him cry out loud and arch his back right off the floor, he panted loudly as Nathan worked his mouth, sucking hard but so gentle around the top of him, feather like and incredible. Alex pumped his hips, eyes closed and held Nathan's head in both hands as he sped up toward his orgasm. It was unbelievable when it came, he grunted hard three times, ending with "fuck, oh fuck..." and gasping as if he was going to pass out. Nathan watched him come down afterwards, eyes closed and panting, every vein standing out across his face and neck.

Alex had such a beautiful mouth and it was a pleasure to watch him blow and lick his full lips as he slowly began to calm down. When he had, he opened his eyes and searched for Nathan's face. They smiled softly at each other then Nathan looked at the clock. "We'd better get going." Alex nodded and let himself be pulled up. They held each other naked, and just stood feeling each other's love, resting their cheeks together. "I love you so much," Alex breathed against Nathan and Nathan tightened his arms around him in return before they let go and headed upstairs to dress.

The hack group that they joined at the stables had only four other riders and the instructor in it. Everyone was in a pair of some kind so it was easy for the boys to hang at the back and talk as they rode. Nathan was an incredibly good rider Alex noted and saw how much love he had for animals. He was kind and careful with his horse, never pulling at her mouth too much or kicking hard. He seemed to know how to make her want to go forward with him. "Where did you learn to ride like that ?" He asked as they walked lazily at the back.

Nathan smiled, "I've loved horses all my life and I've learnt a lot about them, I grew up with the old fashioned lessons when I was really little where you were supposed to dominate your horse so it did what you wanted. I didn't know any better," he shrugged regretfully, "but now, I know completely differently thank God, and I've asked a lot of questions, got tonnes of opinions and then when I still didn't really know what I was doing I read this fantastic book called 'The Man Who Listens To Horses,' by Monty Roberts. He's an amazing guy who watched how the herd interact with each other and he emulated their behaviour in dealing with horses. He created something called 'join up,' where your horse sees you as chief mare of the herd and whatever you ask it to do it will trust in you and do it, just because you've used horse body language which it understands." He shrugged again, "it's simple really, and much kinder."

"Wow !" Alex exclaimed, clearly impressed. "I never knew you knew so much on the subject." Nathan blushed a little, "it was a really great book and I kind of did 'join up' with my friends horse Minstrel when I was about twelve, I knew I did something right because he was completely tuned in to me, but I couldn't have put it into words for anyone else. I just know what feels right with them I suppose." Alex smiled at him, "you really amaze me sometimes."

The ride was over far too quickly, when you are in love everything seems so easy and time whips by Alex mused as they headed home, walking back in the afternoon sun toward his house. As they kicked off their shoes and Nathan slid onto a kitchen stool, picking up a section of paper, idly thrown there earlier, he ran a hand through his hair and his stomach growled loudly. Alex spun around with the fridge door open, "Ok ok, can't you see I'm working on it already ?" He rolled his eyes.

Nathan laughed, "I can't help it, I've burnt off a lot of calories this weekend. What are you going to feed me now ?" "Erm...," Alex turned back to the fridge, "how about toasted muffins with loads of butter, peanut butter and or Nutella ?" Nathan grabbed hold of his stomach, "oh God, whack them in the bloody toaster fast, that sounds sooo good !" He groaned as his stomach gurgled again. " Blimey, you eat more than me !" Alex laughed. He poured them each a tall glass of juice, "Ta," Nathan, clinked his against Alex's.

They watched each others faces as they drank for a moment but then Nathan caught sight of the clock and his stomach felt cold, Alex's family would be home in about three hours and this blissful weekend would come to an end. He put down his glass, sighing. Alex turned to look over his shoulder and got the picture too. He looked down at the counter and reached out for Nathan's hand. Their fingers curled around each others and held tightly. He looked up slowly into his eyes, "this is only the beginning." He breathed. Nathan nodded, he knew it. He looked absolutely beautiful to Alex in that moment, it was gut wrenching to think that they would have to ever spend even one night apart but they would get through it and then October would come and their new life together would really start.

"What were you just thinking ?" Nathan asked. "Our future," Alex replied standing up and turning to sort the muffins and spreads out. "I can't wait," Nathan said. "Me neither," Alex sighed and knew 'that' conversation with his family was going to be hard. Even with such a supportive family, barely anyone got married at 18 these days and especially not gay 18 year olds getting a civil ceremony. He put it out of his mind for now, glancing at Nathan who'd turned back to the paper, he'd do anything to keep them together he thought and passed him a plate of Nutella and peanut butter smothered muffins. They ate quickly, as hungry as ever, and cleared everything up until it was all almost back to normal but they left the pile of newspapers strewn about.

"We'll leave those til the last second before Mum, Dad and Sis get back," Alex said as he pressed his body against the sofa back. Nathan climbed onto his lap, stretching his legs out onto the cushions and laying his head onto Alex's knees. He felt so relaxed there. He shut his eyes feeling very tired all of a sudden and carried on talking with them shut. It went quiet for a moment and then he felt the back of Alex's hand stroke down his cheek again. He looked up at him through barely open eyes, blinking hard he sighed. Alex smiled at him and they didn't need to speak. It was quiet for a while until Alex's pocket vibrated, he struggled carefully to retrieve it, slid it open and groaned, his shoulders visibly sagging as he shut his eyes and tapped the phone to his forehead. "What ?" Croaked Nathan. Alex drew in a deep breath and looked at him. "They're an hour away !" Nathan smiled a dim smile and reached up to touch his cheek. Alex turned his head and kissed his fingertips.

" I suppose we'd better make sure we've put this place to rights." He clicked his phone shut and slid out from under Nathan, leaned over him upside down and kissed his lips lightly, "YOU, stay exactly as you are, you look really tired," he ordered. Nathan shook his head, "where are you going while I'm lounging about down here ?" He asked as Alex bounded up the stairs, "just making the bathroom all pretty again and making my bed, two ticks." Nathan looked around, downstairs was perfect now apart from the papers so he tidied them all into a neat pile and put them in the centre of the kitchen consul. He went back to the sofa and lay down, he did feel tired. He set his alarm for half an hour, just enough time for them to have a kiss goodnight before Alex's family emerged and he had to go home, he hoped.

Alex was back down in a flash and looked about the room, there wasn't anything more to do so he padded across the floor to Nathan and perched beside him on the sofa edge. Nathan opened his eyes, "God I am shattered," he husked. Alex nodded, "it's been a big weekend," he smiled. "Hey, lie back against me for a bit will you ? One last cuddle ?" Nathan nodded soberly, he so didn't want to go home. They snuggled around each other holding tightly, "oh I don't want you to go," Alex breathed into his shoulder. "Oh God don't," Nathan replied, "you'll get me all watery eyed."

They were about to snuggle down for a serious half hours sleep when a car unmistakeably pulled into the gravel driveway. Both their eyes flew wide open, they leapt off the sofa, patting it down and fluffing up the cushions, then eyed each other to make sure they didn't look too tousled and sex satisfied. Alex flicked on the tv and flashed to 'Dave,' as fast as possible. Nathan threw himself down on the floor a couple of feet away from him on the sofa. Feet were heard outside, doors shutting and gravel crunching. Nathan turned to Alex, "why did we just do that and act all guilty almost ?"

Alex shook his head, "bloody habit !" He spat, "I feel like a twat now, here I am completely in love with you and I act like a scalded cat when I know they're outside." He sounded really angry with himself. Nathan reached over and squeezed his hand, "hey, it's just that we aren't used to doing this yet, don't worry, we'd have been just as bad at my Mum and Dad's, and maybe that's the problem, this isn't your house, it's theirs." He soothed, just as the front door opened and Alex's family poured in.

There were lots of hugs and kisses hello, shopping dumped on the counter, the kettle going on. It all seemed to happen so quickly and the boys were swept along in the usual family chaos. Nathan wasn't allowed to leave until he'd had tea and chocolate digestives forced down him. It was all a great laugh but soon enough Alex saw him tiring. He glanced at his watch, 6.30pm and they both had an hour of homework to do. He felt a knot in his stomach, they would see each other in a matter of hours, but something wonderfully significant had happened between them this weekend and it was hard for either to let the other go just yet, even for a few hours.

Nathan was squeezed and hugged by everyone and then slinging his rucksack over his shoulder, he and Alex walked out alone onto the gravel. Silent but glancing and smiling over at each other they walked out of the gate and up the hill. When they were a short distance away from Nathan's house, he couldn't stand it anymore. "This is hard," he whispered with a crack to his voice. He threw himself at Nathan and encased him in his arms. "Oh God, I'm gonna miss you so much !" He smacked a tear off his cheek and sniffed loudly. They pulled away, arms still around each other and laughed at one another's wet eyes.

"October, just remember October," Alex gulped. Nathan nodded and drew in a deep breath. "October," he whispered. They embraced again, "I love you," he whispered. A small sob escaped Alex. He pulled away again after a minute and stroked Nathan's cheek, "I'll be waiting by the hedge, 7.55am tomorrow morning, sleep well." He began to back away, Nathan was worried he'd fall backwards down the hill and crack his head but then he turned and jogged away instead. Nathan turned around and started to walk the last of the way home. His head was bowed and he sighed loudly. Just then a rocket from behind came up and clamped his back in it's warm arms. "I love you so much," breathed Alex and then he was gone again, turning once to wave at Nathan who waved back grinning.

It seemed unreal as he climbed into bed that night. As he'd come through the front door his house had been relatively calm, the twins were exhausted and crashed out in front of '24,' his Dad was fiddling about somewhere upstairs and his mum was clamping the iron press onto yet more stuff, this time iron on labels for the twins gym kits. She sipped a cup of coffee as she sat at the kitchen table watching dancing on ice on a little flat screen telly. She smiled as she saw Nathan, then her eyes did a double take. She held his for a moment and he looked down blushing. When he looked up again she was still smiling at him so he made his way to her side and sat down. She patted his hand and got up to fetch another mug, made him a latte and waited.

Nathan drew in a deep breath and looked at her. "So, it was a good weekend then ?" She smiled, feeding two socks and labels into the press before locking it down for a moment. Nathan couldn't help it, a huge grin lit his face and his eyes were all watery, "Oh Mum, I had the best weekend of my life," he gasped. A tear escaped but he didn't care, "I love him so much, so so much." He wiped his eyes quickly before continuing. "Mum," he shook his head and breathed out long and hard again, "he's the ONE. He's the one. I know it."

His Mum kept ironing as she nodded, processing what her son had just said. She looked at him, his body language, his eyes, his flushed cheeks and made a decision. Some mothers would have fought everything that Nathan had just told her. They would say he was too young to know, he'd only just come out, he hadn't thought through the practicalities, but she knew something much more important from her own life experience. If you were willing to take a chance and you really believed in something, it would usually work out brilliantly.

She had enormous faith that this was one of those occasions and as she looked at her lovely happy vibrant son, she wished more people could be so understanding. No one had ever crushed her dreams and she would never do it to her son. She took the socks out of the press and pushed their coffees away. Turning to face him she smiled her most reassuring motherly smile and said, "then I am ecstatic for you my darling, that's wonderful." Nathan's eyes teared up again at her reaction. She pulled him into her arms and gave him a big bear hug, he hugged her back with both arms and let out a little sob. She rubbed his back and when at last they did pull away she said again, "that's wonderful news, it truly is.

Now then, Mr Loved up, off you go and get that school work sorted, then we're getting pizzas so let me know now what you want and we'll order them for about half 8." Nathan nodded and got up, "thanks Mum, thanks so much for being.....well, just the best about this, the best." He gulped, gave her a quick peck on the forehead and headed off up the stairs.

Alison Henderson gulped back her own tears, she again felt blessed to have such a happy family, she shoved any worries about the gay world and Nathan's future far away out of her mind. He was happy and loved and in love, she sighed at the thought. His life would be good she knew it. Contentedly she took the remains of her coffee into the lounge and sat amongst her other children, "thank you God," she whispered up toward the ceiling. "What ?" Mumbled the twins together, "nothing my loves, carry on watching, look you're missing it," she took another sip, adding a small wink toward the sky.

Nathan did his homework in a flash, for some reason he felt utterly unstoppable, English flew by. He shut the books and looked toward his window remembering Alex climbing up the trellis only three weeks ago. He tapped his pen lightly against his teeth and shook his head, how could he be so lucky that everything had worked out so well already ? He walked over to the window and peered out, a huge grin crossed his face and his stomach turned over with butterflies, tomorrow morning he'd see his love again. He flopped down on his back on the bed and remembered the next part of that first night.

It wasn't so much Alex taking him in his mouth, although that had been beyond any pleasure he had ever thought possible, it was the way he'd slipped onto the bed with his eyes locked on Nathan's, insisted he'd close his eyes and then gently stroked his fingers over his cheek bones. Such a feather light touch that had electrified his soul. Just hearing their hearts beating hard and his own shuddering breath had made that one of the best nights of Nathan's life. He shut his eyes and rolled onto his side, so comfortable, so content and suddenly he was asleep.

When his mother came looking for him to order his pizza she smiled at his sleeping form and covered him with a blanket from the foot of the bed. She ordered him his usual anyway, Nathan could smell food at fifty miles so it would probably wake him. Over at Alex's house, after the unpacking, washing and general chaos had died down, he found himself deflated and missing Nathan being around. In just one weekend it now seemed odd to be at home without him. He sighed as he crushed some garlic and ginger, adding both to the wok full of chilli chicken. "You miss him don't you ?" His mum asked suddenly. Alex looked up at her and sighed again. "Obvious is it ?"

She nodded smiling. "But darling it's not long til school tomorrow, and why don't you call one of your other friends in the mean time and catch up with them ? You have a very varied social life usually, don't put all your eggs in this one basket." She warned. Alex looked really angry for a second before he composed himself and turned to face her. "Mum, you and Dad have always been really supportive toward me so I know you can be again now. You need to understand what I have with Nathan. The reason why I'm not seeing so much of my usual friends at the moment is because I've fallen totally and utterly in love with him."

He pressed his fists onto the counter and took a deep breath. "Mum, don't, please don't do what I know some other adults do and start giving me a warning speech about being too young and not knowing my own mind yet etc..because you know what, Nathan is my ONE !" His mum gave him a quizzical look as she poured some stock into the supper. "Darling, why do you think I'm about to start questioning you now ? I never have done in my life have I ? - and correct me if I'm wrong, but whenever I've trusted you it's all worked out for the best.

Hasn't it ?"

Alex looked terrified for a moment as if he still expected an ear bashing but then he threw his arms around her, nearly knocking over the wok and almost crushed the life out of her. "Ok, ok," she laughed, "I need to breath." Alex let her go and swiped at the corners of his eyes, sniffing a little. She tousled his hair which was a little tough as he was four inches taller than her and they smiled at each other, " it will all be ok, trust me. It really will." She assured him but as Alex turned away he wondered how his Dad would react to the news that he'd asked Nathan to marry him. His parents were wonderful and supportive but that might just be a step too far he suddenly realised and it put the fear of God into him.

They'd need all the support they could get if they were to skip uni and start their lives as young as they wanted to and Alex knew for certain that his dad would have a problem with the ceremony. "Fuck," he whispered under his breath and climbed the stairs to his room, he needed to think this through. His dad wasn't a homophobe and he wouldn't try and put Alex off from moving in with anyone at 18, girl or boy, but he also knew that because of long held religious beliefs, he wouldn't recognise Alex's same sex marriage and he would try and dissuade him from doing it. Live in lovers in this day and age were one thing but to make it official would rankle and Alex had no idea how to battle that.

They had never fallen out before but his stomach knotted up with fear as he lay back on his bed. Somehow they would get through this and he would have his dad at his wedding, but boy this was going to be some fight and as he thought about it he began to shake. Maybe this was the only thing that could threaten their relationship. He gulped hard and texted Nathan, "I'm really worried about something. Hold me hard when you see me in the morning ? X."

"Yes of course. Always. Anything. X" Was the instant reply and Alex blew out a shaking breath as he held the phone to his chest. It would be ok. With a boy like Nathan it just would. He felt renewed in strength again as he responded to his mothers dinner call. He had Nathan, he had his beloved who promised "of course. Always. Anything." - and he knew he meant it.

The following morning, Nathan woke up from a very deep sleep. He opened his eyes tentatively and squinted across the room to his dog picture. He drew in a deep breath and pushed the duvet down frowning. Something was wrong, what was it ? Suddenly he sat bolt upright in bed, "I'm really worried about something...." Alex had texted last thing last night.

He fumbled on the bed and found his phone, he snatched it up and checked and felt his stomach sink, what the hell was it ? He knew it wasn't a problem with them as Alex had said "hold me hard," afterward, and you don't write that to someone you're running away from. He gulped though and jumped out of bed.

Two minutes later, dripping from the most hasty and inadequate shower he savagely rubbed his body dry and grabbed at his uniform. As he snapped on his watch, Nathan glanced at it and realised he was running ridiculously early now. His stomach felt so off he had no appetite anyway so he texted Alex. "Am very concerned after what you wrote last night, running bloody early. Want to meet now ?" "Yes," came the instant reply and Nathan belted down the stairs past his mother who felt like a tornado had just touched her. "Nathan ?" She frowned as her normally starving son wrenched open the huge top and bottom door bolts and unlocked the catch on the front door. He turned looking harrassed, "no time Mum. Alex needs my help, something's happened." The door slammed behind him as he ran full whack for the end of Alex's road. What the hell had him so worried ?

He sprinted down the hill, around the next corner and his heart almost stopped, there was Alex, leaning against a garden wall, chewing on a skinny liquorice shoe lace and looking worriedly about him, his face pale. Nathan pelted faster. Alex heard him and looked up, his face morphed into that dazzling smile and his eyes shone as Nathan slowed as he reached him. He was panting due to the speed not the effort and looked red cheeked as he stood stock still in front of Alex. "Well ?" He breathed. "I am thanks, you ?" Alex grinned back. Nathan groaned and momentarily hung his head in his hands. "This is no time for jokes Alex, what is it ?"

Alex reached forward and wrapped himself around Nathan, breathing in the scent of his skin as he placed his face beside his warm neck. "Oh God you smell good," he breathed. In spite of his burning desire to know what ailed Alex so badly, Nathan felt himself melt against the embrace, a different kind of desire replacing his fear. He groaned back against Alex and kissed his cheek, " Alex, my Alex..." he breathed and Alex moved his mouth slowly around and pressed it down onto his.

Their lips parted to accept each other's tongues and their breathing became ragged as their bodies pushed longingly together. They kissed and suckled at each others mouths, moaning and gasping against one another in ecstasy, not wanting to stop. At last they pulled away, Alex staring with moist eyes into Nathan's as he cupped the back of his head, loving the feel of his silky hair underneath his fingertips. "Ich liebe dich," he whispered. "Ich auch," Nathan replied and they kissed again. They stayed in each others arms, caressing each other gently, just looking at one another's faces. Nathan's stomach growled and they both grinned.

Alex glanced at his watch, "we've time for a danish at Nero's near school if we hurry ?" Nathan nodded and Alex tried to bend down for his rucksack but Nathan held him back. "What's up ?" Alex looked surprised and a little concerned. Nathan shook his head, his fear returning a little. "Alex you haven't told me what's worrying you yet ? Come on, what's up ?" Alex blanched horrifyingly white immediately. Nathan felt sick, "Oh God Alex, what the hell is it ?" He stroked his face with trembling fingers. "It's my Dad."

"Oh my God, is he ill ?" Nathan felt even sicker, if Alex's Dad were dying it would be horrendous. "No, no, nothing like that," Alex shook his head and looked down toward his feet. He drew in a deep breath and looked Nathan squarely in the eyes again and said, "but Nate, he might object to the wedding !"

Nathan wasn't sure he'd heard right for a moment, but then he looked at Alex's face and burst into loud peels of laughter. Alex frowned, he hadn't expected this. Nathan held his side and wiped his eyes. Alex raised an eyebrow at him. He couldn't stop laughing, but at last when he'd finished, he smiled, wiping at his eyes again and grinning at the look on Alex's face and his crossed arms of slight annoyance. "Oh God Al, is that ALL ?" Nathan made a 'my God I can't believe it's so trivial face,' at him.

Alex frowned and said, "but what if we can't get married ?" Nathan's laughter returned but Alex started to look quite pissed off so he calmed himself and put both hands on his shoulders.

"Alex, Alex my love," he said, smiling gently at him, "there is no way that your father's reaction would ever get in the way of anything you want to do. I know they usually support you and I can see that your Dad will have a problem with religion and two men marrying, but think about the alternative, he comes to our wedding or looks like an utter prick, is never invited to our house, offends my family who never speak to yours again and if we have children one day, no grandparent sets foot over the threshold. Do you really think he's going to risk all that ?"

Alex looked pale and worried still for a moment, but then at once he smiled and his colour returned. " Oh yes !" He beamed, I never thought about it like that, I just panicked last night and thought he'd throw a wobbler."

" He probably will about the ceremony to a certain extent, but it will pass and he'll most likely want to walk you down the aisle and embarrass the hell out of you in the end." Laughed Nathan. Alex beamed and lay his head against his shoulder. Nathan wrapped him up in his arms. " Oh thank God Nate, I've been so worried, and all for nothing it would seem." Nathan held him tight and loved him, "sssh, it's going to be ok, they're not going to abandon you," he whispered and felt Alex's arms tighten around him.

" I love you so much my Nathan, so so much." Alex breathed and they un-entwined just enough for their lips to meet again. "Me too," Nathan mumbled as they kissed and his stomach let out an almighty growl. They both burst out laughing then quickly bent to pick up their bags, heading toward Nero's for some breakfast, crisis averted and one more day closer to their eighteenth birthdays and the news that they couldn't wait to break.

Chapter Six.

Over the next three weeks life for the two boys seemed to get better and better. They sat in Nero's before school again talking about their future. They had already started a fund for after their marriage and were totting up the total so far. "Ok, so there's my 'untouchable til you're 18 son,' car washing Isa that my Dad set up for me, that hasn't got a lot in it but it's a start. Wait a minute, let me just check my advice slip here...," Nathan fumbled inside a folder full of paperwork. "Aha, ok so in this I have, oh.." he slumped a bit in the chair, "£1100 quid, - shit, that's not going to get us very far !" Alex patted the top of his hand and shook his head, "don't worry, look, I've got my junior ski instructor fees from the last two years, that's all in here and in total it's £4,300."

Nathan's eyes widened in awe, "Christ Alex, you must be good ! The season isn't that long and you've saved that in only two years ?" Alex grinned back at him and nodded but then he bit his lip and blushed somewhat. Nathan was intrigued and raised an eyebrow at him. "Ahuh, out with it Nesbitt-Hall, why are you looking so sheepish ? What did you really do for that money ?" Alex blushed some more and turned away a bit. Nathan steered his hot face back around with his fingers, "come on, tell me !" He said with a 'who's a naughty boy,' edge to his voice.

"Well erm, no I did earn the money as I said, teaching people to ski , it's just that, erm...well, erm...." he looked highly embarrassed. "Alexander, what have you been up to ?" Nathan grinned, only mildly concerned and very curious. "Erm," Alex was redder than Nathan had ever seen him but he looked into Nathan's eyes and continued.

" The thing is, when you're out on the slopes in Avignon or Gstaad, Corcheval, where ever, people can be very nice, they can also be very snotty and demanding. Then you get the women who's husbands are a lot older than them and they're kind of well, the wrong side of 30, at least in their eyes, and they get....kind of complimentary and become very punctual and a bit competitive with each other and they kind of tip you quite a lot to make sure they get you rather than someone else next season."

Nathan pretended to look shocked, "Alexander Nesbitt-Hall, you shameless hussy you !" He burst out laughing at the blushing embarrassment on Alex's face, it was too funny. Alex's lips twitched at the corners but he also looked offended, he tried to get up but Nathan grabbed him by the wrist. "Oh no you don't cheeky, you get back here and let me laugh at you good and proper."

Alex sat back down in his chair with a thump. "Fuck," he mumbled. Nathan laughed and laughed, rubbing his thumb over the back of his wrist to show he meant no harm. Alex tried to pull his wrist away but couldn't, he looked back at Nathan's face again and felt himself about to crack too but wanted to look offended for a minute longer. Nathan saw him start to laugh and a battle ensued with Nathan trying to turn his rigidly set face back round so they could laugh together and Alex trying to pretend that he was mortally offended for a bit longer, only because he was so embarrassed, but it was funny and the more he thought about it the more his cheeks raised into a smile which Nathan could clearly feel.

He jumped up and sprinted to Alex's other side, catching him off guard he planted a quick peck on his lips and whispered, " my sweet boy toy, thanks for coming this morning, I've only got a tenner but try and buy yourself something pretty with it." He threw the note at Alex who gasped and looked as if he'd explode. Nathan sprinted for the door and then seeing the baristas faces, he walked as solemly as possible back to the table. They sat there bubbling with laughter until Alex mock punched his thigh under the table just a bit too hard and realised as soon as he'd done it.

"Jeez !" Nathan yelped through gritted teeth. "Oh shit, sorry, sorry ! Oh crap Nate, I didn't mean to." Alex looked mortified and tried to rub it better but it still hurt so Nathan held him off for a moment. "It's ok, its ok you didn't mean to, I know." He husked through still clenched teeth but he looked in pain. "Oh Nathan, baby I'm so sorry, is it really bad ?" Alex's heart went out to him, he felt terrible.

"Hey, come on, that's going to happen sometimes with two guys messing around isn't it. You just caught me right on the muscle, it felt quite deep but I'm fine, honestly." Nathan smiled and cupped Alex's jaw gently. "Now," he flipped his watch over, "where were we. Arse ! We've only got fifteen minutes left to tot up our savings Al so let's get cracking." Alex nodded and they wrote a proper list in double quick time. In all they had £9,500 saved between them and Alex's earnings from the snow and ski shop where he worked after school once a week would add another £50 a month over the next six. "Ok, that's £300 more. Then I've got that watch that Uncle Jarvis gave me, it's nice but never been my cup of tea so that's going on ebay." Nathan added it to the futures list. "How much will that bring in ?" Alex asked. "bout £500," said Nathan. "Ok, so that's another £800 bringing us to £10,300 in total so far." He sighed and his shoulders slumped a bit, "it's not much for starting a life is it ?" Alex shook his head, it was more than most people their age had but to be able to put a deposit on a flat and not waste the money renting it didn't seem very much. Plus the fact that they wanted to pay for their wedding themselves. Nathan finished off the last of his cappuccino and put everything back into the folder. They looked at each other, a bit deflated about the money but determined.

"Why don't I get a Saturday job ?" Nathan said. "We'll both get them." Alex smiled back. They headed toward school, slinging their rucksacks on their backs and thinking hard about the money. "Two saturday jobs for the next six months sounds like a great plan to me," said Alex, " but what are we going to do right away after we've left school and got married ? We've never talked about that and I don't want to go to uni." " Me neither," Nathan agreed. They walked on thoughtfully and all through the day both were absorbed in working out how to have their instant life together and make it good financially. The end of the day was sunny and glorious and they ambled happily home together talking about rubbish and laughing in the sun.

Nathan glanced over at Alex at one point and saw his shirt hanging open revealing his smooth taut body underneath. He remembered running his mouth all over that delicious stomach and sucking gently and then more firmly on the pink nipples he could see being grazed by Alex's shirt. He groaned suddenly and Alex looked at him, mildly alarmed. "Nate ?"

Nathan blushed and licked his lips. "What is it ?" Alex didn't understand but then he caught sight of a rising issue in Nathan's direction and gasped. He looked around quickly and pushed him backwards up against a deep hedge that partially enclosed them. "Are you feeling randy my baby ?" He husked which didn't help at all.

Nathan groaned and closed his eyes momentarily. "I looked over at you and your shirt was open," he blushed, "I could see that beautiful body of yours that only a day or so ago I was licking and touching, having your nipples in my mouth, making love to you..." he was stopped by Alex's hot mouth pressing urgently onto his, his swollen excited lips covering Nathan's, licking inside his mouth as he crushed his groin against him.

Nathan had to push his head away panting for a moment. He looked back at Alex who held him almost breathlessly, so erotically charged. His hair stood up, muzzed and disarranged, his cheeks flushed hotly and he looked just as he felt. "I wish I could drag you under this hedge and rip all your clothes off right now," he husked, he sounded almost angry. "Christ Nathan, I want you so much." Nathan groaned again and felt himself slide, rigid and ready to burst against Alex through his trousers. He gasped and felt a trickle of sweat run down his back.

"Not helping..." he breathed, finding it hard to get enough breath. Alex looked like he couldn't hold off and would just rip Nathan's clothes off him right here, but just then there were footsteps on the pavement and he was forced to lean away, letting Nathan re-emerge from the hedge, dazed and breathlessly excited.

He didn't know what to do to hide the fact and an old lady was approaching fairly smartly. He crouched down and retied both shoelaces as Alex pulled out his iphone and fiddled aimlessly with it trying to look absorbed. She passed quickly and they were alone again for a moment but two or three boys from school were walking slowly up the hill and a couple of joggers. It calmed their immediate problems but as Nathan rose up and met Alex's eyes again Alex shook his head. "This," he said adamantly, "is too hard, six months seems like a very long time when I want you in my arms and I have to wait." He sighed heavily. Nathan grinned his killer grin and it made Alex's stomach fall over.

"Don't Nathan, don't look so lovely. Hell, how am I supposed to go home now ? So turned on I want to be inside you all night and so in love with you that I don't want to let you out of my sight !" He looked shaken all of a sudden and shivered involuntarily. It tore at Nathan's guts.

"Oh Alex," was all he could say and they walked to Nathan's gate and then stepped just inside where they couldn't be seen from the road or the house then they fell on each other for the longest kiss and held tightly with their hearts hammering against one another's chests. At last they drew apart and laughed with their faces closely together, their eyes moist, overwhelmed with lust and longing. "I'll call you after supper." Alex whispered and kissed Nathan's soft lips once more. It started his heart up again but he had to go. Nathan nodded and released his arms. Alex walked backwards as usual until he disappeared.

After dinner, Nathan did his home work with a troubled mind, he didn't concentrate on what he was doing but he got it finished. He flopped down on his bed afterward and looked up at the ceiling. What did he want to do with his life ? Two things came to him immediately, him and Alex together, that wasn't in question, and secondly America. He wanted to live on the coast in America and run a smart diner style cafe, very New England, whitewashed woodwork, divine cupcakes and the strong smell of fresh coffee everywhere. He would hire two American cooks to make eggs and prepare fresh bagels, soups, bake fresh cakes. There would be granola for breakfast, American cinamon muffins, English muffins at teatime and fruit, toast and fry ups all day long. They would get to know their regular customers and Nathan would sketch local boats, surfing scenes and people and hang them framed around the walls for everyone to buy at a hundred dollars each.

He rubbed his chin. Was this possible ? Well of course it was possible he mused, but do-able ? He wasn't so sure about that. What licenses would they need, could two gay Brits set up a business, at eighteen would they be legal for a business venture ? There were so many questions, but the biggest one was what would Alex think ? Alex, the most successful outgoing sportsman he knew, would this be too sedentary for him ? Wouldn't he want to be surfing all day, teaching people how to flip 180s or entering big high profile competitions ? He wondered, tapping the phone against his lips. It vibrated against them making him squirm with that weird lip tingle that makes you shudder. He slid it open, not needing to read the display and grinned.

"Hey," came the voice he loved. "Hey yourself," he replied. "What are you doing ?" Alex asked. Nathan shrugged and let out a sigh, "actually I was thinking hard about our future, career wise." "And what did you think ?" Alex asked. "I have an idea but I'm not sure if you would go for it or if we could do it," he finished. "Tell me and we'll see," said Alex reasonably. "Ok, well the first thing is that I can see you and I in America, on the coast somewhere, don't ask me which one, just somewhere sunny. The next thing is, I can see our business. I saw it in my minds eye as being called 'Nate's Place,' - now don't think anything funny, it's just the name that came to me and it sounds kind of American too, it's not meant to exclude you."

Alex laughed good naturedly, he was intrigued. "Carry on, I'm not offended." So Nathan filled him in on all the details, décor, types of coffee, brownies, bagels, soups, specials, he and Alex surfing together on their days off, and the sun streaming in through the windows as they sat together over a cup of coffee after they closed up and looked around at their own place, happy and in love. When he finished there was a long pause. Nathan waited, his heart thrummed, was he saying the wrong thing ? "Alex ?" He asked tentatively, "baby ?" Alex breathed out a long breath and said softly, " I can't believe it. It sounds so lovely. Where did you come up with an idea like that ?"

Nathan smiled at the phone, "I don't know, I just did. I think I've always dreamed of it." "Well it's a bloody amazing dream Nate, amazing." Alex breathed. "I have never ever wanted to sit in a stuffy office as a solicitor or business man, ugh ! I thought I was destined to go that way through no other choice and now I have you and look at what you come up with. It's magical."

Nathan's cheeks hurt for smiling, he was elated. "Shall we look into it right away then ?" He suggested. Alex agreed adamantly and they said their goodbyes with the thrill of meeting up next morning tingling through their bodies. Nathan let the phone drop to the bed, he leant his head back, exhausted, elated and excited all at once. He turned onto his side and shifted down on the duvet. In two minutes he was deeply asleep. When his mum came to check on him she frowned at his slim waist and the fact that he was asleep so early again, perhaps he was doing too much.

Tomorrow night she would overfeed him and sit him down after supper for a chat followed by a movie with the whole family so she could keep an eye on him. Movie night could be changed she mused or done twice. She pulled a blanket up over her sleeping son and closed his bedroom window. Why he'd taken to leaving it always open these days she'd never know but there was a slight chill in the air tonight so it was better shut.

The following evening, after a magnificent feast of lasagne, a huge salad and pavlova, the family sat around stuffed and groaning as they watched a movie. The twins chose Die Hard, "90s revival night," they insisted. Their Dad joined in with "80s more like after tonight's supper I thought, but I don't mind crossing the decades," he smiled. "Looks like you've crossed quite a few Dad," Jack teased and got a gentle swipe around the head for his trouble. "Oy, child abuse, I'm phoning Brussels for that infringement of my human rights !"

"Bite me !" Said their Dad in such a correct accent that it just didn't sound cool at all. Much teasing and silliness followed before the rest of the movie could go ahead and then everyone helped with the tidying up and headed to bed. Nathan's mum was no longer too worried, her son certainly ate as if food were in short supply, she'd just try and keep up a little more with his energy output she decided and added a few more groceries to the Ocado list for tomorrow.

Nathan fell into bed, warm, full and happy. He'd had such a lovely day at school, he and Alex had managed to sneak in some amazing kisses in the shadows, he grinned to himself at the thought as he turned out the light. The sounds from his parents moving about and the twins talking did not last long and soon the house was entirely silent. Nathan began to drift into a gorgeous sleep, Alex was there, stroking his cheek softly and saying, "God you look beautiful when you sleep," his fingers felt incredible, dancing lightly along Nathan's cheekbones.

He groaned gently. "You like that do you ?" Alex breathed in his ear and gently kissed it. Nathan sighed, this was a lovely dream, so real. "Hey baby, are you really asleep my love ?" Alex husked. Nathan was confused, this felt so real. He opened his eyes expecting to see nothing, and jumped a mile, there was Alex, perched on the edge of his bed in his grey hoodie looking utterly gorgeous, heartbreakingly handsome. Nathan's eyes flew wide as Alex grinned.

" I really made you jump didn't I ? Sorry," he laughed quietly. Nathan grinned back looking sleepy and with his t-shirt all twisted about him.

"Alex," he beamed, "you're really here." Alex nodded and stroked his cheek again, "I just wanted to be in your arms tonight, do you mind ?" Nathan looked non plussed, "mind ? Why would I ever mind ? You can climb up my trellis anytime." He smirked and Alex threw back his head with laughter, just about keeping it under parent radar level. Nathan flapped back the duvet and Alex slid in. He abandoned his clothes immediately and so did Nathan, he didn't feel sleepy any more.

At 5.30am Alex's iphone buzzed to wake the boys up. They were deeply asleep and wrapped together. It was hard to wake up and come to life. Alex hit snooze on the phone and stroked back Nathan's hair. His eyes fluttered to life and that killerwatt smile slid across his face. He shuddered as he yawned and wrapped his arms tighter around Alex's ribs. Alex kissed the tip of his nose, "morning sweetheart," he grinned. Nathan blinked, so comfortable and definitely not awake yet, "what time did we go to sleep ?" He croaked. "About 12.30am, Alex replied. "Ugh, no wonder I feel so knackered." Nathan snuggled his face into the pillow next to him and groaned.

Alex laughed, "my sweet, look at you. I have to get up and go home now, you know that," he whispered softly as he stroked Nathan's cheek. "Why so early ?" Nathan asked. " Go home at 7am and I'll meet you at 8 to walk to school." "I can't my love, Mum gets up at 6.00am to get some work done and Dad's not far behind her. Your brother and sister are usually around at a sparrows croak, and until we tell everyone our official plans I don't think they'll like me sneaking down the stairs with you, holding your hand and going, 'God Nate, you blew me away last night, literally. I'm going to dream about all those naughty things you did to me all day long."

Nathan's lips went up at the corners and he blushed with it. "That was a wonderful night wasn't it ?" Alex nodded at him, "more than wonderful and I am going to dream about all those naughty things today at school. Especially when you bathed my nipples with your tongue and then licked all the way down my abs until...." He was stopped by Nathan's hand over his mouth, he looked pained, "Christ Alex, I'm already rock hard, do you want to be late going home, cos in a minute I'm not going to be able to let you leave." He pulled his hand away and Alex chuckled naughtily, "I love you," he breathed, cupping Nathan's face. "Ich auch," said Nathan and blinked at him through long eyelashes. They caressed each other's faces and kissed once more before Alex slipped from the bed and dressed. It didn't take long and when he was ready he sat on the edge and pulled Nathan into his arms, they hugged each other without speaking and then Alex kissed him again, "go back to sleep baby, I'll see you by my gate in two hours," he smiled.

Nathan nodded happily and lay back down as Alex made his way to the window, but he sprang bolt upright again. "What am I thinking ? You can't go that way, you'll fall. Let me sneak you out the front door like last time." Alex shook his head, "I won't Nate, trust me, I'm a good climber." He swung a leg over the frame and started to lower himself. Nathan leapt out of bed to watch him. " Careful, careful..." he insisted as Alex moved deftly from brick to tile, ledge and trellis.

He was almost down, four feet to go when he looked up smiling at Nathan's worried face and totally lost his footing. He snatched at the trellis but missed completely and fell flat on his back on the mossy grass. Nathan yelped loudly and covered his face with his hands. Alex lay still for a moment, winded but nothing more. He struggled up on his elbows and saw Nathan' s anxious face. "Oh my God Alex, for fucks sake ! Never ever do that again !" He said angrily, fear making him snap. Alex nodded, "well you were right, sorry Nate, I didn't mean to scare you." "Alex I don't want you to apologise, I just want you to be safe. Did you hurt anything ?" Alex shook his head and scrambled to his feet, "Nah, I'm ok," he beamed !

"Nate ?" "Yes ?" Said Nathan warily, "I love you." "Well no more being a numpty then you idiot, you just about gave me a heart attack." Alex laughed and smiled as he backed up to head for home. "I know, I'm sorry my love, but I'm fine, look," he jumped about on the grass. Nathan shook his head, "idiot, but I love you." "Me too," Alex husked gently. "See you at 8 my Nate, now rest that pretty head," and he was gone. Nathan sank back down onto his bed, pulled the covers up and was deeply asleep within seconds, dreaming of his 8am kisses.

His alarm woke him again at 7, it didn't feel long enough and he groaned, tired. He stretched in the bed and a big smile swept over him as he remembered last night. Alex climbing in through his window for the second time in a month. He blushed as he recalled their passion, Alex's fingers on his chest had felt like fire burning through his soul, when he'd moved his hands down to grip him it had taken Nathan all of four thrusts before he exploded and less than three minutes before he was ready to go again. He'd used his mouth on Alex, sliding his lips all over his firm body, licking and tasting every inch of him, making him gasp and groan to the point just before pain where he'd taken him over the edge, it was ecstasy.

These thoughts got Nathan aroused immediately, he glanced at his clock, he had time if he hurried. He shut his eyes, moving his hands down under the duvet and began to remember Alex's groans and whimpers in detail, it didn't take him long. He tore through dressing and breakfast and was out of the house making his way to him at 7.55am. It was another gorgeous sunny day and he grinned as he approached him, nonchalantly posed against a garden wall chewing another shoelace. He grinned back at Nathan who came straight to him and kissed his mouth. Alex melted back against the wall and moaned, last night was still fresh in his mind too.

They drew apart with moist bee stung lips. "Hello," said Nathan breathily. Alex laughed and blushed a little. They kissed again and began the walk to school. "How are you feeling ?" Nathan asked, "seriously, I'm fine, I only fell a few feet and your grass is pretty bouncy. I'm fine Nate, I really am," Alex assured him.

"But back to your diner idea, I love it as you know, so lets get cracking on some serious research. We've done our savings tally so what next ? Permits, our age, all sorts of stuff like that I guess." Nathan nodded, "yup, we need to get a proper file together on all of this. Plus it will help with the rentals when we tell them we're getting married and what we plan to do." Alex nodded his agreement and they chatted happily for the rest of the journey, making wonderful plans. They agreed on the right weekend to tell their parents just as they reached the school gate. They exchanged a powerful look, nothing more need be said, this was really it. Their plans were going to come to fruition, and very soon at that, they couldn't wait.

The next few weeks were a blur. Nathan's swimming hotted up, he suddenly found himself absorbed in all sorts of competitions. He loved it but it took him away from Alex a little bit too much. They just weren't any good at being apart and though Alex took part in all his usual hobbies and played hockey and football for the school, he didn't feel his heart was in it as before. School seemed pretty pointless when you knew what you wanted to do and he just wanted it to start now.

They got by, and whenever there was a particularly irksome week that took them away from each other too much, Nathan could be sure that he would have a late night visitor at least once that week and made sure to leave his window always open. There were one or two hairy moments where Alex had to leap off Nathan and squash himself into the cupboard for fear of being found.

In a particularly dodgy moment as Nathan's father decided to check on his son, he'd sure he'd heard a moan, the door handle turned just as Alex was bringing him to orgasm. He had to slam his face into the pillow muffling his groans and gasps as Alex slid over the far side of the bed and hid behind it in the dark. Nathan's dad flicked on the light and Nathan raised his head looking red faced, hot and mussed. His father looked concerned so Nathan quickly made a 'thank god it's you,' face and croaked, "Oh my God that was just a dream." He sank his head back onto the pillow and closed his eyes, "just a dream, just a dream..." he murmured convincingly and looked as if he'd fallen back to sleep. Satisfied, his Dad switched off the light and withdrew. He'd had enough boyhood nightmares and vivid dreams himself. He had no idea what was really going on and went to bed entirely untroubled.

Ten seconds later Alex slid silently back on top of Nathan who could at last gasp out loud and revel in the aftershocks of his pleasure. Alex looked down at his hot face and smoothed back his fringe grinning. Nathan smiled back at him, they giggled for a moment. "Was that nice ?" Alex breathed. "Bloody amazing," Nathan whispered. "It was hard to think at all when my Dad came in, parts of me were just throbbing uncontrollably against the bed. It was heaven." Alex beamed, his teeth white in the moonlight. "I love you." He kissed Nathan's mouth gently, "now roll over so that I can stick something special into you."

Nathan giggled almost too loudly and Alex covered his mouth with his hand, "ssh," he smiled. Nathan wriggled over and Alex slid onto his back.

He looked down at every muscle, Nathan looked beautiful in the moonlight. As usual he was careful not to hurt his love, they had got used to using proper lube and it made the pleasure ten times more intense. He eased into Nathan and heard him gasp. It heightened everything when he did that, making Alex groan above him. "God you're so incredible," he croaked between sliding his hips back and forth. Nathan pressed his face into the pillow and gasped. "Oh Alex, my Alex..." he groaned sending Alex into total ecstasy. He pumped a little faster and Nathan could barely contain himself, "fuck, oh fuck," he whimpered as Alex made love to him. Alex tingled all over, he was beyond the point of return. When he came, he buried his face between Nathan's shoulder blades and gasped and gasped.

At last, as he started to come down from the rush, he kissed where his lips met skin and covered Nathan's hands with his, interlacing their fingers. He lay back down on top of him as they gasped slowly back to normal. He didn't pull out, they remained together, feeling part of each other more than ever until some time had passed. At last they rolled around to face each other and just looked and looked. This time felt just as it was, the most special beginning for them both. Nathan stroked Alex's cheek bones until his eyes started to close and soon they were both asleep, wrapped together again in the way that they hoped to be for at least the next sixty years.

Chapter Seven.

A week later and they were just two days away from Nathan's eighteenth birthday. His stomach flipped every time he thought of it, it meant more to him than any of his family realised because of his pledge to Alex. The were one step closer and only three weeks from announcing it at last. They had booked a venue for the tenth, asked two friends to be witnesses and picked out their wedding suits and music. October couldn't come soon enough. They lay blissful in each other's arms again one morning.

"I didn't like that movie last night you know," said Nathan as he leant back against Alex's bare chest. He was trying to get one of those little cup and ball on a string cracker toys to work but was rubbish at it. Alex watched a few more attempts and took it off him, getting the ball in first time he handed it back to Nathan who dug him in the ribs with his elbow." "Oof !" Alex coughed at the impact and laughed at Nathan's irritation. "Crapping bollocks toy anyway," Nathan grumbled and chucked it over the side of the bed.

"Now, now baby," Alex chided and pulled Nathan's head back onto his pecs, "who's a naughty boy then, no 'toys pram out,' this morning please." Nathan giggled and the vibrations made Alex laugh too. Nathan wriggled round to turn on his side and Alex rubbed his shoulders, "hey, look up handsome," he husked, Nathan raised his head enough for Alex to bring his lips down on his mouth. It was such a sweet kiss that it made Nathan groan a throaty rumble. "God I love it when you do that," Alex husked and stroked his smooth cheek making him sigh with pleasure and beam his mega smile. The iphone jumped to life signalling time to move and the boys repeated their usual routine, except this time Nathan insisted on Alex slipping out of the front door but just as he was about to disappear he pulled him close and held his phone up in the air for a photo. It was pretty stunning and made them both grin.

"Send it to me, I want it as my screen saver," Alex smiled. Nathan blushed and kissed him one last time before he watched him back away and then shut the door. The next day Nathan woke with a feeling of elation, he usually woke with his stomach in knots these days, looking forward to seeing Alex and feeling so in love with him. Today was the same but something else made his tummy contract. He sat up and rubbed his head and then grinned to himself, yes of course, his eighteenth birthday ! His parents had promised him a surprise on Saturday, they'd invited his 3 best friends and Alex and that was all he knew. He dressed for school in a great mood, wondering what the day would bring and looking forward to his surprise tomorrow.

He hopped down the stairs two at a time and grinned from ear to ear when he saw his family all huddled around the kitchen table looking surreptitious. As he neared the table they leapt in front of it to form a human barrier, his dad and brother leaning behind the girls whispering something. His mum stepped forward and hugged him, "Happy birthday my darling," she smiled. "Thanks mum," he beamed back at her, just as the lights went out and the twins stepped forward with a chocolate fudge cake blazing with far too many candles. He threw his head back and laughed, "cake, - at breakfast ?"

The twins nodded vehemently, "come on old man, blow out the candles, - OOH NO, wait we haven't finished," Jack suddenly jumped up and down, "dad !" He whispered under his breath. "What ?" Said Nathan's dad looking non plussed for a second until, - "ah !! Yes, yes, almost forgot, sorry son." He smiled at his youngest boy and then cleared his throat dramatically making the twins giggle, "1.2.3...Happy birthday to you,..." Nathan hung his head in his hands as the whole family joined in the screeching chorus at the top of their lungs. It was so dreadful but filled his heart with joy. He looked up with moist eyes and blew out his fifty seven candles all in one mega breath. "Cool !" Said Jack, "not bad for a really old bloke !"

Everyone laughed and Nathan opened his main present, there were a tonne of little ones which they were saving for after school, stacked up in the corner. He tore at the red sparkley paper around it and pulled out a fabulous long tin of derwent 2b pencils followed by a new set of watercolours and gouache paints, six new fine sable brushes and two thick daler sketch books, one with thick white sheets for detailed drawing and the other in an array of pale beige textured sheets. An envelope fell out of the back of the wrapping to the floor, inside was a receipt for a Saturday morning life drawing class, four in a row. He looked up at his family and shook his head.

"This is just too fabulous you guys," he husked feeling emotion welling up in him. His sister shoved him with her shoulder, "don't blub you big sissy, eat your bloody cake !" as she pushed a huge slice toward his mouth. Nathan started to laugh hard, he bit into the soft chocolate sponge and thick butter cream filling as he heard his mother gasp and shake her head at Jasmine for swearing. Jasmine rolled her eyes and watched Nathan try to swallow as much of the cake as possible. He couldn't finish the slice it was so huge. He swished all the crumbs out of his teeth with a swig of tea and looked at his watch, he needed to move, Alex would be waiting.

"Thank you so much everyone," he beamed, getting to his feet. "Want me to drive you son ?" His dad offered. Nathan shrugged and shook his head, "Nah

dad, thanks but I'm walking with Alex and he'll be waiting so I'd better go."
It was hard to leave as the twins kept putting biscuits in his pockets saying he
needed to keep his strength up now that he was old, and his mum kept flinging
her arms around him in mock dramatic fashion going, "my baby's 18 already,
how, how ?"

Eventually he managed to extricate himself from the madness and walked
slower than normal around the corner and down the hill. He beamed all the
way, checking his face and lips with the back of his hands for extra chocolate
crumbs and continually finding them. At last he rounded the top bend and saw
Alex waiting against the garden wall, his face lit up in a big smile once he saw
Nathan. He was carrying a blue wrapped parcel with a huge red bow on the
top. Nathan coloured as he neared him, it was hard having the spotlight on only
him all day, it brought out his shyness but he grinned anyway the closer he
got. He stood in front of him at last and Alex beamed his heart stopping smile
that showed his perfect teeth and reached out with one hand, instantly cupping
Nathan's face he pulled him close and kissed him, open mouthed, sinking in his
hot tongue. It was electric.

He slid the present onto the wall behind him and slipped both his arms inside
Nathan's blazer, popping open all his shirt buttons, one after the other. His
thumbs grazed his nipples making them concrete hard and erect immediately.
Nathan almost buckled under him at the pleasure. He moaned loudly into Alex's
mouth and screwed his eyes up tight. Alex held him tightly to stop him falling
and brushed his nipples again. He began to pant and gasp. With lightning speed
Alex flicked open his fly and sank his hand inside Nathan's Calvin's, he stroked
once up his stiff shaft and re-hooked his fly. He pulled away from a gasping
Nathan, red and flustered to the core, "Happy birthday my darling," he grinned.

"Fuck ! You bastard !" Nathan trembled and Alex giggled with glee. "I'm
sorry baby, is that really unfair ?" He smirked. "Yes !" Nathan growled. "Well I
thought you might say that," Alex smiled naughtily, come with me."

He pulled him by the hand back inside his gateway, up the front steps
and straight inside his house where he slammed the door and rammed Nathan
aggressively up against it. "My whole family's gone already, this is your real
present," he said, his face very serious but his actions softening completely. He
cupped Nathan's face and kissed him in the most intimate way, then without
another word he led him to the sofa, pushed him down on to it and flicked his
fly open again. He ran his hands over Nathan's sculpted abs and saw his body
shudder with desire.

He pulled the waistband of his boxers down, exposing his incredible rock
hard cock. Nathan let out a little moan and raised his hips. Alex bent his head

down while he swept his palms over his quivering tummy and chest, and took his whole shaft fully into his wet mouth. He closed his lips around it in a tight suctioning motion and Nathan almost shot off the sofa. He let out a wail and flung his head back, gasping as if his life depended on it. Alex murmured too, it felt incredible to be able to suck his future husband, knowing they were only a few months away from doing it permanently.

It added an extra frisson to every movement he made and as Nathan bucked his hips, just about to come, he reached for his hand and their fingers clutched together, each seeming to understand the poignancy. Nathan gasped and cried out, filling Alex's mouth with his cum. Alex swallowed hard and didn't stop licking and sucking around his glans until Nathan physically pushed him away gently. Alex raised his head, dizzy from the exertion and looked at Nathan's heaving body, he looked so beautiful as he tried to regain his normal breathing. A minute passed and he opened his eyes.

Alex was by his head soothing him and stroking his hair. He smiled softly down at him, "hello lovely," he beamed. Nathan flushed and smiled back at him, "wow," he breathed. Alex frowned still stroking him tenderly, "I wasn't too rough against the door was I ? I was kind of being silly but also a bit carried away." Nathan shook his head, "no, it had the best effect on me in the world." Alex beamed at him again, his eyes shining with happiness, "I'm so glad my love. Shall we get to school now ?" Nathan nodded and Alex helped him up and into his arms, holding him for a minute before he re-dressed. "My gorgeous one," he husked and kissed his ear as they left the house.

School was great fun that day, there were already three presents piled up on Nathan's desk. He added Alex's to the pile and was urged to open it first. He lifted the lid and found two layers of home made chocolate brownies from the local bakery with a note that just said 'Us soon...', Nathan's eyes were watery when he looked up at Alex, no one else knew why. "Thanks," he mouthed and Alex nodded feeling emotional himself. Nathan offered them around and instantly became the biggest hit in the class. People came up and slapped him on the back all day congratulating him, cards kept arriving on his desk and by the last period, Mr Johnson, their well liked form teacher peered over at him and smiled.

"Looks like you've had a good day there Henderson ?" "I have sir," Nathan blushed. Mr Johnson nodded rubbing his hungry stomach. "I've heard a rumour about some delicious brownies....erm...?" He raised his eyebrows questioningly. "Sorry sir, they were all gone by 9.30am." Nathan replied. "Oh well, it was worth a try." Mr Johnson smiled back. "So, don't forget the summer fair next weekend everyone, I need volunteers and there's a list of requirements and equipment that we're trying to find to make this years go with a bang on the hall notice board if you could all take a butchers, thanks."

He glanced down at his watch just as the school bell rang out across the halls and noisy chatter and chair scraping broke out as everyone got up. "Have a good weekend, bye," called Mr Johnson as he collected up his books and laptop. People departed in all directions as Nathan did his best to stuff all his cards and goodies into his rucksack, Alex took a few left over bits in his. They headed home grinning and enjoying yet another lusciously sunny afternoon.

As they turned into Nathan's drive he looked over at Alex, "what are you still doing with me ? I thought you were coming to my mini party tomorrow ?" Alex pretended to leave, making Nathan snatch at his shoulder and pull him back again laughing, "you know I didn't mean it like that you loon !" Alex grinned, "I know, your mum invited me over for a birthday supper." Nathan's eyes shone, "really ? She did that ?" His heart hammered against his ribs with pleasure. He dropped his bag and threw his arms around Alex who squeezed him back tightly. "It's another step isn't it ?" Alex breathed, looking hard into his eyes. Nathan nodded, "it is," he croaked. "Come on," Alex beamed and dropped a small kiss onto his lips. "I love you," he whispered, "happy birthday," and then led Nathan into the house.

Chaos ensued again as soon as the two boys entered, the twins were going beserk and acting like 9 years olds, chasing each other around the kitchen table, out into the living room, up the stairs and thundering back down them again. The table was so laden with presents and food that it was going to be hard to find elbow room. Nathan laughed when he saw it all. His mum gave him an enormous hug, "happy birthday again darling," she breathed. "Thanks mum."

The food was ready and everyone summoned to the table straight away. They ate roast chicken and potatoes, carrots, peas, mashed potatoes, brocoli and chipolatas wrapped in bacon, stuffing and gravy. "This is like Christmas lunch," said Alex as he shovelled in his last mouthful hungrily. "I know, Nathan's favourite," Alison smiled proudly at her son. Nathan moved his arm to pat his bulging stomach making the paper debris that was mounded up around him crunch and crackle. "Look shall I take some of this off here ?" His dad asked standing up to get a bin bag. "No dad, I like it. Birthday chaos, it's brilliant," Nathan beamed. His dad surveyed the table's madness, stuff just everywhere. "Er..., yes son, brilliant is the description I was thinking of....!" He shook his head and sat down again as everyone laughed.

The party wore on late into the evening, the table looked crazier by each turn and stuff started to overflow across the kitchen floor. By the time Alex had to leave, Nathan's tie and jacket were off, his shirt undone, his hair dishevelled and the house was a veritable pit of paper, left over food and the air hung with the acrid scent of burning candle wax, 57 again, of course. Nathan had never looked better Alex mused as they walked to the gate. He turned to kiss him goodnight and behind him looked through the half open door back toward the table, the chaos and the members of his family all laughing and joking still. It was a very merry scene.

Alex's tummy tied up in knots all of a sudden, he trembled, this was all so wonderful. So wonderful he suddenly felt scared that they could lose it all if something terrible went wrong and their lives didn't work out this way. He frowned without knowing it. "Hey, what's wrong ?" Nathan's forehead creased with concern. Alex shook himself out of the worry. "Ah, I was just having a stupid thought...don't worry about it. I don't know where it came from. I've had such a happy time tonight Nate." Nathan nodded and smiled, "me too. Tell me though Al, stupid or not you looked really worried, what was it ?" Alex didn't want to be a kill joy and started shaking his head but Nathan wrapped him up in his arms.

"No fair, you know I'm powerless as soon as you touch me !" He grinned up into Nathan's delicious eyes. "Yes I do know that, plus it's my birthday, AND I just turned 18 which means I'm an adult now so I force you to tell me, instantly !" He squeezed his arms around Alex.

"God, you're a bossy grown up !" Alex teased. "Yes I am," Nathan grinned, "so tell me schoolboy, what was it that made you look sad and worried ?" Alex drew in a deep breath, he looked worried again. So worried it made Nathan's stomach drop. "Hey, Alex, what is it ?" Alex bit his bottom lip and inhaled deeply. "Oh Nate, I...I was just being silly." He shrugged.

"Out with it, silly or not," Nathan commanded. "Well," Alex shifted and sighed, " I just looked at you, so happy, beautiful, shiny eyed, and I could see through the door behind you to the happiness I'd just been part of and suddenly I got really scared, what if all of this was taken away from me or something happened to stop us getting what we really want and it was such a horrible cold fear. I don't know why I went down that route but it made me feel really sick for a second." He finished looking pale and shivery all of a sudden.

Nathan stroked his cheek gently, " It's ok," he soothed. Alex's eyes had welled right up. "It was so stupid but I couldn't bear it if anything went wrong Nate, I just couldn't." He dashed tears away from his eyes. "Don't my love. Don't think like that," Nathan whispered. "Hey," he took Alex by the shoulders, "listen to me, we can all indulge in the 'what if,' worries, but that's all they are, worries, and no good ever came of them. It's not like you to worry about the worst and you know what they say, if you focus on a negative you're feeding it and it will only grow."

He brushed away a tear from Alex's cheek. "I did have one or two hours of thinking like that about us when we first got together, but our feelings for each other are so strong. Besides, I was never as confident in myself as you and I was never as good at half as many things as you are but I've learnt in the last few weeks to be more like you, to just get on and do stuff and enjoy life." He kissed Alex's cheek and smiled, "you've taught me so much already Al, you're the most positive person I know."

Alex dashed at his free falling tears now, and smiled back at him, "I'm so sorry love, to be like this on your birthday. It's just all so perfect and I got scared." Nathan pulled him close and held him, stroking his head. "I love you so much Alex, I'm not going anywhere, that's for sure. They're going to have to prise my cold dead fingers off you before you can get away from me." "Nate don't !" Alex grimaced. Nathan laughed, " Nothing's going to go wrong my love."

" I know," Alex sighed and looked tired. "Happy birthday Nate, and see you tomorrow for your surprise." As he said 'surprise,' the usual cheery Alex seemed to reappear and Nathan grinned at him. They kissed once more and Alex disappeared. Nathan wasn't unduly concerned, people felt funny sometimes. He went back to his family and enjoyed another mad happy hour with them all before he went to bed surrounded by gifts and gadgets. Just before midnight he reached to turn out the light but his phone pinged. He picked it up and read "Ich..." "...liebe dich," he typed back to Alex and got a kiss in return. Exhausted he clicked off the light and smiled amid his bed of presents. He glanced up at his open window, grinned and fell into a deep, contented sleep.

Saturday morning sprang up sunnier than ever and made Nathan beam with delight. He couldn't begin to fathom the surprise that his family had in store for him and grinned to himself at the thought of it. His stomach tied up in the usual way when his thoughts turned to Alex and they were tinged with a hint of worry about last night, but he quickly shoved that thought process away. He and Alex were unbreakable, there was nothing that would keep them apart. He smiled at the thought and nipped into the bathroom to get ready. Breakfast was a fabulous feast of pancakes, blueberries and maple syrup with scoops of vanilla ice cream on the side with chocolate sauce. Nathan laughed as the twins kept trying to force another two and another two on to his plate.

"Stop, stop ! I can't take this much sugar, I'll be bouncing off the walls like a nutcase !" The twins raised their eyebrows at each other, "well that's pretty much a given," they giggled. Nathan frowned, "what ? What's that supposed to mean ?" "You'll find out," Jasmine giggled again. After breakfast Nathan's mum made all her children do an hour of school work. "Hey, I thought this was my birthday surprise ?" Nathan grumbled. "It is," smiled his mother, pushing him through his bedroom door, but we don't have to be there until 11.30 so go, that's just over an hour away which is perfect timing." She pulled the door shut behind her and Nathan grumpily sat down. Flipping open his art homework list he realised that all he had to do was draw someone he knew well for an hour. Suddenly his mood brightened considerably. He scrolled through his phone until he found the clearest picture of Alex's face then he sent it to his emails and brought it up on his laptop and began to draw.

The hour flew by so fast that he didn't hear his mother's knock, he jumped as she gently opened the door. "Sorry love, you didn't hear me did you,....Nathan ! Darling that's amazing." She gasped. Nathan blushed profusely, he'd drawn the most beautiful pencil sketch of Alex leaning back against what was actually his headboard but he hadn't filled that part in thank God. One hand was up near his face and his eyes were closed as he nodded off. With the angle of the photo you looked almost down his face from above seeing much of his eyelashes, pointed nose and full lips, his collar bones and then the picture finished just below his taut pecs. Nathan's mum picked up the pad, "this is really breathtaking my darling, wow !" She handed it back to him and cuffed his cheek gently, "you really love him don't you ?"

Nathan nodded going very red. "I do." He breathed. "Come on, surprise time," she smiled, changing the mood, "grab a coat and we'll head out." Nathan snatched up his favourite jacket and slipped on his new dark blue converse, Alex's other present to him. When he got downstairs he was frogmarched out of the house by his family as they set off in the direction of the park. Nathan was non plussed. He tried to guess all the way there what on earth they were doing but he still couldn't. As they neared the gate his family's excitement was palpable and the twins became practically unbearable. They made him shut his eyes and each took a side of him, bracing an arm each and walking him forward.

He stepped out gingerly, leaning back a little. "It's ok, the grounds quite even and we won't let you fall," Jack said. Nathan nodded, "ok guys, but I'm not doing this for long." "You don't have to, five more steps and you can open your eyes," Jasmine panted with the effort of steering her big brother. As good as her word, they came to a stop in just another few steps. There was light music coming from somewhere, Nathan recognised the Pierces singing one of his favourite new songs. A funny sound in the background sounded like something being inflated.

"Oh God, guys if this is a hot air balloon I can't, I just can't, you know me and heights !" The twins laughed, "no that's not it," said Jack. "Open your eyes,"

Jasmine whisperd. Nathan blinked against the strong sunlight as he looked up in front of him. His mind couldn't take it in at first. "Surprise !" Yelled everyone at once and Nathan covered his face with his hands, bending to his knees with laughter, "you didn't !!!" He gasped, when he could speak again, his eyes as wide as saucers. "Everyone laughed, including Paul, Simon, Sam and best of all, Alex, as the four of them sprang on to the canvas of a huge bouncy castle in front of him. They wobbled about in the entrance having just all tossed their shoes to the grass.

"First bounce to Nathan !" Alex called, beaming. Nathan shook his head laughing again and ran forward. The four of them parted to let him dive through, converse flying up in the air behind him as he leapt. He hit the bouncy floor on his belly and was thrown up on to his feet, staggered forward and careered off the back wall by his chest. He lay on his back pinging up and down as everyone else herded on like mad animals and started leaping about like loons. It was so springy and had most people double bouncing each other in no time. It was hilarious.

Alex and the twins delighted in flipping over in impressive back flips while Nathan and Sam bounced higher and higher in competition with each other to see who could leave the most air between themselves and the castle. His parents jumped holding each others hands in one corner and ended up shrieking as they accidentally double bounced scarily high and nearly pitched over the high bouncy turrets.

After a while Alex boinged over and bounced up behind Nathan, he wrapped his arms around his ribs and tried to get them to bounce together but it was an accident waiting to happen so they just leapt about next to one another, grinning madly. The twins came and bounced with them both. "Hey, you wait til you see Nathan's amazing picture of you," Jack breathed between bounces. Nathan shot him a frown. "Huh ? How do you know about that ? I only did it this morning." Jack flashed open his gilet to reveal a white t-shirt which said, 'Jesus loves you but I'm his favourite.'

"My t-shirt !" Nathan exclaimed. "I swiped it from your room just after you followed mum downstairs and your sketch book was open on the desk. That's your best picture yet. What are you going to do with it bro ?" Nathan shrugged, he felt red and hot with Alex's eyes on him but when he looked up he saw such a flattered sweet look on his face it made his heart turn over. He smiled shyly, "that sounds wonderful," Alex breathed and lay down on the bouncy floor. The twins got beckoned over by Paul and Simon and sprang off to join them. Alex patted the canvas and Nathan lay down a foot away, nose to toes, looking toward him. Alex gave his ankle a little squeeze, it seemed the least sexual thing to do in public. They beamed at each other.

"Do you like your surprise ?" Alex grinned. Nathan's cheeks hurt from so much smiling. He shook his head, "brilliant, just bloody brilliant." He laughed. He stood up and inched slightly closer to Alex before seeming to wind his arms up, "Oh no, no you don't !" Alex tried to scramble to his feet but it was too late, Nathan had begun to bounce as hard as his sixteen pancakes from breakfast would let him and each time he landed Alex's body shot up off the canvas, higher and higher.

He tried to move about and get his legs under him but he never had enough time between bounces and laughing to quite manage it and ended up a sprawled bouncing mess of hysterics. Nathan's mother hopped over and gave him a 'tut tut' look which made him calm his bounces enough to let Alex lie back and catch his breath. "Thanks Mrs H," he beamed and struggled to his feet. He smacked Nathan's shoulder, "arse !" He grinned as Alison Henderson staggered away. "Catch me ?" Nathan offered with an arched eyebrow, and as Alex lunged for him he leapt out of reach and proceeded to charge around the bouncy perimeter with Alex haring after him.

The springy madness ensued for another hour. Nathan, Alex and the twins were the last ones to get off. They joined everyone else on a huge red and white checked picnic rug by the lake, flopping down exhausted from too much over enthusiastic bouncing. Jasmine looked a bit hacked off at being back on terra ferma. "Don't worry Jas, we'll bounce around again after lunch." Nathan beamed, reaching for a sandwich and tucking in. "Er, yes well we'll have to see about that," warned his mum, " there's a big deposit on this," she said, pointing awkwardly with fingertips full of crisps, "and apparently the biggest cause of no refund is vomit !"

Nathan and Alex looked dumbstruck and simultaneously dropped their sandwiches. Alison giggled and shook her head, "only kidding, but just let lunch settle first, - please." She asked. Nathan rubbed his stomach and shook his head at Alex, "ugh, vomit !" " Don't please !" Alex shuddered. They laughed and lay back on the rug looking up at the very blue sky with the sun on their faces. "This is a fabulous day." Nathan sighed happily. "It sure is Nate, it sure is."

They did leap about after food and there were a few green faces but no throwing up. They bounced around until their legs felt dull, heavy and thudding when they jumped off again.

It was a fabulous day and ended with Alex and Nathan walking slowly back, ten minutes behind the others, heading back to Nathan's to cut yet more cake. "You're gonna be huge by the time I marry you at this rate," Alex laughed. "Shut up !" Nathan elbowed him with a big smile on his lips. His eyes shone with happiness. Alex squeezed his hand lovingly. "Has it been a good birthday then ?"

"The best," whispered Nathan and gave him a knowing look. Alex sighed as they reached the gate, "just three weeks Nate and then we can tell everybody. I wish I could get you an engagement ring in the meantime." Nathan beamed and laughed happily, "do you know I would really like that actually."

They were unseen, just before the gate so Alex took him in his arms and kissed him tenderly. "Then I'll get it for you my love. You can wear it round here until my birthday and then we'll slip it on your finger." He touched Nathan's chest, just below his throat. Nathan gulped and nodded. "I don't know what to say." He husked, emotion cracking his voice. "I do, I love you." Alex breathed and kissed his lips once more before taking him by the hand into the house.

The next three weeks seemed at times to crawl by, Alex seemed to feel it more openly than Nathan, he became irritable and fed up around his family and every time the phone went in the evenings and his mother talked to one of her friends for more than ten minutes he ended up pacing the floor, fidgeting and frowning. He seemed to sleep badly and rise later, dark circles appearing around his eyes. His tension only eased ten days before his birthday, the day that he managed to purchase the ring for Nathan and planned to give it to him that night. It was a smooth round edged slim platinum ring. It had cost him £700, money he'd raised by selling most of his dvds online and a tag heuer watch on ebay. His parents would kill him if they ever found out but he wanted Nathan so badly it meant the world to give him a sign of their pledge.

As they walked home from school that night Nathan took his hand. It was unseasonably chilly and he rubbed Alex's cold skin, making him look up with moist eyes. "Hey," Nathan stopped walking and cupped his face. "What is it ?"

Alex blinked at him, "you'll see, come on, I'm glad we've got this evening to ourselves. I'll see you at yours in twenty minutes." He pecked Nathan's mouth with his and was gone. Nathan turned the corner and walked slowly home, looking back over his shoulder two or three times, walking backward as Alex always did when saying goodbye. He frowned and then smiled as he walked into the empty house, whatever was making Alex emotional would become clear in about fifteen minutes.

His heart beat faster as he took the stairs two at a time and threw off his uniform, pulling on jeans and a dark grey t-shirt. His feet were bare as the house felt so warm. He padded back down stairs and made himself his after school coffee, slipping onto a stool he flicked on the kitchen tv and watched a bit of the news, too much destruction so he flicked to Bondi Vet and watched the Australian sun and surf and the hot tanned vet fix up a run over terrier.

Still not as hot as Alex he grinned to himself as he watched the blonde vet stroke and cajole the injured animal. Barely five minutes passed and Alex was at the door. As soon as Nathan opened it, he threw his ruck sack to one side and cupped both hands around his cheeks, kissing him lingeringly, passionately and with all his love. Nathan almost staggered as they pulled apart and Alex had to brace an arm around his waist quickly, he felt so foggy headed. "Woah ! Wow Alex, where did that come from ?" He croaked. Alex grinned his killer smile and Nathan's stomach flipped over.

All of a sudden he wanted to be naked with his lover kissing him all over, taking him in his mouth. His mind swirled as Alex's eyes bore hungrily into his, knowing what he was feeling. "Oh God," he groaned and Alex walked him backward to the sofa, pushing him down and stretching his lean body out on top of him. He pulled Nathan's T over his head and kissed him hotly on the mouth, sliding his tongue deeply into him. Nathan shuddered with pleasure. Alex kissed down his throat and across his pecs, swirling his tongue around each nipple, making them erect and sensitive. It was like electric shock treatment to Nathan's groin, he groaned throatily. Alex stripped him completely bare and took him immediately into his mouth. Nathan thrust his head back and his hips up.

He panted and licked his lips as Alex sucked him like never before. He felt like he was on some kind of drug, it had never been this intense. Every time with Alex was magical but now he couldn't fathom what was going on, all he could understand was the incredible pleasure waving through his body in rhythmic pounding sweeps. He came so hard that he had no idea where Alex's hands were on him anymore, he felt drunk with ecstasy. As he panted and gasped, coming down, Alex sat and watched him, awed by the feelings that he engendered in him. He moved close to Nathan's head and stroked his insensible forehead until he opened his eyes again. He blushed and smiled up at Alex, "I couldn't even feel your hand on my forehead properly til I opened my eyes just then."

He shook his head, "what the hell did you do to me ?" Alex laughed and kissed his lips. "Just loved you my love, just loved you." Nathan beamed happily up at him as they interlaced a hand with one another and sat gazing at each other.

Alex gently smoothed Nathan's fringe back. "I..., I've erm...got something for you." He said with a gulp. Nathan raised himself up on his elbows, his beautiful body smooth and supple as he moved. Alex felt incredibly nervous, he knew it was what they both wanted but he felt like he was proposing all over again, and he was practically down on one knee too. "What is it ?" Nathan breathed, hoping more than anything that it was what they'd talked about.

His heart started to race hard now as Alex reached back into his pocket. He pulled out something that looked like a small black velvet box in Nathan's periphery but he dared not look down. Alex looked at the floor then he took Nathan's right hand and closed the box into it. "I hope you like it my darling, it's what I've wanted to give you for a long time." Nathan looked down at his closed hand, he started to tremble, especially when he saw the tears silently streaming down Alex's serious face. He unfurled his fingers and blew out a deep breath. He looked up again as Alex swiped his sleeve under his nose and cough laughed nervously. He opened the box.

It was just a simple, small ring, it shone, smooth and polished and Nathan couldn't take his eyes off it. He shook again and looked up at Alex's expectant anxious face. His own tears splashed freely onto his forearm and he cuffed them away with surprise. He sat up folding his legs crossed under him and took the ring out of the box. "Will you...?" He asked, Alex nodded and took it from him. Kneeling up he slipped it onto Nathan's outstretched left hand, holding it onto the base of his finger for a moment before he let go. Nathan pulled his hand up and stared at the ring. "Do you like it ?" Alex asked in a small voice. "I love it," Nathan whispered.

They both looked up and snatched at each other, arms whipping round one another so tightly it hurt but neither cared. " I love you, I love you my Alex, thank you, thank you so much," Nathan sobbed against Alex's shoulder. Alex cried back against him, his body heaving with great racking sobs. Nathan crushed him harder against himself until they both had to pull away. They gazed at each other's wet faces and laughed. Nathan smeared the tears off Alex's cheeks with his palms, Alex brushed his away with his thumbs. "Why am I sobbing my guts out when I've just put a ring on your finger ?" Alex coughed with a little emotional laugh.

"Perhaps because you have actually just put a ring on my finger," Nathan smiled. They grinned at each other and Alex picked up Nathan's hand, admiring how the ring looked on him. "It really suits you," he breathed. Nathan drew in a shuddering all cried out breath, "I know," he nodded, curling his fingers around Alex's hand. "Can you imagine when there are two of them ?" He looked Alex deeply in the eyes and watched him mist up once more. Alex tilted his head back, "oh God, don't start me off again," he sniffed.

He wiped his eyes and nose on his sodden sleeves and smiled back toward Nathan. "Yeugh ! Thank God I'm in love with you, rank boy !" Nathan laughed. Alex beamed and blushed a little but then he frowned and reached out, touching Nathan's arm, "hey you're shivering. Are you ok ?" Nathan nodded, "I think clothes might be a good idea now though." "Sure," Alex jumped to his feet and handed them to him. "Thanks," he dressed quickly and stood up with a stretch, bringing his hand near his face to look at his new ring again. Alex rifled in his back pack, found what he was looking for and took two champagne saucers out of a kitchen cupboard.

He started to unfoil a bottle of Verve Cliquot. Nathan watched with awe as he walked over to join him. Alex had the foil off, the cage uncurled and started to squeeze out the cork. It popped gently and fizzed out a little as he got to his side. They stood next to each other, jeaned, lithe and happy. Alex poured the two shallow measures and raised his glass to toast them. They sipped together, "to us," he said "and our soon to be married life," replied Nathan.

Alex took both glasses and rested them on the side, then he took Nathan in his arms, examining his face at close range, "you look so sexy post orgasm." Nathan blushed and his jaw dropped open. Alex laughed and tenderly kissed his shocked mouth. "I just want to hold you in my arms in bed and make sure this is all real," he breathed. "It is, it's completely real," said Nathan and suddenly looked really tired.

"I'm not being funny but I could go a sleep right now ! I know it's only 5.30pm but honestly I could really cuddle up with you and catch a few hours before dinner." Alex smiled, "what are we waiting for then ?" He reached for Nathan's hand and lead him upstairs. They got into bed and held one another tightly. Nathan reached up and pulled the curtains to as they curled up firmly in each others arms, at once on the way to a deep and very satisfying sleep.

Chapter Eight.

Nathan woke with a jolt, he'd been so deeply asleep, a muscle spasm had shot up the back of his leg and made him lurch to life again. He breathed wildly for a moment, wondering why he felt a clamping sensation around his body and then realised that Alex had his arms around him. He lay back down with his heart hammering but slowly calming. "Sssh, you're ok, it's just us," Alex smiled, gently squeezing him. Nathan rubbed his forehead. "Phew, I jolted awake all of a sudden !"

"I know, I felt you do it," Alex smiled and bent to kiss him. "Evening handsome." He beamed. Nathan blushed and looked at his hand. Alex looked too and stroked the back of Nathan's long fingers. "What time are your parents back again ?" "Eleven."

He stretched and yawned, looking over at the clock, "well that gives us plenty of time still," he grinned. His stomach rumbled making them both laugh, "food !" They said in unison and staggering out of bed, made their way down to the kitchen.

However hungry they were, the boys couldn't settle to a meal. They rummaged through the larder, all kitchen cupboards and the fridge and ended up picking through an odd concoction on top of the kitchen counter. Nathan sat cross legged and shirtless on a stool and Alex ended up the same way. There didn't seem any point in wearing tops when they constantly drew each other close, running their hands over one another's pecs making each other groan, kissing and holding one another against their bare chests. They grazed for a good hour, chatting, laughing and sometimes still discovering new things about each other. It was magical.

Shortly before ten Nathan slopped some yoghurt down his chin and pushed it back up to his mouth with his finger. Alex stopped in his tracks. "Is it bad that I just found that beyond sexual ! Christ !" He groaned. Nathan giggled and sucked the next spoonful in in an over sexualised manner. Alex put down the strawberry tub he'd been munching from. "Oh you are so gonna get it now !" He warned. Nathan shrieked with glee and bounded across the room out of his reach as Alex snatched at him. His heart pounded as his soon to be husband chased him behind the sofas, through the kitchen and back again with a look of such hunger on his face.

Eventually he was caught by the belt loops of his jeans and swung backwards onto the sofa laughing and red cheeked. Alex leapt on top of him and held him down. " Ha ha, mine !" He said triumphantly. Nathan couldn't stop laughing and it was only made worse when Alex said, "turn over." Nathan raised an eyebrow, "don't I even get dinner first ?" "What do you think that was ?"

"This is MY house idiot, - not exactly wining and dining me are you ?" He protested. Alex reached for a cushion, "look, just bite down on this in case the neighbours are listening, there's a good boy." Nathan laughed and laughed, it was such a good sound and set Alex off too.

They couldn't do anything for the next few minutes but lie there and laugh together. Alex loved the way Nathan's body reverberated underneath him. When their laughter subsided he stroked his cheek. "I love you so much," he whispered, gazing deeply into his eyes. He bent and kissed him again and all the laughter went out of Nathan's body. He loved the feel of Alex's tongue inside his mouth. They were both silent except for the gentle kissing noises. When Alex drew away neither could speak, they just gazed into each other's eyes. Eventually Nathan reached up and stroked Alex's cheek softly.

"Only nine days to go and then we can tell everyone," he croaked, his voice full of emotion. Alex nodded and couldn't speak. He kissed Nathan then got up and turned his back to him, he didn't want to cry again, he was definitely turning into a woos he decided. He heard Nathan struggle off the sofa and felt him come up behind him and slip his arms around his waist. Alex leant his back wholly against Nathan's bare chest. They held each other so close, pressed together, loving the feeling. Nathan let his hands wander across Alex's chest and abs, feeling his six pack and smooth pecs. He was so ripped it felt amazing. Alex was in seventh heaven, he shut his eyes and gave himself up entirely to the feeling. He'd want Nathan's hands much lower in a minute but for now this stroking was all he could concentrate on.

He groaned softly, making Nathan move his mouth and kiss the back of his ear. Alex groaned again. "You like that do you ?" Nathan whispered as his hands still stroked across his warm chest. "Yes," Alex husked and then jumped as Nathan's phone alarm sprang to life. He moved to the kitchen counter and snatched it up before it reached its crescendo. Alex sat on the floor cross legged where he'd been standing and Nathan came back and sat in front of him. "Hey," he pulled at Alex's arms, now covering his face. "Are you alright ?" Alex looked up with a far away expression but he was smiling. "That was bliss," he said. "Do we really have to get this place in order right now ?" Nathan nodded and sighed, "yes, for another 9 days we do have to obey our parents wishes, and that includes getting dressed before they come home."

Alex groaned. "Oh shit, I have to do I ?" Nathan nodded and laughed, "c'mon, let's chuck our clothes back on and get this place sorted. Stuff a watchable dvd in there while I just clear up the kitchen, but RUN to get your clothes on if you hear a car door early will you ?" "Okey doke," Alex stood up and ran a finger lazily down the dvd tower until he came to Harry Potter, The Deathly Hallows part one, that would do nicely.

He bent to slip the dvd into the player but shot upright again as headlights swung across the windows almost blinding him and wheels crunched to a stop on the gravel. Nathan's alarmed eyes met his. "SHIT !" They both shrieked and pelted up the stairs, hysteria making them trip up the last step and fall across each other on the landing. They picked themselves up and sprinted into Nathan's room, slamming the door just as his family started to climb the front steps. As they yanked on their tops and righted Nathan's room, he stopped and looked at Alex, "what did we leave on show down stairs ?" "Erm, well the dvd's playing to itself, you didn't finish clearing up so there's a bit of food left out and a dirty plate or two..." He stopped and frowned at Nathan's huge grin, "typical teenagers then aren't we." He laughed.

Alex's face split into a grin too, he moved toward him and stroked his face before kissing him, "well not quite typical," he whispered. Nathan wrapped his arms around him. "I love you," he whispered and squeezed Alex's ribs just as there was a knock on the door and his mum walked in. She cleared her throat and smiled at them, both boys blushed. "Hi Mum," said Nathan.

"Hello darling, had a good evening ?" "Yes thanks, we just came up to get another game for the wii."

"But there's a dvd playing on its own down there ?"

"I know, we changed our minds about it just before you got back." He picked up the nearest game from his bedside table. "I can smash you at cow racing any time !" He grinned at Alex who immediately fell about laughing, "that I have to see," he said. Nathan's Mum looked at her watch, "well I suppose you two had better say your slushy goodbyes alone and then you'd better shoot off Alex." Alex nodded, "will do Mrs H." She withdrew and they heard her singing quietly as she headed off to her room. Nathan sighed and looked at Alex who pulled him close once more.

They lay their heads on each other's shoulders, rubbing each other's backs. "I wish you could stay," Nathan breathed. "Me too," Alex whispered. He reached down for Nathan's hand and held it up, "I wonder if she saw this," he said, looking at the ring. "Bollocks !" Nathan jolted with surprise, "Oh my God, I forgot to take it off in time." Then he looked sad, "and I don't want to take it off." Alex put his finger underneath Nathan's chin and lifted it so that he could touch their lips together. "Then don't take it off," he husked. Nathan frowned a bit and then remembered, "oh yes, our plan...it just means getting a...."

His voice trailed off as Alex bent down to his jacket on the floor and pulled out a little black velvet sleeve from inside the pocket. He held it out to Nathan who took it. Smoothing his fingers over the outside before he opened it he shook his head and his eyes misted up again. "Oh Alex," was all he could say. Alex gulped, "open it," he whispered and Nathan unpopped the sleeve, held it upside down and out slithered a fine platinum chain with a tiny clasp. Alex reached over and slid the ring off Nathan's hand and then threaded it on to the chain, "turn round," he whispered and hooked the chain shut around Nathan's neck, sliding the ring inside his top. He kissed the back of his neck. "I never want you to take that off," he husked against his ear. "And I never will," Nathan whispered back. Alex turned Nathan back to face him and embraced him, holding his body with every sinew of his being. "Sleep well my love," he whispered and kissed his beloved soundly, then he was gone.

Nathan listened for the front door closing and then fell backward onto his bed. He felt elated and on another planet. His mother knocked and came in. She looked at her son's flushed face and his bright shining eyes. "You've had a good evening haven't you ?" She smiled as she moved to his bed and put down some clean clothes. Nathan nodded, a big grin spreading across his face. "The best so far Mum." Alison Henderson raised her eyebrows. "You two really are very serious aren't you ?"

Nathan drew in a deep breath and played with the edge of the pillow case, "yes, we are very seriously in love." He blushed shyly as he said it. His mother smiled and came to kiss him on the forehead. "I'm glad darling, I think Alex is very nice." She caressed his cheek for a moment and then headed to the door. "He is Mum." Nathan sighed contentedly and as his Mother turned to close the door she said, "well in that case I know you'll sleep very well. Goodnight my love," she shut the door leaving him to click off the light still in his clothes, touching the ring close to his heart, with a massive grin on his face.

Royal Wedding fever had hit the nation, some people said it hadn't but everywhere you looked bunting was being erected, street parties organised and red white and blue colour schemes dominated everything. All the shops in the local village had Union Jack paper plates, cups and napkins for sale. Radios, mugs, tea towels, fold up chairs, aprons...all were festooned with the British flag.

"Makes you feel proud again doesn't it ?" Remarked Alex as they wandered to School on the Thursday before the Royal Wedding. "It sure does," Nathan replied and looked very excited. "God I just can't wait to get there tonight. What time does our train get in ?" Alex looked at his phone diary, "erm, 9.15pm," he replied. "Ok, so that's enough time to get onto the Mall and get our tent sorted for about 10pm yes ?" "I would say so," Alex agreed.

No one concentrated at school that day, even the non Royalists were excited just to be having a long weekend. They had been allowed to dispense with uniform for the last day of school that week in honour of the Royal Wedding and most people were sporting some sort of Union Jack T-shirt while several others had bought the 'Thanks Wills and Kate for the four day bender,' tops. Nathan and Alex laughed at Nathan's friend Simon's T as they walked in to lunch, it said 'Kate's wedding list:

Crockery

Cutlery

Croquet set

Oxfordshire

By the end of the day Nathan and Alex were champing at the bit to get home and grab their gear. Everything they needed bar the fresh sandwiches was already packed into rucksacks just inside their respective front doors and Nathan's newly purchased pop up tent was stashed there too. Bed rolls, a torch, and a small Union Jack brolly filled up the elastic strapping and pockets on Alex's rucksack. Two extra fleeces and scarves filled Nathan's rucksack to bursting.

The boys hurtled about grabbing food and water from their fridges, sunglasses and cameras and soon they stood panting on Alex's drive, all kitted up. Alex's Dad came out and laughed as he saw their expressions. "You will make your train you know, there's loads of time still !" "Yeah yeah yeah, come on Dad !" Alex jumped up and down impatiently. They stowed everything into the boot and twenty minutes later arrived at the station. They had 22 minutes left before their train arrived and ended up sitting in their sunglasses on the platform, kit between them, long legs stretched out, grinning with excitement.

Nathan slipped his straw cowboy hat out of his rucksack, evened out the brim a bit as it had got fairly squashed and slipped it on quietly while Alex wasn't looking. "So are you hungry yet or shall we wait to nibble the supplies later, after all we don't know what the facilities will be like at the....What the fuck are you wearing ?" Alex broke off laughing. "What ?" Nathan grinned and shrugged. Alex pushed his shoulder, "you are such a bloody tourist aren't you !"

Nathan laughed and pulled out a copy of the local gazette that had pictures of people already camped up near Buckingham Palace, "careful, I'll buy one of these if you give me any more cheek !" He pointed to a group of people in cheap felt Union Jack hats that had obviously been bought on the Mall. "Christ almighty !" Said Alex, taking the paper and shaking his head. "Sad bastards !"

Nathan flashed him a grin, "I might get you one."

They laughed and teased each other for the next fifteen minutes, until at last the Victoria bound train pulled in and they joined the rest of the Royal wedding bound herd, most with pop up tents who smiled excitedly at them, yep, Royal Wedding fever had taken over this small part of England and they couldn't have felt more proud.

It was mental at Buckingham Palace, the boys were overwhelmed at the number of people already camped at the top beside the fountain, underneath the dark green temporary television broadcasting units. "Oh my God !" Alex exclaimed, "Fuck !" Said Nathan worriedly, suddenly getting a place near the railings seemed unlikely. They began to make their way around the back of the already erected tents, it wasn't easy, there was a huge amount of foot traffic and they had to struggle through railings on either side of one of the huge gates out of the Mall just to cross the road, but at last the crowd seemed to thin as they made their way down the Mall toward Trafalgar Square, but only just.

They could see a good spot where the tents were only one deep so far and headed toward it just as a smartly dressed blonde woman in a high neck cashmere coat with huge buttons stopped in her tracks and gasped. "Nathan !" as she pulled him to her in a big hug. He looked utterly shocked. "Lynette ?" She nodded and pulled her husband's hand, "Stewart look !" She beamed and Stewart embraced Nathan too.

"Hiya kiddo, wow, we didn't expect to see you here !" Nathan grinned and turned to Alex, "my auntie Lyn and uncle Stewart, Alex Nesbitt-Hall, my other half." Lynette did a slight double take for a second, they'd never discussed Nathan's sexuality though she had always suspected as much. In the British way she quickly shook off her mild surprise and warmly shook Alex's hand, "very nice to meet you Alex," she smiled. "Likewise," Alex beamed and shook Stewart's hand too.

They exchanged 'how are your parents, we must all get together soon...etc etc kind of pleasantries for a moment before the boys began to get noticeably twitchy. "Look, we'll let you go," Lynette smiled. "I know you need to get a good spot. Have a wonderful time and see you soon." Nathan hugged them both again, Alex waved them off and the boys headed sharpish to the spot they had their eye on. Twenty minutes later both boys sat on a large white and yellow edged ground sheet belonging to their neighbouring campers who turned out to be very welcoming and promised them a spot on the railings for a perfect view tomorrow.

Someone had cracked open a bottle of Rose and three generations of female relatives, two early teenage children and two close friends were quickly becoming wonderful new friends. Everyone started exchanging stories and chatting about their excitement for the next day. At about 1am Nathan got restless and said he and Alex would go on a chocolate and booze run around Trafalgar square. The others had been dropped off by the mother Linda's husband, and had brought more than enough food, they didn't want anything else so the boys headed off alone. It was becoming a little cold and breezy so they fleeced up and headed down the Mall.

Trafalgar Square was madly busy, there were tourists everywhere and despite the time of night, three nearby souvenir shops were doing a rip roaring trade. There were no bottles of wine to be found as licensing laws meant all the alcohol cupboards were locked up so Nathan just grabbed a couple of huge bars of Fruit and Nut and headed out of the supermarket back into the crazy melle with Alex. "Hi Nelson, thanks and all that," he said, peering 150 feet up into the air at the statue aloft his column.

"Idiot," giggled Alex as he craned his neck to take a quick look upward too. "C'mon, let's get back to the party," he smiled, reaching for Nathan's hand. They walked slowly through Wellington Gate with its huge stone arches and wandered lazily back toward their mini camp along the pink tarmac of the Mall. Buckingham Palace loomed Golden in its illuminations at the far end and the boys wondered about what was going on inside it.

On the way from Victoria they had passed The Goring Hotel where Kate Middleton was staying on her last night as a single woman. It's cobbled avenue was blocked at both ends by a heavily armed phalanx of police officers and concrete blockades while helicopters circled over head. Alex looked up into the lit sky, you could barely see a star for all the London light pollution but still the evening was beautiful. "Can you believe we're actually part of all this ?" He marvelled. Nathan shook his head, "it's amazing isn't it. Seeing all these flags really does something to me. I feel patriotic in a way I haven't for a long time." Alex smiled and squeezed his hand. "I know what you mean."

No one got much sleep that night, in fact Nathan worked it out to be about 20 minutes by dawn. As the sky started to lighten at 5am, he emerged from the tent leaving Alex dozing and went in search of a hot cup of tea. It took 40 minutes standing in a huge queue that stretched right across the grass of St James's park. When he returned and passed around hot chocolates and tea, they all sat huddled in sleeping bags and duvets looking stunned and bleary eyed. "Did you get any sleep at all ?" Asked Linda, "about twenty minutes," Nathan yawned.

"It was all just too exciting to switch off and then there were those mad rugby squad people singing 'Jerusalem' and 'Another Country' all bloody night, plus the over head helicopters. I don't think many people slept." Linda laughed, "no, we didn't do much better." She pointed at her shattered twelve year old son Patrick, slumped in a thick duvet against the railings. " Did you see those two girls in wedding dresses being interviewed by the Daily Mirror at about three o'clock this morning ?" "Yes," Nathan nodded, "everyone's gone a bit mad, which I really like actually." "The best of British eh ?" Linda beamed.

Just then the zip undid on the tent and out crawled a very knackered looking Alex, shivering to the bone. Nathan smiled at him and pulled a dark blue fleece out from underneath his own, "here, I've been keeping this warm for you," he said. Alex stumbled over and pulled it on without a word, then he almost fell to the ground beside Nathan and snuggled into the nook of his arm grunting gently, making him laugh. "Not awake yet my love ?"

Alex shook his head looking moody and shut his eyes. Nathan stroked his face and smiled over at Linda who passed him a bag of M and S sweet chilli flavour crisps. "Thanks," he breathed as quietly as possible and tucked into his noisy snack, trying not to crunch too loudly. Linda giggled quietly at his efforts. They chatted on together as Patrick and Alex dozed through the brightening dawn. Half an hour passed and Alex came round enough to yawn and rub his eyes and join the chatter again.

He smiled groggily at Nathan who pecked him on the lips and grinned back. "Here, eat this." Alex pulled himself into a better position, crossing his legs for stability. "Yum, thanks," he said, tucking straight into the large apple pastry that Nathan had bought him earlier. More people started to arrive and a whole circle of collapsible canvas chairs soon sprung up behind them. "We're going to have to be careful when we take down these tents whispered Nathan," "I know what you mean," Pat, Linda's mother interjected. "We're being encroached upon." They all giggled.

7am rolled on, yet more people arrived. The crowd slowly swelled and swelled and by 8.30am the masses were getting edgy at the tents still taking up so much room. No one said anything pushy, they just started to shuffle forward, millimetre by millimetre. Alex yawned and then smiled at Nathan, "let's take them down, shall we gang ?" He leant behind Nathan to Linda's family who all agreed and one by one they folded up the pop ups and slid them back inside their flat round carry sleeves. By 9am a line of canvas chairs were their last line of defence between the swollen crowd and the boys front row position. Their newly formed gang took it in turns to leave the rail and go to the porta-loos or snack venders. Alex disappeared off and came back fifteen minutes later in a Union Jack cowboy hat and sunglasses. Nathan held his sides as he laughed and slipped on his own straw hat. The waiting around now seemed interminable but at last things started to happen.

A phalanx of smartly dressed policemen arrived in their white cotton gloves to tumultuous cheers. Next came the beautifully groomed police horses, then the cold stream guards began to march about and at last, at last, the Royal Family. Alex got a fantastic picture of Prince Harry in one of the bullet proof ceremonial cars. Nathan snapped the Queen in her lemon yellow. Beatrice and Eugenie were easily spotted and at last Kate Middleton with her father, sitting up high in a car with an elongated dome which showed her off to perfection. She was very slim with her long dark hair brushed loose down her shoulders and a long veil covering her face below her glittering tiara.

Her shoulders showed lace and the women in the group all wondered if her entire dress was lace overlaid or just the bodice. Barely a few minutes passed and suddenly organ music from the abbey played out across the tannoys. A long cheer and protracted mexican wave moved through both sides of the crowded Mall. Then hush fell for the exchanging of the vows and the address. Each time Kate and William made it past another important commitment, a great cheer went up until finally, with the crowd at a standstill, the deacon pronounced them man and wife and the Mall erupted. Alex and Nathan hugged each other, people cracked open bottles of champagne and all of a sudden everyone was singing Jerusalem amid a sea of flags. It was such a spectacle and the boys loved it.

Not long afterwards the coaches and cars made their way back up the Mall, cheers rang out from every quarter but the best was saved for last. Up came the new Duke and Duchess of Cambridge in their open red gold and black State Landau, dark bay police horses and grey outriders cantered along the pink Mall and in a flash they were gone. The elation was palpable, this truly was a happy couple.

Everyone raised their paper Union Jack cups and drank their inch or two of shared Champagne and then the dust kicked up as en masse they made their way toward the balcony for the flypast and the kiss. There was a lot of waiting around, it was getting hotter and the night of no sleep caught up with the boys. They felt shattered and barely able to go on but as they surged forward with the sea of people and found themselves in front of the palace, they knew they had it in them for one last bit of fun. Alex squeezed Nathan around his waist as they looked up, waiting for those doors to open.

"Not long now, and then we can tell everyone about our special day," he beamed. Nathan blinked back at him, "I can't wait," he whispered as the doors above swung open and the crowds erupted again. Kate and William were dazzling. They waved as the people cheered, grinning with joy. "Kiss, kiss, kiss," everybody chanted, and blushing, William turned and kissed his new wife then pointed to the sky ahead. Everyone turned round to see a World War

II Lancaster Bomber thundering up the Mall with it's two jet fighters on either side. They powered noisily over Buckingham Palace. "Wow," mouthed Nathan. "That's what Kate just said when she saw us all down here," smiled Alex.

"Did she ?" Nathan looked amazed. More noise from above made the boys turn around again, Harriers tore over the palace and then a third group that neither of the them could identify. "Kiss, kiss, kiss," chanted the people all around them and again William blushed deeply as he kissed his wife for twice as long to the tumultuous rapture of the crowd below. As the doors closed on the balcony, Nathan and Alex looked at each other, squinting into the sun, hot, dusty, unbelievably tired and completely in love. "Victoria here we come," Alex said. "Hallelujah to that," Nathan answered as full of wonder and incredible memories they made their way out of the crowds and headed for home.

Chapter Nine.

The rest of the weekend was a tired blur back at home. Both families let their shattered boys conk out for most of the time. Saturday was taken up by the Royal Wedding's total domination of all television channels in the UK, some of which Nathan caught between sleeps and kept trying to point himself and Alex out to his family. Sunday came and went in a flash and suddenly Bank Holiday Monday seemed almost over too. Alex hadn't seen Nathan since Friday evening but they had texted each other non stop whenever they were awake.

It had been a phenomenal event on Friday and the joy of it had stopped them missing each other as badly as normal. They had so much to talk about via text, and the rest of the time they were sleeping for England. The few days whipped by because of it all and suddenly it was Tuesday morning, Alex's birthday. Nathan did as they'd discussed and sprung an 'impromptu' dinner invitation on his family for tomorrow night at Alex's house, the boys would cook. His parents looked mystified for a moment but then accepted after reviewing the calendar, as Nathan knew they would. He'd already checked out their availability earlier.

Alex did the same with his Mum and Dad, his sister was booked away until 10pm that night with the Henderson twins at a swim and bar-b-q at the most popular girl in their year's house.

Alex got the same answer as Nathan and told his parents to be ready to eat for 7pm. He waited for Alex outside his gate this morning, beaming as he saw him emerge into the sunshine. What was it about him that always made Nathan's stomach drop with excitement. Alex looked up and cracked a huge smile when he saw Nathan's smiling face. He drew up close in front of him and they cupped one another's cheeks with their palms, kissing each other's mouths with such tenderness. Alex groaned and Nathan folded him against him. "Happy birthday my darling," he whispered against his hair. Alex squeezed both arms around Nathan's ribs in return. A tingle of excitement made them both gasp as they drew apart to look at each other.

"What time were you born ?" Nathan asked. "7.15am," Alex happily replied and then grinned at Nathan's expression. "So you're already 18. Happy birthday," he smiled. Alex nodded and looked down as Nathan drew something out of his bag, "let's walk a little way, I don't want you undoing this right in front of your house," he suggested. "Ok," Alex replied as they walked around the nearby corner, both stopping to perch on the edge of a low brick wall.

Nathan handed Alex the small red wrapped package with huge outsize red bow. " I would never guess that red was your favourite colour," Alex raised an eyebrow as he pulled the bow apart. "Shut up," blushed Nathan, "just undo your frigging present !"

Alex slid the bow off the small red box and ripped open the paper. Inside was a neat black cardboard box. He upended it, letting the lid hit the ground in his hurry. His heart hammered as he hoped madly to find a particular gift inside. He shut his eyes as he opened the small black velvet box that had tumbled out into his palm.

He blew out a deep breath and opened them again. It was a ring. A polished platinum ring and it matched Nathan's. He squeezed his eyes shut against the tide of emotion welling up inside him. "Thank you," he croaked with out looking up as he pressed his thumb and forefinger into his eyes and sniffed. "Hey," said Nathan, "it's supposed to make you happy." Alex raised his eyes as a tear streamed down his cheek, he coughed out an embarrassed laugh, "it does make me happy, it's the best present I've ever had," he said, dashing the moisture from his eyes with the back of his hand.

"I love you so much, thank you my love," he whispered. Nathan grinned, "you really like it ?" "I love it," Alex pulled the ring from the box and held it up. Nathan took it from him and lifted his left hand. He pushed the ring onto Alex's wedding finger and then raised his hand and kissed it. He let out an involuntary sob himself and heard Alex laugh at him. He pushed at his own eyes, laughing at his emotions overflowing as Alex threw his arms around him and hugged him hard.

They clamped one another against each other's bodies for a minute until they drew apart and once more both dashed at their eyes. Now Nathan's looked more red than Alex's which Alex delighted in pointing out and laughing as it took some of the focus off him. "Shut up," barked Nathan roughly, a half smile playing at the corners of his lips. Then he looked aghast all of a sudden and the colour drained from him, "shit !" He exclaimed.

"What ?" Alex felt anxious at the look on his face. "Oh no," Nathan sunk his face into his hands. "Nate, Nate, what is it ?" Alex put all the packaging he'd been bundling up back on the wall. Nathan dropped his hands and said sheepishly, "I'm so sorry Alex, I forgot the chain !" Alex beamed at him and cuffed his ear, "you silly, that doesn't matter in the slightest, we only have to hide them until tomorrow night and I have a decent chain this can hang on for one day anyway. Don't worry, really love." Nathan shook his head but smiled his perfect Nathan smile, "I am a numb skull but I'm glad you've got a chain." "Me too," said Alex and then looked at his watch. "Come on, last day of lessons before everyone knows, lets go and make the best of it," he grinned and they walked toward the school.

Alex had a lot of cards that day, and a chocolate fudge cake from his friends, as well as a massive tin of homemade short bread from the catering staff who always fancied him for their daughters, - news of his boyfriend hadn't made it as far as them yet. Double English was even more fun than usual as they had to write a short fictional piece in practice for their As, and Alex chose to write about two young men who meet at school and become closer and closer until they fall desperately in love, marry and move to America and run their own business. He only just got the story finished in time but was very pleased with it.

As the day drew to a close everyone wanted to know what he was doing for his big birthday bash, he always threw the best parties. They were actually all already in on it as they'd been sent secret invitations two months before. Alex's parents had hired a huge paddle steamer with a fantastic restaurant on board and they were going to float down the river on Saturday, eating at sunset and dance and party their way back up it again afterwards. The last bell went and the whole school began to empty out. Nathan and Alex walked home together, they couldn't see each other tonight as Alex had hockey practise so they talked all the way home to make up for it. "What do you think we should cook our folks tomorrow night ?" Asked Alex, looking a bit nervous. Nathan's face lit up immediately.

"Ah, I actually have the perfect recipe for this, and it takes such a short amount of time to prepare and cook and looks really impressive too." Alex looked thoroughly cheered. "Great ! What is this miracle dish ?" "Your parents are ok with fish aren't they ?" Nathan checked. "Yeah, they're fine with just about anything," Alex shrugged. "Ok good, well here's the plan. Parmesan herb crusted smoked haddock loin with buttered baby new potatoes, green salad and for afters, chocolate and raspberry cream meringues. What do you think ?" Alex stopped walking, looking crestfallen, "Nathan ! I thought you said it was simple ?" Nathan laughed. "Honestly Al, it really is. Look, ring me tonight after hockey once you've read my email, I'll spell it all out and you'll see how easy it is but how impressive sounding. I promise it will work, and be easy with two of us as well."

Alex didn't look convinced but he trusted Nathan so he shrugged, "well ok." They'd reached his gate and he had to run in to change and make it back in time to the pitch. He turned to Nathan and took his face between both hands, kissing him suddenly, lovingly, groaning gently as he crushed his body against him. He pulled away a little, panting against Nathan's face, "God I feel like I haven't had your body for such a long time," he breathed. "You haven't," said

Nathan. " Well that will be rectified very soon," he husked and kissed him once more. "Goodnight my love," he scanned Nathan's face with longing in his eyes pecked his warm cheek and was gone.

Nathan turned to walk home and within a few minutes was out of his uniform, sprawled on his bed in jeans and a long sleeved T, bawling his eyes out. When his mother came to check on him for dinner he couldn't hide the uncontrollable sobs and she immediately came to him, fearing the worst. Some calamity must have befallen him but she couldn't fathom what. She so prayed he hadn't broken up with Alex or picked up a disease. "What, what is it my darling ?" She asked anxiously. Nathan just sobbed afresh against her, great racking wet sobs that shook him. It took minutes for him to calm down and then she held him away from her to look at his tear strained red eyed face.

"What is it my darling ?" She asked kindly, smoothing the wetness off his cheeks and reaching for a box of tissues. Nathan rubbed at his eyes and took one of the tissues, then he said in a broken cried out voice. "Oh Mum, it's me, I'm just being so stupid. I've got the man of my dreams, I'm young, I'm healthy and yet today I had one of those horrible self doubt moments." He sniffed and his mother smoothed his hair. "Is Alex being nice to you ?" She asked. Nathan smiled, "he's always nice to me." His face creased up as if he were going to cry again though. "The trouble is," he sniffed, "what if I'm not worthy of him ? What if I can't make him happy ? I don't want to be anything but the best in life, and especially for Alex and sometimes I think I just fall so far short." He sniffed again and then looked up as his mother put both hands on his shoulders and turned him square to her.

"Now listen Nathan, you are my son. I love you no matter what, that is true, I'm biased. - but, you are one of the most worthy people I have ever met, you're kind, handsome and sweet with a great sense of humour and are just starting off in the world. Alex I should say, is getting a pretty good bargain in you, and don't you forget it. I know you love him, which is wonderful, but never ever compare yourself to anyone and feel you fall short. You are you, and loved for all the things that make up you, not for what you can or can't do, right ?"

She looked a bit stern but Nathan was smiling. "Ok Mum," he nodded. She dabbed the last moisture from his face like a child and he let her. "Thanks," he said, a bit embarrassed. He shook himself. "I think I'm just really tired from Thursday and school and just thinking about my future etc...." His mother nodded and hugged him into her arms again. She let him rest against her for a minute and then got up to finish preparing dinner. She looked at her watch, "ten minutes," she said, "then I want to see a lot of food going into that body, alright ?" Nathan laughed softly, "I will, don't worry," he smiled and lay back on his bed, closing his eyes for a ten minute recharge.

Alex's evening wasn't going swimmingly either. After the first 17 minutes of the game he was down at A and E having his hockey sticked nose x-rayed. It was seriously bruised and hurting a lot, there had been so much blood that his games kit was drenched. He thanked God that Nathan couldn't see this as he'd be so worried. Luckily, being bloodied, he was seen pretty fast and was at home tucked up in bed with painkillers and an ice pack by 9.30pm. He wanted to call Nathan but was waiting for the painkillers to kick in so that he didn't have to tell him about the accident tonight.

Back at Nathan's, things were looking up. After a huge portion of lasagne, he was beginning to feel much happier again. His mother winked at him from across the table as if to say, 'see, told you it's all ok.' He smiled and yawned and excused himself sooner than usual but his mother didn't mind as he made his way up to his room, he needed the sleep.

At ten, Alex rang. He sounded a bit coldy and slightly distant but said such wonderful things to Nathan that he lay back and felt elation wash over him once again. They had a brief chat as both seemed very tired, and agreed to meet at Alex's the next day for school.

In the morning, Nathan made his way down to Alex's gate feeling a bit worn out. He'd slept well eventually although he'd tossed and turned to start with after his crying fit. He looked ok but definitely tired around the eyes and a bit withdrawn. It had shaken him to feel so low about himself. It wasn't a wholly new experience for him, self doubt and deprecation, but it had got much better in the last few months and he wasn't keen to go back to feeling bad at times.

Alex groaned as he looked in the mirror before leaving the house. His nose had been confirmed broken but luckily didn't look too hideously swollen, it looked puffy but the worst thing was the panda eyes it had given him. Two black eyes was not the look he had been going for on the night he announced his engagement. It didn't look awful, being incredibly good looking meant that he looked more the injured hero than anything else. Still, he didn't like it. He shrugged at his reflection and yelled goodbye, swinging the door shut behind him. The bruises would be gone in a week or two and Alex's heart thrummed with excitement instead as he turned his thoughts to Nathan about to meet him just outside the driveway.

As usual, Alex got there first. He leant against the wall and squinted up at the sunny morning. It was gorgeous, but would do nothing to hide his wounds. Foot steps fell on the pavement nearby and he looked up to see Nathan's lithe frame coming toward him. His tie swung loose and his shirt hung open at the neck. He wore gold steel rimmed Ray bans and he looked fantastic. He grinned as he got near. Thankfully the tint of his sunglasses and the sun so high combined to blind him to Alex's bruises temporarily. They crossed the last three feet between one another, grins plastered across their faces and embraced, wrapping each other up in their arms and sinking their lips together immediately. This morning's passion had them kissing noisily, their lips smacking together and each groaning with utter pleasure.

They pulled away to gaze into one another's eyes and laughed blushing, as they gasped for breath. "Morning," said Alex. Nathan grinned and raised his glasses up into his hair. Alex scanned his face as if seeing it for the first time. Nathan paled, worried that Alex would notice his puffy eyes and shadows. He bit his lip self consciously for a moment but then his eyes adjusted to the light and his brain seemed to wake up and grasp the situation. Alex's face was all bruised. "WHAT THE.....? Alex what happened to you ?" he cried anxiously , wrapping his hand around Alex's chin to get a closer look. Alex sighed, "hockey," was all he said. Nathan looked pained. He gingerly traced the bruise under Alex's right eye with his finger tips, "my poor love. Does it hurt ?" Alex had painkillers stashed in his bag and was actually quite keen to take some as his sinuses throbbed badly. He was about to lie but hated telling any fib to Nathan and he wasn't very good at it. He shrugged, "yes unfortunately at the moment it does but I've got these," he pulled out some ibuprofen. "Well take them right now then," Nathan implored and Alex did just that. They were about to walk away when he put a hand on Nathan's chest then onto his cheek, "hey, you don't get to walk off scot free either you know. What's with the sad look and puffy eyes this morning ? Have you....?" He stopped and peered more closely making Nathan back away a step, he really didn't want to discuss this.

"Nate have you been crying ?" Nathan looked at the ground and then off in the direction of school, " I think we should keep walking," he said. "Wait wait wait just a second there, no you don't." Alex ran right round in front of where he'd turned and held his arms. "Nate ? What is it ? Tell me ?" Nathan squirmed uncomfortably on the spot. He closed his eyes, "oh Alex, please don't make me tell you." Alex frowned with concern, "Nate ? God you have been crying, why ?" He pulled him over to the wall. "Come on, sit here," he commanded. Nathan tried to protest. "Nope, we're not going anywhere until you tell me !" He demanded. Nathan's shoulders sagged as he put his face in his hands. " It's embarrassing," he murmured. "I don't care, it was enough to make you cry, and for some time by the look of you so I want to know. Tell me. Please ?"

Nathan looked up into his concerned, bruised face and loved him all the more. "Ok," he straightened himself as if bracing for what he was about to say. "God this really is embarrassing but ok," he turned to look Alex in the eyes. "I just had a moment, a wobble. I wondered if....., erm. I wondered if.....well if I..., Oh God..." "If you what ?" Shrugged Alex. "If I would be able to keep you happy, if I was worthy of any of this and if I was interesting enough to keep you forever and I just kinda got a bit upset because what if I'm not, I..mumph !!"

The last word was completely indistinguishable as Alex's mouth pressed firmly against his, shutting him up immediately. Alex's arms came up fully around him and held him while his tongue pushed deeply, hotly into his throat. Nathan panted and groaned with ecstasy, Alex kissed him on and on. He unbuttoned three of Nathan's buttons and slipped his hand inside his shirt caressing his firm smooth chest and grazing across his nipples. Nathan gasped at the electric touch and felt Alex caress his groin lovingly for a moment before he let go and removed his tongue. He gazed into Nathan's eyes, God he wanted to take him here and now but instead he said, "never ever think such a stupid thing again. I love you and there is nothing unworthy about you. If you said your life's ambition was to be a dustman who crocheted on the side I'd say great, good for you, as long as you come home to me at night that's all that counts." Nathan started laughing. His killer smile lit his face and his eyes shone. Alex grinned at him and shook his head. "You daft lemon." Nathan laughed even harder.

"So last night I got a stick in the conk and ended up in A and E and you blubbed your eyes out for a sudden wave of self doubt that made your brain spout utter bollocks ?" Nathan nodded, laughing so loud that Alex joined in. They wrapped their arms around each other's necks still laughing. "You big twit," Alex murmured and hugged Nathan so tightly. The back of his hair tickled at Alex's cheek, it smelled so clean and felt so soft. "I love you, idiot," he breathed and Nathan squeezed his ribs in return. "Me too," he whispered, loving the feel of Alex in his arms. They pulled apart at last and sorted themselves out for school. Alex looked at his watch. "Shit, run !" He gasped and Nathan sprinted after him laughing at his gangly legged mucking about run. "Stop it, I can't run when I'm laughing," he giggled. Alex grinned back over his shoulder and did it even more.

School was a disaster that day, the first lesson was awful as they were both told off soundly for being late. It didn't go well when Alex pointed out that they were now adults and he didn't appreciate being spoken to like that. Art didn't go well when Nathan realised he'd got the perspective on a still life totally out. At lunch they both huffed noisily into the canteen and thunked down at their table looking totally pissed off. Even the shepherds pie was gross. Nathan pushed it away and folded his arms. Alex looked up at him and smiled gently. "It's not the best day is it ?" Nathan kicked a table leg, "it's shite !"

"Hey," Alex put a calming arm on his, "it's gonna be fine." Nathan huffed and then leant his head into his hands, "Oh God, how did you know ?"

"What that you're shitting yourself about tonight ? Oh only because I am too." Nathan's head snapped up, "you are ?" Alex nodded. Nathan huffed again, "well how come I look all arsey and pissed off and you seem all bright and breezy then ?" Alex laughed, "no point actually getting stressed is there ?" Nathan glared at him for a second and then couldn't help but smile a little. "No I guess not. Rational bastard !" Alex giggled and got up to toss his lunch in the bin, it really was inedible.

The boys sat in General English, for the last period of the day. Though they now had desks next to one another in every other class, they sat two rows and three desks away from one another in GE. Nathan had been absorbed with a piece of writing for the last twenty minutes and only looked up to check the time, he was enjoying this last part of the lesson. Fifteen minutes to go, just enough time to finish.

He glanced over at Alex and all thoughts of finishing his work went out of the window. He looked pale and in lots of pain, rubbing between his eyebrows. He could hear his low moan across the room. No ruck sack under the desk which would mean he'd left it and the painkillers in his locker. Nathan bit his lip, he wanted to do something. Mr Carter glared at him as if to say 'get on with it,' so Nathan motioned his head toward Alex and shrugged. Luckily Mr Carter followed his gaze and frowned when he saw him. He was a fair teacher and seeing a boy struggling, especially the most popular boy in the school wasn't something he liked.

As discreetly as possible he wandered down the aisle between the desks and leant down when he reached Alex. He whispered something at first and Alex gingerly shook his head without looking up. Mr Carter squatted in front of him and reached out to touch Alex's forehead. He frowned again and then stood up. He leant toward Joe Glaister, the nearest boy and spoke quietly to him, pointing to the clock, the boys work and then shrugged and gestured toward Alex. Joe took a look at him and immediately put down his pen. They were quite good mates and he didn't like seeing his friend in pain.

Carefully Joe and Mr Carter lifted Alex up until he stood. He pushed them away as they both tried to support him and looked a bit moody which made Nathan smile, he'd be alright after some painkillers. Joe stayed on one side of him as he groped along the wall and out of the classroom. Nathan looked up at the clock, seven minutes of class left, well his essay would no longer be perfect but it would be good enough.

When the bell went Nathan checked his mobile immediately and burst out laughing as Alex had written, "dying slowly outside on bench nearest steps,

146

ugh...come save me."

Nathan threw his essay on to the pile on the front desk and headed outside. He laughed when he saw Alex sprawled on the wooden bench with his shirt over his head. He walked over and gently pulled it back into place. "Not that I dislike looking at your fine body," he whispered so that no one else would hear, "but I'd rather not walk home with an erection today !" Alex groaned, "I'll never get an erection again at this rate....!" He moaned. Nathan laughed and rubbed his shoulder. "Poor baby, don't worry though, we've got loads of time, honestly this dinner takes no time to cook at all. In fact we'll make it even easier. Just in case something happened I bought a spare pudding so we'll only make the first course from scratch?"

Alex groaned again but opened his eyes, shielding them from the sun and looked up at him. Nathan stroked the side of his face and looked concerned. "Look, we don't have to do this tonight if you're not ok ?" Alex gave him an angry look. "Are you kidding me ? If you think a bloody smack between the eyes is gonna keep me from one of the best night's of my life you've got another thing coming !" "One of the best nights of your life ?" Nathan raised an eyebrow. "Ok ok, so I'm bricking it, same as you but this is one of the best nights of our lives Nate as this is where we get to say who we are and what we want together. Ow !" He put both hands over his eyes. "Stop talking," Nathan suggested and pulled his book out of his ruck sack as he sat cross legged on the ground in front of the bench. Alex dropped a hand down so that it rested against his shoulder. Nathan gave it a quick peck and settled into his reading.

Twenty minutes later Alex started nudging him with his foot. "Gerroff," grinned Nathan as he did it again. "Lie down and recover, I'm reading."

Alex sat up slowly behind him and slipped a little kiss onto the back of his neck. "Race you home ?" He smirked and made to get up. "Oh no you don't ! You just bloody well wait here like a good boy !" Nathan snapped the book shut and pushed Alex back down onto his backside on the bench. He sat next to him and shook his head, "what are you like ? You look awful by the way." "Thanks, that's just what I wanted to hear." "I mean, you big numpty, that we're walking back slowly, you're drinking masses of fluids and lying down while I cook, no argument."

Alex looked deeply into his eyes. "I do love you so," he said seriously. Nathan blushed and took his hand, "come on, let's go and cook for our folks," he pulled Alex up and put his arm around his waist just in case. It made the walk home extra special and although Alex didn't really need it any more they walked incredibly slowly, touching every tree and bush on the way, pointing things out to each other as if seeing it all for the first time. When they got to

Alex's they had the place to themselves as his Mum and Dad were staying out until 7pm to give the boys their space to prepare.

Nathan made Alex shower and change immediately, then he fed him a slice of bread, buttered and filled with a few slices of cheese and tomato and gave him an enormous glass of squash. "Eat and drink that here and then lie on that sofa for a bit while I sort dinner," he dictated. Alex smiled at him, already looking better after his shower and wearing a dark grey sweatshirt, white T peeping out underneath and dark blue jeans. "God you're bossy !" He replied. "Yes I am, and you have to do everything I say !" Nathan grinned at him.

Alex was impressed at his organisation, while he'd been in the shower he had foil covered a large baking tray, melted a cup of butter, finely chopped some curly parsley and mixed the two in with breadcrumbs, parmesan and seasoning, filled a pan of potatoes with water and dressed the table for dinner. "How long was I upstairs for ?" He asked in awe. Nathan blushed, "I've made this dish lots of times," Alex felt his heart flutter as he looked at him. "I can't wait to tell them all tonight," he said quietly as he got up to follow his advice and climbed onto the sofa.

Five minutes later he was asleep. Nathan checked he was ok and then got on with finishing the preparations. It had taken them much longer to get home than normal and although it was a quick dish to prepare Nathan looked at his watch and saw that they only had twenty five minutes to go.

He drained the potatoes and put them back in the pan with butter and seasoning and swirled them around in the residual heat. He then spread the breadcrumb mixture onto smoked haddock loin portions that he laid out on the foiled tray, poured a little extra butter over the top and covered the fish with a large piece of foil until they were ready to go in the oven. He then took the white wine from the fridge and uncorked it.

He glanced at his watch, with nothing left to do he just had time for a quick shower and change. He had a fresh set of clothes in his ruck sack. Taking a check on Alex he hurtled up the stairs and into the shower, it didn't take long and he was down stairs again with minutes to spare. Refilling Alex's squash glass he headed over to him and crouched at his side.

"My love ?" He whispered and stroked his cheekbone. Alex stirred immediately. "Oh, hi....mmm, nice sleep..." he murmured. Nathan glanced at his watch, "I'm glad to hear it, how are you feeling ?" Alex yawned and sat up. He rubbed his neck and forehead. "Yeah, a lot better I think thanks. He ran a hand through his hair and blinked hard. "What time is it ?" "Five to," Nathan replied.

Alex's eyes flew wide open, "five to ? Oh bollocks, you really have done everything yourself haven't you ?" Nathan shrugged, "you needed the sleep."

Alex grimaced, "Oh Nate, I'm so sorry," he took Nathan's hand and they pulled each other close. "It doesn't matter at all, as long as you're safe and well, that's all that counts," Nathan breathed into his hair, just as the door bell rang. The boys looked at each other and laughed. Alex slid off the sofa and went to let their parents in. Nathan passed behind him and slid the top layer of foil off the fish before sliding them into the hot oven.

He came up beside Alex to kiss and hug all four parents, it was weird doing that together in Alex's house and they all looked slightly lost for a moment. Nathan noticed that all four of them had dressed up which made him blush, they must know it was an important evening, but what would they say at their announcement. He poured everyone a glass of wine which his mother then helped distribute. "You look nice Alex," she smiled. "Ooh but I didn't notice those bruises straight away, how blind of me ! Poor you, what happened ?"

Alex blushed a little, "only hockey practise, I'm ok though," he answered. "Does it hurt ?" Alison asked, concern written all over her face. "Yes it does, he had to leave English early for a lie down today," interjected Nathan. "Ta Nate," Alex blushed deeply and looked embarrassed. "Oh don't be shy about it, it's only your Mum and Dad and us, mmm, what is that lovely smell darling ?" She came to stand beside Nathan at the oven. "Smoked haddock loins," he said and opened the oven to show her.

Dishing up didn't take very long at all, soon everyone sat around the table and tucked into their fish. It was an immediate hit and Alex was amazed at how divine it tasted. "My God, how did you do this ?" He asked. Nathan smiled at him, "I'll show you some time."

Alex squeezed his arm in affectionate return, his dad saw and putting down his cutlery said, "so come on you two, what did you want us round to dinner for ? You've got this lovely house and us all at your disposal so what is it ?" All four parents stopped eating and turned their attention fully on the boys. Nathan felt his ring through his top and his heart underneath sped up with adrenalin. Alex saw the gulping look on his face and took his hand firmly in his. Although their parents knew that their sons were gay and accepted it, the boys weren't usually so tactile in front of them so all eyes moved as one to the joined hands.

Both boys looked a bit nervous but Alex looked deeply into Nathan's eyes and he knew he'd do anything for him. He turned to face the 'panel.' "Well er... the thing is, you know how we feel about each other," the dads both coughed at this but Alex continued, "so to cut a long story short, I proposed to Nathan six weeks ago and he said yes. We want to get married. We have a date, a venue, a colour scheme, a cake and these so far." They pulled their chains up from inside their tops and displayed the matching engagement rings.

To say there was a stunned silence doesn't quite describe it. The boys sat stock still, their legs trembling slightly under the table. They gripped each other's hands more tightly. At last Alison Henderson spoke first. "Darling that's a wonderful goal, when ?" "October the 10th," Nathan answered immediately. No one spoke again for a moment until Alex's dad said, "this year ?" They nodded. "Alex that's too soon, I don't think you should go for a date just within the first college term," he shook his head. "I'm not going to college Dad, neither's Nathan." All the parents looked aghast. "But you both have places..."Alex's mum joined in. "Not any more, we turned them down," Nathan said. The silence that followed seemed to be an angry one.

"Look, we have a plan. We're not two brainless 18 year olds who just thought about this yesterday. Ever since I fell in love with Nathan I could see my whole future with him. We've both saved up some money and made a budget. We can afford to pay for our own wedding, we want to leave school at the end of term and immediately work. We're going to rent somewhere together until we can afford to buy." Alex finished. His mum and dad looked at each other and then his father leant forward and squeezed the back of his hand. "Look Alex, - and excuse me Nathan for speaking my mind as I do genuinely admire you and think you're good for my son, I've certainly never seen him this happy." Nathan nodded, - "but Alex this is too young, it's not the homosexual aspect of it. That is hard on parents at first but we love you and are absolutely ok with it as you know, it's just too young son. What do you know of the world ?"

Alex seemed to sit up taller, "Dad is that your only objection, really ?" His father shrugged, "well yes it is actually."

"Then please listen to me, you don't need to be worried. What do I know of the world ? Not much as yet, obviously. I think I know a lot but I have only been here for 18 years so you're right, I have lots of learning and finding out to do but I want to do it all with Nathan. Don't you understand ? Look around you at all the failed marriages these days and all the lonely people not finding their soulmate til they're 40 ! I've found him now ! Isn't that the best thing in the world ? When I'm forty I'll be able to say I met the right man 22 years ago and we'll have an even stronger relationship than we do now, - unbreakable."

He sat back in his chair looking revved up. Nathan blushed slightly and looked at his dad who said, "boys, that's a very simplistic view of the world, I mean yes, people can meet their soulmates at your age and a life together from 18 does work, it has for many people but in this day and age ? Do you think that's likely ?" Nathan's face looked like thunder, "Dad ! Of course it will bloody well work ! - and if as you seem to be saying 'in this day and age' modern life makes it more unusual for people to find someone so young, why aren't you just going 'hallelujah' instead of trying to put us off?"

"Now come on son, I didn't say you can't do it...." Nathan suddenly looked furious. He stood up so fast that his chair flew backwards and would have smashed to the floor had Alex not caught it. "Look," he was red with anger and breathing hard, " I knew we'd get some rubbish about this but we thought we were lucky with you four as our parents, normally you're so supportive and then when we say we're getting married you go all 'ooh no, um ah, should you do that, moan grumble.' And don't say it's not the gay thing because it is. If I was sitting here now with a pert bouncy 18 year old girl you'd be all 'oh well you are young but obviously so in love,' and you'd be cracking open the champagne."

He physically trembled with rage now. "I love a man, I'm happy and I WILL MARRY HIM !" He shouted, turned on his heel and sprinted up the stairs to Alex's bedroom, slamming the door and slumping down beside the bed with his head in his hands, angry, scared and shaking with fury.

Alex looked at the four stunned parents and stood up, "well I wouldn't have put it quite like that but I agree with him," he shrugged. "Sorry everyone but pudding will have to wait for a little while, that is if you'd still like to stay." He threw his napkin onto the table in disgust and ran up stairs to find Nathan.

When he pushed open his bedroom door and saw him slumped on the floor, head in his hands and quivering with rage, he went to him and wrapped both arms around him. Nathan's body was rigid with anger, Alex cuddled him close which was hard to do as he was so unyielding. "Sssh, we'll get through this, it's ok," he soothed. Nathan kicked a nearby cd across the floor and looked with watery eyes up into Alex's face, "I'm just so fucking angry !" He cried. "I know, I know, ssh my love," Alex held him. "It's not fair Alex, I know we can do this without them but I don't want to have animosity and a fight just to do what I know is right in my heart." He cuffed the tears away from his face.

"Do you know my lovely neighbour on the right, Mrs Raleigh ?"
Alex nodded and smiled, "great lady."

"Yeah she is, Kate's one of the kindest women you'll ever meet, but Christ Alex, she had this sort of shit from her parents," he sniffed, "she met the right guy at 21, they had a bit of an accident and she was pregnant but she loved him desperately. She told me that all she'd ever dreamed of since she was 14 was being with a wonderful guy and creating their own little family. So you would have thought that now she had it all, they just needed to get married, but no. He turned out to have no back bone as he was terrified of telling his parents.

He followed their university dream, not his own. He was so afraid of his parents and so was she, neither of them could get the courage to walk away from what was expected of them just so they could be together." "So what happened after that ?" Alex asked as he stroked Nathan's hair. Nathan drew in a heavy trembling breath. "She felt ashamed, she didn't keep the baby. He went with his parents on their usual summer holiday for two months, leaving her to cope with the grief and her supposed shame alone.

The fact that he didn't tell his parents everything and come and get her and support her and put her first almost destroyed her. Her parents found out and her mother told her that she musn't keep looking for Mr Right and hoping that each boyfriend might be the one. She said that put men off ! What kind of mother is this woman ? I mean for fucks sake Alex, can you imagine doing that to a daughter ? She'd already sent her away to boarding school at 11. Kate said she felt like a burden whenever she came home, never matching up to her mother's exacting standards and then here she is with the love of her life, she's 21, it's all happening for her and yet because of the selfish parents, - on both sides, it all goes to pot. She didn't get married til last year Alex, she was 41. That's 20 YEARS to get over that shit, 20 YEARS !"

He trembled violently again and Alex smiled and hugged him more. "Hey hey hey, ssh, come on," he soothed. "Now listen Nate, that story is terrible. I can't imagine staying sane through that disappointment let alone being such a kind and normal person as her but you've got to realise the differences here.

Look, first of all, we're two men. At the first sign of no support you've fired off like a cannon and basically told everyone to stuff it you're doing it. She didn't do that." Nathan smiled at this so Alex carried on. "This isn't twenty years ago, this is today and life IS a lot different, youngsters do get listened to more but aside from that, if they don't, they just go ahead and do what the hell they like anyway." Nathan giggled and nodded, his rigid body beginning to relax. "It's gonna be ok Nate, really. I'm not her spineless boyfriend, she shouldn't have married a creep like that anyway so good for her and didn't you say that she got married recently ?" Nathan nodded. "Is she happy ?" "Yes," Nathan beamed, "so happy, she says it may have taken all this time but it was worth it. He's the love of her life."

Alex rolled his eyes and Nathan laughed. "So duh, what the hell are you worrying about anyway ?" Nathan shrugged, rubbing his eyes, "I'm sorry, I just...God it hurts Alex, not getting the 'oh my God you're engaged' reaction when my life is so amazing now that I have you." He gazed up at him. "Oh Nathan, my Nathan," Alex reached down and kissed him with all his love. They pulled apart, gazing into each other's eyes. "It's going to be ok," Alex smoothed his fingers along Nathan's forehead and kissed it just as there was a gentle tap on the door and Alison walked in.

Alex and Nathan stayed where they were so she pulled out the chair at Alex's desk and sat down. She leant her head on her hand and looked kindly at Nathan. "Better now ?" Nathan looked down at his hands, mildly ashamed for his outburst but still determined not to let their parents put them off. "Yes," he said and nodded. His mother saw the hard line of his mouth and the cheek muscles working away. He was still very tense and it made her feel sorry that any of them had upset him.

"My darling, no one wants to split you and Alex up," she started, making his eyes fly wide open with alarm. "Split us up ?" He fumed. "I said we DON'T want to do that," Alison waved her hand at him in a calming gesture. She continued in her softest voice. "Alex your father's very sorry, he feels like we've spoilt your evening, both of you and he was so impressed that you went to so much trouble for this, we all are. Please come back downstairs." Nathan didn't move, "Mum, I'm 18, so is Alex. I'm trying to handle this well, maybe stamping off in anger didn't seem too mature but we just want your support. Are we going to get it ?"

Alison stood up, "come here," she beckoned with out stretched arms. "It might take a few days for the dads to come around, but we'll work on them, I promise. No one's going to stand in your way darling, no one." Nathan's lips were still in a rigid line but he looked at Alex who nodded gently.

As the three of them came back into the kitchen Alex's Mum looked on the verge of tears, she came over immediately to Nathan and hugged him. "I'm so sorry you felt badly because of what Christopher said, he only wants Alex to be happy." She squeezed Nathan's arm, "Me too," he replied, "it's the most important thing to me." Alex came and put an arm around his waist. No one moved for a moment and the dads still looked uncomfortable until Alison nudged her husband, "er, David...come on...!" She stage whispered. Her husband frowned and then went to the freezer where he pulled out a bottle of Verve Cliquot while Caitlin retrieved six champagne flutes and set them on the counter.

The dads busied themselves with pouring out exact measures, they whispered together before deciding on who was going to speak. Nathan's dad then tapped his glass with the end of a spoon making his son cringe out the word, "dad," in a 'you dope,' kind of voice. David Henderson cleared his throat still obviously uncomfortable but he looked his son in the eyes, "Nathan, your mother MADE me do this...., no only joking," he quickly added, noting his wife's death stare. "No seriously you two, we only want what will make you happy and so do your parents Alex. I think we do get worried about your age, we get worried about a lot of things about you but that's what being a parent is all about. We support you both boys and we love you Nathan so congratulations." He raised his glass to Alex's Dad's "here here," and they all sipped.

Alex pecked Nathan on the mouth making him jump back a step in surprise. "They've got to get used to it," he shrugged. Nathan blushed and put his hand to his ring under his t-shirt. "Yes, and that's another thing," his mum strode across the room and spun him around without warning, unclasped the chain and pulled Nathan's ring up out of his T. "Could you two PLEASE actually start wearing these on your fingers now the cat's out of the bag. It's playing havoc with your clothes, distorts everything!"

Nathan gasped and Alex's eyes almost bugged out of his head. "You knew?" They both choked in unison. Alison rolled her eyes, "oh for goodness sake! Of course I knew, a mother spots these things you know." She looked over at Caitlin who shrugged back looking utterly mystified, "don't look at me, I had no idea!"

"Well anyway, please wear them now," Alison asked and the boys grinned at each other. "Ok," beamed Alex, putting down his glass and taking Nathan's ring from him. He slid it carefully down his future husbands finger making his heart thrum loudly. Then he reached behind his own neck and undid his chain. He let the ring drop into Nathan's palm and felt his heart speed up too as Nathan reached out and softly unfurled his hand, sliding the ring all the way down to the base of his finger.

They looked up misty eyed, without letting go of each other's hands and then reddened quickly as the realisation of their parents watching such an intimate moment came back to them. "Erm," Nathan said shyly and looked up, sure he'd see two angry fathers and two embarrassed mothers but to his amazement all four looked misty eyed. He burst out laughing as Alex cautiously looked up, took in the moist eyes and joined in his amusement. Both mothers laughed at being caught looking soppy, and a tear actually escaped Caitlin's eye. "Mum!" Alex put his head on one side as if to say, 'oh come on,' and she laughed at her own emotional state.

After some serious sniffing, tissue handing out and both dads clearing their throats loudly, pretending they just had something in their eyes, it was time for pudding. Nathan brought out a Tarte Citron and cream and divided the whole thing up while Alex made some coffee. They ate the second course a much merrier group and as the evening wore on the boys so obviously loved wearing their rings, that their happiness seemed to rub off on their parents, helping all four get used to the idea a little more. Alex's dad caught his son mouthing 'I love you,' to Nathan out of the corner of his eye and saw how it made Nathan's eyes light up, his grin broaden and his cheeks flush. He watched again as he discreetly squeezed Alex's ringed hand and looked down at it so fondly. He didn't understand gay love but he did understand love and it made him well up inside to see his son so cared for.

It got late and everyone started to tire. The table was a mess, a sure fire hit for a dinner party. Alex yawned, Nathan smiled at him and stood up to collect the plates. "Oh no you don't, we'll wash up. It's a school night you two, go on, off you go home Nathan." Caitlin said, standing to start clearing up. Nathan didn't reply. When Caitlin looked up both he and her son were giving the 'uhuh,' arched eyebrow look. She laughed as they started rotating their engagement rings and muttering, "could we er what do they call it, erm vote now ? Get married, stuff like that at all ?" Alex mumbled to Nathan who shrugged, "yeah, you know maybe you're right, hmm," he looked back at Alex's mum who coloured slightly.

"Oh you two ! Yes very funny, I can't treat you like kids anymore, sorry. - but Alex you'll always be my baby." Alex groaned and sank his face into his hands in embarrassment. Nathan loved it and laughed loudly. "Aw sweet !" He giggled, getting a smack on the thigh for his trouble which just made him laugh more. "Come on, walk me to the gate you, my olds are looking a bit knackered," he said cheekily, loving the mock outrage on his parents faces.

"Olds ? Olds ? Did you hear that ? Good God !" His mother said to his father who pretended to be desperately offended and turned away whenever Nathan tried to talk to him. "Dad, dad, stop it...!" He laughed as his father swung his head from one side to the other to avoid him. "Dad," he laughed again. "Ok, well just to let you know, you 'young' parents, that I have a key and if you're staying to help clear up as I know you will as you're both totally OCD about that sort of thing, then I will say goodnight to Alex at the gate and see you at home, ok ?"

His parents continued being silly for a moment until he got up from the table at the same time as Alex so his mother winked and said, "seriously you two, it was a lovely meal, thank you so much." She came around their side of the table, hugged Nathan and hugged and kissed Alex, "welcome to the family," she smiled, making him grin with pleasure. "Thank you Mrs Henderson," he husked, genuinely moved. "Night mum, night Dad. Thanks for letting us use your house Mr and Mrs NH," Nathan said. They thanked him too and once the hugging and handshaking were finished, he made his way down the front steps with Alex.

They meandered to the gate slowly, hands in their pockets, both grinning, they hadn't stopped all night. As they got past the gate and slightly toward the road, hidden from view by the tall hedge, Alex turned to him. The look in his eyes made Nathan's heart beat so fast he had to bite his lip. "Don't, I'm going to need that very shortly," Alex chided. Nathan laughed heartily, his eyes twinkling like never before. He looked deeply into Alex's eyes and blushed profusely. "God you look amazing," Alex shook his head. "It was hard to keep my eyes off you all night."

Nathan choked back emotion, shaking slightly with the intensity of it all. Alex moved toward him, cupping the back of his head with one hand and his cheek with the other, he slid his lips softly onto Nathan's. Long and slow he kissed him, Nathan groaned with pleasure. When they pulled apart it was only to look back at each other and embrace again, holding on, loving one another, lying their cheeks against each other.

At last they parted and looked into each other's eyes. "Goodnight my love," Nathan breathed. Alex looked down at their entwined ring hands, "I'm never taking this off," he whispered. "Me neither."

"See," said Alex, "I told you this would be one of the best nights of our lives." He kissed Nathan again and watched him as he began to walk home, turning around and walking backwards in their habitual way. "I love you," he whispered quietly. It carried crystal clear back to Alex on the night air, "and I you." He breathed. He saw Nathan's smile light up once more in the darkness before he rounded the next corner and was gone.

Alex crunched back across the gravel looking up at the warm orange light coming from his parents house. It had been a wonderful evening in the end. He inhaled deeply, it had gone their way, it really had. He shook his head and smiled to himself. How did people get this lucky? He stood on the gravel and let the light breeze ruffle his hair as he looked straight up at the stars above. Some one was watching them, making it all come out alright, that was for sure.

The front door opened and Nathan's Mum and Dad came out, they were still talking, nineteen to the dozen on the front steps for a few minutes until at last Nathan's Dad virtually yanked his mum away, laughing and mock pleading with her about his beauty sleep. He was a handsome man, still lithe at forty six, Alex had never thought about it before but it did bode well for his future with Nathan. He smiled at the thought and got caught mid grin by Nathan's Mum who jumped at him loitering in the darkness.

"Ooh Alex you scared me for a sec," she smiled. "Sorry, I was just coming back in." He replied. She patted him on the arm, "well thank you for a lovely evening and congratulations again," she smiled warmly. "Thanks so much Mrs H, good night to you both," said Alex one last time and wandered across to where his parents stood in the door way, waving until Mr and Mrs Henderson rounded the hedge and were gone.

Chapter Ten.

In the delicious daylight that dawned warm and inviting the following morning, Alex stretched and smiled, happier than he had ever been in his life before. He skipped out of bed toward the shower and emerged downstairs with the most enormous grin on his face. He stayed that way all through breakfast. His mother put a plate of crispy bacon and scrambled egg in front of him. Alex smiled thankfully at her but blew out his cheeks and patted his stomach, "Mum, I just don't know if I can handle that this morning, I don't feel that hungry."

"That's because you're all dopey and loved up but you're eating it if I have anything to do with it. You two barely ate a scrap last night, did you know that ? You tasted both courses, oohing and ahing about how scrumptious they were and then gabbled on all night without swallowing much more than another forkful. Nathan's mum noticed too so get that down you, I expect she's doing the same this morning to him. You can moan about us on the way to school, now eat !" Alex laughed and grinned back at her, his eyes twinkling with happiness, "ok Mum, just for you," he began forking up his food.

The phone sprang to life just as Alex picked up the morning paper. He shovelled in the last mouthful of bacon and began to read about William and Kate not having their honeymoon til later in the year but just having a few days off to relax for now. "Smart move," he muttered to himself but then his blood ran cold. "OH NO ! OH MY GOD !" His mother gripped the work surface as she cried into the phone. Alex felt goose pimples run up his spine, she looked dreadful. His heart began to thrash against his ribs, what on earth had happened ? Then things got so much worse.

Caitlin turned toward her son, tears streamed down her stricken face as she clutched the phone with trembling hands. She nodded as if the person at the other end were standing in the room with her and husked, "ok, of course. Yes I understand. Keep us up to date." Then the worst bit of all, "yes, I'll tell him," she said, looking straight at Alex and hung up. Alex began to tremble, he couldn't keep his hands still but his body was rigid. "Mum ?" He shook his head, he didn't want to ask her anything. Slowly she moved toward him. He backed up, knocking over the chair and stumbled up against the fridge door. "Mum," he squeaked, shaking and dreading her words. "Oh God Mum, what's happened ? Please don't let it be him, please don't..." his mother gripped his shoulders, painfully hard. "Ow, Mum, oh God, oh God, what, what's happened ?" Caitlin let out an involuntary sob. "There's been an accident," Alex shrieked, he knew nothing yet but his stomach contracted. He shook his head but his mother nodded. "It is Nathan, I'm sorry my love but he slipped on the steps up to his house last night and hit his head. He...," she could barely manage to go on seeing her sons contorted streaming eyes. "He's unconscious Alex, he fractured his skull."

Alex must have let out such a scream but he didn't remember it later. The last thing he felt was breakfast coming up again and the room lurching and spinning away from him, then he couldn't feel his hands, pins and needles starting at his finger tips, working their way right along the length of his arms making them feel like useless rubber flippers.

He came round again, breathing oddly, feeling like something was wrong and as if he'd just run a marathon. He licked his lips, they tasted bad. He opened his eyes and saw his worried mother sitting beside him on the edge of the sofa where he lay. His father stood over him looking incredibly anxious. Alex was confused and then he remembered the last thing he'd heard. His guts knotted up again, his mother snatched up the bin she'd set beside him, he threw up and up, his body shaking and his eyes streaming until he lay down again panting. He couldn't speak for a moment. His father picked up the phone and started speaking to someone in the far corner of the room as his mother reached for a flannel and wiped his face and lips.

He shivered so she covered him in a blanket from the back of the sofa. He lay still for a moment, she didn't speak as she watched him. At last Alex rolled his face up to look at her. He felt weak as a kitten. "Is it true, what you just told me ? Is it true mum ?" Caitlin had to steel herself not to collapse at the pain in her sons eyes, it tore her to bits inside. She gulped and nodded, "yes Alex, I'm afraid it is." Alex's stomach tied up again but he didn't throw up, it just hurt very badly. Tears streamed down his face as he looked into her eyes. She dabbed them with a tissue. He shook his head. "Will he live ?" He whispered as the tears kept coming.

Caitlin dug her nails into her palm to stop from sobbing at the way he asked. "I don't know Alex, there's nothing more that I can tell you for now apart from he's in hospital and we're waiting to hear. Your dad's just phoning the school to let them know what's happened." Alex screwed his eyes up and sank his face into the cushion. This couldn't be happening, it just couldn't.

They heard nothing further for several hours. Alex lay curled up on the sofa as the seconds ticked by, suffering as badly as anyone could. He didn't eat or drink and shook most of the time. Several people tried to reach his mobile but he couldn't talk to anyone, the rest didn't know what to say and stayed silent. Facebook became jammed with horrified enquiries but no one had any information to share yet.

Around 2.30pm the phone rang again, Alex's body jumped in response and he stiffened as his father took the call. He sat on the armchair opposite Alex and his mother and nodded at them. "Yes, I see," he said into the phone, looking grave, "and then we'll see after that scan or what ? Right, yes, and when do they think that his condition will improve if that's the case ? Mmm, mm, I see. So for now we just have to wait while the initial swelling abates ? Right, ok, yes of course I'll pass all of that on to them both right away. Thanks for ringing again David. We'll stay by the phone so don't worry about the time, we won't be getting much sleep here. Alex ? He's, er..." Christopher Nesbitt Hall looked at his desperate son and felt like his heart would break, "he's not doing too well David, I won't lie, this is very very hard for him. Mmm, I know. Well look, we'll do the best we can here and know that we're all praying for Nathan. Ok, speak later, our thoughts are with you, bye." He hung up.

Alex crept up into a sitting position, weakly holding onto the edge of the sofa, his heart in his mouth. "Dad ?" He croaked. His father put down the handset, "ok, well he's in intensive care, he's got a five inch fracture running from above his right eyebrow around to just below the right ear. The good news is that it's a straight fracture, as in no bone got depressed into the brain. David said the next forty eight hours are crucial but the doctors think that within that time the swelling should go down and we'll be more able to see where we are. He'll phone as and when they have more news."

Alex swayed against the sofa, there was some hope but he felt breathless and impotent, it was the worst feeling in his whole life. He looked sick, clammy and totally broken as he looked at his mother. There was nothing of the usual Alex about him apart from his devastating looks but now those looked macabre against his pale slick faced terror. "Mum," he whispered and she grabbed him in her arms and held him as tears burst from him in a hysteria that terrified her. She held her son as he gasped uncontrollably against her, sobbing to the point of retching, unable to breath normally. It took both his parents arms and combined voices to eventually calm him. They rationalised that no one knew the outcome yet and that he couldn't give up for Nathan's sake. After repeating this over and over again it seemed to sink in a little at last. His father stayed beside him, holding his trembling son in his arms, almost hurting him as he squeezed him tightly, but he needed it. He soothed and supported, finding hopeful but not unrealistic things to say as Alex's mother made a strong pot of tea and brought a steaming mug with three sugars in it over to the sofa.

"Darling," she turned his face toward her with a finger to his chin. "You're going to drink this," he shook his head. "No, you are going to. As soon as it's a bit cooler you're drinking it and then it's upstairs for a bath and change." Alex shook his head and his father mouthed 'oh come on,' at his wife but she knew what she was doing. Either they could let Alex go to pieces and completely give in now, or they could build him up for whatever was to come. If they let him succumb now and Nathan did die, she couldn't see Alex recovering for years and she wasn't about to let that happen.

The three of them sat and talked, at least Alex's parents did, he lay in his fathers arms shivering from time to time and drifting off to sleep with exhaustion. Two hours later he woke with a start. He was covered in the blanket and felt sleep addled and confused until the reality hit him again. His empty stomach gurgled horribly. He sat up and rubbed his eyes. He was a dishevelled mess in his school uniform, spattered with bile, his mouth felt terrible. He rubbed his neck and surveyed the room, his parents sat at the kitchen counter with mugs of coffee and a plate of uneaten biscuits.

Alex got up and wobbled over to them, dragging the blanket behind him. They watched him nervously but let him make his own shaky progress across the room. He shivered as he lowered himself on to a stool by the counter and his mum reached down and wrapped the blanket tightly around him. She turned to the work top and brought back a plate with a hot waffle and maple syrup on it, Alex blanched and shut his eyes, it reminded him of Nathan. "Not that," he whispered. Sensing why his mother tossed it straight in the bin and filled the toaster with four slices of bread. Jams, marmite and butter already nestled together in the centre of the consul.

Without asking, his mother buttered the toast when it popped up and put the stacked plate in the centre of the consul. Everyone silently took a slice, Alex added jam to his, not knowing why but just doing it out of habit. He bit into the slice and forced himself to chew. He was so hungry but had no interest in the actual food. He managed the whole slice though and began to sip the mug of coffee his mother placed beside his plate. She flicked on the small consul top tv and saw with a spec of hope that Alex was actually slightly distracted for a moment. His father got up and whispered with his mother before disappearing out of the front door. Alex didn't really care why, he was clinging on to sanity, just breathing, eating and drinking would do him for now.

After he ate and drank, Alex got forced into a bath. His mother sat with him while he shivered in the hot water. He didn't care that they were not normally a nudey kind of family, he couldn't care about anything until Nathan was ok. Once he was dry and dressed again, she made him bring some school work down stairs, he couldn't believe it when she said he should do one piece of home work. It seemed ludicrous but he at least opened the file next to him on the sofa and though most of the time he stared into space or dozed, from time to time he did glance at it and once or twice turned a page, it would have to do for now Caitlin thought and tried to carry on with running the house.

How is it that when your heart feels beyond broken and you can't see a way forward, things like washing machines, aeroplanes and cars still work Alex wondered as he sat doing nothing but listening to life going on within his house and somewhere outside too. He ran his finger along the bottom of his t-shirt, would Nathan ever lift it up and run his hands under it again, stroking Alex into ecstasy, just because it was him. A sob escaped him but he jumped at the same time as his little sister tore through the front door. It was such an unexpected relief to Alex to see another face. He looked up at her as she stood stock still for a moment, then she ran to her brother and flung herself into his arms.

They cried loudly on each other as Caitlin escaped to the larder and wept silently against her sleeve. After a few minutes their sobs calmed enough for Jess to pull away and sit half sprawled across her big brothers tucked up legs. She didn't want to break contact with him just yet, he clearly needed all the help he could get. They began to talk and for the first time that day Alex could actually be more human. His sister told him that the news was all over school, no one knew what to think and there was wide spread shock. They talked about mutual friends as well as what Jess had been up to and after half an hour Alex sighed and leant his head back on the sofa. "I'm sorry bro, you're so tired aren't you ?" She looked contrite. "No, no I'm ok," Alex shook his head but then he broke down again, his face collapsing completely as he sobbed. Jess leaned across and held him in her arms. She squeezed him tightly while he cried.

"He's going to be ok Al," she croaked, "he really will I just know it." Alex cried harder, no one else called him Al but Nathan. He shook his head against her shoulder. "I don't know how I'm going to get through this, I don't...." he sobbed. Jess squeezed him again, "be strong for him Al, be strong for Nathan, he's going to need you now." Alex cried and cried as she held him.

The next few days were the most awful that Alex had ever had to endure. His parents made him go to school the next day which though horrendously hard, was an absolute god send. He never stopped thinking about Nathan and with his own bruised face still healing and devastated eyes he was quite a shocking contrast to his usual self. Everyone tried to help and by the end of the day he was inundated with cards, cds, dvds and all manner of good luck charms, gifts and boxes of brownies, chocolates and biscuits to take to Nathan in hospital.

That thought cheered him a little on the way home in the car, he could actually go and visit him soon he hoped and actually ate supper almost cheerfully that night, determined to visit Nathan the next day. But after supper Nathan's dad phoned again and said that he was in and out of consciousness and had been moved to a surgical ward in case they needed to alleviate pressure to the brain. At this information Alex sprinted to the bathroom and threw up his entire meal.

He spent the night sobbing, dozing and waking fitfully. Saturday came and went with no news and only agony for Alex as he sat numbly in front of the tv, insensible to it's programmes. The only times he seemed to come round were when his sister could sit and talk to him. She had a way that worked or perhaps it was just their nearness of age his parents thought, but they were grateful for it, whatever the reason.

On Saturday evening Alex's hockey mate Andy nipped over. He sat beside him for a while, insisting on watching Top Gear on Dave. He didn't like the look of his friend, it frightened him. No one had seen Alex lose it like this before. He noticed the ring on Alex's wedding finger but didn't like to either ask or congratulate him in these circumstances. They watched the programme and Alex did his best to pull himself out of it for his friend but it just didn't work.

As Andy rose to leave, Alex walked him to the door. He looked thin and dishevelled, and horribly shocked. Andy squeezed his shoulder, "I'll see ya mate," he smiled grimly, Alex nodded and shut the door. Without saying a word he shuffled off to bed where he slept immediately for three hours before waking in a panic and after remembering why, tossing and sweating uncontrollably all night long.

When Caitlin wandered down to her kitchen, tying her silk dressing gown cord as she went, she yawned and tried to think about what she could offer her ailing son to make him eat, at least a little. It was a gloomy start to the day so she switched on the light and jumped at Alex sitting in dark blue sweats and a grey t-shirt, huge dark circles under his eyes and his hair sticking up to the ceiling. He looked into her eyes with dead pupils. It made her stomach hurt to see him like this. She gulped back her fear and switched on two more lights and the tv.

"Morning darling, how did you sleep ?" She smiled, dreading the answer. Alex shrugged. Caitlin ignored it and set about making breakfast. Jess was sleeping in as she'd had a busy week so no one would get Alex talking for at least another hour she reasoned so she made him a cup of sweet tea and carried on. It was awful to bustle about a normally happy kitchen with this silent, dead inside shell of a son but Caitlin didn't know what else she could do.

She made coffee and toasted bagels, pancakes with blueberries and maple syrup and porridge for her husband. Ten minutes later he emerged, took one look at Alex and knew it was pointless talking to him. He picked up the newspapers, put the supplements in front of Alex and a small stack of pancakes. "Alex," he said gruffly, making sure to jolt his son's attention in his direction.

It worked and Alex looked a bit taken aback for a moment which was at least a change from his vacant staring. "Eat these pancakes, your mother's gone to a lot of trouble, I don't expect to tell you again." He stared hard into his son's eyes, it worked. Slowly Alex nodded, he looked a bit bemused but looked down at the food and picked up his fork. "Sorry dad," he whispered. "That's ok, now eat up," his father finished and hid his grim expression behind The Times.

Alex was a quarter of the way through his pancakes and coffee, it had taken quite some time but at least he was doing it. His mother was stuck into Sudoku while his father ate and read the paper. Time seemed endless, but then the phone sprang to life. Alex couldn't bear to show emotion, he slumped further over his food, hoping that whatever it was wouldn't make it all come up again. Caitlin picked up the handset.

"Hello ? Oh hi David, yes, we're all here." Alex started to feel sick, he put his head in his hands but then his mother appeared beside him holding out the phone, her face unreadable. "Alex, Alex, it's for you, take the phone," she said carefully. Alex looked up at her, he didn't understand. "Take the phone darling," she slid the handset into his palm and curled his fingers around it. "Listen, go on....," she encouraged. Alex's terrified eyes didn't leave her face while he took the phone. "Hello ?" He said gingerly.

Nothing happened at first and then a very husky croaking voice said, "Alex, I want to speak to Alex." Alex jumped from his seat, his legs visibly trembling as he held onto the consul top. "NATHAN ?" "Hi, oh Alex I wish you were here, I hurt all over," husked the voice. Alex's eyes were as wide as saucers, he couldn't believe it. Tears sprang from them immediately. He crashed himself back down onto the stool, crushing his eyes shut and crying "Nathan, Nathan, Nathan,.....oh my God !" He pressed his forehead into the counter top and sobbed and sobbed.

His mother took the handset and spoke softly to Nathan for a moment. Alex sat up shaking and red faced. He dashed the tears away from his eyes with the backs of his hands and motioned for the phone. "Hello ? Oh my love," he sobbed.

"Sssh, don't cry Al, please don't," whispered Nathan, sounding very tired. Alex heard it and pulled himself together as much as he could, "I'm sorry Nate," he snuffled, "God I've just been so worried about you." "I know....look, I'm very tired now, need painkillers too. Come later, please ?" "Of course I will," Alex stood up again, "I love you," he said. "Hmm, too," Nathan mumbled, worn out already. Alex looked at the phone and didn't know how to feel. He was utterly utterly shattered. He sat back down as his mother took the handset.

Looking up at her he said, "he's awake !" "I know," Caitlin smiled, "and that is very good news my darling. Now you're going to see him later aren't you ?"

Alex's head snapped up, more alert than he'd been in days. "Yes !" He agreed sounding excited and surprised all at once. "Well then you'd better get upstairs and sort your room out. Have a shower and start to pack up all the things you'd like to take to him. Don't overwhelm him with everything everyone gave you from school in one day ok, he's going to be very tired, pick out the things you'd like best to take in today. Your Dad and I will drive you in at 3pm so off you go and start getting sorted out."

Alex bounded out of his seat, a man with a purpose, "yes, I'll get ready right away, thanks mum," he sprinted off up the stairs. Christopher looked at his wife and rubbed his chin, "Caitlin, don't you think that's asking a bit much of him after the state he's been in recently. I mean look, he's hardly eaten any breakfast and he must have lost half a stone in only a few days." He said worriedly, but his wife smiled knowingly back at her husband and said, " I know, but didn't you see how his face lit up just then. Don't you get it darling ? All he needs is hope and suddenly he's got it. You wait and see, when he comes back down those stairs he'll be like the old Alex again, he won't be completely better yet, we'll know that but you wait and see the remarkable difference in him, just from that phone call." Christopher leaned in and kissed his wife, his eyes shone deeply into hers, "I think," he breathed, "that you are a pretty remarkable woman, did you know that ?" "I do now," she grinned and kissed him back.

Alex leapt into the shower, shampooing and conditioning his hair, he rubbed his poor tired bruised face with a soft sponge and ran the water very hot. It made him a bit dazed when he got out but as soon as he was dry he looked in the mirror, his hair shone and he stood up very straight, some of the normal Alex was back already. He tore into his bedroom and picked out all Nathan's favourite clothes on him then he piled up all the things the friends at school had wanted him to have and started sorting them into smaller piles for maybe two or even three visits. If it were three he hoped the third would be Nathan's welcome home party. He sighed at the possibility of not having him well enough to hold for a long time but then shook himself out of it, he had a lot to organise, he wanted to put some music together on his Nano and lend it to Nathan as it had more memory than his. He set about getting it all done and put some music on in the background.

Nathan lay in his hospital bed feeling relieved. His head throbbed horribly and the machine he was hooked up to for pain management stopped when he'd had all that he could for the next few hours. It was hard to bear the last hour just before it kicked in again, but he knew he was getting better.

Yesterday had been the most frightening day of his life. He'd been left alone for only half an hour in the night, but the pain had been so bad that he thought he was about to die. He'd tried to call for help but couldn't make his voice loud enough and his hands were too weak to press the emergency button. Everyone had left the room thinking he was asleep. He'd had to lie there trying to will a nurse to come back or one of his parents while he concentrated on watching the minutes tick by thinking, 'don't die, don't die.'

He wondered if he'd ever tell Alex of all the other horrible things he'd gone through in the last few days. Some of it he didn't remember thank God. He had no memory of falling and hitting his head, the first thing he remembered was trying to take a sip of water 12 hours after it had happened and throwing up and up. He remembered them lifting his hand as if it weighed nothing to push in the canula even though he tried his hardest to clamp his hand to the bed, not wanting a needle anywhere near him.

He tried not to think about how one of the junior doctors had frowned above him and turned to the registrar saying, 'sir, why isn't he answering me ?' - when all the while Nathan had felt as if they were having a conversation. To him he'd answered every question, sighed a bit, shifted uncomfortably in the bed and groaned in pain. In reality when he told his mother about the incident she looked rueful and said that he didn't need to worry now as he was already so much better, but at that time he hadn't actually done or said any of those things, he'd just thought them. His body never moved a muscle.

When the shock subsided, Nathan decided that he would never ever turn anybody's life support machine off, not even if doctors told him there was no brain activity, he just wouldn't do it after that horrendously surreal experience.

His mum bustled about at the end of the bed and Nathan felt irritated, he snapped at her and then immediately apologised. "Mum I'm so sorry, I keep doing that," he whispered, tears springing to his eyes. "Don't worry darling, it's common with a head injury they say, but you're getting so much better all the time ok ? Maybe you can't see it but those around you can." She smiled kindly at her son. Nathan nodded gently. It didn't hurt to move carefully, the pain was just there all the time, and the tiredness.

He shifted in the bed, "Mum, I'm starting to get bored." Alison beamed at him, "that's a wonderful sign my love, I think you'll be out of here shortly. Besides, Alex will be here very soon don't forget, actually, in," she glanced at her watch, "just under two and a quarter hours now." Nathan looked anxious, "Oh God mum, what if he goes off me, seeing me like this !

It might change his mind about me ? - and I'm so grumpy all of a sudden, I might bite his head off ! Shit, Mum I'm scared, I don't want to lose him." He blinked back another tear. His mother came to sit on the edge of the bed and looked down at her injured son.

" Nathan, he loves you, and his parents will fill him in on your mood changes on the way over here. He won't be expecting a miracle." She stroked the unhurt side of his head and smiled kindly. "It's all going to be alright darling, you'll both get through this, I know you will. Now close your eyes and rest for a bit. I'm not going anywhere so if you get really bored or it hurts too much you can talk to me." Nathan nodded carefully again and shut his aching eyes as his mother pulled the covers up over him and tucked him in. It did help, he felt a bit safer with her there and he didn't mind being treated a little childishly for now, anything to make time speed up and get him back into Alex's beautiful arms, away from this irritableness and pain. He fell asleep.

Chapter Eleven.

Alex's mother tapped lightly on his door, he'd been playing music and packing for a while. When he didn't answer, she swung the door open and smiled at her son. He was deeply asleep, better than he had been for days. Three neat piles of cds, chocolate bars and other goodies were piled up on the floor, the nearest beside Alex's rucksack so she carefully packed them all in. She propped the bag up by the door and walked over to his bed.

She liked what he was wearing, he looked his usual self again in cared for clothes and freshly washed hair. She looked at her watch, she was sorry to wake him but he wouldn't miss seeing Nathan for anything. She gently shook his shoulder, Alex stirred sleepily then snapped awake and leapt bolt up right on the bed breathing hard, "what what, is he ok ?" He looked terrified but his mother's face was smiling and calm.

He put his forehead in his hands and rubbed before looking up again, "sorry, sorry....God, I panicked then." He shook his head as she sat on the edge of the bed. "It's alright darling, you just jumped awake a bit too quickly, everything's fine. It is time to go though." Alex glanced at the floor and nodded, "hey, where's all the...." "I packed the nearest pile into your rucksack, it seemed right, is that ok ?" She asked. Alex smiled, "thanks mum, that's great. He put his hand under the pillow and pulled out a thick white envelope that just said, 'Nathan.' - "For when he gets down and needs to hear good things," he explained and got off the bed to slip it into the rucksack too.

"I think that's a lovely thing to do Alex. Now come on, let's go and don't be nervous," she ushered him from the room. "I'm not nervous Mum, I'm sick to my stomach with worry still but at least I'm going to get to see him and kiss him hello again," he beamed at the thought and his cheeks flushed for the first time in days. She hugged him and kept her arm around him as they made their way out to the car.

Outside Alex's dad was already behind the wheel. Alex stowed the rucksack and was about to get in when he thought of two more things and sprinted back inside. Christopher turned to his wife, "I just can't believe that's the same boy ?" He gasped. Caitlin squeezed his knee gently, "I know," she smiled.

Alex reappeared incredibly quickly with one of his pillows and wearing his striped grey hoodie. He jumped into the car and they were away. It didn't take long to get to the hospital but just being there was pretty horrible. At once Alex clammed up once more and went very white. His parents put an arm each around his shoulders in the lift and as he looked from one to the other, both smiling encouragement, some of his colour returned again.

Sooner than his racing heart could handle, they were at the doors to the ward. Nathan had been moved just that day to an empty room at the far end of it to help him sleep so they had to walk amongst several occupied beds with people in all different states along the way. Alex felt terrified, it smelt oddly like plasters and floor cleaner mixed with something he didn't recognise but he didn't like it.

His parents ushered him on. There was a mini corridor between Nathan's room and the end of the ward, the three of them crossed it, glad to leave the big strange room behind them, Alex shuddered to think of Nathan being somewhere like that for the last few days. They knocked on his door and his mum opened it. She looked pretty terrible, tired beyond belief and thin. The same thoughts about Alex ran through her head but neither said so. She smiled as she saw them and turning toward the bed said, "darling you have a visitor." She patted Alex's shoulder and gently pushed him past her into the room then she left to sit on the four green pvc seats outside with his parents, shutting the door firmly behind her.

Alex turned around, his heart in his mouth and saw a very bruised, panda eyed looking Nathan staring back at him. He'd wondered how he'd feel at this moment and stood unmoving in shock for a moment. Then he ran forward, falling on his knees and kissed Nathan full on the mouth. It was hard to kiss while putting no pressure at all behind your lips but somehow Alex managed to do it. Very softly he stroked his fingertips down Nathan's cheek under his hurt side. Nathan groaned.

Alex pulled away only a few inches and stroked him still. He gazed deeply into Nathan's eyes. A tear spilled out of them and splashed off his nose onto the floor.

"I've missed you so much," Alex breathed. Nathan nodded gently, his eyes looked so black and sore. "Does it hurt very much ?" Asked Alex, thumbing the uninjured part of his head. "Yes," Nathan husked. He looked pained as he stared into Alex's eyes, "this is so awful," he whispered. "I know," Alex agreed. He shook his head, "oh Nate, this has been the worst time of my life. I was so worried about you." Nathan blinked slowly. "I'm sorry," he said.

"What ? What are you sorry for ? You didn't do anything !" Alex looked incredulous. "Well, apart from depriving me of my engagement nookie that is," he half smiled. Nathan grimaced back at him, "my head !" He winced and moved uncomfortably in the bed. Alex felt sick and didn't know what to do. "Do you mind that I ran in and kissed you first ?" He asked.

"Why would I ever mind you kissing me ?" Nathan husked. Alex grinned and rested his chin on the backs of his crossed hands on the edge of the bed. He sighed and closed his eyes. When he opened them Nathan looked at him. "You don't look so good yourself, what's wrong with you ? Why are you so thin ?" Alex coloured a bit and gulped. "I, er... well you see, the man I love is in hospital and I just," he looked down at the floor and shrugged unhappily. Nathan sighed deeply in obvious pain. Alex looked at him with a grim look, he felt suddenly so miserable about everything over the last few days.

Nathan studied his face. "I need to go back to sleep Al, I just hurt so much, sorry." Alex shrugged again feeling even more miserable and tried to keep himself from crying, "it's ok," he said in a small voice. Nathan shut his eyes against the pain, so desperate for more sleep but just managed to say what he wanted to. "Hey, Alex," he said. "Yes Nate ?" "Do me a favour would you ?" He whispered, his voice growing more tired each moment. He reached a hand down to meet Alex's, they immediately entwined. "I'm going to be a bit off and moody for a while but it's just the pain talking. Knowing this, will you still come and see and me every day from now on ?"

"Try and bloody stop me," Alex said defiantly.

"Will you also marry me in October ?" He breathed gently and just about managed to open his eyes again. Alex's face split into a huge grin, "yes my darling, yes I will," he husked, tears of happiness in his eyes. Nathan grinned back at him before the pain overwhelmed him. "Good," he whispered softly and turned his face toward the pillows, shutting his eyes and immediately falling back to sleep.

Alex sat still at his side for a minute, he watched his chest rise and fall, rise and fall. He looked carefully at his bashed face and injured head and at the drip in his hand. When he was certain that everything was as well as it could be he got up and retrieved the rucksack from where it had slumped off his shoulders to the floor. He opened it up and slipped out the letter and the Nano, placing both within reach, then he re-zipped it and stowed it inside the little bedside table next to Nathan. He stood up, loathe to leave him and dropped the softest of kisses on his head before backing out of the room, watching him until the very last second.

Alex slept that night, he slept and slept so deeply that he woke up the following day not aware of time in any way shape or form. He sat up groggily at first letting his body acclimatise to the daylight then staggered out of bed. He was refreshed but slightly drunk on sleep still. There was no movement in the house which seemed weird, he was sure it was past 6am and no one stirred. "Mum ?" He called and tip toed down the corridor, his parents bed was perfectly made, odder still.

"Jess ?" He called after his sister and found her room empty and neat too. His heart beating with the beginnings of concern he wandered downstairs and found one place set at the kitchen consul. There was a note on his plate. Smiling he padded over and flipped it open. "Alex," it began, "the school knows that you've been under the weather this past week, they know that it's because of how you feel about Nathan.

We've told them you're getting better though and we left you sleeping today so you'll be back soon. I've dropped your sister to school, Mum's gone to that National Trust place with auntie Sue so you have the place to yourself. Nathan's dad rang at 10am, he had a good night, he's still in a lot of pain but they're talking about releasing him to his parents care in about a week if he keeps improving slowly like this. Sounds like good news to me son. Get some food and relax, we'll see you later. Ring if you need. Love you, Dad. X"

Alex smiled a half smile and put the letter down on the counter. He was happy that everyone was being so nice and particularly happy that he knew Nathan was getting better but the last few days had been so terrible. He sat down on one of the stools and looked at the breakfast plates, he wasn't hungry. Physically he felt much better but emotionally he was as blue as could be. He put his head in his hands and sighed. Across the counter top his phone buzzed, he snatched it up. "Head hurts, miss my Alex," was all it said.

Alex pressed his cheek up against the screen, screwing his eyes up, he felt sick, elated, still scared and wondered how much more he could take. When would he see Nathan lope across the room with his long lean legs, that killer smile igniting his insides. He so wanted to be taken in his arms, to have him back in his. He'd never known gut wrenching pain until the accident but now it was a familiar daily event. His hands trembled for a second as he typed back, "Your Alex loves you, what can I do for your head ?" "Kiss," was the one word reply and suddenly Alex was grinning again.

He understood why everyone had left him alone. He had to pull himself together for Nathan. If he was to get better he needed Alex to be strong, they couldn't both go to pieces. He straightened up and ran a hand through his hair. "It's coming up shortly, I'll see you at 3pm. X" he typed, and pulled two slices of bread from the bag, shoving them into the toaster. He flicked the kettle on for some coffee and ran upstairs to dive into the shower, he only had an hour and a half after his marathon sleep. Five minutes later he emerged clean and sparkling.

He bundled up the second lot of presents for Nathan and slid them into an

M and S 'bag for life,' hurtled back downstairs and shoved down the toast and coffee at a rate of knots. He looked at his watch, it would take 35 minutes on the bus and they ran every fifteen. To be safe on time he needed to leave now. He grabbed his keys and sunglasses and was about to head out of the door but thought of something else, sliding everything onto the counter he sprinted back up the stairs, sprayed his throat with some Hugo Boss and dived back out of the front door.

Alex made it to the hospital with a few minutes to spare, Nathan's Mum was sitting outside the door when he got there, she stood up and hugged him straight away. "Well you look a bit better," she smiled. Alex nodded, "I think I have to be, for Nathan. It's hard but I just want him to get better." Alison nodded and patted the seat next to her.

"The nurse is in there so I said I'd give him some privacy for a few minutes. I'm sure he wouldn't mind if you were in there at the same time though ?" Alex shook his head, "I know he wouldn't, but barging in half way through a sponge bath or something probably isn't what he wants me to see first," he half smiled at her again. Alison looked intently at Alex, he did look better but she could see the enormous strain he'd been under. She squeezed his hand, "now look, I want you to help us out as your in-laws if you can." Alex nodded, "Anything, what can I do for you ?"

"When Nathan comes home he's going to need everyone a lot for the first couple of weeks, he's lost a lot of weight, he hasn't any strength and it's just going to take a couple of months to get him properly back on his feet. Sometimes, with my husband, the twins, the cat and just life in general, well what I'm asking Alex is if we can take it in turns to look after him ?" Alex's eyes filled up and he gave her his killer smile, she wasn't stupid, she knew he needed to be part of things, she knew how desperately ill he'd become too because of the strain. He leant forward and hugged her, she hugged him back. Just then the nurse appeared.

"All finished," she smiled, then pointed at him. "I really hope you're Alex ?" He nodded starting to stand up. "Well thank God for that, he hasn't stopped bleeting on about you for the last ten minutes." Alex reddened and smiled from ear to ear. "Can I go in now ?" He asked looking at both women. The nurse patted him on the shoulder as she walked away. Alison nodded, "of course," you never need to ask. "Thank you," he drew in a deep breath and walked inside.

Nathan lay on his back looking up at the ceiling, his bruising was looking worse before it got better and his stomach looked so concave through his grey pjs. Alex had kissed and held him in those so many times it made his stomach turn over to see them on him now, badly hurt and in pain. They looked intently at each other. "More stuff from people at school ?" Nathan asked with his husky voice. "Ahuh," Alex nodded and walked over to sit carefully on the edge of the bed. He propped the bag up between his feet. "How are you feeling ?"

Nathan closed his eyes and opened them again slowly, "the pain's pretty constant and I feel kind of surreal, it's hard to explain." Alex nodded and put his hand gently on his forearm. Nathan moved his arm up until their hands curled around one another's. Alex looked down at their joined hands and smiled. "That feels so good," he said. "Yes it does, the more you touch me the faster I'll heal, I think." Alex looked up from their hands, his eyes examined Nathan's face, "well then I'd better hurry up and do this," he breathed as he bent across the bed and touched his lips to Nathan's. It was a gentle kiss, again without pressure, as he pulled away Nathan kept his eyes shut for a moment. Alex wondered if he'd hurt him, "Nate ?" Slowly he opened them and sighed deeply. "When I'm better will you give me one of our normal kisses ?" He pleaded. Alex looked pained and stroked his cheek with the backs of his fingers, "oh baby, yes of course I will ! I just don't want to hurt you at the moment, I know you're very sore." Nathan smiled and then winced, his head was throbbing from being awake for most of the day.

"I can't wait for that," he whispered, his strength deserting him already. Alex watched him carefully and though it took all his reserve, he knew he had to leave even after such a short time. Nathan's eyes began to close, "I'm sorry, I just get so tired," he whispered. "Nothing to be sorry about, I told you that," Alex whispered as he stroked the good side of his face. Nathan let out a sort of purr, "I wish you could stay and do that all the time." His voice got quieter and quieter.

"Me too," whispered Alex, "Me too." He stood up and leant the bag against the bedside table,"goodnight my love, sleep well," he walked quietly out of the room.

He blew out a deep breath as he stood leaning against the closed door for a moment and then looked over at Alison. They smiled weakly at each other. "He is getting better," Alison said quietly. Alex nodded, " I know," he looked down at the floor and shuffled his feet. "This is so hard on you Alex, I know that, but I think what you decided to do in staying strong for him is the best thing for you too."

Alex inhaled deeply and didn't say anything. "Go home," Alison said, not unkindly, "have lots of food, love from your family and sleep, come here every day and see him, that way you'll both get through it better and faster." Alex drew in another deep breath and walked over to hug her goodbye. She embraced him with motherly concern and sent him on his way.

Alex arrived home just as his mother appeared having picked up Jess from school. She was thrilled to see him looking so much better but she also noticed the slightly slumped shoulders and pre-occupied look that just wouldn't leave, not matter what he did. "How's Nathan ?" She asked as Alex climbed onto a kitchen stool. "Yes he's ok," he sighed, trying to offer up a smile.

Jess passed him a drink and a doughnut, "eat this, you're too skinny," she said in a demanding tone. "Er..no thanks to the doughnut," Alex pushed the plate away. "You eat it or I'm telling Nathan !" She warned. Alex's stomach felt cold for a second, it still hurt to think of him lying there so ill but he remembered his positive path forward and slid the plate back in front of himself. "Alright terror," he tried to smile at her. She winked back and started to help her mother unload the groceries.

After he'd eaten his doughnut, Jess pulled Alex by the hand and took him upstairs. She lay on his bed reading while he caught up on some school work. It was so good to have her around, despite his promise to himself to be strong and not let Nathan down, he was finding it hard. After dinner she curled up next to him on the sofa to watch 90210. "What do you think of the gay crumpet in this ?" She suddenly asked.

Alex laughed, "well, not much so far. I quite liked that Ian bloke but then they made him a totally unbelievable fraudster just to get Teddy's attention, - who by the way in real life is 33 not 17 !" "No ?" Jess looked shocked. "Yup," said Alex quite assuredly.

"How do you know that ?"

"I googled him one night."

Jess laughed, "ooh I'm telling Nathan," "It was BEFORE Nathan, you cheeky girl, when I could only dream...!"

He looked wistful for a moment and Jess wondered how to distract him again. She was about to channel surf when Alex's phone buzzed. He picked it up and read for a moment then his wide grin broke through and his cheeks flushed a little. Jess smiled, "that has got to be Nathan texting you ?" Alex nodded and started tapping back.

Another moment later and the phone vibrated again. This time Alex's eyes became watery immediately, "Oh Nath..." he breathed. "What's he sent you ?" Jess asked, slightly worried at her brothers face. He turned the phone toward her.

"His mother must have taken it for him," Alex croaked. It was a picture of Nathan in his bed with his eyes shut, lying on the non hurt side, bruised and with the drip clearly showing but most of all, patting the empty space on the bed

173

beside him. "Oh, Alex that's sad..." said Jess. She peered at the picture more thoroughly, "he looks very bruised and tired but apart from that, he must be getting a lot better because he's kind of joking with you, so that's a good sign isn't it ?" Alex nodded, "yes, it is."

"Hey, let's send him back a picture of you ?" Alex shook his head, "no...., well doing what ?" Maybe it wasn't a terrible idea he mused.

"Erm, just look like you are now, kind of sweet and missing him, I know, touch your engagement ring and look hard into the lens with a bit of a smile, he'll like that, you know it'll say 'look I'm missing you too !'" "Yes sir, David Bailey," Alex saluted.

"Who's David Bailey ?" Jess asked, clambering into a better position to take the photo. "Never mind," Alex shook his head at her ignorance and did as she suggested with the ring.

"That's a really good photo," she said, staring at the phone. She showed it to him. " Yeah it is," she pressed send and Alex took the phone back to look at Nathan's picture again. He leant back on the sofa and sighed. Jess nudged his leg.

"Thanks for being so great sis," Jess nudged him a bit harder grinning. "Ow !"
She laughed at his reaction, "come on, let's watch something crappy and mind numbing, ooh look, 'The Only Way is Essex."

"Oh God, that really is mind numbing crap," Alex smiled. Ten minutes into the programme they were busy dissecting the characters. "I wouldn't marry Mark if I were Lauren," Jess shook her head.

"He's a wide boy twat," Alex answered making her giggle. "Ooh ooh, what about Joey, now he must be gay I mean look at him, what do you think bro ?" Alex shook his head, "no I don't think so, I just think he's really prissy and no one's as important to him as him." They carried on analysing everyone and wondered if Arg and Lydia really would get back together or not. Neither could decide if he'd actually cheated on her but she seemed pretty determined not to have him back at any rate.

Over the next few days Alex went back to school and did his best to distract himself. He threw himself back into lessons, he wasn't allowed to do hockey yet as some of his bruising hadn't died down and the bloody health and safety gestapo stepped in. Nathan's progress was slow but he did improve. Every day for the next week after school, Alex would hop on the bus to the hospital and tell him as much as he could about the outside world. Their talks got a little longer gradually but the head injury meant he tired really quickly and often Alex went home trying not to be deflated from yet another cut off conversation.

He missed their talking.

As he sat on the bus on the way home one night he felt quite tearful. It was great to be able to see him and to kiss him lightly but none of it was normal yet, he didn't have Nathan's attention, not fully, nobody could until his battered brain calmed and all the swelling completely receded. In no way did he hold it against him but boy did he miss him. As Alex looked down at his rucksack, trying to visualise which piece of home work to do first, two tears splashed across it, he dashed them away looking angry for a moment.

"Excuse me," a woman's voice spoke from the seat across the aisle, he looked up, they were almost alone on the upper deck, bar one teenager at the back, totally away with his ipod. Alex looked at the woman, "sorry were you talking to me ?" "Yes I was," she said with a kind smile, "I'm sorry to interrupt and I don't mean to pry but you're awfully young and nice looking to seem so upset, is there anything I could do to help you ? Do you need to borrow a phone and call somebody or anything ?"

Alex felt genuinely taken aback at her kindness. "No, that's really nice of you though, thanks for asking." He sighed and smiled back at her, "I've just come from visiting someone in the hospital that's all..." he trailed off.

"Oh dear I'm so sorry, they didn't erm, well they didn't...pass away did they ?"

"No, but it looked that way a week ago and it's been so tough, I'm trying to put on a brave face but seeing him lie there unable to really talk to me as normal because he gets so tired or is in pain, it's really hard. I miss his arms around me." Alex blushed, why was he telling her so much ? "Sorry that's a bit personal," he mumbled. "No it isn't, it sounds pretty normal to me. Believe me, I've heard so many hospital stories nothing could surprise or shock me. Is it your father ?"

"No, it's my fiance," Alex gave her a half smile, waiting for her shocked response. "Oh no, poor you," then seeing Alex's amazed expression she said, "it's not a shock, my son's gay too. He's a lot older than you though and we had the civil ceremony a few years back now. He emigrated to Australia last year with his husband." She smiled, "it's quite nice to talk to someone who's obviously as in love as Keith is with Simon." She shrugged looking wistful. "I miss him."

Alex's eyes were wide with surprise, "wow, I didn't expect you to say that !"

The bus turned a corner and he spied his stop in the near distance. "Well it was very nice talking to you, I hope you see your son soon, at least you can go on a lovely holiday when you do," he said, sliding his rucksack onto his shoulders. "It was good talking to you too young man, forgive me but what's wrong with your fiance ?" Alex looked grim, "he fell and hit his head very hard, he's got a fractured skull." The woman sat bolt upright and immediately opened her handbag, they were almost at the stop now. "Here, take this," she pushed a cream coloured business card at him which said 'Headway.'

"I run a charity for victims of head injuries and a support group for their loved ones," Alex's head snapped up, "I can't believe it...!" The woman laughed as the bus began to brake. "Fate !" She smiled and Alex nodded, "bye, and thanks," he waved the card, slipped it into his jeans and shot down the stairs off the bus.

Later that night Alex discussed the woman he'd met on the way home and showed his parents her card. "I know this charity," said his dad, "mm, good people. You know if you two are serious about a job as soon as you leave school, you might want to look into this place. You've unfortunately got an insight into how people will be feeling who get in touch so this could be just the ticket for your first employment. I'd ring her up and offer a few free hours a week if I were you son." Alex chewed thoughtfully, "Yeah you might be on to something there dad."

On the eleventh day since the accident, Nathan's mum rang to speak to Caitlin. "Don't tell Alex it's me so I can fill you in on Nathan ok," she started. "Absolutely," Caitlin answered and kept her face expressionless as Alex ate his breakfast a few feet away. "Right, well mother to mother this is what I want the boys to know and what I don't want them to know. Nathan had what they call a linear skull fracture which is the best to have apparently in terms of good prognosis," "Ok," Caitlin answered carefully so as not to give away any clue about who she was talking to.

"However, he did have a tear in the dura, the membrane around the brain, which accounts for the severe bruising and panda eyes, as the crack extends round into the lower skull. That's why he's been a bit more poorly than just a straight fracture. There was a heavy risk of infection hence the intravenous antibiotics. Anyway, he can come home tomorrow is the good news. He's not as well as he might be because of the shock that he went into after the event, he's lost twelve pounds in twelve days." Caitlin gasped and then jumped as Alex looked at her, "oh good god Sue, you spent as much as that ?" She quickly improvised feeling foolish.

Alex checked her expression carefully, before returning to his food. It was probable that his mother's shopaholic friend Sue would over spend so his thoughts quickly turned back to what to bring to Nathan that afternoon. "Well done," Alison said, "anyway, so he's coming home tomorrow and the best news is that he should make a full recovery. We've decided not to tell him about the dura or quite how far down the injury extends though. I can just see the two of them looking up 'linear skull fractures,' on the internet and becoming terrified so if we can keep it between us I'd be grateful."

"Of course," Caitlin answered. "Well don't spend any more money today then and let me know what time you're dropping that off tomorrow won't you." "I will, it will be so wonderful to have him home Caitlin, I just can't tell you. Thanks for all the support you and Christopher and of course Alex have given, it's been so hard, I don't know how we'd have got through without you. "You would have done the same for us" Caitlin answered, "well it means a lot to us. How's Alex today ? He seemed a lot better yesterday ?" "You're right," said Caitlin carefully, "a really big improvement there, it's been tough though, it really has, they love each other so much."

"I know, I'm looking forward to the day they sit down to dinner together again and come home with those big silly grins on their faces," "Me too," smiled Caitlin.

"I'd better go," Alison, answered "take care and I'm sure we'll see you at some point tomorrow." "Will do, bye for now," Caitlin smiled and set the handset back in its cradle. Alex frowned, suspicious. "Mum ?" She turned trying not to look caught out, "yes ?" and started folding some laundry. "What's she dropping off tomorrow, and how come she knows so much about me and Nathan ?" He asked with an edge to his voice.

" Well she knows about you two because she's one of my oldest friends and as for what she's dropping off, never you mind !" she sounded slightly pissed off, "something which I am looking forward to is all you need to know, nosey !" Alex blushed, "sorry, I didn't mean to be." It suddenly dawned on him that maybe it was something girly that he really didn't want to know about. His mother squeezed his arm, "don't worry about it darling, right, now I must get on, wolf that lot down then it's off to school with you." He smiled back at her and did as she asked.

Nathan hadn't been told about his release date either, all he'd been asked by his mother was to think of what he would most like to eat. His appetite had been awful since the accident and now the shock had worn off he really needed to eat to aid his healing and speed it up ten fold.

He frowned, "Mum I still feel like I've been run over by a truck, I just can't think of anything appetising at all !" Alison looked at her son and tried to recall all his favourite things. "Ok then, we'll go through a list, when anything grabs you tell me and that's what we'll try." "Ok," said Nathan. His mother began, she made him laugh a few times with some daft suggestions as well as roast dinners, burgers and sandwiches. Nothing seemed to appeal at all until she got to cereal, "Shreddies !" Nathan exclaimed suddenly. "Oh my God mum, I really want a big bowl of shreddies with milk and too much sugar !" His mother laughed and patted his leg, "alright darling, then that's what we'll get you," she smiled and got up from his bed to head for the near by Tesco local.

Forty minutes later she poured milk over and heaped two teaspoons of sugar onto a mound of shreddies in a home bowl and handed it to him. Nathan fell on it like a starving man and started shovelling the food down. "Wait wait just a second there darling, you're stomach can't manage being stuffed like that just yet." He nodded and slowed down a little, grinning at her from behind his bulging mouthful. She was right though, as his stomach filled he quickly became too stuffed to eat any more and lay back moaning gently on the bed.

"Oh God I'm going to burst," he groaned. She smiled and kissed him on the forehead, beginning to pack things up for the night. "Well I hope not, that would mean getting you home tomorrow would be difficult and having Alex over to celebrate for a bit even harder." She turned back to him and saw his eyes wide as saucers. "Is that true ?" Alison nodded. Nathan's face split into a huge grin. "I'm going home tomorrow ?"

"Yes my love you are. Your Dad's doing the night shift with you tonight so I'll just ring and find out where he is, I'll be back in a sec." She left the room as Nathan grinned up to the ceiling. He felt elated. Gingerly he raised himself up on his elbows and reached into yesterday's M and S bag that Alex had brought, sliding out his favourite T-shirt. It smelt of Alex, his warm skin and his aftershave. He slipped it up by his head, its smell was intoxicating. He drifted off to sleep with his cheek nestled up against it, imagining Alex's there instead tomorrow. He had the best sleep.

In the morning Nathan woke to only a little pain and tiredness, he was definitely on the mend. To his embarrassment he was to be wheel chaired to the car as a precaution but he had a fair few tests to complete before they would actually let him home. His father made him a big bowl of Shreddies with lots of sugar again and a cup of tea. He sat up in bed to eat and drink and watched the news while he ate. David sat at the foot of the bed watching the news one minute and filling in the Times crossword the next. "You can really do that can you Dad ?"

Nathan looked impressed. His father smiled slightly shyly for a moment and shrugged, "it's not really as hard as people say it is." Nathan looked amazed, "you do know that there's a reputation attached to people who complete it within a certain number of hours don't you ? Like you should join Mensa type of reputation." His dad smiled and shrugged again. Nathan sighed, he was starting to feel a bit agitated all of a sudden, he didn't know exactly what time he'd be allowed home but he couldn't wait. Just as he was starting to wonder how he'd pass the hours, a nurse came in with the doctor and a lot of questions began.

It was embarrassing to have to say whether he'd been to the loo that morning, had it been both, had he managed alone, all of that kind of stuff. Nathan knew they had to know and that they were used to it every day but he still reddened. All his answers seemed to satisfy them and then it came to walking. He gulped, he had been out of bed to the bathroom several times but the thought of actually being up and around now on a daily basis suddenly scared him. He realised that the trauma of the fall might be making him very wary but he was still scared.

"So," the consultant said, "shall we see you walking?" Nathan swung his legs over the side of the bed as his dad stood up, ready to lend assistance. The nurse came to his right side, ready to be his safety net should he stumble. He stood up and felt a slight headrush. "How's that?" Asked the consultant. "It's ok, I feel a bit light headed but I think it's the excitement," Nathan said truthfully. The consultant smiled, "can't wait to go eh? That's a good sign. Well let's take a little walk with you, just down to the other end of your ward and back ok?" Nathan nodded, stepping into his Crocs and wandered through the held open door. The four of them walked slowly to start with until he started commenting on things around him, even to walk through the slightly creepy feeling ward was a refreshing change for him.

At the far end they turned around and walked back, slightly faster this time and to everyone's joy, he was distracted enough by his surroundings not to have to concentrate on putting one foot in front of the other. It seemed entirely natural. When he got back to the room there were a few more tests, a couple of bloods, blood pressure, etc...then he was encouraged to go and have a bath. Luckily his en-suite loo also had a tub, it wasn't the nicest one he'd ever seen but it would do the job and as his dad stood by and watched him lower himself into it his heart beat faster, going home was imminent.

Chapter Twelve.

Alex handed in all his homework at school that morning, there was a lot as he'd caught up on the few days he'd missed but at last it was all done. He was still trying to be positive and threw himself into lessons with as much attack as he could. He seemed low to those closest to him but it was a vast improvement on the previous week. His teachers still saw how thin and drawn he looked but he was alert and participating again so they left him alone and hoped it would pass.

At lunch he sat and talked to the guys from hockey, they sorely missed his skill and wanted to know when he'd be allowed back on the team. They chatted as they ate and Alex had the usual invitations to rugby games, parties and concerts but try as he might he just couldn't be completely himself. There was a big hole in his heart. He glanced over to the next table as his hockey mates messed around, lunch was almost over. His heart lurched as he saw Nathan's two best friends stop and talk to a couple of the guys from his art group. They were obviously talking about him and it made Alex miss him all the more desperately.

He sighed and sagged a little in his seat just as his phone buzzed in his pocket. He fished it out and read, "since you aren't in hockey, will pick you up at the same time as Jess today. Be ready at 3pm, love mum. X" He touched the phone onto 'vibrate only' and got up as the bell went. He didn't really care what time he was being picked up, apart from texting Nathan to let him know when he'd be coming over of course. He rubbed his forehead as he walked into maths, 'be positive, be positive,' he whispered to himself but his face was grim as he took his seat. If he didn't get a proper Nathan hug soon he'd go crazy. Glancing up at the clock he saw an hour and a half left to go. "Good," he thought as he opened his 'Applied Maths,' text book, at least at home he could bury himself in a dvd with Jess for a couple of hours, thank God for her. He sighed and bent over his work wishing this day would be over and his mood so much better.

Alison and Caitlin had been in constant contact through out Nathan's injury. Today they were both excited and nervous for their sons, running about getting everything done while trying to remain calm and not give the game away to Alex, besides, they didn't want to build his hopes up in case something went wrong. But it didn't. Caitlin collected both her children at 3pm, noticing immediately that Alex's mood had shifted down a gear again but she wasn't worried as she knew what awaited him very shortly.

When they got home Alex didn't seem keen to get changed right away, he flung his stuff in a corner and slumped onto the sofa. This was no good, but Caitlin had a plan. "Alex I saw some jeans that I thought would look good on you today, I couldn't resist them, go and throw them on will you ? If they're no good I'll take them back tomorrow." He rolled his eyes, he really wasn't in the mood but his mum was so good to him he acquiesced. "Ok," he replied and grabbed his rucksack on the way.

Alex looked at the jeans neatly folded on his bed, a new t-shirt sat next to them. He quickly slipped both items on and smiled at himself in the mirror. It lifted his mood so much that he dabbed on some Hugo Boss and gelled his hair up too. Slipping on his favourite blue converse he was pretty damn happy with the look. He'd wear it for Nathan he decided and bounded down the stairs to thank his mum. She looked up at him as he ran and threw his arms around her.

"Thanks mum, it's a really fab outfit, I love it, and you !" Caitlin laughed at her son, it was good to see him happy. "You soppy nitwit ! But I do love you too." She squeezed him back. "Now then, sorry to ask love but I'm a bit behind with stuff, would you do me a favour and drop these brownies and that lasagne off at Nathan's house for me ? I know they haven't had much time to cook so I thought I'd do something nice for them."

"Yeah sure, want me to go now ?" Alex asked. "I can do it and be back in time to make the 4.00pm bus to the hospital if I hurry." Caitlin hid her thoughts very well, "good plan love, take a jacket, it's going to get chillier later." "Right," said Alex and reached for his coat by the front door. He slipped it on and put the lasagne and brownies into a bag, blew a kiss to his mum and was gone.

He walked happily up the hill, nothing to take to Nathan today so he could drop the food off and just hop on the bus outside his house. There were a few bits left over from people at school but he'd take them tomorrow he decided, space it out a bit. He turned the corner nearing Nathan's and despite knowing he wouldn't be there, he was glad to be able to be in those familiar surroundings again. Perhaps he'd ask Alison if he could go up to his room, have a closer look at that dog drawing, pick a top to take him to wear on the day he left hospital.

Yes, that was a husbandly thing to do he thought and smiled as he crunched across the gravel and walked up the steps to his front door. As he stood on the top step and rang the bell, Alex's heart beat increased, he felt a bit breathless all of a sudden, as if he expected to see Nathan anyway. He shook himself and thought, 'don't be stupid !' The door swung open. Alison Henderson beamed a warm hello and ushered him in. She looked much better than a few days ago Alex was pleased to note, Nathan must be well on the way to recovery.

"How lovely to see you again Alex," she smiled, "oh that was so kind of your mum to do that," she thanked him profusely as she peered into the bag, but then she stood there oddly and seemed to glance nervously over his shoulder. He frowned, "are you alright ?" She nodded and patted his arm, "yes I'm fine thanks, I tell you what, I'll just go and put this little lot in the larder, please stay for a quick cup of tea will you ?" Alex was desperate to run outside and jump on the earliest bus but he didn't want to let her down and he felt sorry for her too, he knew how she must be feeling.

"Erm, ok well just a quick one," he smiled, "I'm heading off to see Nathan shortly." She was already half way toward the walk in larder, "great, well go through to the living room, I'll be right in."

"Right," Alex dropped his jacket onto the back of a kitchen stool and turned to walk into the living room behind him.

For a moment he couldn't believe what he was seeing. As he stepped over the threshold, a movement caught his eye and then with a huge double take both of them locked on to Nathan.

Getting up from the sofa, pale, less bruised, smiling and dressed in a white T and jeans was his Nathan. "Hello my love," he whispered. After a stunned second Alex gasped,"Oh my God !" Nathan blushed at the look on his face. Alex crossed the floor in a second and took his lover in his arms. He squeezed him tight, then pulled away a little and asked, "your ribs are ok aren't they ?" "Yes," said Nathan so Alex squeezed them tighter. Nathan laughed and for the first time in two weeks, totally forgot about his head.

"But I do need to breath," he giggled. Alex loved the sound, it set his heart racing. He pulled away and looked into his eyes, "have I really got you here ? Are you really back ?" "Yes," Nathan breathed, "and I want a proper Alex kiss." "No need to ask," Alex breathed, taking his face in both hands he pressed his lips on to Nathan's and kissed him with every fibre of his being. When he stopped Nathan felt genuinely breathless. "My God, one of those a day and I'll be perfect in no time,"he gasped. "You already are," said Alex, stroking his red cheeks and kissing him again.

"Ahem...erm, I'm sorry to interrupt this lovefest but someone has to take about four hundred huge pills right now so can you break apart for five seconds before resuming your activities ?" Alison stood blushing in the doorway, but she couldn't be happier.

They still stood with their arms around each other and Alison had never seen such a dramatic improvement in someone's bearing in such a short time as Alex. He was a different person from the one who'd come in just seconds before. He shone, there was no other description. He turned his head and pecked Nathan's cheek lightly before letting him go.

Nathan lowered himself carefully on to the sofa as Alex lowered himself to the floor. Alison hadn't exaggerated that madly on the pills after all, some of them were huge and Alex's heart thrummed with worry for a moment at the number. Two big oval black ones, two mini white aspirin types, two two tone pills like antibiotics and two small red ones. "How many times a day do you have to take those ?" He gulped. "Four," said Nathan, trying not to think about it as it scared him too.

"Why ?" Whispered Alex nervously. "Just to keep the swelling down, and any pain and infection away," Alison answered in her most 'it really isn't anything to worry about,' voice. The boys looked at her, wanting that to be the truth as she passed the pill cup and water glass to Nathan. He started to swallow them two at a time.

"Look at your faces," Alison forced her most reassuring smile, "I know what you need," she disappeared out of the room for a moment. Alex looked into Nathan's eyes, he blinked slowly back at him. "I can't believe you're really here, it's so fantastic,". Nathan grinned and coloured, "it's so wonderful Alex, my heart's hammering like mad." Alex gave him his killer grin. "Oh God that smile," Nathan trembled and leant back against the sofa. Alex laughed his lovely laugh, making Nathan's face widen into an even huger grin. Alison walked back into the room with a plate of brownies and had her week made. "Well look at you two ! Left alone for thirty seconds and you're the happiest people around."

Nathan looked at her, he reached down for Alex's hand and felt his fingers curl around his hand. "It's just so good to have him back mum," he smiled at Alex who looked completely blown away with joy. "I said you were the soppiest people ever and I'm right !" Alison smiled. "Now I'm leaving these here, I've got to go to the supermarket and I'm taking the twins, - lucky them ! Your dad's out until 6pm so you two now have the place to yourselves for a bit, enjoy and be good," she winked, picked up her canvas shopping bags from the kitchen counter and was gone.

" I just love your mum," Alex stated. Nathan grinned and then reddened at the way he was staring at him. "I still can't believe you're back," Alex breathed, shaking his head and moving up onto his knees. He leant across Nathan and thumbed his left cheek very gently. It felt so heavenly Nathan closed his eyes for a moment. When he opened them Alex nodded toward the fracture site, "can a I touch you there ?" He asked nervously. "Very gently, yes," said Nathan.

Alex took his left hand, he found he was shaking a bit, and carefully, as light as a feather, smoothed his fingers over the wounded area. "Does that hurt ?" Nathan gently shook his head, "no." Alex took his fingers away, he'd wanted to be less scared of what had happened, somehow feeling the hurt part and knowing Nathan was healing under it did that.

He sat back on his heels and held Nathan's hand, " so you can get up and walk about now can you ?" "Well yes but not for long, I need to put some weight back on as I lost too much too quickly so I really haven't got much energy yet," said Nathan. "You're telling me, look at that concave stomach !" Alex looked appalled. "You're a fine one to talk, cocktail stick ! I've seen more meat on Frankie Detorri's whip. What the hell happened to you in the last two weeks ?" Nathan raised an eyebrow as Alex reddened and looked down at his own non existent stomach which growled right on cue. Nathan laughed but Alex kept his head down, sometimes the last two weeks took it out of him so much and suddenly he felt well and truly shattered.

He didn't want to dwell on why he'd skinnied down so much too. "Hey," said Nathan, sensing his depression. "Alex," he breathed, "I'm sorry, I know this must have been hard for you. Has it...., has it been bad ?" Alex looked up but didn't meet his eyes, " I don't really want to talk about it," he said in a quiet voice. "God I'm sorry Al," Nathan manoeuvred himself into a sitting position. "Hey, come here, please," he whispered kindly.

Alex moved to sit beside him. Nathan folded his legs up and drew him into his arms. Alex buried his face into Nathan's shoulder, he wasn't going to cry, he just needed to be held so much. He sighed as Nathan kissed the top of his head and said, "are you ok my love ?" Alex sighed again and spoke with a muffled voice against the shoulder, "it's just been so hard," he gulped. At first it was a huge shock and I thought you might...., I thought you were going to....., I thought,.... I can't say it," he shook his head. "You thought I might die ?" Nathan finished for him. Alex squeezed his ribs and winced, "don't !"

"I thought I might too," Nathan said in an awkward voice. Alex pulled away and looked into his eyes. "Did you ?" He was horrified. Nathan nodded and gulped, "yes at first it was so awful, I've never had pain like it. Nothing made sense either, I thought I was going mad. Then there was the night when the pain was so bad and nobody was around, I was alone for half an hour that's all, but in that time I was too weak to call for help and I thought I was dying. All I could do was concentrate on the clock and think 'don't die, don't die.'" He gulped going very white. Alex felt sick, "fuck Nathan, why the hell didn't you call me ?"

"I couldn't even do that, I had no energy to pick anything up or even move my fingers properly. There were other strange things, awful times," he blanched again, " I don't know if I want to talk about them now..." "Sssh," Alex folded him into his shoulder, careful to mind his head. They held each other, their hearts thumping from the weeks of utter fright. "You're ok now," Alex whispered, "you're ok now my love." He rubbed his back soothingly, "I've got you, there's only forward and better for you now Nate." Nathan rubbed him back, "I'm sorry it was so hard on you, I really am."

"Don't be, it wasn't your fault, and it's in the past now. Let's look to the future. How long til your head heals properly ?" "Another six weeks," Nathan answered. "So let's organise a really special relaxed weekend, just the two of us for then shall we ?" He pulled away to smile at Nathan who looked back lovingly at him, "I'd love that." He said softly. "Me too," said Alex and kissed him full on the mouth.

They lay back against each other, sighing gently as all the stress and pain started to ebb away. Nathan shifted down onto his back and Alex came with him. Tiredness overcame them both and when Alison returned home she had to immediately quieten the twins, pointing out the boys and covering them with a blanket. As noiselessly as possible the Henderson house got on with homework and supper and all the usual things.

They slid the living room door half closed and checked on the sleeping couple from time to time. By nine o'clock David was yawning and rubbing his eyes, he'd been getting up at 5.15am for the last few weeks to make a bit of extra money and it was taking its toll. He kissed Alison as they stood looking at the two boys. "What they must have been through this past few weeks," he shook his head and wrapped an arm around her. "It's been tough as his dad let me tell you, but my God Alison, if it were you in that bed I think I might have died of shock."

Alison's stomach leapt with butterflies, even after nineteen years together her husband still shook her up inside. "Don't," she whispered, "it doesn't bear thinking about." They watched the boys for a moment longer and then turning out a couple of lamps, left them sleeping in the dimly lit room and headed up to bed.

Alex's leg jolted them both awake, that sudden shock of a muscle spasm that doesn't hurt but makes you jump. "What the fuck !" He sat up immediately. He took in the dimly lit surroundings, blinked hard and rubbed his eyes looking back at Nathan who smiled sleepily up at him. "We fell asleep ?" He beamed groggily. "Must have," Nathan croaked. They both giggled, "Brilliant !" Alex smiled and then twisted his watch around to look at it. "Christ !" He breathed. "What ?" Nathan looked concerned. "It's bloody 1am !" "No!" Nathan grinned and propped himself up on his elbows, "cool, I feel like a properly naughty teenager now."

Alex threw his head back and laughed making Nathan press his finger to his lips. "Shit, sorry !" Alex giggled. They grinned again at each other and Alex reached over to stroke his palm down Nathan's cheek. "God, it's so good to be able to do this with you again, I just can't believe it," he whispered. Nathan lay back down on the sofa and nodded gently, " I know it's the best." He looked tired Alex noted and got off the sofa to fetch another blanket. He pulled it up around Nathan's chin and crawled underneath the side which draped off the edge of the sofa, wrapping it around his shoulders so that he sat next to his head on the floor. "What are you doing ?" Nathan asked groggily.

"You need some sleep my love," Alex reached up to cup his face. Nathan shut his eyes and groaned gently, "ok," and was at once asleep. Alex gulped as he watched him. His heart hammered worriedly for a while but Nathan slept peacefully, his chest rising and falling rhythmically and at last Alex's concern dissipated. He still watched him for a minute but then felt his own eyes begin to close and let his head droop to the edge of the sofa. He didn't expect to fall asleep that way but it just felt so nice to rest there for a moment before he got more comfortable. He prayed for Nathan's strength to return incredibly soon and for his skull to heal 100 per cent. He screwed his eyes up at such intense thoughts and felt so foggy brained that he couldn't be bothered to get up and make himself more comfortable, he'd just wait for a minute or two...maybe five.....he drifted off to sleep.

Addled with sleep, Alex felt a gentle hand lift his head and re-lay it onto a pillow. It made him sigh with delight, was it his imagination or was this pillow warm ? He opened an eye and looked up at Alison bending over him as he lay beside the sofa, she was tucking a thicker blanket around him. "Sssh, oh I'm sorry, I didn't mean to wake you love," she smiled. "It's got a lot chillier and you didn't look comfortable." Alex nodded sleepily and she touched his cheek affectionately. "Go back to sleep, it's only 5, I had to get up to do a bit of mending for the twins. I'll try not to disturb you again til 7am." She smiled and with drew to the kitchen. Alex was so tired and felt so cared for that he found it easy to drift back into a delicious sleep.

He woke again just after an hour later. The smell of fresh coffee and hot croissant filled the room making his stomach gurgle with hunger. He raised himself groggily up and looked at Nathan, pink cheeked and sleeping. He smiled with relief, he must be mending well now, he thought. Another stomach rumble and Alex had to investigate such delicious smells. He wrapped the thick blanket around himself and headed into the kitchen where he found Alison watching the news quietly and taking a tray of croissants out of the oven.

She slid them all onto a plate to cool and smiled at him, "good morning again." He nodded, "sorry to disturb you but my stomach wouldn't let me sleep any more." Alison laughed and pulled out a stool, "that's alright, sit. Everything does smell enticing I know. That's partly why I did it I think. My subconscious wanting to prod Nathan back to normality at every opportunity." She shrugged and looked toward the door. Alex understood entirely, "he'll be back to that sooner than either of us imagine I think, but in the meantime I don't blame you for trying to prompt him. I look for normal things with him virtually every second and I'm probably missing a million of them already because of it !"

They smiled kindly at one another. Alison sat at the consul and poured them both a coffee as she passed Alex the croissants, he took two and heaped blueberry jam onto the first before reaching for the nutella and going to town with it on the second one. As he ate, the hazelnutty chocolate spread was so tasty he sighed. "Hmm, the little things really cheer you up in a situation like this." Alison laughed.

"In a situation like what ?" Came the throaty husk from the living room door. They both jumped and turned to see a smiling Nathan with his hair all over the place, standing eyeing the food hungrily. He was wrapped in a soft orange and red checked blanket that was falling off his left shoulder and covered his right, all the way up to his ear. Alex grinned to see him and Nathan gave him a heart stoppingly lovely look back.

"Nutella !" he then exclaimed with a huge hungry eyed grin. Alex pulled out a stool and patted it, "we knew you couldn't resist, come and sit." Nathan blushed and made his way to the chair beside him. He sat carefully, not used yet to not worrying about his head, and smiled at both of them. Alison turned away to top up the coffee and Alex pulled Nathan's face toward him, kissing him full on the mouth. "Hello my love," he whispered. Nathan coloured enough for his mum to know what they'd been doing when she turned around but she didn't mind in the slightest, he was getting well, he was happy, and nothing else mattered more.

They couldn't stop grinning at each other as they ate, Nathan was hungrier than he'd been in weeks. He got through two nutella laiden croissant, one with jam and a slice of toast with butter and marmite plus a massive handful of blueberries. He groaned slightly and patted his belly afterwards. Alex glanced at it making him redden again, "yup, I can practically see that tummy getting huger already." Nathan laughed out loud and ran a self conscious hand through his hair. He looked back at Alex shyly and realised that they were both thinking the same thing, suddenly they wanted to be Nathan and Alex again, naked, groaning and loving each other with their hands.

He bit his lip and turned away. Alex swept a trembling hand through his own hair and turned away too, he didn't want to get hard at the table but he was already getting there fast. He couldn't stop thinking of Nathan lying in his arms gasping, close to coming while he stroked him and stroked him. Christ his hard on was rock solid now. He couldn't move. "Alex, would you get me some more milk please ?" Alison asked without looking up from the morning paper. Alex went white and looked straight at Nathan who frowned for a milisecond and then got it instantly.

He slid from his stool and padded gently across to the fridge, "here you go mum." He put the container down by her elbow. Alison looked up and noted Alex's white look and Nathan's sudden helpfulness, she'd missed something, that was for sure. She eyed them both with interest for a moment as she added more milk to her coffee but then something caught her eye and the milk crashed to the floor. "Oh !" She yelped. "Nathan you're bleeding !" She jumped up, grabbing a tea towel and pressed it to his face where blood streamed from his nose.

Alex thought he'd pass out. "NATHAN !" He screamed, and scrambled around the consul until his arms were firmly locked around Nathan's ribs. Between them, Alison and Alex lowered him to the nearest stool where he scowled angrily at them and with some effort pushed both off. "I,...am NOT...," he puffed with the effort at trying to detach Alex's hold on him, "made of bloody spun SUGAR !" He roared the last word, snatching the tea towel out of his mother's grasp and wiping at his already stopping nose bleed.

There was a stunned silence. He turned to look from one to the other. "For God's sake you two, you're going to have to stop acting like that, you scared the shit out of me ! It's just a nose bleed, I had them before the accident and I'll have them again, it's nothing to do with my head and I feel fine ok ?" Again silence. Nathan looked at their troubled silent expressions and sighed, "alright, I'm sorry, I know you both care, it just scared me when you reacted like that but I promise you I do feel fine."

He looked at Alex who rubbed his chin thoughtfully and exhaled slowly. "Alright Nate. Look I'm sorry too, it's just easy to get scared that's all, - I care." Nathan picked up his hand and kissed the back of it, "I know my love, thank you for that." Alison cleared her throat. " I didn't mean to panic darling, or to scare you, sorry." She shrugged. Nathan leant forward and hugged her, not letting go as she held him tightly back for a minute. "I love you mum, thanks for everything recently."

A little sob escaped Alison before she let go of him and shook herself back to normal. Alex smiled at her and then rubbed Nathan's arm. "But can we just at least check you out a bit, please ?" He nodded, "ok, what do you want to do ?" "Has the bleeding stopped yet ?" Alex gently pulled away the towel, tilting

Nathan's head back very slightly to look for blood. "Yes it has," he replied. "Can I clean you up ?" Alex thumbed his cheek gently. "Sure," Nathan smiled and let him fetch a clean towel and bowl of warm water. Alison rose to clear the plates and mop up the milk, then kissed her son lightly on the head, drama over. Her heart slowly returning to normal.

Alex worked very gently on Nathan's face. There had been a lot of blood in the first spurt, and it was all the way down his throat and chest. As he slid the damp towel up and down Nathan's skin, caressing his throat through the cloth, Nathan closed his eyes and prayed his mother didn't see. It felt so good. Alex rubbed carefully at the blood on his chest and accidentally grazed one of his nipples. Nathan let out an involuntary gasp making his mother's head snap up. He reddened but thankfully his erection died immediately, "shit I forgot to thank one of the nurses." He improvised. His mother smiled and shook her head, "nevermind darling, I'm sure you did it more than once every day knowing you. We'll send them all a big thank you card anyway so no one will be left out, how about that ?" He smiled at her, "thanks Mum, great idea." Alison shut the dishwasher and set it going before brushing his cheek gently and disappearing upstairs to dress.

Alex watched her go, listened to her steps disappearing toward her bedroom and then pulled Nathan to him and kissed him with all his passion and pent up longing. "Christ !" Said Nathan afterward, "fuck me !" Alex beamed and stroked his cheek, "God I'd love to, I really would...." He moaned. "Oh Alex," Nathan's arms came up around him, encasing his back and they kissed again as if nothing had ever happened. Nathan totally forgot about his head, until Alex's forearm grazed the area and made him jolt away from it. "Hey hey, shh, it's ok, I only brushed against you there." Alex soothed.

Nathan nodded and bit his lip. He didn't know what to say, he was so turned on and ready for Alex on one hand and so scared of hurting himself on the other. He trembled as Alex pulled him close, "it's ok, it's ok. I know what you're feeling, I do, but we'll be doing it soon enough I promise my love." He kissed the back of Nathan's neck and held him safe and close. "I love you so much." "Me too," breathed Nathan against his skin and they held each other for a long, long time.

Chapter Thirteen.

Every day after school for the next week and a half, Alex roared round to Nathan's and had dinner with him and his family, usually staying until late or falling asleep with him, clothed on top of his duvet, facing his sleeping beloved until Alison gently shook him awake to go home or to move to a blow up mattress on the floor. He was having breakfast on a rare occasion at his own home one morning when his mother said gently, "you know I think we need to have Nathan and his family round here for dinner. How about tomorrow night ?"

Alex's face lit up, "brilliant mum, cool ! I'll tell him after school today." "Wait, wait, wait...hold your horses sunshine, come back here a moment," Caitlin grabbed her sons sleeve as he bounded off his seat. "Just sit down for a moment my love." Alex frowned but did as she asked. "What's up mum ?" Caitlin drew in a deep breath, "now darling, don't be annoyed, - at least not until you've heard me out ok ?" He looked at her suspiciously, "go on." "The thing is my love, look, I'm a mum, well.... I just think between you and I that it might be nice if you left Nathan to his family for one evening.

They suffered so much, as did you when he was in hospital and they haven't had a night of just caring for him themselves. His mum hasn't got to be the mum again since he's been home, in the best sense, because you're always there. It's entirely understandable but at the same time maybe it would be a wonderfully kind thing to do to just let them be there for him tonight and then take the pressure off them having to cook for and look after you too for once. What do you say ?" She looked worriedly at her son who'd gone a bit white.

Alex sank his head into his hands and groaned. When he looked up he shook his head. "Mum I never thought of it !" He whispered. "Of course I'll do that for them. I'll miss him terribly but one night I can manage." Caitlin smiled at him and reached over to squeeze his hand, "phew, I thought you were going to be really angry with me !"

Alex smiled back and picked up his toast then put it down again, "but what do I tell Nate ? He'll be expecting me." "Why don't you tell him the truth. He probably hasn't thought of it either." She shrugged and started to clear away the breakfast. Alex nodded. "Yes of course, right, excuse me, I need to go and ring him right away." He disappeared into the living room for ten minutes then came back looking a little forlorn but red around the cheeks too. He plonked himself onto the nearest stool shaking his head. "What ?" His mother slid a bowl into the crockery cupboard and reached for another to dry off. "Nathan." Alex shook his head again and looked up at her. "He really is the most amazing person in the world, how did I get so lucky ?" Caitlin smiled, " I think he thinks he's pretty lucky too."

The next two weeks sped by, dinners were now alternated between the two houses to make it easier on Nathan's family. Caitlin insisted on Alex taking his own bed linen over and bringing it home again every few days to be laundered. The dads made sure he stuck to hockey practice and cross country after school as he was wont to skip it and run home early if one or other didn't make a point of enthusing him at dinner the night before. Nathan recovered slowly at first but by the beginning of week three his weight began to creep back up as his appetite fully returned, his eyes brightened and his movements became more relaxed and easy, less fearful. It was a wonderful time.

Another week passed and the boys sat around Alex's kitchen eating a lazy, late breakfast one Saturday morning. Alex smiled a red cheeked knowing smile at Nathan, they'd embarked on their first sexual night since the accident and coming all over each other had literally blown them away. Afterward Nathan gasped and puffed like a train but he'd exploded easily after six weeks of nothing and his whole body felt better for it, every nerve ending had sung with pleasure. He grinned back at Alex who placed a hand on his knee, "so, where shall we go in two weeks time to celebrate your head officially mending ?"

"Vienna," said Nathan without a thought. "Vienna ?" "Yes, I want to see the beautiful architecture, draw a building or two, swim in a hotel pool and go out for coffee and pastries at all those lovely street cafes." Alex laughed and shook his head, "not that you've thought about it or anything then ?" His mum wandered into the room and reached for the coffee pot, "what are you two looking so cosy about ? - well, when do you ever not look like that," she rolled her eyes in mock exasperation.

"Hi Mum, we're going to Vienna in two weeks time for a long weekend to celebrate Nathan healing. He's officially ok on the 29th." Caitlin smiled at Nathan as she sipped a little of her coffee, "oh thank goodness, that sounds like a wonderful idea guys, and how fabulous that you're nearly there now Nathan, good for you." He blushed nodding gently, "I know I can't wait, that's going to be such a great trip." He turned to Alex, "I've had another idea too. I know where I want us to go on our honey moon, I hope you don't mind, I did want us to go to the Maldives like you, but I've had a lot of time to look up beautiful places and to think about it all and I'd like to do two very different destinations." "Go on," Alex said, looking intrigued.

"Well how about the first week at this place in Colorado, it's a ranch, a dude ranch where you can ride every day western style, rope cows, camp out at pack camp one night and live tv and communication free for a week. Then we fly back home for the second week, jump on a short connecting flight to the south of france and stay in this lovely hotel in Cap Ferrat, the Grand Hotel Du Cap Ferrat to be precise. It's five star but they're doing a special deal this October only, to commemorate Hemmingway, who the bar's named after and who stayed there fifty years ago this year.

I had a brochure sent on each place so if you like the look of them we can book it over the next few days." Alex shook his head when Nathan finished. "That sounds incredible ! The best honey moon in the world. I love it Nate, let's do it." Nathan shrugged, "well wait til you see the brochures yet, you might not like either." Alex shook his head, "no need, I trust your judgement entirely." Nathan felt a shudder of pleasure, no one had ever said that to him before and truly meant it. It meant more than Alex could ever know and just made Nathan love him all the more.

"Ok, so let's book Vienna first," Alex slid off his stool and fetched his laptop, clicking it on and sweeping his arm across the granite consul to check for dripped tea or jam before he felt safe to put it down. They spent a happy half hour checking out hotels and deals until they found a central hotel in the heart of Vienna, close to all the most beautiful buildings and with incredible recommendations. "That looks fab," Alex grinned as they poured over it. "Sure does," Nathan agreed. They settled on the 29th July to 1st August and once they'd booked the room and flights, they clasped each other around the waist, grinning from ear to ear. "Oh God I can't wait," Nathan's voice cracked with emotion.

"Darling, my darling boyfriend," Alex husked against his ear. Nathan laughed at the wording making Alex crack up too and squeeze him even more tightly around the ribs until he almost couldn't breath. They pulled apart with red faces and Alex thumbed Nathan's glowing cheek, "beautiful," he breathed. Nathan blushed more deeply in return as a coy smile lit his face. "Alex..." he chastised gently. "You're gonna have to get used to hearing that," Alex grinned.

Two weeks crawled by. Suddenly with such an exciting 'let off the leash,' moment in the offing, Nathan was climbing the walls. He still couldn't chance running around outside or cycling, climbing anything, skate boarding, nor even swimming. Three days before they were due to fly to Vienna he had his final run of tests back at the hospital. He wanted to go alone despite Alex's desperation to go with him. In the end he relented that his mum could drive him there and sit in the different waiting rooms for him but no one else.

As he waited for her to get her coat and bag, Alex sat sullen and put out on the sofa beside him, moodily turning a five p over in his hands and looking at the floor. "Hey, come on, don't be like that..." Nathan asked, sounding a little hurt himself. Alex shrugged and looked across at him with a tight lipped expression. " I just don't understand it, we're getting married in a couple of months time, I'm going to be your husband and you won't even let me come to the most important thing that's happening to you at the moment."

Nathan shook his head and reached for his hands. "Alex, look at me. Sweetheart you are the only person I want instinctively at my side at all times, but this has been something so terrible and so frightening for me. If I have to be in a hospital with you scared shitless I want it to be because I have to put you through that, but on this occasion I don't. My mum can come, you can worry yourself to death in comfort here and I'm the only one out of the two of us who actually has to be in that horrible place with the terrifying memories again.

You see for me that's what it is, it's a horrible memory of when I honestly thought I might die. I don't want you there to be part of that thought process any more. You visited me when I was on the mend and I knew it, let's keep it that way. If God forbid I fall and break a leg, fine, come running to my side but please, this time, just let my Mum sit and sweat with me and let you be the wonderful reward I come home to, please."

Alex scanned his imploring worried face and sighed, "sure, I think I do understand. I just hate to let you go through this without me as much as you want to save me from it." Nathan squeezed his hand, "thanks." "Maybe that's why we're perfect for one another, we don't want to put each other through crap."

He smiled at Alex and turned at hearing his mother come down the stairs. He stood up, shrugging into his jacket. "Or maybe it's because we're just completely head over heels in love," he said softly. Alex blushed in response as he stood up, "Christ I'm going to worry about you so much this afternoon. Come back to me safe and sound my Nate won't you." He demanded, linking his arms around Nathan's neck and kissing him full on the mouth.

Alison became engrossed in the bottom of her handbag suddenly, and miraculously free as they broke apart. Slightly red faced she smiled at the two of them, "ready my love ?" Nathan nodded and broke away from Alex who stood rooted to the spot as they headed for the front door. "I'll come right back and tell you everything straight away," Nathan turned in the open doorway. Alex nodded, forcing on his most encouraging smile and then sank back onto the sofa trembling as soon as the door banged shut behind them."Fuck, fuck, fuck !" He whispered into his palms.

"Not quite how I'd have put it but I understand how you feel." Alex jumped as his Dad walked over to the sofa and gave his shoulder a reassuring little squeeze, he blanched immediately. "Blimey Dad, you nearly gave me a heart attack !" "Sorry," his Dad replied and smiled down at him. "I know you're going to worry so I want you to come and help me with something to keep your mind off things today." Alex groaned, "Oh God, not a 'keep Alex busy,' job ?" Christopher laughed and plucked his coat from the hooks by the front door, "yup, get moving, we're all set, just waiting for you," he snatched up his car keys and jangled them noisily. "We ?" Alex raised an eyebrow as he made his way over to pick up his fleece from the kitchen counter.

He zipped it up against the outside chill as his dad held the door open. "Yes, we, - move." He was virtually shoved over the threshold and a few seconds later, belted into the front seat and turning left out of the drive. "So where's this we then ?" He asked again. "You'll see." Alex leant his head back and shut his eyes, feeling sicker inside at the thought of Nathan down at the hospital without him than he was letting on. He found it slightly comforting to keep them shut for a couple of minutes, he hadn't slept well last night anyway, but then the car swung left onto gravel and came to a gentle halt.

He opened his eyes, feeling pretty exhausted, and looked up at Nathan's front door. He sat up worriedly for a moment but his dad put a comforting hand on his arm. The front door opened and the twins, Alex's sister and Nathan's dad poured down the steps in a merry stream and all clambered into the car in a silly mood. Alex glanced at them all feeling that it was in pretty bad taste to be so cheery. Mr Henderson understood immediately and gave his shoulder a slightly painful scrunch, "he will be fine Alex, trust me, I'm his dad and I know he will."

Alex gulped and wished people would stop saying that. His sister squeezed herself awkwardly across David and grabbed her brother around the neck, "ooh you're such a numpty sometimes but I do love you," she laughed. Alex coloured with frustration and wished he was on his own as they backed out on to the road. His black mood prevailed for another ten minutes until the silliness of the others started to rub off on him. "Did you lot OD on sugar at breakfast this morning or something ?" He asked a little grumpily. The twins, David and Jess all turned to grin stupidly at one another and then back to Alex where they nodded in unison. "Ooooh yes !" Jess exclaimed and they all burst into riotous laughter.

Alex shook his head, "what the hell did you eat ?" "Erm, well a huge stack of American pancakes with strawberries, blueberries and Canadian Maple syrup, then, even though Dad said no at first, you know that huge bar of chocolate that we bought at Cadbury world in Bourneville ? Well we ate half of that, it was delish !!!" She giggled. Alex looked astonished, "what ? Between four of you wispy little people, - not you David, sorry, but between you skinny minnies and

David, you ate 2.5 kilos of Dairy Milk for brunch ?" The twins and Jess nodded dumbly, their cheek dimples practically reaching their ears.

"You morons !" Alex said in shocked awe, "you're gonna have the most enormous sugar come down later today !" They all grinned back at him, "yup, but for now we're a ridin it high !" Jack guffawed and slapped his sisters palm high up in the air. Alex groaned and turned back in his seat, this was worse than being the only sober one at a mad party with slobbering gibbering drunk teenagers giggling all over you. "Give me strength !" He whispered through gritted teeth, making his father giggle as he glanced sideways at him.

"Don't you bloody start !"He admonished but then couldn't help his lips beginning to turn up at the corners too at the silly look on his fathers face. "Hey did you snaffle some too because I didn't see you ?"

"Nope," grinned his father, "it's just the pious look on your face, it's hilarious." "Shut up," Alex growled, trying to look afronted. "Ooh," the sugar rush crowd in the back seats cooed. He giggled and tried to pretend it was a cough. Everyone screamed with laughter. "Busted !" Jack shouted and Alex's hearty laughter rang out around the car making everyone else set off into peels of raucous laughter again.

When they pulled up at a pretty farm gateway with a rather twee old fashioned sign over head that read "Millets Farm," Alex couldn't think why it rang a bell. "Oh my God !" He suddenly remembered, "strawberry picking ?" "Not just those but raspberries too, and if we get enough, we're all making jam later today." Jess explained as they scrambled out of the car and headed toward the punnet collecting shed. "Oh good, just what you lot need, more sugar !"

His sister giggled and picked up two cardboard punnets before skipping off toward the neat rows of low growing plants with straw in between each one. Alex picked up two punnets too, and in spite of his worrying, he found himself feeling a lot happier surrounded by their silliness. He squinted up at the sun and thought, 'thanks God, thanks for this daft lot, but most of all, make my Nathan get the best results today, please, please. Thanks.' He looked back toward the field and headed over to the others, already bending amongst the plants and springing away every now and again with a small shriek at the size of a big hairy spider or two, and that was just his dad, he thought to himself and giggled as he squatted beside the first fat strawberries and started to fill his punnet to the brim.

It was absorbing work picking strawberries, well for the non sugar junkies anyway. Alex worked fast and scared off at least four enormous steroid spiders in the process of filling his first punnet. When it was almost too heavy to lift and the metal handle threatened to break away, he knew he had enough and looked toward the rest of his posse who were redder than they had been on the journey in. His sister had squashed strawberries running down her cheek and bleeding into her long brown hair as if she'd been in an accident.

For a second Alex blanched at the sight. He shut his eyes and swayed where he stood. "Please let him be ok," he whispered under his breath. Opening his eyes he saw his worried father closing the short gap between their rows and shrugging at him. "Son ?" Christopher Nesbitt-Hall looked anxiously at his white faced teenager and hoped he wasn't going to pass out.

Alex curled his lips together in a tight line and nodded toward Jess, Christopher didn't get it for a second and then he visibly blanched too. "Christ !" He said and looked back at Alex. "He's ok now, I'm sure of it." He squeezed his son's shoulder and watched him nod. "No seriously Alex, I mean it. Besides," he nodded back at the sugar rush gang who were now actively engaged in springing about squishing strawberries into each other's ears and down the back of one another's tops, "you can't possibly let that bunch of hopped up loons get you down, I know what you thought when you saw Jess just then but I ask you, how scary does she look now ?"

Just at that moment Jess looked toward them and waved, grinning manically. Alex looked at her, still shaken and rigid but then burst out laughing, as hard as his lungs could bear. She squinted back at him, "what ?" She mumbled. "Have I got something in my teeth ?" Alex couldn't stop laughing, his sides started to hurt. Jess stood there in mock perplexity with an over ripe strawberry squashed into and protruding from her from front teeth, a teeny tiny one complete with stalk, pushed into her right ear, four huge juicy ones, again all with stalks, entwined in the top of her hair like some bizarre crown and a couple of oddly shaped ones poking out from underneath the left shoulder of her once yellow top, now a lovely orange and red striped mixture of colours. Alex laughed so hard he had to cross his legs.

He bent double toward the strawberries and saw another huge spider peg it out of the undergrowth straight toward this dad's shoe. "Dad," he managed to squeak and poked his father in the calf. "What ?" Christopher looked toward him and then down at where he nodded and leapt away from the eight legged attacker. "JESUS !" He bellowed, making Alex scream with laughter even more and sink to the ground. His dad grinned down at him and snuk a surreptitious look at his watch. He wondered how Nathan was doing and made a mental note to pack up in half an hour. He wanted Alex showered, dressed and engaged in jam making or whatever the heck they all decided to do later, just in case the news wasn't good.

'Better he's in his own home,' he told himself grimly, just in case. He was no actor and looked down again, jumping at the frightened look on his son's face. "Hey, what's that look for ?" "What was your look for ?" Alex bounced back. "If you must know, I'm not overly thrilled at being surrounded by 8 legged things that want to scuttle up me at any second Christopher improvised." Alex's face split into a grin, his dad was the worst arachnophobe he'd ever known. "Come on then, let's take our punnets to get weighed shall we." Alex struggled to his feet, brushing off dust and straw from just about everywhere as his dad breathed a silent sigh of relief behind him.

Alex had 4 lbs of strawberries and his dad 3, they needed another 3 lbs from the sugar drunk gang to be able to make enough jars of strawberry jam for everyone to have one. It took a while to cajole the strawberry soaked troops into line but at last they had everything weighed, paid for and bagged. The grandmotherly lady at the tills tittered at their appearance, Alex shook his head, they were one hell of a mess. "Well done for driving dad," he said sarcastically, making Christopher groan and put his head in his hands. "Oh God my car...!" He breathed. "Oh well, I know a good hand valeting place, I'll take it in tomorrow."

The journey home was nearly as mental as the one going out, until the 2.5kg sugar rush hit its peak and the four chocolate laced loons had a massive come down. All at once the car went very quiet and Alex looked around at four very subdued fruit stained people, their eyes drooping as much as their mood, and within a few minutes they were all asleep. He turned back to his dad who glanced quickly at him and smiled, "nice when they're asleep eh ?"

"Do I sound really old for my age if I agree ?" Alex replied. Christopher laughed and ruffled his hair. The rest of the journey passed in absolute silence which was lovely at first, but as they pulled into his road, Alex's butterflies started again and he sort of wished their crazy banter was still going on. Especially when his dad had to cajole everyone out of the car in a miserable heap and almost carry them all to the bathrooms. Nathan's dad, Alex and his sister had the first showers, the advantages of a big house with three bathrooms, as the twins and Christopher waited for one to become free. The twins kept silent and sulky looking, their eyes drooping so Christopher sat at the breakfast stools and read the paper, leaving them to their listless slump on the tiled floor as they waited.

Thirty minutes later and everyone emerged, fresh, dry apart from their hair, and slightly brighter looking but still fairly sullen. Christopher didn't like the affect it was having on his pale cheeked son. Quickly he got everyone sitting around the kitchen consul, handed out hot drinks and biscuits and broke out the UNO. Most of them groaned saying it was a stupid game that no one had played in years, but after one addictive round and several chocolate digestives, they were all placing bets on themselves winning. Some of the earlier silliness kicked in again and the afternoon was away.

It's amazing how much noise six slightly knackered people and one pack of cards can make Alex pondered as he dealt the seventh game. He shuffled the cards and flicked one at each person in the round and back again until they all had seven each. He was determined to win this go and bit into a malted milk with ferocity. Win it he did. He thrashed the others who then pounced on him, well, the younger ones anyway, and dragged him to the nearest sofa, holding him down and tickling him until tears streamed down his cheeks. "Stop, stop.... please, no more...ha ha," he giggled breathless and red.

The chocolate biccies seemed to have done for the twins again and they were as crazy as earlier, Jess had to forcibly push them off, "ok, he's had.... groan, enough, puff,....I said, get...,off, him, NOW ! You big sugar freaks !" She laughed as they rolled off the sofa and chased each other into the kitchen. "Dad I'm SO hungry," said Jack, "can I get some jaffa cakes from the shop ?" "No you bloody can't," David replied, "you've had enough sugar to stun a whale." Jack's face sagged. Christopher got up and started to rummage in the fridge, "I'll make us all some cheese on toast ok guys ?"

Jack beamed. "No Chris, you really don't have to.." David Henderson started to protest. Chris held up a hand, "I insist, you drugged my kid with chocolate, the least I can do is stuff yours with saturated fat ?" He shrugged and everyone giggled. David got up to re-fill the coffee pot, "Thanks Chris, that's really nice of you." "Don't mention it," he patted his friend's shoulder and felt his stomach turn over. Nathan had been a long time. He hoped so much for everyone's sake that it was good news.

It didn't take long to make six rounds of cheese on toast, soon the consul was full with ketchup, Worcester sauce, slices of ham and tomato to make it even more tasty. The kitchen smelled lovely, fresh coffee, cheese, toast....and now only the odd, "please pass the ketchup...," or "who had the Worcester last ?" - could be heard amongst the odd rustle of pages being turned as everyone settled down to flip through newspapers and magazines. They were a deeply contented lot, if only it hadn't been for Nathan's tests and the waiting game they were playing, it would have been a perfect day. Alex unconsciously rubbed his hands clean on his jeans and sighed as the thought came back to him. His father glanced across the table and tried to smile reassuringly just as the front door opened. It went silent immediately.

"I'm alright," grinned Nathan. The kitchen erupted.

Their joyous cheers could be heard all the way down the street. Alex's dad saw his son's face go from chilled terror to total ecstasy in half a second and he couldn't have wished for anything more. Everyone howled with joy at Nathan's declaration and after much hugging and shrieking they pulled him over to the sofas and all gathered round him in a crazed chattering group gazing intently up at him for full details. He laughed aloud at their expressions, "God this feels like something out of the Waltons !" He exclaimed. "Yes yes, all very well but come on, fill us in !" His sister demanded.

Nathan went in to full details about the tests, all except the toilet questions, no need to talk about that. It didn't take long and as he finished, Christopher placed a round leather tray in his lap with a plate of cheese on toast on it, "eat," he commanded. "Oh no, I....." "EAT !" Everyone chimed at once. "God such bullies, ok ok !" Nathan laughed and tucked in immediately. "So, he's fully healed and can go back to normal life but he just has to watch it for the next year, try not to injure himself there again as it wouldn't do to have two such injuries in a short space of time. Other than that, we have our Nathan back." His mother concluded while Nathan ate.

Their eyes met for a moment and hers threatened to go very watery but she pulled herself together, this was a celebration and a moving forward moment and she wouldn't forget that. But no one else would ever know how much she and her son had cried in the hospital at the good news. It had been such a hard day but now she sat up taller in her seat and shook herself mentally to enjoy their celebrations.

"Now then you two, about this wedding," she smiled. The two young lovers beamed at one another and fell into a tight embrace as the shrieks of joy filled the rafters once more.

That night Nathan and Alex were too exhausted to make love but as dawn broke, they instinctively reached out for one another. Alex almost wept seeing Nathan's flushed beautiful face and hearing him gasp in ecstasy as he brought him over the edge. Nathan returned the favour and Alex had to cover his mouth with both hands to stop from crying out so loudly that he woke the house. Sated, they lay gasping and sweaty in each other's arms. It was a comfort to both to be able to feel their breath on each other's skins. As their breathing slowed, they couldn't seem to take their eyes off one other. "I love you," breathed Alex.

"Why do you love me ?" Nathan grinned. Alex's smile met his, "because I can't live without you. Because when I look at you I see everything that's good in the world and I want only you for life," he whispered, stroking and stroking Nathan's hair with his caressing fingers. Nathan gasped and shut his eyes for a moment. "Wow," he whispered back, blinking gently at his lover's face. "I love you too." He husked.

"Why do you love me ?" Alex breathed. Nathan blushed and his cheeks dimpled under his smile, filling Alex's stomach with butterflies. "God when you do that," he groaned.

"I love you because when I'm with you I can feel that my soul is truly alive," said Nathan, "It's like you switch me on and no matter where I go or what I do that day, people tell me that I 'shine,' and it rubs off on them. I never have a bad day when we wake up together. That day can always end well, whatever life may bring." A tear threatened and spilled down Alex's cheek. Nathan thumbed it sweetly away and then pulled Alex's mouth to his.

They were one and would never be parted now. Every touch set nerve endings alight. They began again, gasped, held their breaths, and rolled their bodies together once more. Their hips locked, hardnesses conquered each other, sweat dripped from their brows and their lips found every morsel of skin to suck and make electric with desire. Higher and higher their passion drove them as their slicked bodies sparked against one another and all they could do was hold on, wrapped tightly in one another's arms barely breathing, uttering little gasps of incredulity. Alex's wet face slid down Nathan's soft cheek, he groaned in ecstasy. Tangled together, under the bedding and in it, they never wanted this moment to end until finally they drifted off into a deep sleep, irreversibly woven together for life.

Chapter Fourteen.

A few days passed with life getting back to predictability and no-one in either household had ever been more thankful for it. The wedding was coming together and Nathan had gone back to swimming, just once a week to start with. Alex got left in charge of organising their celebration weekend in Vienna and now scanned Trip Advisor for any bad reports on the hotel they'd chosen. Satisfied that they had chosen well, he printed off a few notes on the best places to see and sloped over to the sofa.

It was heading toward later afternoon and he felt very tired. Too much time on the net had made his eyes ache. With no one else home he sprawled out on the big squashy sofa cushions and moaned, rubbing his forehead with two fingers. As sleep threatened to overwhelm him, he gazed out of the long windows up at the clear blue sky and smiled to himself. It was one of those golden moments, Nathan was well, everyone seemed so happy and as he lay there, Alex felt so blissfully comfortable. He wore a soft grey Holister top that felt glorious against the skin and long legged dark blue jeans, rolled up once on each side. Warm sun filtered across his body, warming him gently as he drifted off to sleep.

He dreamt that soft dreamy lips attached to the most handsome boy in the world touched his and grinned as he stretched awake and blinked up at the dreamy boy above. "Hi," whispered Nathan stroking his cheek. Alex scanned his beautiful face, his shining eyes and cheeks flushed with love. His dark hair was slightly damp around the edges as it framed his face and he bit his lip shyly at the look Alex was giving him. "God what a lovely way to wake up."

Nathan blushed even harder and grinned down at Alex who lifted his head until their lips met again. "Is it just you here or is anyone else around ?" He asked. Nathan shook his head, "just us." "Thank God, get your clothes off immediately."

Nathan laughed as Alex tried to strip him with both hands. "I don't think we're going to be alone for that long," he giggled, trying to wrestle Alex's fingers from his clothes. "How long do you think I want to take ?" Alex raised an eyebrow naughtily and tried to push him down on the floor making him giggle all the more. " No, stop...., ha ha," he laughed and they rolled over a few times, fingers burying under each others shirts until a key in the lock backed up Nathan's prediction and they reluctantly dropped their hands from each other but didn't bother to get up. Alex's dad walked in, saw the two of them with flushed cheeks, snuggled up together on the floor and rolled his eyes, "blimey you two, there are bedrooms here you know !"

The boys giggled and Nathan blushed self consciously but then gasped as Alex started to say wickedly, "but Dad, Nathan wanted me the minute he got back, what was I supposed to....mmumph !" He didn't get any further as Nathan planted both hands firmly across his mouth and sat up looking mortified, "that... that just SO isn't true !" He gabbled shaking his head at Christopher. "I know, don't worry Nathan, I'll get Alex back for that one soon."

Nathan blushed further, Alex sat up with his hair all over the place and a naughty look on his face still. "Alex..." Nathan shook his head, "you're in one of those moods aren't you ?" Alex grinned in reply and Nathan put his head in his hands. "Lord save us," he pleaded then looked up again at him, watching him smooth back his hair and stare intently back. Alex exhaled noisily and cupped Nathan's cheek, still in a silly mood but serious for a moment. "I love you."

"Ich au," said Nathan. "Ok, you do all the talking in Austria." Alex replied, raising Nathan's hand and kissing it. Nathan reached out and stroked his cheek. "Before we do anything else tonight my love, I am absolutely starving so get in that kitchen and whip me up something amazing would you ?" Alex bowed low, silliness overflowing again. "Your wish is my command," he said gravely before struggling to his feet and offering Nathan both hands, but as he pulled him up he whispered "I love you," once more in his ear and winked before heading into the kitchen and starting to clank around with the pans.

Christopher reappeared from the downstairs loo at this point and seeing Alex busy in the kitchen looked at Nathan, "oh well done, I really didn't want to cook tonight. Come on, you deserve a g and t in the garden for getting Alex to do it, lets catch the last rays of the afternoon." With that he grabbed his pre-prepared g and t tray and headed down into the front garden where he set it underneath the green canvas umbrella and pulled plastic zip sheets off two squashily covered garden chairs.

Nathan and he got settled and were soon toasting life in general with a clink of crystal. Nathan held his glass up to the light and lay back against his chair. Christopher passed him a bowl of frazzles and he smiled with utter contentment as he sipped his gin and crunched away, a light breeze fluttering his fringe and his husband to be cooking delicious food in the back ground. Christopher glanced over at his blissful expression, "I'm so glad to see you better Nathan, you're really very happy aren't you?" Nathan nodded, " I don't think life gets much better than this." Christopher nodded and sipped his gin before lying back against his lounger, "if you think this is good, just wait til the wedding, I really did love mine." He smiled sounding slightly wistful. Nathan held the cold glass to his flushing cheek, "I can't wait for mine either," he said softly and shut his eyes to enjoy that thought in the sun.

The morning of their Vienna weekend arrived early, very early. Alex groaned and stretched in Nathan's arms. "Oh God it's too early !" He moaned and pulled the duvet over his head. Nathan laughed and slipped it off him again, kissing his forehead in the process. Alex looked up into his waiting eyes, there was so much love in them. "God I love waking up to this view," he breathed. Nathan blushed and smiled softly at his lover caressing his cheek lovingly with his finger tips. "Even if it is fucking four bloody a.m. !"

Nathan threw back his head and laughed loudly before Alex shushed him. "No one else is awake yet you loon !" "Oh yes, oh well, maybe now they are." Nathan grinned and sat up, stretching hard toward the ceiling. It really was difficult to get moving so early and they both stumbled groggily out of bed, trying to pad around as noiselessly as possible. It didn't take long for them to slip into their clothes and shove the last few bits into their rucksacks.

Nathan wasn't a fabulous flier and didn't look forward to the flight but with Alex at his side he knew he'd be ok. "Ready ?" Alex smiled and rubbed his arm just as a soft knock made them look round and Nathan's mum walked in looking awake and fresh in a way that only mums ever do at that time of the morning. "All set ?" She smiled. The boys held up their passports and boarding passes. "Sure are," they said as one and blushed. "It really is sickening how in tune you two are," Alison Henderson laughed and passed Nathan a small black zip up lunch box from M and S. He blushed again, "mum !"

"Now don't be like that," Alison smiled and turned him around like a small child, much to Alex's great amusement as he laughed and made faces to wind his beloved up. Alison zipped up the rucksack and spun her son around again, it's just a couple of sandwiches, brownies and two drinks, indulge me, I'm your mother." Nathan groaned and put his embarrassed face in his palms as she hugged him and Alex laughed again. As they pulled away from the embrace and Alison followed the boys out of the room she cuffed Alex lightly on the ear, "cheeky, stop embarrassing him !" Alex ducked and rubbed his head, "ow, child abuse, make her stop Nate, please, please !!!" "Oh get away with you !" Alison giggled and let Alex put his arms around her for a great big bear hug.

They loved each other deeply now, almost as if real mother and son after sharing so much anguish over the boy they both loved irrevocably. "Bye mum, thanks for the food." Nathan squeezed Alison as if he would never let go and there were tears in her eyes when he did. "I'm coming back you know." "I know," she nodded and thumbed his cheek. "Take care of him Alex," she nodded at her 'other son.' "You know I will," Alex kissed her cheek and they were gone. Alison didn't lock the door behind them, she stood and looked out of it for a while before closing it gently and sitting down to a private coffee and the news. She was so lucky she mused as she gripped the hot mug and smiled at the sun just beginning to rise through the living room windows.

Terminal 3 wasn't a patch on T5 Nathan decided as they found their way to the BA bag drop section. Nothing seemed easily sign posted and it was badly laid out. "Blimey, imagine being foreign and coming here !" Alex echoed his sentiments. "Snap, just what I was thinking. This terminal's shite !" They headed up an escalator toward a Costa Coffee, "Come on, we've got ages yet and I need one of those pretty badly," Alex nodded at the steaming cups people were carrying toward little tables. "God yes," Nathan agreed and they installed themselves into a clean corner table and were soon sipping the revitalising stuff.

"This feels so good." Alex smiled, "I can't believe how lucky we are ?" "I know," Nathan blew on his coffee and grinned. "I can't wait to see Vienna, don't laugh but I really want to go to the butterfly house." Alex shrugged, "I'm not laughing, even big butch straight blokes like butterflies you know." Nathan nearly choked on his coffee with laughter, "ha ha, I don't care whether they do or not, it just seems a bit girly. Still, I like them. Especially those massive blue ones with huge wings. What are they called ?" "Big blues," said Alex. "Oh crap, what a mong brain I am !" Nathan reddened severely. Alex raised an eyebrow at him. "Er excuse me, did you just call yourself a 'mong brain ?'" Nathan started to clutch his stomach at his expression. He laughed so hard that along with Alex, the two people at the next table started laughing too without knowing why. After a good while had passed they began to calm down again but tears of laughter still streamed down their faces. Each reached up to brush them away from each other's cheeks and grinned at just being alive, in love and so utterly, utterly happy.

Once in the air Alex kept holding onto Nathan's sweaty hand. He wasn't too bad apart from gripping the seat edge every time they heard a whir or a clonk. Suddenly he shut his eyes at the loudest one yet and gulped. "Oh baby," Alex said, with genuine sympathy. "Hey it's ok, the seat belt sign's just gone off and the stewardess is walking toward us with your drink, no she really is honestly !" He smiled encouragingly at Nathan who looked in the same direction as Alex and reached out his hands as the stewardess got to them.

"There you are my lovely, let me know if there's anything else I can do for you, ok ?" Nathan blushed and took the little bottle of gin and can of tonic. He looked slightly guilty as Alex cracked it open for him and poured all the gin into a tiny plastic glass with enough of a splash of tonic to just about balance the taste and no more. "Do you think it's really ok to drink gin at 7.55am ?" Nathan grimaced at both his concern and the first sip. Alex gave him an, 'oh come on,' kind of look. He chuckled at it, "ok, ok, I was just asking…"

Being up above the clouds again was strange for Nathan, after his accident it had an all consuming affect on him. He was quiet for a few minutes as they reached their ultimate altitude and the plane hummed quietly along. Beneath the wing which his window overlooked, the top of the cloud plane looked so regular and smooth in its formation. Every now and again a gap permitted the view to the fields below. Even from this height Nathan was amazed that you could still make everything out.

He turned back to Alex and got a kiss for his smile just as breakfast was delivered. They munched on their egg rolls and sipped back the tea and orange juice. When breakfast was cleared away they started to flick through the duty free magazine and played, 'pick out the most disgusting 'fugly' present for one another possible.' It was fun and of course one of Alex's deliberate distraction techniques. They did stumble across a really decent watch with a slim chrome dial and deep chocolate leather strap. It wasn't expensive and Nathan eyed it for a moment before turning the page, "no point in wasting money we're trying to save," he shrugged and kissed Alex before disappearing to the loo.

As soon as he was gone Alex collared the nearest stewardess and spoke fast, she smiled warmly at his plea and soon he held a black leather box which he managed to hide just in time for Nathan's return. Once re-buckled, Nathan looked up at the little monitor to check their progress. "Arse, still an hour and five minutes to go !" He groaned. Alex took hold of his hand and unfurled his fingers before gently placing the box in them. Nathan did a double take and stared up at him with wide eyes. "What the….? Alex what's this ?" Alex smiled, "just open it."

Nathan popped the fastener on the front and opened the lid. He misted up when he saw the watch. "Hey…" He started to protest but Alex gently put a finger to his lips. "It's only a little something to say I'm so ecstatic that you're ok and to thank you for coming away with me for this weekend when I know how much you hate flying." Nathan gulped and took the watch out of its box. Alex reached over and turned his wrist around to buckle it on for him. Nathan's heart thudded in his chest. He watched Alex's beautiful, chiselled profile. What had he done to deserve such a fantastic guy ? Some people waited til they were 40 to find a love like this and some people never found it. He shook his head as Alex turned his wrist over again and looked up at his face.

"What ?" Alex coloured this time, something sweet was going on in Nathan's mind and it made his tummy turn over with excitement. Nathan reached out and thumbed his warm, smooth cheek and gazed deeply into his crystal clear eyes. "You're just so damned beautiful, on the inside and the out aren't you," he breathed. Alex's eyes filled up as he bit his lip. "I....," he couldn't speak so Nathan leaned forward and kissed him. "When we land I'm going to kiss you properly and show you how much I'm in love with you," he whispered close against his mouth.

Alex whimpered and choked back a tear. "Oh God you always get me like this," he gasped, as quietly as possible so as not to piss their neighbouring passenger off too much. Nathan grinned, "I love you so much," he whispered. Alex pressed his face into Nathan's shoulder and shuddered for a second before he looked up with red eyes. "Christ Nate,.....I, I....well fuck me !" Was all he could manage. "Later," beamed Nathan making them both giggle. He ran his thumb carefully under each of Alex's eyes and wiped the moisture on his jeans. Alex snorted and trembled, overwhelmed at his feelings. Nathan held his hand and felt him shake. "That's how you make me feel too," he husked. Alex smiled back at him and shut his eyes. Nathan did the same. Underneath him the plane hummed gently as it flew, they banked a little and his stomach tingled with only a morsel of fear because in his hand was the hand of his beloved, the best, the most handsome, the loyalist person he had ever met and he felt one hundred per cent total and utter happiness.

The boys woke with a slight jump, "I'm sorry," said the smiling stewardess, "but it's time to put away your tables and put your chairs upright, I can see you've got your belts on. We're coming in to land." Nathan rubbed his sleepy eyes. "Really..., oh." He looked at an equally knackered Alex who yawned arching his back. "Rrrrr, ah that feels so good," he stretched his fingers up to the ceiling where they brushed the plastic above. They were coming down through soft billowy cloud now which bumped them around for a second and temporarily blocked any view. Nathan paled and clutched the seat.

"It's ok," Alex rubbed his arm and then looked over at their neighbour to his right. The man had gone back to a slump and snored gently. Alex turned back to Nathan and pulled his face around, "come here gorgeous," he put his lips on Nathan's mouth, kissing him softly at first and then with complete passion, pressing his tongue in deeply. It was so hot that Nathan groaned longingly and felt himself harden. He pushed Alex away quite forcibly and lay back panting with his hands flat to his grinning lovers chest.

"Christ Alex," he panted, red faced and fiery eyed. Alex tried to press in again for more of the same but Nathan held him off. "No ! Shit Al, look at me...!" He whispered fiercely. "You've got me so hard already !" "I know," Alex smirked as they heard the undercarriage come down. "Took your mind off the turbulence though didn't it ?" Nathan's face was a picture. He looked totally shocked. "Oh my God ! Yes ! That worked a treat !" All fieriness immediately went out of him as he caressed Alex's face. "You're wonderful."

"You too." Alex sat back in his seat and took Nathan's hand as the plane swung a bit across the runway on its final approach before landing safely on Viennese soil. It was a good thing that the boys were young and healthy as the hotel's online description of its proximity to the heart of town was a load of rubbish. They hiked across four lanes of traffic, crossed an unexciting graffiti strewn, walled part of the Danube and down two unappealing side streets before reaching it. "Ok that was a bit crap !" Alex frowned. "Foyer looks nice though," Nathan smiled as they puffed up the red carpeted steps to the front desk.

They smiled kindly at the receptionist who seemed about as helpful as a chocolate fire guard. After filling out the necessary paperwork she shoved the room card at them and pointed up the corridor with a fake smile of about half a second. Nathan saw the look on Alex's face and led him quickly away. As they tramped down the hall feeling the weight of their bags now after so much walking, Alex grumbled, "customer service obviously fantastic here. Vienna, 'nil point,' England 1." Nathan giggled, he didn't disagree. "Right," he looked down at the key card, ok, room 150, here we are."

They had to play with the card for a moment or two til the green light flickered and the door unlocked. "Bring back frigging keys !" Alex mumbled crossly. They poured into the room, tired from the early flight, gagging for some lunch and then stopped dead. The yellow walls were absolutely hideous, and the twin beds looked clean but tiny. Nathan strode across to the window, "Erm, Al, I don't think this is the view you requested is it ?" Alex joined him and gasped going red. "The fuckers ! Right." He slung his bag back over his shoulder. "Come on, I know we're bloody starving and I'm sorry to get pissy but we asked for a view. A brick wall eight inches away is NOT a view !"

Nathan snatched up his ruck sack and ran after Alex as he fumed. They got back to reception where the receptionist eyed them suspiciously. After hearing their complaints she still seemed relatively unbothered but handed them another key card, one floor up. No help again, no one carrying bags, ok it was only two rucksacks but still. Nathan bit his lip, it was hard not to laugh, both out of total gnawing hunger and the furious expression set on Alex's handsome face. Room two was worse.

At the door of room 3 the boys panted with the exertion of going all the way around the hotel in fifteen minutes. It was just as bad. Nathan didn't speak, he just nodded at Alex as they made their way back to reception for a third time. They just caught sight of their receptionist getting tapped on the shoulder by her colleague, glad to pass the buck. "Ich ?" The girl whispered in a bad stage whisper and rolled her eyes before coming over. "Yes YOU !" Alex snapped. She stopped with her mouth set in a sharp line on her sour face. "I may be young and I may be gay, but that doesn't make me stupid !" He fumed. Those rooms were all unacceptable. Give us the room we deserve. We booked a four star hotel room with a view and a double bed. Give it to us NOW !" He shouted the last word. The receptionist put up her palm in a defensive gesture and started to try and tell Alex to calm down and that they didn't have any better rooms.

"Don't lie to me !" He roared and slapped his palm on the desk. It made Nathan's groin ache to look at him. He was incredible. The girl trembled for a moment and then just about disguised a sneer as she reached over for another key card. She tapped on the PC keyboard and handed it to Alex. "Room 239, in the new part of the hotel." She pointed again , Alex picked up his rucksack and slung it over his shoulder. "Come on sweetheart," his face softened a little as he took Nathan's hand. "I just have a feeling about this one." They tramped back up the same corridors again and then wound round to the right this time, snaking up some slate tiled stairs which were impeccably maintained.

At last they reached the door just off a small modern landing which looked nothing like the rest of the hotel. The card made the lock flash green and they were in. Both stopped dead. It was like being in a different hotel. "Oh my God !" Said Nathan as he took in the smart dark carpet, dazzling white bed linen, modern wall mounted lamps, wet room, flat screen tv and two fully stocked glass fronted mini bars. "Bugger me !" Said Alex and dropped his ruck sack where he stood. Nathan was at the window, he parted the modesty curtains and looked down. "There's a view too." He let the curtain fall back in to place and stood up.

"That's not a bad idea by the way..."

Alex frowned, "What ?"

"What you just suggested..." He smiled.

Alex frowned more and was about to shrug, "but I just said, bugg.....ooh ! Oh I see...!" He grinned. Nathan stood six feet away from him and slid his belt out of his jeans, it fell to the floor. "I thought you were hungry ?" Alex gasped as his body turned from one need to another, more pressing. "I'm fucking starving," Nathan breathed unpopping his fly. Alex caught his breath and pulled his t-shirt over his head. They stood still for a moment, quivering with heady need and then ran at each other. They had never made love like it before. It was powerful, desperate, groaning lust that drove them. Ripping at each other's clothes they were instantly naked and pressed together, panting and shaking. There was no time to grab the lube. Alex flipped Nathan over and used his saliva on his fingers and shaft. He applied one after the other to Nathan's tightness and had never heard him come so loudly in his life. When he exploded too it was two strokes behind Nathan and he thrust so hard he was genuinely afraid that he'd hurt him. He squirted so much that he felt dizzy beyond all memory. He flopped onto his back, puffing and gasping, desperate to know if Nathan was ok but physically unable to check for another minute. Instead he reached out and was thankful to feel Nathan's damp body rising and falling as gaspingly as his own.

Eventually he sat up and rolled on his elbow to look at his beloved. "Nate, Nate, , my God I'm so sorry, are you ok ?" He gasped. Nathan sat up puffing still but nodded, then his face split into a huge grin. "Abso-fucking-lutely !" He beamed. "Where the hell did that come from ?" "You, it's all you," gasped Alex.

"Well I sure as hell started it but after that....,phew....!" He shook his head. Alex blushed deeply and looked incredibly worried. He leant across Nathan, pushing him gently back into the pillows. "My love, are you ok ?" He looked so anxious. "Alex I'm fine, I really am. You got me so damn fucking turned on there's no way you could have hurt me." Alex visibly relaxed, "thank God," he smoothed the backs of his fingers down Nathan's cheek. "I love you." "Me too, and if you don't do that to me at least once a week from now on I'm going to be very disappointed," Nathan breathed. Alex looked totally shocked. "Really ? You liked it ?"

"Well that might not be good for my body to bang it about so hard every time, but once in a while, Christ all mighty Alex.....it was,.....just amazing !" Alex grinned down at his love and stroked his cheek again. "What did I do to deserve you ?"

"Everything you've ever done because you're perfect," Nathan whispered. "No one's perfect," said Alex.

Nathan smiled,"but you are to me. My perfect love Alex, and nothing will ever change my mind." Alex gulped back his emotion but his eyes were watery. Idly he played with Nathan's fringe, "marry me in October then ?" Nathan blushed and nodded with shining beautiful eyes. "Good," said Alex, "just checking," then he pulled him to his feet and they dressed to go in search of some lunch.

Ravenous as they were, the boys didn't go far before finding food. Turning left out of their hotel and heading toward the town centre Nathan remembered their passing a yacht shaped cafe on stilts above the river which looked sort of fun so they tried there. It had shallow teak steps with long treads to make the walk up to the eating deck seem even more boat like.

"Well this is quite cool," said Alex turning around to take in the 360. "Shame it's not prettier though," he added, as they both gazed at a little sandy beach and a few tired sun umbrellas gracing the opposite side of the rivers edge. Next to the tiny beach the depth of the river wall had been graffitied to the max. It could have been arty graffiti but just didn't quite work, instead looking tired and a little dirty. "Hmm, I see what you mean," Nathan agreed as they found a sweet little wooden table with wicker chairs in the sun.

Both slipped on their sun glasses as the clouds parted all the way, chasing the earlier greyness out of the sky. "You look cool," said Alex. Nathan chuckled and showed a lot of teeth with his smile, it made Alex grin too. "I love being here with you already," he husked just as the waiter appeared. "Me too," said Nathan. The waiter was surprisingly good looking with chocolate brown hair, piercing blue eyes and a slim tanned frame. He was quite flirty but it was lost on either boy. As he walked away with their orders Alex looked after him, more in curiosity than anything else.

He looked back to see Nathan watching him but there was nothing to fear for either of them. He nodded after the waiter and Nathan smiled, "I know, he was pretty handsome." He frowned, " but the thing is, I know when someone else is good looking, it just doesn't have an effect on me anymore, do you know what I mean ?" Alex beamed back, "completely. I looked as he left because I'm not used to seeing other gay guys our age and especially in another country, I mean there just aren't that many at school," he shrugged, "maybe ours is unusual in that way ?"

Nathan sipped his coke and laid his head back on the seat. "Maybe," he sighed idly as the warmth of the sun made him zone out a bit. "Hey, gorgeous...!" Alex poked him with his toe under the table, "no going to sleep on me, oy, stop that immediately !" Nathan giggled and heard footsteps behind him. "Look," Alex whispered conspiratorially, "that handsome waiters back again. You'd better wake up, what if I flirt with him ? Quick !" That just made Nathan giggle even more. The waiter came and put down their food, asked if there was anything else and left again. Only then did Nathan look up, stretch and lazily pick up his fork to try the strange concoction before him. Alex eyed him huffily so he put down his fork and grinned at him, nudging him back under the table, "hey, grumpy !" Alex crossed his arms and pretended to turn away, Nathan giggled and poked him with his toe again.

"No, no, it won't work, just because you know I only have eyes for you. You could at least pretend to be jealous from time to time." Nathan threw back his head and laughed, he couldn't stop, even when Alex started to look genuinely a bit pissed off, it just seemed funnier still. He was gasping and holding his ribs when he suddenly saw something different in Alex's expression. He was actually tight lipped and shiny eyed as if holding back emotions that threatened to over flow. Nathan sat bolt upright and reached across the table. "Alex ?" He said worriedly. Alex struggled with himself, he didn't want to be a pain in the arse on their first day but he felt so overwhelmed with a moment of 'what if I lost him,' that he had to reach under his sunglasses and press his fingers to his eyes.

He dared not look at Nathan, a small sob escaped him. "Shit !" He whispered and jumped up from the table to go and cling on to the rail over looking the Danube. Nathan was beside him in a second, he put his arms around him immediately and pulled him close. Alex sobbed and sank his face into his shoulder. "Alex, Alex, my love, my baby....what is it ?" He wrapped him tightly in his embrace and rocked him gently. Alex cried and cried in his arms. Nathan held on to him, utterly alarmed, soothing him over and over. He'd never seen Alex cry so much. He didn't know what to do but wished so hard that he could make it better for him. Eventually, when his crying began to ease, Alex turned around in Nathan's arms so as to shield his face, embarrassed beyond measure and scared of saying something off putting but Nathan was having none of it.

"Oh no you don't. After sobbing like that in my arms for ten minutes I want to see your face." He firmly helped Alex turn toward him and lifted his chin when he tried to turn away. "Hey !" He said anxiously at the look of agony on Alex's face. "Hey, come on, what is it ?" Alex breathed out a long deep breath and licked his lips. "I must look like shit."

"You never do," Nathan thumbed his cheek softly, his heart thrumming still. "So come on Al, what got you so upset, you're really worrying me ?" Alex winced as if that hurt to hear. "Sorry."

"I don't want you to be sorry, not at all, you've done nothing wrong. I just want to know why you're so upset ?" Alex slumped against the rail behind him and looked ashamedly at his feet for a second before he looked into Nathan's eyes again. "I....," he gulped, obviously finding it difficult to speak. "I just...., Oh God," he shook his head as if he couldn't do it. Nathan trembled, he was so frightened he started to feel a bit angry. "For fucks sake Alex, please !"

Alex gazed into his eyes, his own filled up again, tears spilled freely down his cheeks, his face crumpled, "Nathan I thought you were going to die !" He sobbed, breaking down again.

Nathan yanked him close, knotting his arms around him as he sobbed and whispered into his hair, "I'm so sorry, I'm so sorry my darling for putting you through that." Alex sobbed more but raised his pained wet face just enough to shake his head, "and then I saw that waiter and I knew that there were more ways than one to lose you and I just couldn't bear the thought, I...I,....I felt sick and helpless and I just...., I'm sorry, I'm sorry," he sobbed.

Nathan felt his own eyes over spill, he felt like his heart would break. "Oh

Alex, oh my Alex," he croaked and rocked his beloved in his arms as he cried against his chest. It took many minutes before Alex could calm down. All the while Nathan held him, smoothed his hair and kissed it, sometimes rubbing his back. At last, exhausted, Alex staggered from his grasp and looked at him. He felt horribly shy at what he'd just done and wiped the back of his hand across his eyes to dismiss any remaining moisture. He couldn't help the odd air sob escaping him as his breathing adjusted. His lips were red and bee stung looking, his face red, damp, flushed and so exhausted. He shook his head again as Nathan's eyes met his.

"I'm so sorry," he shrugged as if he didn't know where to begin to apologise. Nathan's expression grew shocked. "I'm sorry, did you just apologise for thinking I might have died, being upset about it and also for loving me enough that you can't bear the thought of someone else coming along and whisking me off?" Alex smiled and chuckled gently for a moment, "er yes I did actually," he gave Nathan a heart breaking look and ran his hand through his hair, letting out a shuddering breath. "When you put it like that it does sound kind of silly," he searched Nathan's eyes and saw only love in them, love and concern.

Nathan caressed his cheek still, looking anxious for him. "I love you so much, I'm really ok now and I will be for a very long time. I'm sorry that you had to go through those horrible horrible feelings. It was an awful time all round. I wish you'd let this out sooner so I could have held you at home in bed but I'm glad it's at last come out."

Alex nodded as a shorter shuddering breath left him. Nathan looked deeply into his eyes. "As for the other thing," he sighed and shook his head. "I don't get jealous, I really don't because I know for a fact in the very heart of my being that you and I are meant to be together. It just feels so right that you could line up a hundred of the hottest bodied men in the world in front of both of us and we'd turn around and go the other way for a cup of coffee !" Alex laughed at this. "So I can't get jealous, it can't happen as I just feel so part of you it's hard to explain."

"No it isn't," Alex croaked, "because I know what you mean. I don't get jealous either, but I've never felt such a feeling of impending loss before as I did when you had your accident. Suddenly I knew what it was to maybe have your entire reason for living ripped away from you and it made me physically sick, I passed out from the pain. My dad had to take care of me. I wanted to die if you did." Nathan sobbed out loud and clutched Alex to him, he hugged him as if he would never let go and cried softly into his hair. "Oh my Alex, I'm so sorry, I didn't know any of this," he sobbed.

"It's ok," Alex said weakly. They stayed holding and rocking gently together while their lunch got cold, was surreptitiously taken back into the kitchen and brought out again when it was noticed that they were now both perching on the lower rail of the fence above the river, holding hands and talking. "I will NEVER want anyone else," Nathan squeezed Alex's hands while he looked into his eyes. "Me neither," Alex air sobbed one last time as he looked groggily back at him. "And though I said I don't get jealous, I can't guarantee I will never get a moment of anxiety about losing you, I've had a few already and it scared the shit out of me !" Alex looked surprised, "you did ?"

"Of course!" Nathan shook a little as he looked at the floor for a moment, " Alex you're the most popular, clever boy in school, why would you be interested in me ?" Alex looked utterly taken aback, his brow quickly furrowed in annoyance, "don't you ever question that about yourself, not ever do you hear ?! You're the sweetest, loveliest, most incredibly handsome guy on the planet, what you need to ask yourself is why anyone would not be interested in you !"

Nathan blushed and bit his lip, "do you think so ?" He asked with a little self conscious smile.

"What ? Are you crazy ? Of course I bloody do ! Everyone who meets you must want to go out with you." Alex shrieked. Nathan laughed coyly, but it felt good to be so flattered. He only wanted what he'd got, Alex's love, but to have him say all those lovely things made his heart swell. Alex leaned in and kissed his lip, "now do you see why I was so scared of losing you ?"

"No," Nathan answered honestly, "because despite the nice things you said, I don't see myself like that and I probably never will. I think I'm quite nice looking," he blushed, "and hopefully kind and well meaning, but I won't ever have a massive ego or believe that everyone else thinks I'm so marvellous either. It's just the way I'm made." He smiled shyly.

Alex shook his head, "Well thank God I've got you, and you really don't know your own worth. You're everything to me Nate, everything." "And you are to me too, never forget it." Nathan husked as they leant forward and kissed each other softly, lingeringly on the mouth. When they drew apart Alex thumbed Nathan's cheek. His stomach growled, "I'm bloody starving !" Nathan grinned, "then let's eat."

Alex had a kind of sausage and mash for lunch and wolfed it down in barely a minute. Nathan had mash too but with spinach, poached egg and a little bit of crispy bacon. It was delicious but incredibly salty. As they lay back in their chairs waiting for the bill Nathan glanced over at Alex through his glasses. He loved him so very much, it amazed him that he would be the one to be afraid of someone taking either of them away. He mulled this over, if anyone should worry it should be himself he mused, but he'd meant what he said, it wasn't just something to say, he really did feel so connected to Alex that he simply never worried about it.

There were hundreds of gorgeous men out there but it was as if none of them counted, they didn't engage Nathan's brain and he knew it was the same for Alex. The bill came, they paid and left, getting out the map they headed into the picturesque town away from the graffiti and were soon strolling down prettier little streets, stopping to take pictures of red brick and gold painted churches, sculpted white columns and old shop fronts. There were a lot of shops and a small crowd had gathered outside the cathedral where a group of late teens were street dancing. They were brilliant so the boys stopped to watch. A minute later a man hardly older than them approached with a folder full of information about Viennese music, he was dressed in a white wig, frock coat and pantaloons.

"You like Opera ?" He began, and flicked open his folder full of show times and prices. "No no, that's ok. Thank you," Alex smiled and headed away from him toward the cathedral door. Nathan, close on his heels, put his arm around his waist and pulled him close. Alex turned toward him, Nathan slid his sunglasses into his hair to look at his eyes, he was definitely much better than earlier but so tired, what with their early flight, the room debacle and his crying episode, Alex looked really shattered. Nathan kissed his eye lids, Alex kept his eyes shut afterwards and groaned, "do you want to make me fall asleep on my feet ?" "Sorry," Nathan laughed and then caught him by the hand. " I know, let's go to that Fortnum and Mason lookalike," he pointed up the street straight in front of them, "and have some gorgeous tea and cakes, - purely for market research for our diner/ cafe later of course !" "Well if it's necessary for research, count me in," Alex beamed as they headed off toward a pretty four storey stone building with sliding glass in its arched doorways.

Once inside they were blown away. All the shelves were impeccably tidy and clean with wonderful displays of lots of old fashioned style tins and bags of pasta, candy canes, jars of jams and preserves, chocolates and bon bons. "Wow, this place is beautiful !" Exclaimed Alex. Nathan nodded, "it's pretty fab isn't it ? Everyone's really smiley here too." "Can you blame them ? I'd smile if I worked here !" Alex beamed back, completely his old self again. "Come on," he said, smoothing his fingertips down Nathan's cheek, "let's check out upstairs." They tramped up the wide wooden staircase hand in hand and came out into a light room with big arched windows. Half the room had more shelves of sweets and chocolates and the other half was a neat little cafe with small round tables and high stools. "Let's go there," Alex picked out the place he wanted to sit and headed toward it. Soon they were sitting at a little ledge table by the windows in front of a long mirror. It reflected the oak ceiling beams right across the room and made it seem huge. "Gruse got," said a cheery young waitress with dark hair. "English ?" Said Nathan tentatively. "Yes of course," she shrugged with a smile and produced an English menu. "I come back," she smiled and disappeared. "This is great," beamed Alex, "I'm loving it already." "Me too," Nathan grinned and kissed him lightly on the lips then they both fell on the menu.

"Phlot you...., think, that ith..." mumbled Nathan with a huge mouthful of lemon meringue pie, pointing across the square to a large white memorial of some kind with gold figures at the top. Alex raised an eyebrow at his over stuffed hamster cheeks, "you are quite disgusting sometimes aren't you ?" Nathan giggled, nearly choking on his pie. A bit of meringue shot out and bounced off the mirror. He blushed and looked squarely at Alex, his eyes twinkling with laughter. "Pig !" Alex laughed, shaking his head. "Ahuh," nodded Nathan, chewing down his mouthful quickly and licking his lips. "God that's seriously amazing !" He looked down at the last few mouthfuls, "you've gotta try a bit Al."

Alex did as he suggested and dug in, a look of pure bliss slid across his face to the point where he closed his eyes and groaned gently. Nathan shuddered, seeing him do that suddenly made him want to tear all his clothes off and make him scream in ecstasy. When Alex opened his eyes again Nathan was white and staring at him. "My God, what is it ?" Alex asked quickly. Nathan slowly shook his head and casually slipped his napkin fully across his lap. Alex frowned and then threw his head back and laughed.

"Shush !" Nathan breathed, alarmed as a couple of other tourists glanced over. Alex laughed a little less noisily but reached up to stroke his face. "Oh Nate you are priceless and I do love you." "That's all very well you cheeky fucker but no more groaning over pastries in public ok ? I'm 17 not 70 ! " Alex hid his mouth with his napkin at this point but Nathan could see his cheeks bulging with laughter. He rolled his eyes and smacked Alex's knee, "yes, very amusing ! Knob !" Alex still laughed, finally making Nathan's lips turn up at the corners.

"Ah look, you're laughing too, bless !" "Fuck off !" Nathan laughed. "Anyway," he added, turning in his seat, "what do you think that thing is ? It's some kind of memorial that's for sure." Alex leant against his back and linked his arms around his waist to peer out of the window as well, "I don't know, let's look it up in a sec. Oh and by the way, you're 18 not 17, I know old age is creeping up on you but..." He was stopped mid sentence by another whack on the knee and fell about laughing again. "What now ?" Nathan shrugged. Alex shook his head and backed away slightly in case he needed to run. "That," he giggled, "what ?" Nathan frowned. Alex took his hand and effeminately slapped his own knee lightly with it. "That sweetheart, it's just the gayest thing I've seen you do...." Nathan's eyes blazed for a second, his cheek muscles clenched along the jawline. He slapped down his napkin and made to get up but Alex was too fast for him and sprinted off across the room to hide behind a big rotating shelf of sweets, laughing.

Their waitress, realising it was high jinks but still keen not to be short changed, came over and put down the bill. "Danke," said Nathan and gave her a 20 Euro note. He waited for his change while keeping Alex in his peripheral vision. "Fillen danke, cheers," he nodded, pocketing his coins, and casually walked toward the top of the stairs as if he didn't know where Alex was. As he stepped out to descend the first step, a small smile played across his lips, out of the corner of his eye he watched him tip toe toward the other stairs at the back of the room and crouched to turn and follow him, he was so going to enjoy this.....

Alex crouched low behind another shelf and giggled to himself. Just one more check before he sprinted off he thought and carefully raised his eyes above the tins of sweets and preserves in front of him to look toward the other stairs. Fully expecting to see Nathan he was bemused, only a second ago he'd seen him pay so where the hell had he....... "JESUS CHRIST !" He Screamed and leapt into the air as Nathan whispered evilly into his ear"hello my pretty..."

Alex trembled with fright for a millisecond as Nathan gripped his sides, "worked like a charm," he guffawed. "Bastard !" Said Alex, furious at having been beaten at his own game but elated at Nathan being able to muck about again. "You arse," he grinned and slipped his arms around his waist looking deeply into his eyes.

Nathan caught his breath, "are you going to kiss me right here ?" He gasped with excitement, "yes," said Alex and pulled him close, pressing his lips fully onto Nathan's and kissing him hotly, passionately until he groaned for real. "Oh my God."

"My thoughts exactly," panted Alex, as they rested their foreheads together. "This is going to be such a beautiful weekend," husked Nathan, cupping Alex's head in his palms. " I know," Alex answered breathlessly and kissed his mouth again with all his desperate longing.

Chapter Fifteen.

After their cakes and coffee, followed by languorous delicious kissing behind the sweet shelves, the boys left with their arms wrapped around one another's waists and headed out onto the flag-stoned streets to take in the rest of the sights. They pulled out Alex's Time Out guide to Vienna and put little stars next to everything they wanted to see. "Wow that's a lot of stuff for a few days," Nathan commented. "Too much babe ?" Alex looked concerned. "No, don't worry, I'll just sleep really well and we'll have to keep stopping for cake too !" He grinned. "Oh no !" Alex beamed back at him and gave his waist a little squeeze. "Come on gorgeous, what next ?"

"Erm, I want to go on a carriage ride around the city," Nathan decided and pointed toward a very well kept pair of dark bay horses with their ears covered in matching protectors to the carriage which was painted a deep claret with white panelling. "Ok let's do it," Alex kissed his cheek and they made their way over to the double row of carriages. When Alex asked the price and the boys took a closer look they realised that the whole out fit was run by a bit of a motley crew. Nathan, being the knowledgeable one about horses looked down at their feet and was glad that he'd picked that particular carriage as both horses had neat, well fitted shoes on, unlike a dapple grey pair behind who looked uncomfortable in their ill fitting ones which flopped and clinked on the cobbles every time they moved. He grimaced at the sight.

"Er, I think we have a slight problem with choosing this carriage..." Alex whispered. Hearing a pissed off rather raised voice Nathan looked up at the proprietor of the whole operation, "No, you go there, not this one, you GO THERE !" He gesticulated wildly from under his bowler hat to the front of the teams where a mismatched pair of horses with a ratty looking carriage stood. "I guess we have to go with who ever's at the front," Alex shrugged. "No we bloody don't," Nathan replied. The acid tone of his voice made Alex stare at him.

"We want this one," Nathan said calmly. "NO !" The man got more animated and practically jumped up and down with his cigar bouncing around in his mouth. "THERE !" He jumped and shouted rudely. "No, THIS !" Said Nathan. The man shook his hands at the heavens and pointed to the front of the teams once more. "No it's this one or nothing," Nathan stood his ground. The man became dumb with shock, tourists never argued with him and won ! "You know what, never mind, never mind," Nathan shrugged and reached for Alex's hand. He turned as if to walk off and just when it seemed they'd lost the fight the man yelled, "ok, ok !" Then he mumbled super fast in German to the carriage driver who clambered up and flicked open the door for the boys. Nathan's cheeks flushed, "thank you," he said and climbed aboard with Alex close on his heels. The driver reversed and teased his team out of the ranks with impressive precision and then they were off, trotting down the cobbled streets between sculpted buildings left and right, the Glockenspiel, the Hofburg, The Plague

Memorial, - ah that's what that thing was ! It was wonderful riding in the carriage.

It had a button back claret interior and a hard roof which could be pulled up half way so that you sat up with your head covered if it rained, or you could pull both halves of the roof together for the winter and again drop them both down for a full 360 view on a sunny day like today. Nathan beamed with happiness. He loved horses. They trotted along so smoothly, he had forgotten how this felt. Alex saw the pleasure on his face, "you love this don't you," he smiled. Nathan nodded.

"I'd forgotten how great carriage rides feel this is so unbelievably smooth isn't it ?"

"It is, I love it. You've done it before though ?"

Nathan shrugged, just once, a few years ago. A week before my fifteenth birthday I won a drawing competition and they sent me away for a weekend in London. It was amazing. My Dad took me up on the train, we were met at the station by the hotel car, a lovely dark blue Bentley Sovereign with shaggy blue carpets, I took my shoes off and curled my toes into it, it was really soft," he paused to look at Alex's expression and got a gentle stroke on his cheek for the effort. It felt so nice, he slumped down in the carriage seat a little. "God it's so good when you do that," he croaked making Alex grin, "Carry on, I love this story already."

"Well as I say, the car ride was amazing and we travelled through some pretty but very busy streets, then we came to this lovely art nouveau looking hotel with flags all dangling at a slant outside it and a door man showed us to a great big suite with a black marble tiled bathroom and everything, it was amazing !" Alex sat bolt upright and stared at him, "you were at Claridges ?" "Yeah, yeah that's the name, how the hell did you know ?" Alex looked as if he'd choke, "because it's just one of the most famous hotels in the world that's all, nothing special."

Nathan laughed at his expression. "Go on, make me utterly jealous by carrying on immediately," Alex shrugged turning his face away in mock disgust.

"Ok, well we stayed the night in the most comfortable beds on the planet and the weird thing was that they must have asked my dad what I liked or for a theme or something because of the two big surprises."

"What do you mean ?" Alex frowned, intrigued. "Well we ordered dinner in the suite, dad said why not order all the things I fancied as it was all paid for so we did and it was an incredible feast ! They rolled in a whole round table big enough for four or five people just for me and dad and covered it in silver domed plates then four waiters went one two three, 'ta da,' and we were blown away by the food," he paused to shake his head in disbelief at the memory.

"Anyway, we stuffed ourselves and talked and talked until late into the night. Eventually dad said he was really tired, gave me a massive hug, told me he was really proud of me and went off to bed. Well I was tired too but amazed by it all and I didn't want it to end so I flicked on the telly and opened the mini bar. It was so packed Al, you would have loved it. I've never seen so many sweets, chocolates, mini bottles of champagne, it was fab ! So I cracked open a mini Piper Heidseck, just for the sake of it, grabbed a huge yellow tub of peanut M and Ms and settled back to watch Ricky Gervais, 'Animals,' stand up live. It was sooo funny!"

Alex looked utterly blown away, "and this was a prize for a drawing competition ? Wow ! but what were the two surprises ?" He asked. "Oh yes, sorry I nearly forgot just then, everything came back in such detail. Well in the corner of the living room was a huge parcel, I mean really huge, like six feet long by five feet high, all wrapped up in purple paper with a huge white bow around it. Forgive the next bit of detail but it has to be described for you to get the whole picture." Alex nodded, keen to hear more and beyond happy. He slipped his hand into Nathan's and watched how it suffused his lover's face with pink. His heart skipped a beat every time he saw that, it would never fail to get him.

"I finally went to bed, and although it was late I must have been over excited by the whole experience or something because I woke up really early the next day which was actually my birthday, dad was still out of it so I tip toed into the living room and flicked on the tv again, the funny thing is I really fancied watching something horsey and suddenly on a channel I'd never even heard of before, I found a whole hour of rodeo ! Weird eh ? Anyway, I grabbed last nights m and ms and settled back on the sofa grinning like an idiot thinking 'this is the life.'

I watched most of the rodeo and just thoroughly enjoyed being alive," he beamed at the memory making Alex's heart skip again at the beautiful look on his face. "So did you undo the present ?" Nathan nodded excitedly, his eyes shining, " Oh Alex, it was such a perfect day. I finished my M and M breakfast as the rodeo carried on in the background and then I remembered the present, - doh ! I mean there it was all big and 'hello,' in the corner of the room but I think that's why I just got so used to it being there and forgot about it for a bit, ha ha. I honestly wanted to wait for dad when I remembered it but he wouldn't be up for hours, it was still only 7am, so I couldn't help myself. I stood in front of that big purple gift and just gawped for a moment. Did I carefully cut off the ribbon and peel back the sellotape or did I do a mental mad tearing sess and get it open ?"

"Mental mad sess !" They both said at once and laughed, "snap !" Beamed Alex. "It's funny, I wasn't even in the room and I feel all over excited at the anticipation myself!" Nathan laughed. "Well I did do what we both said, lunacy and teen impatience got the better of me and I ripped at that paper. It didn't take more than a few swipes until it fell away from the open fronted box it had been wrapped around, and there inside, was a life sized black cuddly pony with a white blaze and four white socks !"

Alex's face was a picture, "no way !" "Yes way ! I named him 'Ned.'" Alex fell back against the seat laughing, "I've said it once on this trip already and I'm gonna say it again, sometimes Nathan you are sooo gay !" "Fuck off !" Nathan laughed back. "So come on horse boy, what was the next surprise ?" Asked Alex.

"Well dad got up quite soon after that, I think I woke him up ! Oops, but he was nice about it and loved my surprise which of course he'd known about anyway as they had to ask his approval. So then we went downstairs to the dining room for an incredible breakfast. It's the customer service there, it's just so relaxing ! Dad had a full fry up and me pain au chocolat, coffee, orance juice, fruit, yoghurt.....wow....yummy...." his eyes glazed over for a moment until Alex nudged him grinning, "ok we'll stop for cake again after this and I'm changing your name to 'Dyson,' but could you please continue with your story."

Nathan blushed and giggled, "sorry. So we languished at breakfast for some time, it was amazing. We got the papers and did the crosswords, - you know my family and our obsession for that, anyway, dad kept glancing at his watch hoping I hadn't noticed and eventually I looked at mine. It was 10.15ish by now and I wasn't in a hurry but I knew our stay at the hotel must be nearly over, we'd probably have to leave by 12 or something like that but I'd had such an incredible time and was on such a high I was on cloud nine. Anyway, I asked dad why he kept watching the time and he said what I thought he'd say, that it was for checking out of the room so I said I'd better go and pack my stuff.

He told me he'd done his already and looked a bit nervous when I wanted to go and do mine which I thought was weird but he told me to be quick, leave the bags on the bed and then just as I was about to leg it up the stairs he said a strange thing, he said 'just don't look out of the window while you're up there and please come straight back down here afterwards.'"

Alex frowned, "eh ? Why would he ask you not to look out of the window ?" "My thoughts exactly ! But he looked so serious when he said it that I promised. Anyway, I ran up to the room, shoved all my stuff into my bag, squeezed in half the mini bar's chocs and pelted back down to the dining room. It was hard not to look out of that window I tell you, but I didn't do it. Dad asked me when I got back to the table if I had and I reassured him. He genuinely kind of went, 'phew,' and slumped back in his seat at that. Bloody odd !" Alex shook his head, "What the hell didn't he want you to see ?"

Nathan grinned and sat up in the carriage, he swayed a bit as they turned a corner by the Spanish Riding School, "Ironic," Alex nodded as they went past. "So come on, don't keep me in suspense now Nate, what the hell was waiting for you ?" "Funny you should put it like that," Nathan grinned. "At 11 o'clock precisely, with dad now almost unbearably twitchy, a receptionist came to get us and asked politely if we'd wait outside on the front steps.

I must have looked exactly as you do now, I thought 'what the hell ?' But we followed her to the front door, stood on the top step and she breezed off somewhere. Just as my heart began to race with anticipation I heard them." "Heard what ?" Alex gasped, gripping the seat. "Hooves," said Nathan, "coming my way, clattering on the tarmac. Then around the corner came a dark brown open carriage in mint condition pulled by a pair of immaculate grey horses called 'Lambert and Butler.' The driver was pristine too, wearing a top hat and driving tails, holding a long whip. Dad and I went around London, with everybody staring, up to Sloane Square, past Tiffany and Peter Jones department store, back down Sloane Street and got dropped off at Harrods. I gave the horses a polo and we headed inside. I'd never been before so we did a bit of a tour, bought Mum a present and then sat down to lunch. I couldn't speak."

He beamed at Alex whose face was agog. His mouth hung open. "Pretty much like you now," he laughed. Alex shook his head in disbelief, "my God !" He said at last. "Nate that is an incredible story !" "And all true !" Nathan beamed as the carriage swung onto a cobbled circle in front of the 'Rathaus.' "Gruse got," said the driver and it was obvious that their ride was over. Alex got out first, tipping the man by as much as their budget would allow.

Nathan dismounted too and the carriage pulled away. Alex still shook his head as they began to walk in the direction of the Albertina museum. "Wow," he said at last and looked deeply into Nathan's eyes. "I'm glad that happened to you, you deserve it," he breathed. "Thanks," gulped Nathan, overwhelmed at the compliment, his cheeks flushing.

"Come on Dyson, after that I need more cake." Alex pulled him close into his side as they walked, making him laugh again for the hundredth time that day, and it was still only two o'clock.

They didn't stop for more cake on the way to the Albertina, they were laughing and talking too much and forgot about it. Inside the beautiful old building with it's appropriate horse statue outside and modern additions here and there, it was calm and quiet. People milled slowly from room to room and it seemed the only ones who spoke were them. Nathan had been desperate to see the Monet paintings and having felt obliged to saunter through the Picasso room just because it was there, which neither of them really enjoyed, he gasped out loud as they entered a high ceilinged white washed set of rooms.

"This is it," he breathed and clung to Alex's arm. They passed some other works which were nice to look at but Nathan was breathless with excitement to see the Monet's and hardly lingered anywhere else. Into the third room they turned and stopped dead. There on the wall in front of them, alone in its glory, hung 'The Water Lilies.' "It's stunning," said Alex. "Do you really think so ?" Asked Nathan as they sat down on the squashy white leather bench in front of it. "Yes I do. But why are there two more paintings of the bridge by him on the next wall ? One greener than the other and the other one more pink and purple ? It's the same scene but in different colours ?" Nathan smiled, "good that you asked. Monet loved that lilly pond scene very much, he was fascinated by light and light on water and painted the water lilies many times, also the bridge over the lilly pond too. Only, over the years his eyesight began to fade, and as it faded his colours got brighter and more extreme. So the more realistic colours are his early work and the brighter ones...." "...when he couldn't distinguish colour so well anymore ?" Alex finished for him. "Exactly."

"Wow," Alex was impressed, "and this is only our first day !" Nathan beamed at him. They kissed a quick gentle lip touch in front of the painting. "I've always wanted to do that," husked Nathan. "Good," Alex, looked deeply into his eyes. "Well now that I've helped make another one of your dreams come true how about we go and chase some big hairy butterflies around a steamy room ?" Nathan laughed out loud and then saw the disapproving look on the security guards face.

"Let's get out of here, I was going to suggest a distraction and then you could slip that canvas into your ruck sack but we've been rumbled, c'mon, leg it !" Said Alex as they tip toed from the room eyed suspiciously by the guard then ran laughing all the way under the warm blue sky to the butterfly house.

"Bugger me !" Said Alex as the steaminess of the enormous greenhouse hit him. "Yug !" He pulled at his top as it began to stick to his shapely torso. Nathan gave him an approving look and then pulled at his own t-shirt. "I can't believe this place, it's SO hot....I...whoa !" He exclaimed as an enormous blue butterfly fluttered down and landed on his forearm. It's feet felt so gentle but firmly placed. "Wow !" Breathed Alex, pulling the camera out of its sleeve and taking as many pictures as he could from every angle. "Gosh, that's lovely," he smiled at the last one. He'd caught Nathan side on, his slim waist in perfect perspective broadening out to his ribs and shoulders, his bicep close to the lens, smooth and taut, but best of all was his expression of utter innocent joy, cheeks flushed and lightly damp from the heat he wore a lovely smile which lit his eyes as the butterfly tip toed its way down to the back of his hand. He giggled as Alex turned the camera toward him to show the picture, "ha ha, his feet are really ticklish..." Alex grinned as they looked at the picture together, "how do you know he's a he ?"

Nathan shrugged, "dunno. Wow ! Well done Al, that's a fab photo."
"I can't take any credit, look at my subjects," he smiled, just as the butterfly leapt into the air and winged its way right up to the top of a twelve foot tree. They watched it go as Nathan rubbed the back of his hand, he shook his head as they moved slowly forward toward a small pond, surrounded by thick foliage, "that, was fantastic."

Alex looked at the expression on his beautiful face. "It's funny," he continued, "but when you've been in a situation like mine recently, I know it might sound silly, but those are the moments you dream of that let you know you're alive again. I mean I craved you every minute of the day and I never want to be apart from you like that ever again, but when you're so hurt, just being able to do something really normal, - or I suppose abnormal, like having a huge butterfly tickle your arm, means the world." He looked at the floor, serious for a few seconds as if letting himself realise that he really was ok now. Alex gave him a moment and then slipped his arm softly around his waist and lightly kissed the nape of his neck. "That's wonderful my love," he husked and released his grip, it was too hot to walk around coiled together but Nathan reached out his fingers instead and they meandered quietly that way through the rest of the house.

There were so many beautiful butterflies inside the steamy greenhouse that they stopped and took tonnes of photos, bending their heads together each time to review the results. It was a blissful time. Sometime later, as they stepped back out into the breezy afternoon temperature, Nathan shivered. Alex pulled his polo shirt out of his ruck sack and draped it around his shoulders. Nathan smiled and kissed him in return. "Come on," whispered Alex happily, "let's go and force feed you more cake." Nathan giggled as Alex took his hand, leading him into the high vaulted ceiling cafe next door.

The rest of the trip seemed to fly by. Nathan got tired fairly quickly but after a cafe stop at regular intervals, he was fuelled and ready to go again. In four days they visited one Cathedral, five cafes, three restaurants, the Albertina, the Butterfly house, the Hofburg, two churches, Schonbrunn Palace, took a carriage ride around the city centre, saw the Glockenspiel strike twelve and made love five times. On their last day, the day they visited Schonbrunn, Nathan rested his chin on his hands as he looked out of the window of the 'Gloriette,' where they were at last trying the famous 'Sachatorte.' Alex suddenly laughed gently and shook his head.

"What ?" Asked Nathan, smiling at his laughter. "Oh I was just remembering last night at that little restaurant, 'Figmullers,' I can't believe we stumbled onto the best place to eat Wien Schnitzel in Vienna and you didn't eat it !" Nathan grinned and blushed as he replied sheepishly, "yes well I don't eat veal and my 'chicken schnitzel,' was just as nice thankyou very much !" Alex laughed out loud and stroked his cheek, "ha ha, 'chicken schnitzel !' There's no bloody such thing !" Nathan blushed more and pulled the Sachatorte out of Alex's reach, "piss off !"

Alex lunged for the cake with his fork making Nathan swing it right off the table out of reach until he pretended to look really upset and Nathan crumbled. "Ok, ok, no blubbing in the 'Gloriette,' please, this is a place where you're supposed to rejoice you know !" Alex blew him a kiss and snatched up a massive forkful of chocolate cake making his cheeks swell and a few crumbs drop from his barely closed lips. Nathan raised an eyebrow, he shook his head, "oh well, thank God you're pretty !" Alex 's cheeks dimpled with laughter, he nearly choked on the cake, but once he'd coughed enough to be able to swallow again he licked his lips at Nathan with streaming eyes.

"Hee hee, don't say that kind of thing to me when I've got a huge mouthful !" He wiped at his eyes with the backs of his hands. Nathan grinned, he loved mucking about with him. "I'll give you a huge mouthful later sunshine !" He murmured as he bent to fork up the last of the cake. Alex laughed and laughed and laughed. He didn't care that a few people stared, some grumpily at the amount of noise he was making. This had been some of the best days of his life and he was going to continue to love every minute of it with Nathan.

They lay back against their chairs, loving being in the light airy stone building, just able to peek over the high window ledge out to the steep grassy bank they'd climbed, the incredible marble fountain below and the maze hedges and sweeping gravel path way that led back to the palace, resplendent in the bright afternoon sunshine. "I can't believe this place," Alex breathed as he looked straight up at the ceiling high above. "I know, apparently this was built as only a half celebration ? What the hell would they have built if they'd been really proud !" Nathan snorted and looked around the rest of the room. Alex fished out their Time Out guide and read aloud the story of the Gloriette. "Built in 1775 by Ferdinand von Hohenberg as a monument to the soldiers who gave their lives for the empire, wow ! Originally the planned site for the palace itself, although it was deemed too expensive at the time." He frowned, "funny, why more expensive to build up here than down there ? Oh well." He shrugged and flicked the page over to look for more interesting little details.

" 'The Gloriette,'" Nathan exclaimed, "such a fantastic name." "It's just stunning," replied Alex and rubbed his hand over the back of Nathan's upon the table, "a bit like you." Nathan bit his lip, he blushed and leaned on the window ledge to look out again. Alex's stomach did somersaults, God he couldn't wait to marry this man, more than that, he couldn't wait to have him gasping in his arms tonight. Gasping, sleeping, talking, any and all of it would do. Just having Nathan back again was phenomenal.

"Ok my love, time to get cracking," He looked at his watch and waved at the waiter for the bill. Walking back toward the steep grassy bank a few minutes later, the boys looked back at the Gloriette. "Wow !" Said Nathan. "I agree," Alex crouched down with the camera, "stand by that massive urn for a moment will you." Nathan did as he was asked, leaning back against the cool stone sculpture. He folded his arms, crossed one leg across the other, slid his sunglasses down to shield his eyes and whispered, "ready Urn, say cheese !"

Alex nearly toppled over with laughter. "Shut up you fool !" He giggled and clicked to enlarge the photo he'd just taken. It blew him away. Nathan looked so beautiful, so young, so lean, so handsome but what really took his breath away was that smile, lighting him up from ear to ear. Alex stood up slowly and looked at him, still casually posing but pretending to have a conversation with his static new friend. He caught Alex's expression, "what?"

Alex shook his head, "nothing, stay there...one more," he crouched and took two more of a similar pose, each time Nathan's lit up face made his heart pound. Nathan patted 'Urn,' "nice to meet you mate, cheerio," he crunched toward Alex over the gravel, was met half way and then had all the breath knocked out of him as Alex flung his body around him and squeezed him hard in a bear hug. "Aaarrgghh ! My ribs ! I need to breath," he laughed. Alex let go and grinned at him, then his face softened as he looked into his eyes, "I'm so glad you're well," he husked, he brought up the picture and showed him, look at your smile here. "That's what stopped me in my tracks, just look how happy you are." Nathan took the camera and flicked through the 3 pictures, he flushed with pleasure and bit his lip. Turning moist eyes on Alex he said, "that's because of you."

It was a slow amble back down to the palace after that, there was so much to take in. The Schlosspark – or vast baroque landscape, the Palm House, Tiergarten (Zoo), and sweeping 360 views. It took some time. Once outside the gates it started to pour with rain so they jumped into a taxi back to the hotel to pick up their bags. "I can't believe that place," Nathan remarked, "it's just incredible. Did our guide really say that the most famous incumbent there, Sisi had sixteen children over 20 years ?" Alex nodded. "Shit ! No wonder she had a day bed made to take her meetings in."

"That was amazing wasn't it," Alex smiled, remembering their grand tour around 40 of the palaces 365 rooms. "Her bedroom was kind of creepy with the perspex box they've built to hermetically seal off the bed from the public," Nathan said. "Yeah but look what our guide said, in ten years it hasn't even needed hoovering !" Alex remembered, "and, no deterioration in the bedspread or other artefacts as none of our sweaty salts have been able to reach them." Nathan made a face, "that's so gross, that it's actually sweaty bodies that cause damage to things. Grim !"

"Yep ! Actually, speaking of sweaty bodies....we do have some time....." Alex raised an eyebrow making Nathan laugh and reach for his hand. "No my love, great idea but let me get my feet back on British soil before we do it again, I need to get to the airport without a rush or my nerves will be jangling all the way home." Alex smiled and smoothed a finger along his cheek bone, "of course my sweet and don't worry, I'll be right beside you every step of the way."

Chapter Sixteen.

The boys fell back through the Nesbitt – Halls front door at 7 o'clock that night. They were brimming with happiness, utterly shattered and even more tactile than before. It was a pleasure for their families to be able to wind them up gleefully as they flopped down onto the sofa together, arms entwining, ruck sacks still in place.

"Oy you two, no fornicating in front of your Father's in law," David mock growled. The boys giggled, red faced and squeezed each other tighter still until both mothers made their way across the room. "Ok, ok....!" Nathan disentangled himself and they struggled to their feet, slumping their bags to the floor and grinning at each other. "Could you please both go and have a shower do you think ?" Alison raised her eyebrow at them. Alex grinned over at a reddening Nathan, "sure !" He beamed.

"No, on your OWN Alex !" She chided, "luckily there are 3 bathrooms upstairs so that's at least ONE EACH !" Nathan hid his face in his hands and groaned,"Oh blimey," embarrassed to the core. Alex giggled and grabbed one of his hands, "come on handsome...." he laughed and pulled him up the stairs. "SEPARATE !" Shouted all four parents at once and were pleased to hear different directions of running and giggling upstairs but then only seconds later, one set of feet flew back down the landing into the first bathroom where everyone heard the lock ram home and two voices laughing hard over the thrashing water.

"Oh for God's sake...!" Christopher reddened and made for the bottom of the stairs. "No darling, I really wouldn't bother," Caitlin shrugged, "I mean what are you going to do ? Just don't pay it any attention." Christopher glanced up the stairs and back at the other three who looked slightly embarrassed but turned to get on with helping to prepare supper. His jaw muscle worked over time for a moment, he knew his son was gay, he knew what that entailed, he just didn't want it happening in his house and especially before they were married. Married ! He shook himself, struggling internally, gay men marrying ! He chewed his lip for a moment, he wanted his son to be happy but it felt so odd when he thought of him being 'married' to a man.

He rubbed his chin and looked up to find his wife smiling kindly at him. She put down the vegetable knife and courgette she'd been chopping and came to his side. "I know my darling," she whispered. "It's hard for you, but you're doing the right thing, this is their life and just think how miserable we could make them if we didn't support them eh ?" Christopher sighed deeply and looked at her. He glanced at the Hendersons but they were engrossed in chatting over a recipe. "I don't want to bring them down or anything Cait, I just find this hard sometimes," he shrugged, "I mean I see how happy they both are and I know it must be ok but it's just that marriage for me is about a man and a woman." He gazed searchingly into his wife's eyes.

"But times have changed so much my love and as you say, look how happy they are ? Neither is promiscuous, they aren't messed up mentally, they want to work, marry and start a wonderful life together. Some people should be so lucky ?" She stroked his face. Christopher smiled at her, she was right and he knew it. He slid his arm around her waist and kissed her full on the lips, she blushed as they pulled apart. "And if Alex is anything like as romantic as you are then lucky Nathan, just think, they could be as happy as us for 21 years," she smiled. "And the rest," husked Christopher, looking at his wife with the memory of their first days together clearly in his mind.

She'd blown him away. She was a beautiful woman, - to him at least, and he didn't care what anyone else thought. But better than that, she was incredible inside. She noticed things that other people rarely saw, her attention to simply being 'alive' and 'human,' was amazing. She wanted everyone to have a happy life and it shone out of her. "If Nathan's anything like you then I can see why our son loves him so much," he breathed, "I'm going to show you just how I feel tonight, maybe all night," Caitlin caught her breath and blushed deeply. "They are incredibly lucky if they have one tenth of what we have, incredibly," she beamed, her eyes shining with love and desire, so thankful for the man she'd held every night for the last 21 years.

After dinner Nathan's parents took him home. He was exhausted but so didn't want to leave Alex, his eyes looked misty as they kissed goodnight by the car, all parents keeping a discreet distance. "Hey," Alex squeezed him around the middle, "don't be doing that or you know I'm going to get all tearful too." Nathan snorted and smiled away the threatened tears, but his eyes were still moist. "Oh baby," Alex shook his head and gulped. "God I hate leaving you too, we're meant to be together, but it's only for the odd night here and there now, and by October the 10th we'll never have to sleep apart again ok ?" Nathan chewed his lip and nodded, still struggling with his emotions. He looked down at the gravel and idly toed it with his foot, trying to distract himself. He sighed, "I know, I'm just really tired," he shrugged, "now it feels so strange to be away from you, even for one night. I feel like I'm visiting my parents on a trip and something's missing." Alex beamed at this and closed his arms around him, "oh my love, my precious, it's the same for me, always the same." They held each other, eyes closed, nothing else mattering, until a few polite "aherm," noises from the back ground. They disentangled to look back at the house and saw Nathan's mum and dad descending the steps.

"We'll talk at school tomorrow about where we're going to live, it's gotta be somewhere around here I think, at least to start with as we might need a lot of help from our folks, what do you think ?" Alex asked. "Agreed," Nathan smiled. "Night," they both whispered, their hands lingered together until Nathan's parents opened the car doors. Alex walked back toward the house, backwards. Nathan laughed out of the window at this, he shook his head, this was all so special, was it a dream ? Lucky lucky him to have found his 'one,' so early in life he mused. As the car turned out into the road he closed his eyes, seeing Alex still walking backwards in his mind, grinning, handsome, youthful and so full of life. He hoped that he'd still be like that when he was sixty.

He was in a perkier mood the next morning over breakfast, undoubtedly as he was to see Alex again, crunching through jammy toast and coffee as the news played in the background and his family bundled about around him Nathan felt inordinately happy. His mother winked at him over her Earl Grey which made him blush and look away, she always knew when he was thinking about him. He frowned for a moment, would Alex mind if he broached the flat subject with her without him ?

"Now what's that look for ?" Alison still couldn't help watching her son a little too carefully since his accident, she knew that would pass but luckily it meant she had seen his mood change to slight concern. He looked up at her from his food and decided to give it a whirl anyway. "Well, I'm not worried or anything, don't get concerned mum, I was just wondering where Alex and I are going to be able to afford to live after the wedding ? We were talking about it last night and agreed it would be better to be somewhere close to you guys for now at least as we'll probably need a lot of help, what do you think ?"

Alison smiled and came to rub his arm, "don't you worry darling, would you like Dad and I to do a bit of searching through a few particulars in the area while you're at school ?" Nathan grinned, "Mum that would be wonderful, thanks so much !" He threw his arms around her in a big bear hug. She laughed and squeezed him back. "Ok, leave it with me for a day or two then, now come on, off to school with you." She pecked him on the cheek. He grinned again, pecked her on both, stuffed a huge slab of peanut buttered toast between his teeth and tore out of the front door, scooping his ruck sack up in the process.

Five minutes later he was panting from exertion, licking peanut butter off his lips and running toward Alex's beautiful smile and outstretched arms. He leapt into them, dropping his rucksack and wrapping his legs around his waist.

Alex squeezed him tight and spun around in joy before letting him slide down his body until their mouths met for a prolonged, heart thrummingly exciting kiss. "Mmm," Alex groaned, "that really made me hungry." "Oh yes ?" Nathan beamed, blushing and raising an eyebrow. "Yeah, I love peanut butter !" He laughed. "Arse !" Nathan cuffed his ear.

Alex ducked away, giggling and grinning, Nathan chased him along the pavement, "why does it taste even better in your mouth than on my toast ? Strange huh ?" He teased. Nathan felt his cheeks flame and sped after him. They tustled and teased their way to school, laughing continuously, if this was a taster of their life to come as a couple then Nathan knew it would be pretty awesome.

He waited til first break to tell Alex about the conversation with his mum over breakfast. "Nate that's wonderful news, your mum's seriously brilliant you know," Alex replied, lounging back against the bench they'd commandeered. He tore off a large piece of his chocolate croissant and gave it to Nathan who dropped the whole thing into his mouth and chewed, nodding. "She is," chew chew, "I know, I'm very lucky, well we're very lucky actually, as she's going to be your mother in law." Alex grinned, "yeah," he blushed all of a sudden. It was much harder to make him colour than Nathan who gawped at him for a second, "my God, is there something wrong ? You've gone really red. ?" Alex shook his head and ran a hand through his hair, he looked desperately shy and not like himself for a moment. Nathan shuffled closer to him lying both arms on top of his. "Al ?" Alex looked into his eyes with moisture in his own.

"Hey..." Nathan felt his stomach knot, "What is it ?" He asked worriedly. "It's us," shrugged Alex, a tear dropping onto his knee, silvery and glinting for a milli second. Nathan felt a bit sick, "us?" He trembled, "yes, us," said Alex, another tear spilling onto his legs. "It's just so damn fucking wonderful !" Nathan shut his eyes, blanched white and snatched Alex into his arms, he squeezed him tight for a moment and then said with relief, "it is, it bloody is baby, but if you EVER fucking scare me like that again I'll thrash the living daylights out of you !" Alex roared with laughter and wiped his sleeve across his eyes.

He looked back into Nathan's and and thumbed his cheek, "wait a minute dumb ass, it shouldn't be possible to scare you, I can never have anything bad to tell you about us ok ? You know this already." "I know," Nathan nodded, "but what about when we were in Vienna and you got all scared, you know how much I love you but you still had a panic. I guess we both get scared at the 'what if,' sometimes." Alex smiled at this, " then we're both idiots sometimes." "True," grinned Nathan, "but I still love my idiot." "Me too," Alex breathed, leaning forward to kiss his mouth with a lingering tender kiss.

The bell went for the end of break. "We'll meet at your house on Thursday night to go through the property details that your parents find out about, and I'll set mine on to it too, maybe we can book a few viewings for Saturday afternoon, how does that sound ?" Alex suggested as they wandered back to class. "Brilliant," Nathan beamed, interlacing their fingers together as they made their way up the stone steps and back inside til lunch.

After school on Thursday, all four parents gathered at the Henderson's to eat with the boys and go through the flat details that they'd found. There were delicious smells coming from the kitchen as Nathan appeared fresh from a shower after finishing his home work. He looked so well now after his recovery, Caitlin and Christopher both hugged him hello. "So where's our son tonight ? I thought he was joining us ?" Christopher asked as Nathan took their coats and hung them by the front door. "Oh he is, don't worry," he beamed, "hockey practice, they've got a game on Sunday morning." He looked at his watch, "in fact, a rather muddy individual should be pitching up here with his ruck sack full of clean clothes in approximately two min..." he didn't finish the sentence as there was a knock on the door at that very second and in he came, panting and filthy. "Ah, talk of the devil !" Caitlin smiled. Alex beamed at them all and then made a face as he slid off his boots and hobbled toward Nathan for a kiss. "Oh no, you're bloody limping ?" Nathan grimaced but embraced him warmly, kissing his muddy face and thumbing his cheeks. "Yeah," gasped Alex and rubbed his leg, "I got a hockey stick to the shin just as the whistle blew, not nice. He got me just below the guard." "Ouch !" Winced Nathan as Alex's parents also made a face. "Are you ok darling ?" His mother looked concerned.

"Honestly I'm fine, it's just throbbing a bit now, a hot shower and some of that Nurofen gel on it and I'm sorted," he turned back to Nathan and gazed into his eyes. They both grinned. "You must be starving, dinner's only five minutes away, is that enough time for you ?" Nathan asked as their fingers entwined. "Yeah, that's plenty," Alex gave him his killer smile and kissed his mouth quickly. Nathan's heart sped up immediately so Alex did it again. They both grinned like the Cheshire Cat. "I won't be long," Alex bent to pick up his ruck sack and hobbled loudly up the stairs for his shower.

Dinner was just about getting underway when he reappeared ten minutes later, Nathan slid a large portion of Lasagne onto his plate and filled his salad bowl with a hefty helping of Iceberg lettuce and orange pepper slices, his favourite salad. "Yum," said Alex as he clambered into his seat, limping a lot less and smiling at Nathan. "Hi," he breathed and pecked him on the lips again as he took up his fork. "Hi yourself," said Nathan, colouring. "Do you two ever let up ?" David asked, shaking his head. "Nope," said Alex confidently as they held hands under the table. Everyone seemed starved and attacked their food ravenously so the flat conversation waited until pudding. They sat back in their chairs, slowly progressing through totally unnecessary but delicious home made apple crumble and cream. Alison got up to put on the coffee and pulled out her file of property details that she'd been collecting all week.

Christopher saw this and stepped away from the table to retrieve more information from his laptop bag. "Ok, so we parents, have been doing a bit of research for you two on your home," Alison began. The boys beamed with delight. "Thanks Mum," Nathan smiled. "Yeah, great that you did it Dad," Alex added. "Well we did actually find something quite special," Alison grinned, Christopher nodded, his face lighting up too. "You did ?" Alex's heart thrummed in his chest, this sounded exciting already. "Actually Alex, your father and I went to see this place yesterday and we booked you two a viewing on Saturday morning at 9am," she slid a set of details across the table. Alex picked them up and leaned closer to Nathan. "Wow !" He exclaimed. Nathan's eyes flew wide, "Oh my God ! It's the turret house ?" He blurted, incredulously. "Yes, it is," smiled his mum. Nathan blinked hard, his mouth wide open, "Oh My God !" He gasped again. "What ? What am I missing ?" Alex wanted to join in. Nathan faced him with a still stunned expression. "Do you know that red brick house two roads up from here, turn left, entirely overlooks the view, Dutch gabling at the front and then a turret on the right as you look at it, lovely big windows going all around underneath ?" Alex started to shake his head frowning and then all at once his expression was an absolute picture.

"NOOOOOO !" He looked blown away. Nathan laughed and nodded, "yes my love, that's it. This flat is in that house ! Can you imagine ?" Alex shook his head, wide eyed with astonishment. He picked up the details and looked inside, not actually reading at all, stunned at them even considering the beautiful building. "Yes it's a self contained but mind you, very small flat, within that house," Alison smiled, "and yes, it does have Nathan's favourite feature in it, the turret room." Alex shook his head. "That's wonderful but you know what guys, we are never going to be able to afford the mortgage on this, let alone a deposit." He shrugged sadly at Nathan, "I mean we've been working our arses off at any extra jobs you know that and we have a little bit of our savings left but it's not much after the wedding." His dad smiled at them both and made a 'shall I ?' expression at Alison who nodded.

"Well that's the thing boys, - Alex, remember 'Headway' ? I rang them and spoke to Mrs Brooks-Bank, the woman you met on the bus that day. She was thrilled to hear from me and wants you to call her, she does have a job going if you're interested. Also, we four parents have so far not been allowed by our wayward sons to contribute to their nuptials at all. So we decided that we're going to help you out on the deposit. Call it a wedding present, we'll each pay half and you two then just have the mortgage to manage yourselves. What do you think ?"

Alex's jaw dropped open, he didn't know what to say. Nathan shook his head, "no, it's too much....!" He said in shock. Alex jumped a little in his seat and clutched Nathan's arm.

"Don't say that Nath, how are we ever going to get on the property ladder this early without their help ?" He gesticulated toward the parents. Nathan's heart thrummed wildly, it was a huge commitment to a lot of money and he was scared, what if they didn't make enough ? Alex scanned his face, "I know what you're thinking, but why should we not be able to afford it.

We're young, we're just starting out and people always give youngsters a chance." Nathan made a face, "well they have in my experience anyway," laughed Alex. He took hold of both of Nathan's hands. "Please Nate, trust me. I know we can do this. You're not scared to marry me this young are you, so don't be scared to try something else too." Nathan looked at Alex's earnest expression and felt the strength of his grip, even if he himself doubted his earning potential, clearly Alex didn't. He looked over at his parents, they were happy enough to do this and smiled reassuringly at him. After everything that had just happened to him he didn't feel like sitting still and not taking the chance. Slowly he smiled, "alright then, let's do it." Alex threw his arms around him and squeezed him tightly, "oh thank you, thank you, my love." Nathan giggled, "God I need some air, get off me you." He tried to wriggle out of Alex's grasp.

"Ok you can put him down now," Christopher sighed, it was making him a little uncomfortable at the table. "If we get the flat I'm going to take you in every room," Alex husked as he pulled away. Nathan gasped aloud and completely reddened. All four parents stared at him making it worse and then fixed their eyes on Alex who guffawed with laughter. "Are you embarrassing your fiance again ?" His mother raised an eyebrow. Alex grinned and nodded taking a huge spoonful of his crumble. "Lucky you're so mature eh ?" Nathan shook his head at Alex's hamster cheeks. "You're so gonna get it later !" He said before he had time to consider the implications.

Two seconds after the words left his lips he clapped his hands over his mouth, dying with embarrassment and now claret red. The parents all burst out laughing and Alex coughed, spraying the table with crumbs. Nathan buried his face in his hands and only looked up when he heard crockery being collected and chairs moving as their parents started to clear up. He gingerly raised his head and saw Alex chew down the last of his huge mouthful, he took a sip of water, licked his lips and grinned at his expression, loving every minute of it.

"You cock !" Nathan tried to look pissed off but every time this kind of thing happened, he only needed one look at Alex's giggling face and he just couldn't be annoyed. His lips played up at the corners. Alex stroked one of his cheeks. "Sorry babe," he whispered and kissed him on the mouth. Nathan shuddered. He needed to be alone with Alex tonight, he wanted him so badly.

They helped with the clearing up which got it done in no time. Alison put on another pot of coffee and asked Nathan to get the biscuits from the larder. He brought them over and arranged a few on a plate as Alex stood between them and topped up the milk jug. "Well I'm certainly looking forward to 'getting it later,'" he murmured. Nathan gasped and clutched the side going beetroot red. Alison laughed beside Alex and smacked the back of his hand, "stop it you naughty child !" Alex laughed catching her eye, they were so fond of each other and she couldn't help laughing at how easily he could wind up her son. Nathan's face was hidden behind his hands again as he groaned, "that was in front of my mother."

Alison took the jug and biscuit plate and disappeared to the living room. Alex gently pulled at Nathan's hands and after a few seconds of gentle persuasion Nathan lowered them. He was still red and shook his head at Alex who laughed at the expression on his face. "I'm sorry," he giggled, without an ounce of contrition. "No you're not," Nathan sighed. Alex beamed at him and again Nathan's lips turned up at the corners. "You are so naughty Alex ! Why do you do that in front of my parents ?" Alex shrugged impishly, "I don't know, I think I just love to see you go all red and aghast, you look fabulous when you do it." He grinned his mega watt smile and folded Nathan into his arms, "do you forgive me ?"

Nathan wrapped his arms around him and grinned back, melting against his warm body. "Yes I do, and I probably always will, because I love to see you this happy." "Even though I've got an enormous cheek in doing it ?" Alex looked a little ashamed after all. "Even though you've got the biggest damn cheek in the entire world and I'm gonna kick your arse for it big time when we're alone, yes," grinned Nathan.

Alex threw his head back and laughed. In the living room their parents craned their necks to see their boys embracing and giggling once more. Caitlin smiled as Christopher shook his head, "they'll never change," he tutted and sipped his coffee. "Let's hope not," said both mothers in unison and laughed.

As the alarm sounded on Friday morning, Nathan's mum knocked on the door. "Boys, there's tea here." "Thanks," they said together. Since a polite discussion some weeks back, Alex often spent the night now, but it was on a discreet basis and the boys didn't flout the few rules that the Henderson's had asked them to stick to. Nathan slid into his PJ bums and retrieved the tea. He brought it back to bed and slid once more into Alex's smiling embrace. They kissed lovingly. "Hello my love," Alex breathed down at Nathan's happy face. Last night had been amazing. They'd been so tender with each other, making slow love for hours, caressing and kissing every inch of skin. This morning their connection seemed even stronger than ever. Alex gazed at Nathan and thumbed his cheek. Nathan's heart swelled. He may have had a fractured skull barely a few short months back, but if this was his reward for being brave he couldn't be happier.

"It's going to be tough going to work when we live together," breathed Alex as he gently stroked his chest. "Why?" Nathan managed, though his brain could barely form the words with Alex's caressing. "Because then I can't lie in bed and do this to you all day." Nathan grinned and reached up to cup his face. He looked serious for a moment. "I didn't think it was possible Alex, but after last night I feel even closer to you." Alex nodded and took hold of his hand, kissing the back before interlacing their fingers. "I know, me neither, but I do too." They gazed at each other, content, calm and confident in each others love.

Nothing more needed to be said as they lay together, Alex sinking down onto the sheets and laying himself half across Nathan who idly played with his hair. It was a serene moment. They closed their eyes, snuggled closer and then the door banged open making them leap with shock as the twins launched themselves across the duvet, landing in a tangled heap on Alex's sore shin from the night before and winding Nathan in the process. "Yow !" Screamed Alex.

"You idiots !" Nathan snapped, shocked for a second at their surprise entrance. Jack beamed at his brother, Jasmine laughed at the livid expression on his face. "WHAT is going on ?" Roared their dad suddenly appearing in the doorway. "Ok you two, out ! You know the rules, leave Nathan and Alex alone when they're behind closed doors. Go on, hop it !" Jasmine giggled, "this is your fault," she stabbed her finger at Jack. "Oy, don't blame me, you thought it would be fun too !" "OUT !" Roared their father. "Sorry," murmured Jasmine, not looking it at all, as she clambered off the bed and exited with her moaning grumbling brother.

"Breakfast boys, don't be late," David nodded at them as he shut the door. Nathan flopped back onto the pillows. "Well that definitely won't be happening when we move out of here," he grinned. "No it sure won't," agreed Alex looking pained. He was sitting up rubbing his shin. "Oh God sorry about that, here let me look," Nathan reached out to pull back the duvet. Alex's shin looked purple and red and there was a definite lump. "Ow !" he grimaced. "Let's nip into the shower then I can gel you up and take some of that pain away." He smiled. Alex put his hand around the back of his head and kissed him full on the mouth. "You may have a mental brother and sister," he breathed, still rubbing the leg, "but I do love you." Nathan grinned, "me too."

School was really boring this Friday, it seemed to go on for ever and afterward Nathan had a swimming competition to go to so the afternoon seemed to linger even more. At least Art was his last class before the swimming as he'd recently dropped the last lesson of the day, Biology. Who needed that as an A level he'd rationalised, after all, he didn't want to be a scientist and had missed so much course work already. He drew a sketch of the diner he wanted them to open and tried to put in as much detail as possible. Mr Kinsella, their tutor peered over his shoulder. "That's wonderful Nathan, your drawing's still coming on so much, really good, well done." He squeezed his best student's shoulder proudly and progressed around the class looking at everyone's work.

Nathan began the walk up to the pool after Art. He was in a good mood but the nerves were starting to kick in. He jumped as Alex appeared next to him, sliding his fingers into his palm. "Shit !" He exclaimed. "Ooh dear, bit nervy are you ?" Alex gave his fingers a reassuring little squeeze and smiled his killer smile. Nathan melted against him with a grin, "yes, a bit."

"Don't be, you're bloody awesome and just seeing you in your trunks is enough for most people anyway." Nathan threw back his head and laughed, his cheeks flamed. "What ? It's true," shrugged Alex. "Al...," Nathan smiled shyly and pushed him with his shoulder as they reached the changing rooms. Alex kissed him quickly on the mouth and brushed his thumbs over his cheeks, "you really will be awesome," he breathed and left him to change.

There were six other boys competing in tonight's competition, all from other local schools. The top three would progress onto the next level, county competition. Nathan had no ambitions to go higher than that but winning a county comp would be nice just once so he was unusually nervous tonight. He knew he wasn't as strong as before his accident so he could only hope that his determination would carry him through. Serendipity had him in lane 7, his lucky number. He smiled at the thought as the whistle blew for them to take their marks. He gulped and tried to forget everything. 'Swim for Alex, get him a medal,' he told himself and then the second whistle sounded and he plunged into the water from a flying dive, knifing through the surface with practised ease.

He forgot everything except his stroke and breathing, arm in, head to the side, kick, kick. Same again, arm in, head to the side, precious air intake. He sucked it in quickly. They were coming up to the first turn, he spun himself forward and kicked off the wall, 3 more lengths to go but his lungs were already protesting, these guys were fast. He concentrated on effective breathing, elongating himself through each stroke to glide across the top of the pool. They turned again, he kicked hard and caught a flash of sound, the crowd were cheering already, willing on their favourites with still two lengths to go.

Nathan concentrated on getting to the next wall, it was coming up again, his lungs felt fit to burst. Kick, kick, arms in and out, breathing, breathing, he could think of nothing else. The pain in his chest made him want to stop but he would hang a medal around Alex in bed tonight if it killed him. He feared it might.

The last turn, he soared through the water, breaking the surface ahead of at least two people he was sure, it gave him hope. He had only peripheral vision to rely on but he would give it his best shot, he was beating someone he knew it. Again the crowd roared, were they on their feet ? Nathan kicked harder, his thighs hurting so much as his chest burned. The wall loomed, podium's were being decided, closer and closer, he could see the tiled edge, just a few more strokes, he squeezed every ounce of energy from his gasping frame reaching out for the wall, was he winning ? A cheer went up, his hand hadn't touched yet, shit ! Someone else had won, nearly, nearly there, it was a split second, he stretched and stretched, yes !

He sprang up and down on the spot and pulled his goggles onto his head. The crowd were on their feet going nuts. Lane 2's swimmer was punching the air, ok so that was the first spot decided, lane 4's challenger suddenly leapt about too as he saw the scoreboard which Nathan couldn't see clearly from his end. He gulped, that was two slots gone, damn, damn ! But then everyone cheered again and Nathan spotted Alex in the crowd, he was double punching the air and jumping up and down pointing at the scoreboard. Nathan grinned from ear to ear, straining to read 3rd place. "Well done," said lane 6's swimmer and shook his hand.

"I got it ? Third ?" "Yup," said lane six, managing a sporting smile before he pulled himself out and sighed his way to the changing rooms. Nathan bounced out too and stood up, peeling off his tight hat and goggles. Alex looked ecstatic in the crowd, it made him blush with pleasure. "Well done," said the headmaster, shaking his hand and smiling warmly, "could you stand on position 3 please, we want to give out the medals." "Yes of course, thanks," Nathan smiled and quickly rubbed himself with his towel before slipping on his school fleece and joining the other two on the rostrums.

"Well done guys," smiled the winner. "Thanks Charlie," Nathan shook his hand, they'd met before at several events. "This is your spot really Nathan, we both know that. Great to see you back anyway, I heard about the accident, good job today man. Next time you'll be standing here for sure." Charlie said honestly.

Nathan was touched, "thanks, that's really nice of you." "Just the truth," Charlie shrugged and lowered his neck for the medal, this wasn't like the Olympics, in school competitions first came first in the medal giving which meant Nathan was last. He grinned stupidly as the Headmaster approached and hung his bronze around his neck, it felt incredibly special. The school photographer, a year eight boy, took their picture, all three on the top podium and hurried instantly away, already emailing it to his computer. Everyone shook hands amid great cheering and whistling, group hugged once, and then stepped back onto the watery poolside to head off and get changed.

The crowd whistled its approval of the whole event before immediately starting to disperse. Nathan rubbed his head with both hands, that swimming hat was really tight, he could feel a deep mark from the edge on his forehead. It was cold standing there but he felt a bit dazed with pride, he'd won another swimming medal, it always felt good. He started to amble slowly toward the changing rooms, knowing Alex must be on his way down from the stands, probably parting groups of people with his mega watt smile and built in charm. He smiled at the thought and held up his medal to admire it. It had figures swimming in relief on it, he fingered their shape and felt his smile broaden.

"God that was amazing !" Alex grinned as he appeared suddenly, flush faced at Nathan's side. He shook his head as he beamed at his beloved and joined him in gazing at the medal. "Nate I'm so proud !" He exclaimed, his eyes shining. "Thanks," Nathan grinned as they reached for one another. They held each other tightly, "you were brilliant, just bloody brilliant," Alex said again, still genuinely astonished.

He slipped a little kiss onto Nathan's lips, pulled away and gazed into his eyes. "You were all SO, good, I've never seen anything like it !" He looked stunned. Nathan blushed and giggled. Alex grinned at him and touched his cheek. "Go and shower, I'll be waiting." He urged, seeing Nathan's skin start to goose flesh. "I will, it's a bit chilly. Back in a minute," He pecked him on the lips and was gone. Alex smiled after him, it made his heart pound to think they'd be married in just over two months time. He inhaled slowly and rotated the ring on his left hand. He couldn't wait.

They lay in bed at midnight after another slow gentle sess that night and lazily caressed one another's skin where ever their fingers lay. It was heavenly. Nathan sighed, " I'm so comfy." Alex laughed softly and kissed the top of his head, his hair smelt citrusy and fresh, newly washed. He lay back and sighed too, eyes closed. "This does feel good," he croaked. Nathan snuggled closer, his cheek pressing against Alex's warm chest. "Damn," he groaned and started to slide out of the bed. "No, hey wait, where are you going....don't leave me all cold for a minute without my human hot water bottle !" Alex pretended to pout. Nathan grinned at him and stumbled over to his rucksack, "ok but there was something I promised myself I'd do if I won a medal today so let me just get this," he reached into his bag and began to rummage.

"Oh ok," Alex pretended to try and wake up a bit, rubbing his eyes and struggling to sit up against the pillows. "But I have lube in the bedside...." Nathan shot him a look. "You mean I'm not going to get lucky again tonight ?" He sagged against the bed in mock disappointment. "Shut up you fool !" Nathan giggled. "Oh come out would you !" He said frustratedly into the rucksack. "We did that at school together if you remember," added Alex, from the bed. Nathan nearly fell over with laughter. "NOT helping !" He giggled, "aha, here you are you little bugger ! - don't say it ! " He'd caught the grin forming on Alex's lips from across the room.

He came back to bed holding something behind his back. "Not that you deserve me doing this now as you're such a tease, but here you go. Shut your eyes," Alex beamed naughtily at him and raised an eyebrow, "hmm, shut my eyes for a surprise eh ? Now you're talking."

"Shush ! Be a good boy for once, shut em and shut up," Nathan said sternly, trying not to laugh. "Ok ok, I'm sorry," Alex smiled and shut them. Nathan reached across and slid the medal over his head. Realising what he was doing Alex moved to help it slip down and then opened his eyes as the metal thudded gently onto his chest. He looked down at it, picking it up and feeling the swimming figures just as Nathan had earlier. He'd gone quiet and thoughtful.

He looked up into Nathan's face and reached for his cheek, "it's beautiful Nate, really beautiful." Nathan nodded slowly. They eyed each other, totally content. Alex picked up Nathan's hand, interlacing their fingers and making him smile. "Come here," he whispered and they were off again for the second time that night. It took most of the night. They began slowly once more, appreciating every contour, every muscle, every inch of flesh. By the early light they lay back down again, watching each other's faces in the dim blueness that slipped through the curtains. "I love you," whispered Nathan. "I know you do," Alex caressed him softly as the dawn slowly rose. Nothing more needed to be said.

Chapter Seventeen.

"Erm, you two, YOU TWO !" Alison Henderson stood exasperated outside her sons door. Her husband walked up behind her, resting his hand gently in the small of her back. "Al ?" He asked. "I just can't wake them this morning David. Do you think I should be worried ? Maybe they're not there ?" She shrugged, not knowing what to think. David patted her shoulder, "I'll go in love, hang on, I'm sure they're fine, just overslept." He knocked loudly on the door, repeated the boys names at top decibel and then tried the door. It swung freely open to reveal his son deeply asleep and wrapped up in the arms of his lover, equally deeply asleep. David coloured, embarrassed, he didn't really want to be party to behind closed door goings on but at least their modesty was just about covered.

He picked up Nathan's spare blanket from his toy chest and threw it over them, just as a precaution. "Son, son, WAKE UP !" He said loudly, shaking his son's shoulder quite roughly. Nathan was deeply embedded in a wonderful dream, Alex's lips were all over him and kept returning to his mouth for deep sensuous kisses. He smiled in his sleep but then the picture seemed to lurch or the ground beneath him wobble, what was going on. "Gerroff," he frowned and feebly batted his Dad away.

His fingers touched real flesh as he flayled, feeling shirt sleeve and skin. It jolted him suddenly awake. He lifted his head, confused for a moment. "Eh ?" He glanced up at his father, looked away and then jumped a million miles, colouring profusely as he realised that his arms were firmly locked around Alex's nakedness and his mother standing   in the door way too. "Erm,..." he blushed at his father who clapped him firmly on the shoulder.

"Don't worry son, you just overslept, we didn't want you to miss the flat viewing, come on get up. Mum and I will be having our breakfast, see you down there." Nathan nodded, his cheeks aflame. His mother smiled kindly from the doorway. Alex began to stir as David Henderson crossed the thresh hold, closing the door behind him.

It took Alex a few seconds to fully cognate too but then he leapt out of bed looking totally dishevelled, hair in every direction. "Fuck, fuck !" He screeched, eyes like saucers as he stared at Nathan who collapsed back onto the bed in fits of giggles. Alex panted and looked about him wildly for another few seconds. He gulped and ran a hand through his hair.

"Did your father just see us, NAKED ?" Nathan was laughing too hard to answer at first, but then he sat up and nodded. Alex looked even more horrified.

Nathan clutched his sides, "but don't worry, just your cock !" "WHAT ?" Alex was beetroot red. Nathan had never laughed so hard in his life. He fell back onto the sheets in fits, Alex's expression was the funniest thing in the world. He gripped his ribs as he cried with laughter, rolling about on the bed with his eyes shut. A second later the mattress depressed beside him and he opened his eyes to see a seething Alex clamber over him.

"Just my cock eh ?" He repeated. Nathan tried to reply but tears streamed down his cheeks and just a squeak came out. Alex's lips turned up at the corners as his body started to quiver too, "just my cock ? I'm going to enjoy this, you are SO gonna get it now." He pounced on Nathan making him screech as his fingers tickled and pinched mercilessly. "No, No !" Shrieked Nathan, screaming and screaming with laughter. Downstairs his parents shook their heads. His dad looked up at the ceiling, "just ignore it," said his mother.

"Please no," Nathan croaked as Alex groped and attacked every part of him. At last when it seemed he could stand no more Alex finally stopped, sitting back on his haunches shaking his head. "Just my cock !" He said again, setting Nathan off into even more laughter. It sounded so good to his ears. He grinned broadly, a very naughty evil look crossing his face. "Oh God !" Gulped Nathan and squealed once more as Alex pounced for the final assault.

They had mucked about for so long that when they finally jumped out of bed there was no time for a shower. "I don't care," whispered Alex, stepping into fresh boxers, "I can have you on me all day long." Nathan groaned and shut his eyes. He opened them, blushing, as they dressed with speed.

"Hungry ?" He beamed as Alex folded him into his embrace and they kissed each other good morning. " Absolutely frigging starving !" "I'm not surprised, not after last night," Nathan breathed shyly, caressing his chest. "Me either," husked Alex. The look in his eyes took Nathan's breath away. He gasped and chewed his lip. Lucky lucky me, he thought as they took each other's hands and made their way down to breakfast.

David Henderson knew teenage boys could eat, but he'd never seen anything like it. They stuffed so much food in it was unbelievable. Alex's mounded plate looked ridiculous to start with. "You'll never get through that," David said incredulously. "Watch him," shrugged Nathan, well used to Alex's serving sizes by now. He went back for a second round, more toast, more scrambled egg, two croissant and another yoghurt. It all disappeared quickly into him.

He patted his stomach afterwards which barely even seem as if it bulged. "You're digesting that already aren't you ?" David looked astonished. Alex laughed and nodded, draining his tea cup. He flicked his wrist over and glanced at the time. "Shit we'd better go Nath. Ooops !" He clapped his hand over his mouth for swearing at the table. Alison rolled her eyes, "nevermind," she smirked, "go on you two, you don't want to miss the appointment. We'll clear up."

The boys slid from their stools and fished their coats off the hooks by the door, shrugging into them in double quick time. Nathan rolled his wrist round and nearly swore too, "blimey we'd better hurry. Thanks mum, Dad, see you in a bit." They banged out of the front door and tore out of the drive. David got up to slowly stack the dishwasher. "They'll be sick at that rate !" Alison laughed, "honey it wasn't that long ago that you were their age. They won't be sick, and they'll come back in 45 minutes looking for biscuits." David looked appalled. "Was I really like that too ?" Alison leant over and kissed him softly on the cheek, "yes my love, you were a total glutton til you were 30."

Nathan and Alex pelted up the hill once they got out of the drive. It didn't take long to get to the turret house but they ran extra fast just in case and arrived just after 9. The estate agent smiled warmly. She had two teenage sons so 9.02am was a refreshing level of lateness. "Hello boys, don't worry, don't worry." She waved her hand at them as they started to apologise, "it's a Saturday, I almost slept in myself so no problem. Anyway, who's Nathan, ok nice to meet you, so you must be Alex ?" They got through the introductions followed by a bit of chat about how lovely Alison was, Nathan blushed a lot and Alex started to hop about getting fidgety.

"Sorry, you really want to get in and look don't you ?" The estate agent understood his eagerness and turned to unlock the door. "Now you know it's the top floor flat don't you," she began and talked all the way up the stairs until they got to it. Alex squeezed Nathan's hand as she put the key in the lock. "Oh God this is it," he whispered nervously, "our future home !" He crossed his fingers and scrunched his eyes shut. The door swung open and they stepped inside.

The view from the huge living room window made them both stagger. Alex looked dumb founded, "oh..my..God !" Nathan whispered. "Ali by the way," said the estate agent, "my name's Ali." "What ? Oh, oh yeah, like my mum, Alison is it ?" He said distractedly. Ali shook her head, "no I'm Alicia but everyone calls me Ali." "Right, right...." Nathan wasn't really listening. Like Alex he was blown away. He moved across to the window, stunned beyond belief. It made him remember that first fantastic weekend in Alex's front room, it was the same view only much higher up. Alex slid silently to his side and they looked out together. "Could we, could we really afford this place ?" He breathed, touching the glass lightly with his finger tips.

Their breath fogged up the pane, lingering as they turned to look about the rest of the room. It was small, big enough only for a coffee table, maybe a small sofa and chair and the tv. "My bookshelf and sketching books could go there," Nathan pointed to the far wall before another door way. "I've got a great rug that would fit under your leather chest, we could use that as our coffee table, put it just here ?" Alex pointed to a bit of floor not four feet away from them. "That's a great idea," smiled Nathan. They looked up at the tidy finish, cream walls, white ceiling and coving, glossed skirting, chrome light switches and plug sockets. It was stunning. "Can we see the bedroom ?" Nathan asked.

"Bedrooms." Replied Ali. "Eh ?" The boys frowned. "There are two," she corrected. "Oh my God," breathed Alex, "and that's all we seem to have said since we got here !" They followed her into bedroom two first. It was tiny. Sweetly finished, modern, perfect in every way, just like the living room but very small. "You can fit a single bed and a bedside table in here, and there is a teeny tiny built in cupboard at the end of the bed before the window but that is it for this room I'm afraid," Ali shrugged slightly regretfully. The boys looked anything but, they grinned at each other, still blown away by the whole place. "Yes but it is still a second bedroom," smiled Alex, "and that, we did not expect." Ali looked pleased and lead them into the kitchen. It was really small but had nifty little space saving devices in just about every corner.

Two cupboard doors were glass panelled, made from light wood with long cylindrical chrome handles and the other two solid wood. There was a corner cupboard with open glass shelves for stacking cups and crockery. Nathan looked very happy. "Are you thinking what I'm thinking ?" Alex asked him. He blushed and pointed to the top shelf, "how about wine glasses at the top, water glasses on the next and everyday mugs on the bottom shelf. I kind of thought plates and dishes in that cupboard beside, the nearest glass panelled one."

Alex nodded and let out a little laugh, "that was exactly how I imagined it too." Nathan gazed into his eyes, grinning. "You did ?" "Yes I did,"Alex squeezed him around the waist, his heart thumping with excitement at all this becoming so real. Nathan's cheeks hurt from smiling. "It's really happening," he whispered, eyes moistening as he looked into Alex's. "I know," came the whispered reply.

Ali felt as if she'd well up any minute now so moved them on. "Well," I'm glad you like what you've seen so far. Now let's go and take a look at the master bedroom, come on." She gestured for them to follow. Out of the kitchen they went, through the back of the living room, 'we're walking behind our sofa,' Nathan told himself, trying to imagine it as their home. It gave him a complete thrill and his stomach leapt with joy. Ali swung open the bedroom door and let them go in front of her.

"There you go," she said casually. The boys gasped. It was a lovely room again, cream walls, white ceiling and skirtings, obviously newly appointed as the rest of the flat but what blew them away was the long window to their left, showing another perspective of the hill they'd both lived on for so many years. It was stunning. Ali grinned, she knew it was an awesome flat. Not enough room to swing the proverbial but stunning none the less, and they hadn't seen the best bit yet, she couldn't wait for their reactions. "So here's the bathroom," she said nonchalantly and opened a door in the corner, "en-suite of course."

Nathan's hands flew to his face, "the turret !" They went in and stopped dead. Neither could speak for a moment. "This must be a dream," Alex whispered. Nathan shook his head. "Alex !" he couldn't say anymore. The entrance to the bathroom comprised two dark grey slate tiled steps up into a bright light room with a cream tiled floor. Three feet from the window, wooden flooring had been laid and another single long step built up to a vast comfy looking window seat with a balustrade that ran all the way around the inside of the turret's three windows, dropping away every two feet to make the window seat fully accessible.

From the left hand wall a huge chrome sunflower shaped shower head protruded on a graceful static arch, it was encircled by a sliding glass shower capsule from which no water or person could escape unless you had the only side with the elongated vertical hole in it facing out. It had sand blasted sunflowers carved into it at intervals. To its left was a modern low level loo and opposite a free standing roll top bath with a shiny centre mixer tap that looked like a four inch cigar tube with a long oval hole in the top.

Alex was fascinated by it, he stepped up onto the tiles and pushed the tap arm across letting cold water flow free, it cascaded out like a mini waterfall. Nathan gasped. He walked over to the window seat, prodding it with his fingers as if totally disbelieving and gaped out at the view. He couldn't take it in. Slowly he turned around and looked at the long oval mirror hung above the cream scallop edged basin, it too had a cascading waterfall tap.

He shook his head, imagining the room dimly lit by the warm glow from a host of candles. Alex relaxing in the bath, and him on the window seat with a book, wrapped up against an English winter amid a sea of soft cushions as he looked out at the snow. Neither could speak. Ali grinned. "Well I take it you like the flat then ?" Alex shook his head and stared at Nathan. "Like ?" He breathed incredulously. Nathan gazed back at him, the warmth of those penetratingly beautiful eyes made his stomach fill with butterflies. "It's amazing," he whispered.

Ali glanced down at her watch, "I'm sorry," she shrugged, "but I have another client to see this morning, I wish we had more time but I only set aside an hour." The boys stared at her in astonishment. "We've been here an hour ?" She glanced back at her watch, "not quite yet but getting on that way yes, I'm afraid I must go." She got out the keys so they started to follow her to the door. Being big in impact but tiny in square footage it took barely a second or two to be outside the flat again and at once Alex felt breathless and depressed. "I..., but... look Ali, is your next customer viewing this ?" He asked anxiously.

"No he's not," she beamed and lead them back down the stairs and out onto the chilly pavement. Nathan shivered and zipped up his coat. Alex slid his arm around his waist for extra warmth and felt his cheeks rise up in a smile. They shook Ali's hand rather on auto pilot and agreed to her recommendation of having a think about it over the weekend and speaking again on Monday. As soon as she drove off they simply stared in utter bewilderment at each other. "Have a think about it ? Who the hell needs to bloody think about it ?" Alex exclaimed. Nathan smiled his mega watt smile, "I know. Win the lottery yes, but think about it, nope, not needed, no brainer there." They were walking homeward and already turning the corner away from the turret house and down the main road toward Nathan's. A stunned silence purveyed for the rest of the walk until they actually turned into his drive.

"But I mean Nate, do you think we could ever afford the mortgage on it ? Even if our parents do sort us on the deposit. I mean is it possible ?" Nathan slowly shook his head. "I don't know Al, I really don't. The good thing for us is that it is literally tiny, but it's so incredibly well done, and that bathroom..." he trailed off as they stood talking on the gravel. Just then the front door opened, Alison smiled out at them, "come on in you two, it's got really nippy this morning, there's hot chocolate and cake in here." "Yum !" Said Alex and ran up the steps behind Nathan.

They tucked into slices of lemon drizzle cake and hot chocolate with big swirls of whipped cream. Alex practically inhaled his. "God I was starving," he stated as he scraped the bottom of his mug with a tea spoon. David Henderson gawped at his wife from behind his paper and went back to it again, shaking his head. Alex licked his fingers, "that is delish !" He beamed.

Nathan hadn't eaten very much of his, Alex's face fell when he saw, "Nath, are you ok ?" He asked worriedly. Nathan seemed away with the fairies. He stared into his half full hot chocolate mug absent mindedly spooning up the last of his cream. "Nath ?" Alex put his hand on his arm. "Hmm ? What ?" Nathan looked up, "sorry, did you ask me something ?" Alex smiled, "it's ok. You alright though ? You haven't eaten your cake." Nathan looked down and sighed. He let go of his fork and put his head on his hand.

"Oh Alex, I just want that flat so much." "Hey, is that what's bothering you

? Nate we'll get it don't worry. We'll find a way, I promise," he squeezed his shoulder. Nathan looked at the promise in his eyes and smiled, "yeah you're right, we will won't we. However hard we have to work, that's it, that's our first home."

"Well," said Alison, "so you like it that much eh ?" Nathan nodded as he forked up the rest of his cake. "More hot chocolate anyone ?" She asked. "No, I'd love a cuppa though mum," said Nathan. "Ooh yeah, I could go one of those Mrs H," Alex smiled. "Right you are," said Alison and made a pot of Earl Grey. The half past tens-es party moved into the living room where they all loafed about on the sofas for the next half hour. The boys started to chat about the impact that the flat had had on them and soon they couldn't stop. David Henderson even put down the Times and listened with a big smile on his face as they gabbled away.

Having described every single detail of the place the boys were now onto how to afford it. They got out a pad, pen and Nathan's phone to check their sums. Guessing how much 'Headway' might pay Alex at his first job was pretty tricky, especially since he hadn't even spoken to the woman from the bus yet and he had no idea what the job entailed so they wrote down £15,000 per annum. Nathan was hunting for something in the baking industry, despite Alex nagging him to do a drawing exhibition. That didn't feel to him as if he were pulling his weight enough, nope, he had to get a proper job at the same time as Alex, and it might as well be something that they could draw on later in terms of experience.

Alison disappeared upstairs to grab her handbag, reappearing barely a minute later and left the men alone together as she went to meet a girl friend for some shopping followed by lunch. An hour later and David's ears felt like they might bleed from hearing the boys go on so much. He had no chance of reading the rest of his paper so joined in, helping them answer lots of questions. Eventually when he caught a glance at the time, he stood up, stretched, yawned and snatched up his coat and car keys. "Right, I'm off to collect the twins from swimming and then we'll be at your Grandma's til 4pm so see you later boys." He was just about to leave when he turned on the door step, "oh and by the way, we're eating at Alex's tonight as a family so be there by 6pm ok, bye," and he was gone.

"But...!" Nathan went to follow him but David disappeared too quickly. "Damn, I really wanted to go and see 'Abduction' with you tonight," he sighed, sinking down on his haunches to rejoin Alex. "Yeah me too," Alex frowned as he leant across the floor and crossed out a wrong sum on the notepad. He sat up and looked at Nathan, "that was weird actually," he looked thoughtful, "I think they're up to something." "Do you ?" Nathan was intrigued, "what though ?"

"Don't know, but definitely something." He tapped the end of the pen against the pad and then flicked his wrist over, "damn, that's me gone too my love, hockey time."

Nathan followed him to the front door. "Have fun, don't get injured," he said between kisses. Alex laughed and looked at him with shining happy eyes, "and what are you lazy bones gonna do while I'm out and about thrashing the other team ?" "I'm going to learn how to make Mars bar Pain au Chocolat using a recipe I found online yesterday," Nathan said proudly. "Yum !" Alex looked almost pained with longing, "sounds scrummy, I can't wait to try them later." They hugged each other tightly once more and he was off, running up the road toward the school.

The day sauntered by for Nathan, he pulled out his as yet untried Mars bar Pain au Chocolat recipe and went to work. It was absorbing making a new dough that he wasn't used to and learning all the unfamiliar steps. He had never flattened and chilled butter before and then folded it into the dough. It was a protracted process, folding and chilling, folding and chilling until at last the the pastry was made and covered with cling film to chill overnight. That wouldn't please Alex. He smiled at the thought of his usual post hockey sag that always required copious amounts of food so he quickly set about making soft chewy chocolate chip cookies instead. He glanced at the clock, he still had 45 minutes, perfect. After clearing up the pastry debris he set to work on the cookies.

From a protracted recipe to a pretty instant one with immediate results felt good and he realised once again how much he truly loved creating things. Making something from scratch that would bring a smile to people's faces made him thrill with happiness inside. He beamed as he creamed butter and sugar together in a bowl, poured in one egg and an extra egg yolk, a good splash of vanilla extract and stirred away. He felt so relaxed and happy. This was the life. He flicked on the tv and leant against the kitchen units as he added the flour and broken chocolate pieces to the mix. The dough came together, stiffening considerably until he had to set it down and pull chunks out to roughly shape into small balls with his hands. Once he had two full trays he slid them into the oven, checked the temperature and set the timer. He cleared up until the kitchen was spotless and sat down in front of the tv with a big grin on his face to wait for Alex.

The cookies were ready in a trice, two 'accidentally,' slipped into his mouth as he left them out to cool and cleared up. He groaned, they were unctuous and delicious. With everything sparklingly clean, he washed his hands and sat down to watch Redbull X-fighters, amazed at the way they got their motorbikes to do 360s while 100 feet in the air or how they did handlebar stands, Cordobas and side running. He shook his head as Danny Torres took to the stratosphere. This guy was on fire today, thrilling the Chilean crowd with his amazing stunts. Next up Nate Adams, Nathan couldn't deny the guy was brilliant but Torres had something and he couldn't help hoping that for once he might take the lead and get a bit of the rewards he justly deserved.

The key clicked in the lock and in clattered a dishevelled flush cheeked Alex. No mud today as the ground was so hard from a few days of no rain, red knees though, which Nathan noticed immediately. "Oh no," he groaned, "are you hurt again ?" Alex beamed and shook his head. "No I'm not, but even if I were, what is that heavenly smell ?" He followed his nose and gasped when he saw the cookies, snatching up 3 at once and stuffing the first one in. He closed his eyes with bliss, "Oh my God," he breathed, "a hot body AND you can cook, what more can a guy ask for ?"

Nathan laughed, grinning from ear to ear as Alex walked toward him and kissed his lips longingly. "Wow," he husked as they pulled away. "What was that for?"

"Because I love you and I haven't stopped thinking about how much I want you all day. Fancy a shower....?" He raised his eyebrows. Nathan's heart sped up in a second, he could feel his chest pound and his groin grow instantly. He nodded slowly, looking deeply into Alex's eyes and took the offered hand to follow him upstairs.

As soon as they were under the water, soaped, fresh and hot, they couldn't get enough of each other. Nathan groaned wildly, panting with pleasure as Alex licked and sucked on his neck, running his long tongue from the base of his throat up to just below his ear. "Oh fuck," said Nathan, rock hard and oblivious to everything but Alex's hard wet body and the delicious things he was doing to him. Alex's own heart wanted to crash out through his chest. When he got Nathan in this state he could barely control himself.

He encased him in his arms and kissed and licked his beautiful body, concentrating on his smooth, lean chest and perfect pecs. He lapped at his nipples and heard him gasp before moving down his body, cupping Nathan's hard round buttocks in his hands he pulled his hardness into his mouth, swirled his tongue around the glans and sucked him like never before.

Nathan threw his head back with a gutteral yelp of ecstasy, so glad that his family were out. He speared himself at Alex and had to grip onto the wall behind him when he felt a pre sucked finger push all the way up between his cheeks. "Oh Christ, oh God," he gasped, pulling Alex's head deeper onto himself with one hand until he took one huge breath, emitted a deep grunt and exploded into his hot throat. It was so dizzying and fantastic with Alex, every time felt wonderful, but these passionate all consuming, needful desperate sessions were beyond belief. He panted long and hard as Alex stood up with a grin and steadied him with his arms. "Fuck I need a lie down now," he whispered. Alex laughed and laughed. Nathan grinned and ran a hand through his wet hair. They smoothed their fingertips down each others cheeks, gazing, each into the others eyes with absolute love. "Want to go to bed ?" Alex said softly. Nathan nodded.

Chapter Eighteen.

"No I'M making lunch," said Alex for the 50th time as they got dressed. "You baked all morning so let me do something nice for you." He shrugged as if it were a no brainer. "I thought you just did," Nathan said shyly. Alex flushed and looked at him with his heart thrumming. "We could....skip lunch...?" He said with a grin just as Nathan's stomach gurgled for England. "Or perhaps not !" Nathan giggled and headed for the bedroom door, he really was starving. "That's a lovely idea but I need to eat so come on," he ran down the stairs, two at a time and headed straight to the fridge but Alex caught up with him as he opened the door and lifted him clean off his feet, swung him round and pointed him in the opposite direction.

"No cheeky, my turn to cook, now sod off and do something else, scram !" Nathan made a 'tsk-ing,' sound, shrugged resignedly and headed for a kitchen stool where he rummaged in the consul drawers for a sheaf of recipes and starting hole punching them into a skinny file while Alex got on with lunch.

Nathan's three best friends came around that afternoon and joined him and Alex on the Wii. Everyone was rubbish at cow racing so they switched to carnival games. Simon brought his Ipad. Having failed miserably at most of the carnival apart from frog throwing, he decided to play Angry birds. Alex then got his Ipad out as well to try and beat his score but kept over speeding up his birds so they over shot their targets. It was such a laugh but Nathan couldn't keep from thinking about the flat. He had a brilliant afternoon, but every now and then he'd catch Alex watching him, giving him a knowing look, understanding his preoccupation entirely. He coloured on catching Alex's eye one more time as he got up to grab more pringles and cokes from the larder. He was just about to turn around when he jumped a mile, Alex was right up behind him. "Shhh !" He giggled, "sorry, I didn't mean to make you jump."

He cupped Nathan's anxious looking face and kissed him with utter love. "Don't worry my sweet, we'll get it."Nathan smiled back at him, "how did you know I was thinking about the flat ?" "Because you haven't really stopped all day have you ? I can see it in your eyes." Nathan closed his arms around Alex's waist and laid his head on his shoulder with a sigh, "I hope we do," he breathed. Alex wrapped him up in his arms, "we will my love, for you I'll make sure I promise."

Without warning, the larder door wrenched open so hard on its hinges that it nearly flew off. Nathan and Alex practically leapt out of their skins as all three of their friends burst in, squashing them up against the shelves. "Woooo ! Caught you snogging !" They chimed, laughing hard at the apoplectic look on Alex's face. "Christ guys, you nearly gave me a frigging heart attack !"

Nathan pushed Simon away from him as hard as possible, "get....out....of....the...larder...you ARSE !" He laughed and then yelped as something jabbed him in the backside. "Ow....! Right that's it, everybody out, I've just been spiked by a pineapple."

As all five of them tumbled out in a giggling heap, Nathan rubbing his backside, the front door opened and in poured his family, fresh from his Grand mother's house and full of ice cream. "Hi," he blushed at the smirk on his mum's face and his dads raised eyebrow. "How was lunch mum ?" He hugged her and took the six shopping bags out of her hands. "I see the shopping was a disaster then ?" Alison laughed and cuffed him gently on the arm. "It was wonderful thanks, and how was your day, or shouldn't I ask ?" Nathan shook his head and grinned, "it was great mum. Actually the guys are just off. We're eating at Alex's I hear ?" "Yes," said Alison, rather oddly Nathan thought but he didn't have time to think about it as his friends all started to head toward the door and he had to say goodbye.

After they'd gone, he and Alex flopped down on the sofa together, sprawling across one another and searching down the side of the cushions for the remote. They giggled as they fought each other for it. Alex's fingers reached it first so he held it away from Nathan's grasp.

They rolled around on the sofa, giggling and laughing as he tried to snatch it and fell to the floor on top of each other with a loud thump. "Oy !" Snapped Alison, fearing her son's head hitting something. Her heart raced. The boys looked over at her, Nathan struggling to do so as he was trapped under Alex. "Yerrrssss.....?" He giggled. Alison eyed them for a moment and then started to laugh herself. She shook her head, "I think I know what makes you right for each other, it's just hit me." "What's that ?" Asked Nathan as he fought Alex's tickling fingers and shrieked rolling out from under him, struggling to get up. "It's your matching levels of maturity !"

There wasn't much time left before Alex's house beckoned. The boys were of course starving again. At ten to, the merry Henderson band plus Alex made their way down to his house and strode in behind him. Caitlin hugged her son as if she hadn't seen him for weeks. "Mum ! Gerroff me !" He wriggled, embarrassed. "Ah, sweet !" Cooed Nathan teasingly. They were still in a silly mood which seemed to rub off on the rest of the party making dinner hilarious. No one said anything important for a whole three hours and it was only when Jess challenged the twins to beat her on X-box that the parents finally looked at each other in that secretive way of theirs. Alex nudged Nathan and suddenly they were both more serious, something was definitely going on.

"Ok, what is it ?" Alex asked. "We know you're up to something so come on, and dinner, - though lovely as usual Mum, was not just to make sure we all ate so what is going on ?" The fathers exchanged 'shall we ?' looks and checked their wives faces. After a couple of nods Christopher got up and moved to the top drawer in the little table just outside the downstairs loo. He pulled out an A4 envelope with a thick letter inside from the look of it, and something distorting the paper at the bottom. Alex frowned, "what the...?" Christopher and David both looked at the envelope and then at the boys. They seemed reluctant to hand it over for a second. "Now you two," Chris began. "No don't," Caitlin grabbed his wrist suddenly, she looked anxious. Christopher stayed calm and put his hand over hers.

"No, look I said I would just say this before I hand these over. It is after all, my right as a father so I just want to do it before we go any further." He looked back at the boys faces and saw that they had linked arms and were staring at him in consternation. He looked from one to the other and then seemed to re-think his next move a bit. He sighed and rubbed his chin.

"Oh hell you two. Look before I,...sorry, we." He motioned to the other three, "give this to you I was just going to check that this is what you really want, you know for good, because if it wasn't...., well.....?" He couldn't continue. Alex had pulled Nathan even closer and now looked at his Dad with angry eyes. Nathan gripped Alex's hand, how could his father even consider that there was ever a second of doubt in either of their minds ? Hadn't he been watching them ? The room was silent, the others wished Christopher wouldn't go down this route and all at once he wished he hadn't too. The boys looked on the verge of becoming really upset and Alex was already furious.

He looked at them, tensely gripping one another as if someone threatened to break them apart and suddenly he realised that someone had, him. He wondered what the hell he was doing. What exactly was he worried about ? He knew he couldn't stop his son being gay but it wasn't really about that. As he looked at his quivering angry eighteen year old, Christopher realised that he would miss his only son more than he'd been willing to acknowledge. He ran a hand through his hair and stood up with the envelope, walking over to Alex he motioned for him to stand up. "I'm sorry son," he shrugged and when he looked into Alex's eyes there were the beginnings of tears in his own.

He cleared his throat roughly and handed him the envelope. "You're my son and I love you, I just didn't want you to go this early I suppose. I hope you're both very happy." Alex just gazed at his father. They were almost the same height now as he'd grown again over the last few months. He looked anxiously into his Dad's eyes before turning over the envelope in his hands. "Go on," Christopher gave an encouraging nod. Alex didn't know what the hell was going on, he still felt very nervous and a bit angry at what Christopher had just said, but he was being really sweet now too.

Alex turned to Nathan for reassurance. "Go on Al," he smiled. Alex reached into the envelope. He read only the first sentence before he gasped "Nooooooo !" Reached into the bottom of the envelope and pulled out some keys, then he launched himself at his dad. "Thank you, thank you, thank you," was all he could say as father and son held tightly, understanding and incredibly proud of one another. When he pulled back, Alex looked at his father's shining eyes and then at the other three who all looked pretty welled up too.

"What ?" Said Nathan, getting to his feet. "What is going on ? Please will somebody tell me ?" Alex turned slowly around and held up the keys. "See my love, I told you I'd get it for you, I did promise !"

Nathan's hands flew to cover his gaping mouth. He looked at Alex with huge eyes. "The flat ?" He whispered. "Yes, my love, the flat. It's ours."

All hell broke loose. Nathan screamed aloud and flung himself at Alex, beside himself with joy. Tears streamed down his cheeks. He cuffed them away roughly. "Bloody hell, all I seem to do is cry !" He stamped his foot and made Alex laugh his head off. The twins and Jess sprinted into the melee of hugging, jumping around and rejoicing. They insisted on knowing what was happening and screeched with excitement when they heard.

"No way !" Said Jess and gave her brother a huge hug. She was so glad for him after the recent stress of Nathan's accident. She kissed him on the cheek feeling lucky to have such a good brother. Her stomach pinged a bit as she'd miss him terribly but it was the right thing and she loved Nathan so much as well. "Hey, where exactly is it again ?" She asked. Nathan explained. Her eyes flew wide open. "Oh my God, everyone, shush....shh... SHUT UP YOU LOT !" She got on a chair to yell at them. "Jess," chided Caitlin gently, thinking her daughter a little rude. "No mum, I'm not being impolite, it's just why don't we all go and see it ?" She grinned. Everybody went silent for a second and then looked at each other.

"That's a brilliant idea," smiled Alex. "Yes, that's a nice plan darling, when were you thinking ?" Caitlin softened. "Well what the hell's wrong with now ?" Jess beamed. Alex and Nathan gasped and clutched each other. "Bloody brilliant ! Come on everyone," Nathan grabbed the keys as Alex ran for their coats. The twins followed and chucked Jess hers. "Wait, wait, wait...What, you want to go right now ?" David looked like he thought they'd all taken leave of their senses. Everyone looked at one another and then back at him. "It's past ten !" He tapped a finger on his watch. Silence again and then everyone burst out laughing and headed toward the door in a mad flood of excitement.

"Come on," said Nathan, catching his father's sleeve as he passed him. "I'm getting you a Saga catalogue tomorrow by the way," he whispered as he let go of him by the coat hooks.

David reached for his jacket as the words took a second to make sense. He was the only one left on the door step as the others all bundled down them and out across the gravel in record time. "Oy !" He yelled to Nathan's departing back, "rude !" He slammed the door behind him and ran down the steps to catch them all up but he was already laughing at himself. Ten o'clock ! He'd be looking at electric recliners soon thinking, 'that looks comfy.' He shuddered at the thought and found his wife's arm. She gave him a knowing look and he nudged her in the ribs. "I love you," she whispered as they headed up the hill. "Thank God," he replied.

"Apparently I'm getting a 'Saga' catalogue tomorrow by the way." Alison guffawed. "Shut up," David grinned, tickling her and making her shriek with laughter all the way to the top of their road.

In no time at all they were all chattering and laughing outside the building. The twins looked up to the turret, "woah, fabulous !" Jack grinned, "yes ! I'll be coming round here ALL the time after school now, that's for sure." "You won't," said Nathan and Alex in unison. They exchanged a look, this was theirs now, their private sanctuary. Nathan's stomach filled with butterflies and Alex chewed his lip. "Come on," he lead the way inside and everyone piled up the stairs.

He had barely unlocked the door before the twins and Jess hurled themselves across the threshold and ran about in a mad frenzy. At that pace they'd seen the entire flat in about two seconds flat and came back to where Nathan and Alex stood discussing with their parents where they'd place everything. "Brilliant but bloody small !" Said Jack breathlessly. "Yes and no bathroom which is a bit of a shag...I mean bugger, er well anyway," Jas giggled, "why isn't there one ? You don't, share with downstairs or something awful do you ?" She made a face.

Alex laughed, "no you numpties, if you'd bothered to slow down at all as you hurled yourselves around here, your brother could have shown it to you. Nate, do you want to do the honours ?" Nathan gave his fingers a quick squeeze, "I sure do," he smiled. "Come on you ingrates, form a line behind me." Jack, Jess and Jas all fell in and marched behind him into the main bedroom. "Duh ! We've been in here already dumb dumb !" Jas teased her older brother. "Oh I see," Nathan said patiently, stepping to the corner of the room, "so how did you manage to miss this then ?" He swung the door wide. Bathed in moonlight, the turret bathroom looked even more exquisite. "What the....?" Jess was blown away. She stepped gingerly inside. The twins followed with their mouths open, "oh my God, this is amazing Nathan." Jas turned to her brother, shaking her head. "It's so beautiful." The three of them wandered slowly about the room taking everything in.

They touched every surface, gazing in awe at it all before settling on the window seat to take in the view. "It's so amazing," Jess whispered, shaking her head as she looked out across the houses below. "Huh, you can see your garden from here Nathan." Nathan stepped up to join her and followed the direction of her finger. "Oh yes !" He said delightedly. His mum and dad joined them in the door way, followed by Caitlin and Chris. "Wow," said Caitlin, "this is a stunning room but it really looks amazing in the moonlight doesn't it. Ethereal and truly beautiful." She joined the youngsters at the window. "Mum this is unreal," Jess shook her head. "Can I have a house like this when I get married ?" Caitlin laughed, "if we can find one darling, why ever not. You'll need a good job though, these mortgages don't come cheap."

Amazed and thrilled as they were, soon everyone started to yawn, and the merry crowd left the flat and ambled back toward their houses, the boys hung back. Nathan rested his head on Alex's shoulder. "You tired my love ?" Alex curled his arm around Nathan's head to rest his hand in his hair. "Hmm, pretty much." He husked.

"Oh crap !" Alex suddenly jolted. "What ?" Nathan looked at his pale stricken face. "Oh God, Oh God Nate !" He turned looking absolutely shocked. "We've forgotten to send out the invitations yet !" "Shit !" Nathan blanched, his eyes wide with horror. "Well how far away is the 10th ?" "Five weeks." Alex whispered. He looked like he might pass out. "Oh my God. How did we do that ?" Nathan started to tremble a little bit. "Al you did pay the florist didn't you ?" Alex looked pissed off for a second. "Sorry," he rubbed his shoulder. "I know we did all that weeks ago but do me a favour, can we just go through the check list tonight when we get back, please and if you don't mind, let's run the invitation cock up past my mum. She's brilliant at saving situations like this." Alex's cheeks lifted up into a smile as he hugged his waist, "I knew you'd know what to do." His eyes shone as he gazed at Nathan in the moonlight.

Alison didn't react very much at all when the boys flew in, breathless and pale, each blurting out between them what they'd done. Nathan was pretty stunned, if not to say a little offended at first. "Mum !" He demanded, "didn't you hear us ?"

She looked up again from the newspaper she'd been pouring over and raised an eyebrow. "Nathan, of course I heard you, but it's not the end of the world by a long chalk and you've told most of your guests when it is so they've already saved the date anyway. Now calm down, both of you and let's go through all of this and make an easy plan that we can implement tomorrow and you can go to bed happy."

"Thanks mum," Nathan smiled, still looking a little nervous. Alison got out a notepad and scribbled down the address of the wedding venue, the time and the people she knew were coming to it. "Now, you two have both sets of parents, the twins, Jess, Paul, Simon, Sam, Rupert, Ollie and Chris coming to the actual wedding, yes?" They nodded. "Ok, we know they're all coming because we've all spoken to each other so much in the past few weeks so don't worry about them. Now how many people are you seating at the breakfast?" She looked up. "Fifty," said Alex. Alison scribbled. "Right, now in honesty, how many of those people are really firm on the date and have told you they're absolutely coming?" Alex looked away and starting tapping his fingers trying to count everyone that he could be utterly sure had said yes. After a minute he grinned. "41!"

Alison and Nathan both looked relieved. "Phew," she said and wrote that down. "Your caterers are all booked? Music etc...?" Nathan nodded. His cheeks flushed as the reality of it actually happening in almost only a months time hit home again. Alex saw and squeezed his thigh under the table. Nathan gasped an involuntary moan of pleasure and slapped his hands over his mouth in embarrassment. "Stop that," said Alison very calmly without raising her head from her notes. The boys laughed. "You two!" She shook her head, "the sooner we get you married the better." Nathan's cheeks hurt from smiling and his eyes twinkled. It did something special to Alex's heart every time. He exhaled shakily and kissed Nathan's hot cheek. "Put him down or I'm not helping you!" Said Alison without looking up again. Alex couldn't stop laughing.

They went to bed very happy after all. It was a bit of a cock up delaying the invites but as most people had confirmed verbally already, they could breathe a little more easily. Alison gave them an extra £100 towards purchasing the invitations which thrilled Nathan. He'd decided on their second choice at first as his favourites had seemed too expensive but now they could afford them. He snuggled closer under Alex's arm and heard him groan gently in his sleep.

"Is it me or did this summer's school holiday seem ultra short to you?" Alex asked the next morning as they got dressed. "That's because it was," said Nathan. "Don't you remember, they're trying that new break the year up thing so we get those two shorter breaks instead."

"Is that what that was? Christ I thought I was going mad! Yesterday I was reading through my diary and wondered why I was at school on July the 26th and then again at the end of August. Blimey I'm getting old !" Nathan laughed at his expression. "Come on oldie, get your kit on I'm starving," he pulled a slate grey T over his long sleeved white top and threw a striped grey Joules hoodie over the top, it really was starting to get chilly. As he bent to retrieve his shoes from under the bed, Nathan stood up to find Alex watching him with a soft expression on his face. "What ?"

Alex smiled and slipped a dark grey sweater over his white T. "Nothing," he smiled, "I'll just never get tired of sharing this experience with you that's all." Nathan blushed hard and curled his body around Alex's as he crossed the room to hold him in his arms.

Sunday was truly lazy. The boys chilled on the sofas reading and nodding off in between bouts of fridge raiding. They'd stayed over at Nathan's again for which both felt a bit guilty. "Psst," whispered Alex. "Yes ?" Nathan glanced over at him. "Do you think your mum minds me staying over so much, or us come to that, you know the whole couple thing going on here all the time ?" Nathan shook his head and put the book open on his chest. "What are you reading by the way ?" Alex motioned toward it. "The Ilyiad," Nathan replied. "Eh ? The who ?" "Homer," said Nathan. "Aah ! Yes of course, but why are you reading that ? I thought you gave up Classical studies last year ?" "Well I passed my GCSE in it if that's what you mean," Nathan teased, "but I just wanted to take a look again. I don't know it as well as I know 'The Odyssey.'" "O..K..." whispered Alex in a 'you've lost the plot,' type voice. "Uneducated peasant," Nathan laughed and got 'The Death and Life of Charlie St Cloud,' bouncing off his shoulder for his trouble. It hit the floor with a papery thump.

"Why are you reading that !" He asked with ill concealed contempt for Alex's reading material. "My sister gave it to me so I thought I'd try it, ok ?" Alex tried to sound hurt but failed. Nathan smirked and picked up The Ilyiad. "So how is it then ?"

"Well if you must know it's a pile of utter pants." Nathan let his book drop to the floor and giggled as Alex giggled back.

There was only a week left of term which made the boys smile over breakfast the next morning. "I just can't wait for this week to be over !" Said Nathan excitedly as he crunched through his toast. "Me too," Alex smiled. His stomach flipped as he caught Nathan's eye, knowing he was thinking the same thing. Five weeks and they'd be married. "Now what's that soppy look for this time you two ?" Alison poured them both a big mug of tea. "Er....hmm," said Nathan unhelpfully and looked coy as he put the milk back in the fridge. Alex rested a foot on the stool next to him and re tied the laces. Alison looked from one to the other and then slowly got what was making them all jittery. "I see," she smiled. Nathan caught her eye this time, blushed and looked away. She couldn't help herself, walking over to him she wrapped him into a big motherly hug and kissed the edge of his hair. "Oh my baby boy," she breathed feeling pretty soppy too. Nathan coloured considerably and struggled in her grip, "oh blimey mother, please...." he struggled more, totally ineffectually. She didn't hug him often like this and she prolonged it for as long as she could. Alex grinned at the look on Nathan's face and found the whole thing really sweet.

At last Nathan managed to disentangle himself and shook his head at her. "What are you like ?" "Er...., your mother ?" Alison raised an eyebrow which made him giggle. "Go on you two, get your stuff and get cracking or you'll be late." They looked at the clock, both gasped and sprinted for their things. As they tore back down the stairs and out past Alison, Nathan did a lickety split u-turn, hugged and kissed her on the cheek and was out and running across the gravel behind Alex. Alison stood in the silent aftermath and sighed, she'd really miss them both in a few weeks, but she consoled herself that they would be only just around the corner for a good while to come, and started to clear up the breakfast things and mentally pick out her outfit for the wedding.

The week went quickly at school, at least the first two days did and then everything seemed to slow down. Alex felt irritable on the walk home after school that day. They'd saved the invitation situation, all of those had gone out that morning after a hectic evening of writing, searching addresses and stamping the night before. Their suits were ready, the celebrant and wedding room booked. In fact the room was a real stunner. An 18th century morning room inside Thornbury Hall, the local Palladian mansion. It could seat 50 but there would only be 15 family and friends to that bit as it meant so much to them, they wanted to keep it intimate.

Nathan and Alex had divided the different tasks between the two of them so that each would have a few surprises on the day. Being in charge of the flowers had not been something Alex relished at first but as he'd talked to his local florists and got to know one particularly nice helpful polish girl, he'd begun to enjoy the task immensely. He had booked a tri coloured theme, white, purple and yellow. Dotted around the reception room were going to be bouquets of purple trichelium, white anti-ryhnhams and yellow roses, the same in the morning room where they would be married. In the centre of each table at the reception there were going to be shallow chunky rectangular vases with spiral shaped yukka stems growing and each person could pluck a stem, place it in their mini enamel flower pot/ place name holder, and take it home if they wanted to.

Everything had been thought of. Still he sighed and looked annoyed as they walked home together. Nathan smirked slightly at his rattiness. "What ?" He said grumpily and totally unlike himself. "Feeling a tad huffy are we ?" Alex looked enraged for a second, turned very red, mouthed and fidgeted and then plonked himself onto a nearby wall and put his face in his hands. "Fuck !" Though it came out very muffled. Nathan couldn't help but laugh, Alex was never like this. He watched him for a moment and then sat silently on the pavement in front of him. It was an unseasonably hot autumn day and the stone felt nice and cool through his trousers. He got out his blackberry and flicked through a few things while he waited for Alex to calm. It didn't take long. Soon he moved to sit cross legged in front of Nathan, gently removing the blackberry from his palms and setting it aside for a second. He closed his hands around Nathan's and shook his head.

"I'm so sorry Nate," he sighed. "Hey," Nathan shrugged happily, "don't worry about it, it happens !" Alex looked guiltily into his eyes. "I'm not normally such an irritable arse though am I ? I know I've been a moody shit all day." Nathan laughed, "c'mon now, don't give yourself such a hard time, but you can tell me what's wrong though ?" He raised a questioning eyebrow. Alex looked down and fiddled with his laces. A couple of tutting adults manoeuvred with deliberately exaggerated movements around them. "Oh get over yourselves, we're only talking !" Snapped Alex. The couple mouthed and looked as if they were about to come back and have it out but Nathan's sweet imploring face and apologetic look decided them and they walked on. "Twats !" Alex spat and poked a leaf at a join between two pavings. He looked up to see Nathan smiling kindly at him, no judgement, just support and love. Suddenly he launched himself at him, wrapping his arms around him, burying his head into his shoulder.

"Oh Nath, I don't want fifteen people in the room, I don't want them all staring when I say how much I love you. It's too personal, I just want you, I just want you." He clutched at Nathan's body tightly as the words rushed out of him. More people wandered past on the pavement, this time politely looking away as they deemed that some crisis must be happening and in the British way, left them to it.

Nathan squeezed him back and caressed him, pressing his cheek up against Alex's. "Then we won't have fifteen people in the room, that's settled," he said easily. Alex pulled away to look at his face. He looked astonished. "But, isn't this what you want ? Our three best friends each and our immediate family ?" Nathan shrugged, "sure it is, but if it's not going to make you happy then that's fine with me." Alex searched his face and then shook his head. "God I'm being so selfish !" He struggled off Nathan and stood up. He paced around for a moment and ran a hand through his hair. "What the hell's wrong with me ?"

Nathan got up and pulled him close, holding him lightly and rubbing his back. "I think my darling, that what you have is called the pre wedding jitters." Alex stiffened for a second in his arms, mouthed and shook his head, stood still, mouthed again though no words came out either time, and then let himself be pulled into a firmer embrace. He softened and melted into it, curling himself against Nathan's loving arms and body. They held each other and slowly the tension began to ebb away from him. Nathan's hands calmly caressed his back and at last, with sleepy eyes he pulled out of the embrace and looked at him. "I'm not usually hysterical," he said. "No you're not," Nathan agreed, "but if you are going to be at any time, then I'm glad it's about this. It just shows how much it means to you." Alex smiled and reached for his hand. "You always say the right thing Nate. I love you." "Me too," Nathan replied as they shared a soft, tender kiss in the middle of the pavement.

That night the boys moved to Alex's mum and dad's. Left to their own devices while his parents took Jess to a ballet evening, Alex more than made up for his earlier grumpiness. "Can you be all pissed off tomorrow as well please," panted Nathan as he lay sweating lightly across Alex's chest on the floor of his bedroom. Alex laughed his low throaty laugh. "Mmm, then do that to get me going again," Nathan breathed and they rolled across the floor laughing and kissing and starting up once more.

Since dinner at 10pm wasn't a crazy concept for any teen, Caitlin and Christopher never batted an eyelid when they returned home with their shattered daughter to find the boys cross legged on the kitchen stools eating bowls of noodles. Caitlin secretly loved that they did things like that, it reminded her of her own teen years and how everything was always so easy, you just did what you felt like when you wanted to. "Shall I get the cake ?" Alex asked as he stuffed in the last huge forkful of his noodles. Nathan couldn't speak as his mouth was so full but he nodded enthusiastically. Alex jumped off his stool and headed to the fridge where he pulled out two massive slabs of chocolate fudge cake and set them down on the counter while he retrieved two spoons. "Sure that'll be enough ?" Caitlin teased. Nathan coloured and looked away. If she knew what her son had just done to him for the last two hours she'd know it wasn't.

He bent low over the plate to hide his feelings and spooned up the cake as fast as possible. "Cheese for afters ?" Alex grinned, whacking down a huge pot of square cheesy nibbles. "Cheeselets !" Nathan cried through chocolate smeared lips. He beamed at Alex who laughed and leant across to kiss his chocolatey mouth. Caitlin rolled her eyes, "oh for goodness sake you two. Roll on October the 10th !" She smiled. "Night darling," she kissed Alex's cheek as she passed and gave Nathan's shoulder a squeeze. "Sleep well boys." "Night," they both called after her and then reached across to thumb the chocolate off each others faces. Their expressions turned soft as their fingers brushed one another's cheeks.

"This is a great life," Alex said as he looked deeply into Nathan's beautiful eyes. "It really is," Nathan whispered. They sat talking long into the night, finger tips touching, caressing hands and faces. Sometimes they moved from furniture to furniture, always facing one another to talk and look, to laugh and love. They stretched legs across one another and slumped comfortably against each other in various positions, never breaking eye contact, never leaving off softly speaking. Hours drifted by, slowly, slowly as each moment filled. They felt present and alive like no other time in their lives. Moonlight finally gave way to a new dawn as they padded barefoot onto the cold kitchen tiles and slid onto the stools together. Alex held up Nathan's hand in his, their elbows resting on the granite consul together. He kissed it and blinked slowly, his long soft eyelashes framing his lovely eyes. Nathan stroked his cheek, not speaking. Alex looked deeply into his. They didn't need to speak any more just now. Sitting, just being this way was all that mattered in the world. What a wonderful, wonderful night.

Alex leant forward eventually, kissing Nathan's lips with absolute delicacy. "I'll make us something to eat," he whispered. Nathan simply nodded happily. They began to chat again as the sun came up, utterly in love with being alive and with each other.

Wedding fever hotted up around the two houses in the few weeks left before the wedding, except that is, for Nathan and Alex. Since that one day of Alex's semi melt down, it had broken their nerves and now all they thought about was how to furnish their new flat and make sure they both had jobs. Alex had spoken to and finally met up with Rose from 'Headway,' or Mrs Brooks – Bank as she was officially known but she refused to be so formal with any of her staff.

They had a wonderfully informal interview over mugs of PG Tips and Custard Creams. They talked about Rose's son in Australia a fair bit and Alex was intrigued to hear all about someone just like him who'd already got married and started their same sex life together. It all sounded so great and made his chest pound with excitement as she spoke.

Suddenly Rose flicked over her wrist and gasped a bit at the time, "oh dear, I knew this would happen, I always talk far too much !" She smiled. Alex put his mug down and made to get up, he'd never had an interview before and didn't know the etiquette. Rose stood up too, "oh, do you have to go somewhere ?"

She looked a little anxious as if she'd detained him unnecessarily long. "Erm, no, not at all," Alex shrugged looking nervous. "It's just you said you'd talked for too long so...," he shrugged again, flushing slightly, hoping he hadn't blown it.

"Relax," Rose smiled and squeezed his arm in a motherly fashion. "Alex I think you're just what we need. I can't pay you a vast fortune but it should be enough with your fiance working too and I think you'll like it here. You've got the job." Alex's eyes flew wide with astonishment, he was used to achieving things in life but this still blew him away. "Oh my God !" He breathed through his palms, "thank you, thank you so much Mrs Brooks-Bank." Rose tilted her head at him, "sorry, I mean Rose." He grinned and couldn't stop himself. He threw his arms around her neck and kissed her on the cheek. Rose laughed and hugged him back.

"Go on, go home and tell your fiance. You start this Monday at 8am ok ? We finish at 4.30pm so we start a little earlier and on Friday's I'm afraid it's a 7.30 start but then we finish at 3pm." Alex nodded and grasped her hand, shaking it with profound gratitude. "I just can't thank you enough," he beamed, clasped her once more and tore out of the room in case it was all a dream. He heard Rose laughing softly behind him as he sprinted out of the front door. It refreshed her to find some one so likeable and so close to her son in personality. She missed him terribly and having Alex around would be a blessing to both the charity and herself. She made a couple of notes about him, passed the information to her HR manager and headed out to lunch.

When Nathan walked in from his own interview that day, he looked dejected and Alex dreaded telling him the good news. He sagged on his seat at the kitchen counter as Nathan walked over to him. "Hi," he sighed and pecked Alex on the lips. He made to walk away but Alex pulled him back. "Hey, that's not a 'hello Alex,' kiss ! Come here and show me some love." He teased. Nathan didn't look into his eyes but shrugged and let himself be pulled into a hug, then he sat down looking at the floor. Alex felt awful for him but decided that at least one of them having a job might cheer him up after all. "Look Nate, I'm sorry things must not have gone well for you today, I really am, but the good news is, we can get started on paying our way on the mortgage soon anyway. I did get the job and I'm sure you will get one incredibly soon too."

There was silence and then a naughty smile started to lift the corners of Nathan's lips. At last he looked up into Alex's face with twinkling eyes. "Who says I didn't get the job ?" He grinned. "WHAT ?" Alex was torn between needing to thrash him for winding him up and absolute joy so he decided to go with the thrashing first. "You little.......!" He jumped off his stool lunging for Nathan who leapt out of reach screeching with laughter and hurtled away from him across the room. But Alex had always been faster. He sprinted for all he was worth, catching Nathan's sleeve and tackling him hard onto the sofa as he attempted to long jump it. "No, no !" Screamed Nathan as Alex pinned him firmly and tickled him mercilessly.

When Caitlin walked back into her house, she found her son tangled half naked with his soon to be husband, shrieking with laughter beneath him on the living room floor. Alison followed her inside, clutching a chocolate fudge cake from Waitrose in her arms. They both stopped and stared at the boys. "Aherm..." Caitlin cleared her throat loudly. Neither heard it so Alison thumped her handbag noisily onto the counter top. Both boys heads snapped up. They coloured as they looked at their mothers and giggled. Caitlin smirked slightly under her mild disapproval. Their joy was always infectious. "See," sighed Alison, "matching levels of maturity." The boys lay back against the carpet, laughing softly as they got their breath back.

As the mothers turned away to unpack food shopping, Alex kissed Nathan's mouth. "I love you," he whispered. Nathan grinned back and stroked his cheek. They jumped up, Nathan retrieving Alex's top from where he'd thrown it behind the sofa. "Thanks," he smiled. Nathan watched his muscles flex as he slipped back into it. "What ?" Alex beamed at the expression on his face. "God that was a lovely sight," Nathan whispered. Alex giggled with pleasure.

"Right, you're making us both a little queasy, so into the kitchen you two and start helping !" Caitlin called making them jump. "Sorry mum, can't." Said Alex as he wandered past her to the fridge, grabbing two Baby Belle's and chucking one to Nathan. "We're going to Ikea for some cheap stuff for the flat, then Cargo so no can do today." Caitlin shrugged, "Alison and I will just have to eat this cake then. Oh well." She lifted the plastic dome from the fudge cake, a delicious chocolatey aroma filled the air. Nathan joined them and groaned. Both mothers laughed and rolled their eyes. "Alright, alright, a slice each before you go, I'm sure we can permit that," Alison smiled and reached for some plates as the boys wrestled each other to the cutlery drawer. Alison looked at Caitlin as they giggled and fought each other. "I've said it before and I'll say it again, roll on October the 10th !" Caitlin watched her son dive at his lovers ribs with pinching fingers as his yelping laughter filled the air. "I couldn't agree more !"

Chapter Nineteen.

"Oh my God, oh my God !" Nathan sat bolt upright in the dark, breathing hard and confused for a moment. Alex struggled awake beside him and sat up, rubbing his eyes. He squeezed his arm. "What's up baby ?" Nathan rubbed his face, ran a hand clumsily through his hair and said, "3 DAYS AL ! 3 DAYS !" Alex grinned, his eyes shining in the darkness. Nathan shook his head. "How is that possible ? How did this come around so soon ? I mean I can't wait to marry you, but I know I'm going to look like a moron ! I don't know why, I just am, I mean it's me, it's you ! How did I get so lucky ?" He ranted.

Alex leaned back and parted the curtains behind them, a little moonlight filled the room. "Right which one of these is going to make you calm down ? I flip you over and take my pleasure right here and now and I can tell you I feel damn horny this morning, especially with all that panting you just did, or I put something thick and hot in your mouth for you to suck on, you choose ?" Nathan turned slowly to face him, his expression an absolute picture. His mouth hung so wide open and his eyes were saucers. "Ah, option two I see, come on then." Alex started to push his boxers down making Nathan burst out laughing. He did it so loudly that Alex clapped his hand over his mouth. "Shush !" He giggled.

Nathan lay back with the hand still in place. Alex gazed down at him, shaking with laughter. "You're not going to fuck it up my love, don't worry, you can't do. I'll be right at your side." He stroked his cheek softly with one finger. It was heavenly. Nathan closed his eyes momentarily, when he opened them again he saw such a lovely look on Alex's face. He reached up and cupped his cheek. "I was being a bit silly wasn't I." "Yes," Alex nodded, "but I don't care, I will always love you." Nathan gulped, "really ?" Alex nodded.

"I will always love you just as much, more if it's possible," Nathan breathed. "Not possible," Alex whispered and bent to kiss him with every bit of his mind body and soul.

Two days before the wedding the boys sat at Alex's house on the kitchen stools, eating again, while excitedly chatting about it. "It's weird that you two are getting hitched on a Monday but then you are weird !" Jess grinned, strolling into the room and helping herself to one of Nathan's chewy chocolate chip cookies. "God these are AMAZING !" She groaned, taking a huge bite and sliding two more cookies into a piece of kitchen roll. "Ignore her !" Alex shrugged and got a poke in the ribs before she disappeared upstairs with her haul. "Ow !" He pouted and heard her laugh as she shut her bedroom door. The phone rang, Caitlin lazily reached for it while she too bit into another cookie. The boys shared a copy of Evo. They were just drooling over a Testarossa when Caitlin jumped a mile. "Oh my God !" She gasped with real shock.

"Mum ?" Alex's head shot up in alarm. Nathan's heart thudded in his chest, oh please not one of his parents he prayed. Caitlin got up with the phone and took it into the living room. They spun round to watch her. She paced about from side to side, nodding and whispering a lot before abruptly hanging up. She crossed to the front door almost at a run, snatched up her coat and keys and was about to disappear. "MUM !" Alex remonstrated, "what the hell's happened ?" Caitlin looked utterly distracted. "Erm, er...I've got to nip out, nothing serious, no one's injured. Erm,...yes. I'll see you...in..., erm....a bit," and she was gone.

Alex was absolutely flabbergasted. "What the ?" He frowned at Nathan who shook his head, "don't ask me, I have no idea what the hell that was." He scratched his head, "funny thing though, I don't actually feel worried. I mean your mum was pretty weird there that's for sure but she said no one's hurt and I believe her." Alex nodded, "yeah, I believe her too but what the hell was that and why didn't she just explain ?" Nathan flicked a page of the magazine, "hmm," he rubbed his chin.

"Hmm ? What are you thinking Nate ?" He looked up at Alex's questioning face and then a cold horror started to slide down his spine. "Oh shit Al, I think it's something to do with the wedding." Alex blanched white. "Fuck !" He rubbed both hands up and down his face. "It is isn't it." Nathan nodded. There was a split second of understanding between them before they leapt up and sprinted out of the house.

They pelted up the hill and around the corner into Nate's drive way, flew up the front steps and burst in to find Caitlin deep in discussion with Nathan's dad while Alison talked quietly and calmly on the phone in the living room. David and Caitlin both jumped guiltily when the boys stormed in. Alex lead Nathan over to the kitchen stools and sat down in front of his mum. Nathan put a reassuring hand on his shoulder. "Dad," he nodded. "Well ?" Said Alex, looking deeply into his mothers eyes. "It's the wedding isn't it ?" Caitlin looked nervously at David who steeled himself slightly, drew in a deep breath and said, "yes lads, I'm afraid there is a problem but we're trying to resolve it immediately. I was the one who phoned your mum just now and we've already been able to half rectify the situation, we're just making a call or two to see if we can sort the rest." Alex nodded, not quite sure how to take it in. Nathan gripped his shoulder feeling as non plussed. "Dad what does that mean ? What problem ?"

"Ok, don't panic but there was a problem with the celebrant, he put the wrong date down in his diary and consequently we do have to move the day you get married on as he's fully booked til March 2012 otherwise." Alex's face fell, "move the day ?" Nathan looked stunned, "but Dad, move it to when ?" David looked at the boys anxious faces and then back at Caitlin who shrugged, "there's no choice David, we have to tell them." "I know," said David. He looked squarely at them, inhaled a long deep breath and said, "tomorrow."

Alison strode back into the room. She smiled and hugged her son and kissed Alex on the forehead. "Now then you two, the caterers can do tomorrow, they were booked but a 21st had to be cancelled so they're free, the florists and staff at Thornbury said as long as we parents and maybe the twins, Jess, Ollie and a few of your other friends etc....turn up first thing in the morning, it is possible to get your reception room dressed in time too. I've also just spoken to Paul and Simon, they can both do it. So now I suggest we all get out our phones, I'll run off some copies of the guest list. We each call our own guests and tell them what's happened. A tick means yes they can make it, a cross unfortunately not. Ok let's get to it." Everyone got to work.

An hour later and the five of them were sprawled around Nathan's parents living room, lists of people and phones littered the furniture. No one spoke for a few minutes until David kissed his wife and whispered, "I'm going to make the coffee." He disappeared into the kitchen. A phone rang and Nathan and Alex sprung upright. "Mine !" Nathan dived on his blackberry. "Yup, ahuh, ok, - fantastic ! Yes, see you tomorrow, thanks so much for phoning back. Yeah see you then, cheers, bye." He snapped the phone shut and sprang up and down on the sofa. "Yahoo that's another yes for tomorrow !" Alex beamed at him excitedly, "so how many does that make now ?" Nathan hunched over the lists, counting up the ticks and sat up with a broad smile. "Forty !" "No way ?" Alex's smile stretched from ear to ear. He hugged Nathan with all his might. "Only ten to go and we've got the full set !" Alison's phone rang, she took it into the kitchen as David looked lost in there, trying to find the coffee pot. "Yes, I see, alright then. Thanks Sue. No, no don't worry at all, honestly. Yes, see you soon. Bye." She switched off the phone, pulled the cafetiere out of a nearby cupboard, handed it to David and walked back over to the boys.

"Auntie Sue ?" Nathan looked disappointed. "Really ?" Alison nodded and dropped a kiss on her son's head. "I'm sorry my love, but she's taking a tour group around that National Trust property and she can't let 20 people down at short notice who've all paid already." Alex slid his arm around Nathan's shoulders. "Sorry Nate," he said quietly. Nathan gave him a small smile, "it's not your fault Al." Alex gazed deeply into his eyes. They touched foreheads for a moment and sighed. Another phone sprang to life.

Half an hour later and the final tally was in. Forty one people were definite, three were out so they had to wait to hear back from them and six had prior engagements that just couldn't be changed. "That's not bad," said Alex and then winced as Nathan buried his head in the edge of the sofa. He hoped he wasn't crying. David and Alison hoped the same thing. "Erm, well I need to iron Jas's dress for tomorrow." Alison excused herself awkwardly. "Right, yes. I need to do something too," said David, completely unconvincingly so Caitlin simply shrugged and followed them both, sliding the living room door to as she left.

Alex slid off the sofa and curled his body around the back of Nathan's. "Don't cry my love, please don't. It's all going to be ok," he soothed. Nathan pushed back against him and then struggled round to face him. His face completely dry. "Hey I thought you were upset ?" Alex frowned, confused. "Upset ?" Nathan gazed up at him with groggy looking eyes. "I'm absolutely shattered that's all. At first it was a big shock of course but we've saved it all, and tomorrow I get to marry the man of my dreams one day early. How the hell would I ever be upset at that ?" "Oh Nate," Alex breathed, his eyes welling up. "How do you make me this happy ?" He bent to kiss his soft lips, they pulled apart with watery eyes and then embraced each other tightly. "I love you so much," whispered Nathan. "I love you more," Alex replied.

So as to keep them both in good spirits, neither set of parents would let the boys do any more. "Look, you two paid for and organised just about everything for this wedding, so let us sort this all out for tomorrow now ok ? I know you want to nip back to Cargo for a few bits for the flat and you can't stay together tonight remember so I should make use of the rest of the day right now." Christopher suggested as they all stood around in the kitchen hugging hot coffee mugs. Alex looked at Nathan, "well we do need a few more things and I don't know about you but I don't want to come back from honey moon with a list of stuff to buy, what do you think ?" "I agree, come on, I'll drive, Mum can I...." he didn't need to finish his sentence as Alison threw her keys to him. "Thanks," said Alex, impressively snatching them from mid air. "Show off !" Nathan mumbled.

Alex laughed his low throaty rumble as they headed out. "God don't do that in the car will you," Nathan moaned, "I'll crash !" Alex laughed even more. "Oh God, and I can't have sex with you tonight either," Nathan wailed as he over revved and shot out of the drive way nearly squishing a pensioner in the process. Alex beamed beside him, tomorrow was going to be so incredible.

Cargo was pretty busy, full of well mannered browsers, couples mainly. It did Alex's heart good, he felt like a proper grown up, shopping with his fiance.

They filled two baskets easily, picking out shell pictures for the bathroom, a couple of landscapes painted on canvases for the living room and two really nice big claret coloured squashy cushions for the sofa. Next they got new tea towels, a bright yellow bathmat, two new deep chocolate bath sheets and a whole host of multi coloured silicone coated kitchen utensils.

"I think that's it," said Nathan, getting out his Cargo card and handing it to the assistant. Alex watched the display and handed over half the cost in cash. "Ooh I've just remembered something I wanted. Meet you in Costa, Waterstones, quick coffee ?" "Alright," smiled Nathan and began to pack up the stuff.

Alex shot to the back of the store and found what he was looking for. Making sure Nathan had gone he slipped back to the till and got them to de-price and gift wrap it for him. It didn't take long and a few minutes later he was on the escalator to the first floor coffee shop. Nathan had found a spacious window seat over looking the heart of the shopping centre. He loved people watching and stared out of the window, a copy of 'Where's Wally,' face down on the table in front of him. "Thank God they had it," Alex smiled as he joined him. Nathan looked up, "had what ?" "This," Alex handed him the gift wrapped box. "It's just a little wedding gift Nate, something I know you want." Nathan looked totally taken aback. "Alex," he said softly, clearly touched. "Go on, open it," Alex smiled. Nathan pushed aside the book and took the box, he blushed slightly looking very sweet. He prolonged the pleasure by carefully picking apart all the tape they'd used to secure the gold and yellow striped wrapping paper, detached the sticky gold bow from the top and stuck it onto his chest, then he gasped as he read the box. "Al !" He smiled and undid the top. With a little difficulty he extracted a brand new sparkling cream Dualit kettle with ergonomic handle. "It's beautiful, you know I've always wanted this." He hugged it to himself, grinning, "I know it's daft to get excited about a kettle but I love it !"

"Careful, you'll be snogging the toaster next," Alex laughed. "Shut up !" Nathan reddened, but set the gift aside and kissed Alex's mouth quickly. "Woah ! Hold up there, that's no thank you kiss, gimme a real one."

"Alex !" Nathan grinned from ear to ear looking incredibly self conscious. "No one's here, look !" Alex shrugged and peered over his shoulders. He turned back to Nathan, raised his eyebrows with a devilish grin and pulled him close.

He kissed him with such a passion that Nathan totally forgot where he was for a moment and groaned loudly. Alex laughed softly, his tongue still in his mouth. Nathan pulled away, blushing and horribly embarrassed. "Bastard !" He breathed, sinking his face into his palms. Alex laughed and laughed, he loved turning him on and winding him up this way. His heart skipped a beat with excitement. "I'm so sorry Nate," he laughed. "No you're frigging not," grumbled Nathan from within his palms. He gingerly raised his head and noticed three elderly people who'd just come in staring at them. "You little fucker !" He whispered.

"Permission to always be badly behaved, wind you up and turn you on in public please ?" Alex giggled. Nathan shook his head with fire in his eyes. "You just wait til tomorrow night Alexander Nesbitt – Hall, you just wait !" "Oh yeah ?" Said Alex, leaning his languid body right across the table, an unmistakable look in his eyes. "What are you going to do with me tomorrow night then ?" Nathan shook his head, all three elderly people and two hovering baristas had heard it all.

"You, utter,...utter..!" He couldn't complete his sentence and simply buried his face in his palms again and groaned, but Alex saw the corners of his lips turn up as he hid his flushing cheeks. "My love...," he whispered erotically and thought he'd explode with mirth as Nathan put his head to the cold table top, his shoulders shaking with laughter.

They went first to the flat on their way home, and nailed up the pictures, slid the kitchen implements into the enamelled cream utensil pot and added the cushions and bath things to their rightful places. Alex enjoyed laughing at Nathan struggling with technology. "Fucking piece of crap !" He swore, shaking the infra red cable detector and placing it on the wall again. It beeped and told him nothing for the third time in a row so he eyed it angrily and tossed it over his shoulder. It hit the floor with a thud. Alex giggled under his breath, picked it up, strode over to the wall, held down the on button and waited.

"Clear !" He declared and watched Nathan's expression in mock innocence. "What ? Something wrong ?" "Give me that !" Nathan grabbed the detector back, peered at the now empty screen and chucked it over his shoulder once more. "That's £6.99 I won't be seeing again !" He muttered as he applied the hammer to the nail for the last time. Alex guffawed with laughter and returned the gadget to their tool box. Together they angled the final canvas in place and stood back leaning against the window ledge. Alex slid an arm around Nathan's shoulders. They'd done it beautifully, he'd rarely seen a fresher yet cosier flat. It took his breath away.

"I can't believe we've done this, and we'll actually live here very shortly." Nathan shook his head, " I know, it's amazing isn't it. Tomorrow night will be our first night here as a married couple and then it's off to Heathrow for our honey moon." They didn't need to speak after that. Just standing there taking it all in was enough. Each marvelled at the room, it's two small goat skin tables with tall lamps baring stiff cardboard monochrome shades, the thick, soft sheepskin rug that nestled under Nathan's leather chest, now doubling as their coffee table and the new cream sofa with its soft throw in deepest red and the claret and cream cushions.

Newly hung pictures brought the walls in a little making the room hang together, cosy, friendly, yet minimalist. Beside the right arm of the sofa stood a chocolate brown leather magazine rack, stocked with all the latest reads. A matching leather clock ticked lazily on the end wall. "That's a bit loud," said Alex softly. "Yes," agreed Nathan, "I'm pretty sure Mum and Dad are giving us a clock tomorrow, I think I overheard something I shouldn't have so we can probably replace it soon." Alex squeezed him closer, it was so great looking about, taking in everything in their new home.

They could both see into their bedroom from there. Nathan smiled as he looked at the claret red and gold duvet cover, new deep filled goose down pillows and single John Lewis throw cushion. Cotswold Co New England style bedside tables carried a lamp each on either side and on the window sill stood a shallow rectangular glass vase with three spiralling Yukka stems, growing as a sign of prosperity. Above the bed hung an ornately framed print of Nathan's dog drawing and on the right hand wall a framed 'Monsters Inc,' cell that Alex had managed to blag through sheer charm on holiday at the studios a few years before. He smiled at the memory, that had been an awesome trip, but nothing would ever compare again to the future holidays he would take with the love of his life. He sighed with contentment and looked at his watch.

"Let's head back to yours shall we ? It's getting on for 4pm and I'm pretty sure our parents will be trying to get us back into our own houses for the night within the next couple of hours." Nathan gulped at this. Alex felt it and caressed his cheek. "I know, I don't want to be apart tonight either. Can we text each other do you think ?" Nathan bit back his emotion as it threatened to overspill, "I don't see why not ? We won't skype or anything, just texts." "Good," Alex grinned and stood up. He turned to face Nathan, surprised him with a soft kiss and reached for his hands. "Next time we step through that door you'll be my husband." Nathan's heart sped up, "and you mine," he replied breathlessly.

They took a last look around, hugged one another tight with excitement and headed back to Nathan's house. Alex was right. Things were under control but the mothers looked tensely at their boys. "You two should be saying goodnight soon," Caitlin looked from one to the other with an anxious expression. "It is tradition."

Alex rolled his eyes, "yes mum, and we always go to bed at, ooh look, 4.07pm," he answered sarcastically. Nathan's dad smirked in the back ground. Alison laughed gently. "Come on Caitlin, we'll kick you lot out in about an hour, how's that ? In the meantime please sit down and have at least two of these will you, they're fresh." She offered up a plate of delicious smelling scones. Nathan's eyes lit up. "Yum ! I'll get the jam and stuff," he beamed. "Dyson !" Mumbled Alex softly, making him giggle as he retrieved the clotted cream from the fridge.

It was such a fun couple of hours as the nine of them sprawled all over the living room stuffing down thickly laden scones, vast mugs of tea and laughing copiously. Time flew and soon Caitlin began to sneak little glances at her watch again, unnoticed by no one. Alex caught Nathan's eye and saw a millisecond of sadness cross his expression. He needed to find out why. "Come on husband to be, help me carry this stuff through to the kitchen," he struggled to his feet, overladen with plates. Nathan stood immediately and took some off the top. They wandered through as everyone chattered on and knocked back the last of their tea.

"So," said Alex as he bent to slide the plates into the dishwasher, "what's up with you ?" Nathan looked a bit taken aback. "Eh ?" "I saw that fleeting look of worry, what's that all about Nate ?" He asked, concern in his voice. Nathan looked non plussed for a second and then the penny dropped. "Oh...., oh ok," he nodded and looked a little shy. He picked at a rivet on his jeans. Alex squatted down beside the dishwasher and pulled Nathan down too so they couldn't be seen. "Come on beautiful, what is it ?"

Nathan blushed and exhaled in a slightly exasperated way. "Oh I was just being silly," he shrugged. Alex ran a hand around onto his backside and caressed it. "This hand is moving all the way around your body in a minute unless you tell me, I'll make you rocket right here, don't think I won't !" He tried to look threatening and serious, Nathan laughed. "Ok, ok," he shook his head, "and by the way, please never use the expression 'rocket,' while we're actually doing it as I won't be able to stop laughing."

"Yeah yeah, whatever," grinned Alex, "enough of your distraction techniques young Henderson, what's up. Tell me, please ?" He said the last word softly and caressed Nathan's cheek. "I told you I was just being silly Al. I can't wait to marry you and moving into our flat is so wonderful, but just for a second while we were all mucking about in there I thought that I might miss being part of all of that stuff and I felt a little sad." Alex shook his head, "you daft twit !" "See...I...," Nathan started to interrupt, but Alex slid a hand across his mouth.

"No you lemon, let me finish. Of course you're going to feel a bit sad, odd, disoriented, any or all of the above, and so am I ! I mean neither of us has ever lived away from home before so what do you expect ?" He shrugged, removing his hand. Nathan smiled, "so you think so too ?" "Duh !" Said Alex, making them both laugh. They stood up to retrieve more plates and utensils for the dishwasher.

"Besides," said Alex as Nathan rinsed a couple of things under the tap and passed them to him, "you and I are gonna be round here so often for the first few months that they'll get heartily sick of the sight of us and we'll save a fortune on food. Good eh?" Nathan laughed, grinning from ear to ear. "I really do love you," he smiled his killer smile at Alex who shook his head. "Me too. Oh God don't look at me like that when we have to be apart tonight. Blimey Nate...."

He didn't have time to finish as his dad appeared behind him, gripping his shoulder in a no nonsense manner. "Ok, enough chit chat you two. Thanks for clearing up." He looked at his watch, "it's that time guys, so you have two minutes to say your soppy good nights and then we're carting this one home until tomorrow." "But, I...." Alex tried to protest then looked at the wall of parents and knew he needed to go. His stomach flipped over, excitement banged his heart hard against his ribs as he turned his gaze back to Nathan's rather pale face. They were feeling the same and gulped at each other, but it was only one night Alex told himself and walked toward him.

The parents removed themselves for a minute. Alex reached down and linked hands with him. "You ok?" He breathed. "No," said Nathan truthfully, he was full of nerves and didn't want Alex to go. "We'll be fine Nate," Alex caressed his cheek, Nathan closed his eyes at his touch. Alex's arms closed around his body, holding him close and kissing him with utter gentleness. When they pulled apart they simply stared into one another's eyes. "My Alex," whispered Nathan, his fingers trembled as he touched Alex's smooth face. "I love you," Alex whispered back.

"Oh for goodness sake! You're seeing each other in eighteen hours!" Christopher had been sent from the living room to get Alex and witnessed their heart rending good nights. His exclamation made them jolt with fright. "Christ dad! Don't do that," said Alex, his arms still around Nathan who grinned and turned red. Alex shook his head and looked back at him.

"This is it my love, I know we'll get no peace unless I leave now so sleep well, text me. Remember that I love you and I'll be thinking about you all night," he kissed Nathan once more on the mouth. "For God's sake," Christopher mumbled in the background. Nathan grinned as the other parents appeared. "I love you too," he whispered. Alex thumbed his cheek and turned toward Nathan's mum and dad.

"Thanks again for a lovely day," he smiled, "and for making such a gorgeous son." He hugged them both. Alison kissed him on the cheek and laughed. "Get away with you you cheeky boy." Alex grinned at her and shrugged on his out held coat. "Not that you want me to go or anything....?" He raised an eyebrow at his parents. "Car !" They said in unison and ushered him and Jess toward the door. "Come on," she said kindly and took her brother's hand. "The sooner you're home, the sooner it's tomorrow."

Alex gave her shoulder a little squeeze, headed down the steps and glanced back once to catch Nathan's eye. He blinked hard at the special look that made his heart flip, and followed his family into the car, almost unable to bear the one night between him and utter happiness.

Nathan stood at the window, catching a last glimpse of the back of Alex's car as it pulled away. He remained there as his family put away the last of the afternoon's debris. It was amazing to him that his life had changed so much and yet he himself was exactly the same as he'd always been. Tomorrow really would be the beginning of his life. His and Alex's, no one else's and it made him tremble with anticipation. He stood for some time looking out at the view. They were lucky to live in this part of England and especially on this hill, it was truly beautiful.

He leant an arm against the window frame and gazed out as if seeing it for the first time. The noises from his family in the back ground quietened down and for a while he felt entirely on his own with his thoughts. Slightly further down the hill Alex would no doubt already be home with his family, last minute washing, ironing etc...taking place. He smiled at the image and watched his breath fog up a small patch of glass.

"Here," there was a gentle tap on his shoulder, his mother passed him a hot cup of tea. "Thanks," he smiled. She gazed out of the window too for a moment, then reached over and rubbed her sons shoulder. He blinked at her, serene and content. "Want to come and sit with us ? Maybe bung in a dvd ? Jas's choice though I'm afraid," she smiled. Nathan nodded and walked slowly with her into the living room. He linked his arm around her waist, something he never normally did, but he loved his mum and wanted her to know it. She was touched.

"Sit next to me ?" He nodded and for his last night as a single man, curled his arm around his little sister and leant against his mum's shoulder on the sofa, drifting off to sleep half way through 'A Room With A View,' and dreaming of his own George Emerson.

The wedding day dawned with such brightness the following morning that Nathan was sure it was a sign that he and Alex were meant to be. Not that he needed it. He'd gone to bed early, slept immediately and then found himself waking off and on for most of the night. Some how he'd managed to get good sleep in between his waking and didn't feel bad. In fact, he felt amazing. He stood alone, gazing out of the living room window, down toward Alex's house.

They had texted only twice last night, the last one that Alex sent back made him want to blub his heart out it was so remarkable. Maybe that was why he had slept so well he mused.

No one else had come down stairs yet but Nathan felt sure his mum must have been up for ages. He was surprised not to see her pottering about in her usual cheerful morning manner. He frowned and glanced at his watch, 7.15am. For a mother of the groom that was surely unheard of? But he smiled and found it hard to worry about how long his family slept for today, as long as they got to the ceremony on time. His heart thrummed with excitement. It was such a beautiful 18th century building that they were getting married in, so many period features, tall elegant arched windows, huge marble fire places, ceiling roses and walls covered in painstakingly maintained gold silk.

The morning room had several long bookcases on either side, packed with neat rows of classic books, button back leather chairs and a central chandelier of dazzling 18th century Murano glass sending refracted light rainbowing off every surface whenever the sun warmed it. He grinned to himself, that room coupled with the wedding breakfast downstairs in the cream painted orangery, decorated with its beautiful bouquets were going to make the day his dream come true with Alex.

Now his heart was really thumping. He put the backs of his fingers to his cheeks to feel how flushed he was. Just then the key turned slowly, carefully in the front door as if who ever it was didn't want to be heard and wake everyone up. Nathan stepped out into the room and folded his arms with a grin. Slowly and as yet not noticing him, his mother re latched the door with absolute quiet. She seemed to sigh with relief at having accomplished it, but then jumped with fright and let out a small shriek as she turned and saw him.

"Oh my good God !" She looked utterly flustered. A shopping bag fell to the floor with a soft thump. Nathan walked over and picked it up, "morning mum, sorry for frightening you," he beamed. Alison looked at her sons ecstatic face. "Darling, come here," she held her arms open for him and they hugged one another tightly. "I'm so pleased for you," she cupped both hands on either side of his face as they pulled apart. Her heart thought it would explode with joy seeing his eyes shine with so much happiness and excitement.

"I've got such butterflies mum," he beamed. "I just can't believe today's here !" Alison squeezed his hand and grinned at him. "Come on my darling, let's get these croissant into the oven for a warm through and we can be excited together." Nathan laughed, "ok mum," and followed her into the kitchen.

Chapter Twenty.

Over at Alex's he woke with a start as his phone jumped to life. He punched snooze on the alarm and turned over groaning. He'd slept really well after a tossing and turning start which saw him knocking back half a 'Nightol' at 11.30pm. Not his favourite thing to do as apparently they worked for ten hours. The alarm started again. He groaned and fished around on the bed for it, his hand rummaging unsuccessfully as it got louder and louder.

"Oh for fucks sake !" He roared at last and slashed at the curtains to let in the daylight, spotted the phone and fell on it with anger. With the annoying tone now silenced, he sat up grumpily feeling his hair all over the place, looked down at the dishevelled duvet barely covering his naked groin and thought about Nathan caressing him later on that night. His face slowly split into a huge grin, all sleep gruffness ebbed away and his heart began to bang in his chest with excitement. He yawned, still foggy headed but now a man with a plan and stumbled out of bed for a good stretch. He bent and snatched his pj bottoms from the floor, flung on a t-shirt, shrugged into his Joules hoodie and headed down stairs for a strong cup of coffee to wake himself up.

As he emerged into the kitchen half light, he looked out across their magnificent view and it only heightened his excitement and anticipation. In a world of his own he turned toward the kitchen counter and jumped at his mum sitting cupping a mug of green tea. "Oh blimey, you scared the crap out of me !" He grinned. Caitlin smiled warmly at her son and watched as his eyes moistened and his cheeks flamed. She shook her head, he really was deliriously in love.

"Today is going to be really really special Alex isn't it." He nodded and blew out a big breath, tilting back his head for a moment and dabbing at the corners of his eyes. "Oh mum." He didn't know what else to say and came to sit at the consul, running a hand through his hair before resting it on the cold granite. Caitlin cupped hers over his and patted it gently as she stood up, "let me get you some breakfast my love. Now then, what would you like ?"

It was lovely for both boys to have a few minutes of mother son time, but of course impossible to sustain in Nathan's house at least as the twins, woken by their dad nice and early to be ready for the day in time, staggered groaning and moaning into the kitchen barely a few minutes later, and after three pain au chocolat each, proceeded to hurl themselves around the down stairs in a mental fashion, pinching each others stuff, giggling and yelling at one another in equal measure. Nathan shook his head and winced at Jas's ear piercing screech. "I swear those two are allergic to sugar !" He sighed. Alison laughed and passed him another pain au chocolat, topping up his orange juice glass as she went.

He frowned, "Mum, I'm not going to be able to get into my suit at this rate !" She squeezed his shoulder and glanced up at the kitchen clock. "Just eat what you like my love, now then, I must throw my clothes on and head down to Thornbury, I promised the florist I'd help dress the tables with this late change of plans. You carry on, I'l be back by 11 to get ready." She kissed him on the forehead and dashed up the stairs holding her dressing gown up so as not to trip on it.

They were getting married at 2pm, hours to go Nathan realised as he glanced up at the clock. His heart thumped, maybe he should go for a run around the block. "What are you mulling over ?" Asked his dad as he reached for a croissant and shrugged on his jacket. "Hmm," sighed Nathan. "I know, I know," his dad held up a hand, " not enough to do until 2pm eh ?" Nathan smiled sheepishly, "how did you know ?" "Because I felt exactly the same on my wedding day," said his father kindly. "My advice son," he zipped up his jacket and peered outside at the weather, "throw on the tv for a couple of hours, chill, don't run around like a loon 'using,' the time, it will only wind you up, trust me."

He looked up at the clock, "however, it's a different story for us, time your mother and I were off, ALISON ?" He yelled, going to the bottom of the stairs. "Coming, coming," she emerged at once, her wavy hair in a hurried chignon, dark blue and pink fleece in place over long legged dark jeans and trainers. She looked about 19 and totally happy. Nathan grinned at them as his dad slid his hand into hers and pulled her at a run toward the front door. "Come on cheeky," he grinned into his wife's eyes. Nathan rolled his as he waved them goodbye, but grinned with pleasure at seeing them so happy still. People banged on so much about divorce and the lack of true love these days but that just wasn't his experience. He felt blessed to be surrounded by happy couples, great role models for he and Alex, a true inspiration to them both.

He pottered out of the kitchen and into the living room. Flicking through the Mail's weekend magazine, he saw that The Lion King was just starting on Film 4 and flopped onto the sofa to watch it. It was the right thing to do though very emotional and got him in exactly the right mood to be his soppiest ever to the man he loved in a few hours time. Perfect for his wedding day.

Alex did go for a run. After being force fed bacon and eggs he felt it lying hard against his stomach and went for a sprint around the block, though he was terrified of bumping into Nathan and breaking the tradition of not being seen before the ceremony so he pulled a ratty old hoodie from the back of his cupboard, kept the hood pulled over his face and ran in his shades without looking at his house as he ran past. He made it back intact, sweaty and elated. Extending his run all the way up the hill and around the park had been a good idea and worn away more time. He was thrilled to see it getting on for 11 already by the time he got home.

Everyone else was out by now helping to dress tables and adjust seating plans to accommodate the recent changes so he towelled himself off in the living room with a hand towel off the top of the laundry, grabbed a huge fresh bathsheet flung it over the sofa and lounged in his sweats for twenty minutes while happily channel surfing. It was only when he heard his parents car turn back into their driveway that he flicked off the tv, snatched up his drenched towels and shot into the bathroom for a long hot shower.

He re-emerged downstairs 25 minutes later, his skin a deep pink from the heat of the water, his dark hair shiny and his face lit up. "Son can you go and put some clothes on please ?" His father asked from behind the local Chinese takeaway menu. "Yes you can't get married like that darling !" His mum raised an eyebrow at his appearance in nothing but a big white towel knotted around his waist. "I know mum, I'm just too hot right now, I need to cool down a bit," he grinned and plopped down onto the sofa. Caitlin looked at her watch, "ok, we've all got time for a coffee before we get ready, who wants one ?" "Me," said Christopher before going back to his menu reading.

"No thanks," said Alex and then frowned at his father. "Are you getting eccentric already dad ?" "What ?" Christopher looked up and then followed his son's eyes to the menu. "Oh this, no, we're all choosing our order for tonight in case we get hungry after you two have disappeared, no one will want to cook." He smiled and shrugged. 'After you two have disappeared,' God that made Alex's stomach flip with nerves and he felt himself getting cold all of a sudden in nothing but his towel. He shivered and rubbed his arms as his mum returned with the coffee. They chatted for a while, the three of them. Joined after a few minutes by a breathless Jess who came barrelling back through the front door, a huge grin on her face. "God that place looks AMAZING !" She beamed and flung herself onto Alex's lap.

"Oh thank God, I was getting a bit cold, I needed a massive heavy lump to warm me up," he teased. "Oy !" Grinned Jess and pinched his ribs. Time passed slowly for the happy group, chit chatting about nothing and everything and then at last, 'D day,' as his dad jokingly called it. "Ok," said Caitlin, that unmistakably motherly tone in her voice that no one argued with. "Let's get changed everyone. We've got an hour and a quarter and then we HAVE to leave, no two ways about it so go." She took the empty coffee mugs into the kitchen, loaded them into the dishwasher and followed her family up the stairs.

Alex lead the way and as he shut his bedroom door and looked at his suit pressed and ready, hanging on the outside of his cupboard his heart skipped a beat. 'Oh my God, oh my God, this is really it !' He thought and set his alarm again for forty five minutes time. He lay back on the bed, tempted to 'amuse himself,' but refrained, the only man to make him explode today was going to be his husband. He shivered with over excitement, wriggled under the duvet and picked up his psp but he couldn't concentrate and picked up his diary instead. Reading about how he'd felt for Nathan from the start took him back and soon he was totally absorbed. He'd only got to their first encounter when his phone leapt to life. He gazed at the screen finding it hard to believe 45 minutes had flown so quickly by but it was true. He shut the journal and sat up, nerves jangling but his heart singing with excitement. He slipped off the towel, trying not to think about Nathan touching him later as he stood naked for a moment and then began to dress.

The Lion King wasn't quite finished when Nathan's mum gave the same directive to her family. Nerves gripped his stomach as he also switched off the tv and followed the rest of his troop upstairs. He had to open both windows and stand naked in the cold draft for a moment before he could calm his breathing enough and turn to the dark charcoal grey suit with matching waistcoat hanging outside his cupboard. A truly nervous smile slid across his face as he reached for his boxers and slid them on. This was it, he was really getting married. He looked at his left hand where the ring should be and prayed that Jack wouldn't loose either of them before they'd been blessed and were never taken off again. He grinned and looked up at the suit, it was time.

Everyone gathered downstairs in Nathan's house, milling nervously about the living room fiddling with cuffs and stray locks of hair. His dad kept glancing at his watch and back up at the stairs. Finally he huffed and said, "Alison where is he ? We really need to leave now !" Alison saw the time and felt a bit anxious too. "I'll give him a call, wait here, I...." she gasped and didn't go on. "Sorry for the hold up," said Nathan quietly as he came down the stairs. He stopped at the bottom, grinning at his family's shocked faces.

"Oh my God !" Whispered Jas and held her fingers up to her eyes. Alison handed her a tissue, she'd need one herself in a second. No one else spoke at first until she crossed the floor and carefully embraced her son so as not to crease him. "You look stunning darling." He coloured and looked around at the rest of his family. "You do," croaked his father, unused to saying that to any man but overwhelmed at the emotion brought on by his handsome son. Nathan shone.

His dark hair spiked naturally upward with it's short choppy cut, it gleamed with health. His face, clean shaven, smooth and lightly tanned glowed with happiness and he looked tall, lean and so desperately handsome in his perfectly fitted dark suit. He wore the jacket open to show off the exquisitely tailored waistcoat underneath, a crisp white shirt under that, dark grey silk tie flecked with blue, a white handkerchief placed in his top pocket and black patent leather shoes gleamed on his feet. He fiddled with his cufflinks for a moment which only made him look like an extremely lithe and beautiful young James Bond. Jas, Alison and David all shook their heads to look at him, they were dumb with emotion.

"Bastard !" Piped Jack all of a sudden. "What ?" Three incredulous expressions snapped his way. "Well, look at him !" Huffed Jack, "I'd get all the girls if I looked like that, not bloody fair !" Everyone else, including Nathan, burst out laughing. "Come on," said Alison, walking over and kissing her youngest son on the cheek, "into the car you lot." "What ?" Said Jack and shrugged as he was herded out of the front door. "I'm just saying."

Nathan shrugged on his long trench coat, it made Alison wonder why she'd never suggested modelling to her son, seeing him like this. He was breath taking. He moved forward but Alison got in his way. She seemed to be deliberately blocking his view for a moment on the top step. He tried to dodge around her. "Er Mum, you're kind of getting in the way ?" There was a strange honk from behind her, unmistakably from one of those old fashioned brass car horns with the rubber bulb on the end.

"Mum ?" Nathan grinned at her, what was going on ? Then he raised his eyes and saw his whole family beaming as they held open the doors to a British racing green 1927 Morris, glinting in the sun. It had a black canvas roof and detachable windows, thankfully attached today against the chill. Nathan's grin reached from ear to ear as he descended the steps. "Wait !" Shouted Jas and ran forward to snap his photo quickly. Nathan laughed and walked over to the car. He walked all around it. It was beautiful with it's glass water gauge on the nose, side flip engine panels, black wheel arches and red leather interior.

"Come on," Jas jumped up and down with excitement, "let me take one of you next to the car, one foot on the running board." He did as she asked and then slid into the front passenger seat. "No you have to go in the back, chauffeur style," Jack urged. "Ok," Nathan felt sublimely happy, all of this was just wonderful. A bit of re jigging on who sat where, and they were off, his dad drove slowly out of the gravel drive, getting Jack to indicate left by sticking his arm out of the passenger window. "No way, that's not how you indicate !" Nathan laughed. "Sure is," Jack beamed over his shoulder. The long piece of white ribbon tied from the nose of the car to either side of the windscreen, vibrated in the wind as they drove along. Many people turned to stare and every time David honked the horn making everyone in the car cheer. It was a fabulous journey.

Twenty minutes later, they turned into the long drive at Thornbury. Nathan's heart started to hammer with nerves. He drew in a deep shaky breath and wondered if Alex was there yet and what they'd both do when they saw each other. Jas closed her hand in his, sensing his tension. He smiled at her and gulped with slightly pale cheeks. "Don't worry, you look amazing Nathan," she whispered. He let out a tiny choking noise and gripped her around the shoulders, "thanks sis." "You smell really lovely too," she added and hugged him back.

The car swung round in front of the hall and Nathan felt slightly sick. How would he last all through the day with nerves like this ? He sat in the car while his dad went in for a moment. "What's going on ? Can't I get out yet ?" He frowned as the twins disappeared inside. "It's nothing to worry about darling, we just decided between the parents on who was getting here first and how, I know you said it didn't matter to you and Alex but we wanted to make it special so he got a surprise car this morning too, and he's supposed to have got here first. I suggested that as I thought you might be nervous, do you mind ?"

Nathan blushed and clutched her to him. "Oh mum, thank you. I am nervous, I didn't think I would be but I am. It does make a difference." They separated and she gently thumbed his cheek. "Good, but you've no need to be nervous, Alex loves you," she smiled. Just then David reappeared with a big grin on his face. He opened the door, "he's here Nathan, ready and waiting for you." Nathan's eyes flew wide, his hands went up to his cheeks as he tried to steady his breathing. He felt sweaty under the arms, thank God for a dark suit.

"Calm, gently,....calm." Said Alison and slowly inhaled a deep breath. Nathan watched her and copied gratefully. Once more and again one for luck together, and he was calm enough to get out. They walked inside the stone arched doorway, met on both sides by a small row of smiling staff who took their coats. A glossy dark haired girl walked smartly toward them and shook Nathan's hand. "A very warm welcome to you all" she beamed. "My name's Natalie Sinclair and I've been co-ordinating everything for Nathan and Alex today." As she clipped smartly ahead, waving everyone onward, Jack looked at Nathan, pointed at her back and made a finger down his throat motion. "Shut up !" Nathan snapped, more tensely than he'd meant to. Jack looked at his immediately contrite expression and shrugged it off. "Sorry bro."

"Me too," Nathan whispered. They were already outside the morning room and came to a stop. "Seriously man, good luck, I know you're gonna have an amazing day," Jack reached up and hugged his big brother tightly around the neck. "Yes you are," said Jas and did the same. His parents both nodded at him, each squeezing a hand and disappeared into the room. Natalie shut the double doors behind them and turned to face him. "I hope you don't mind but Alexander asked me privately if you could come in with him as he said you might both be rather nervous. He's waiting in here. Is that alright with you ?" She looked a little concerned in case it wasn't. Nathan gulped hard and looked at the door that she gestured toward. Behind that ornately panelled wood waited the man of his dreams. "God I'm so nervous," he blurted suddenly. Natalie laughed, "well that makes two of you then."

"Does it ?" Said Nathan with a grin, suddenly feeling quite a lot less anxious. "Yes it most certainly does," she smiled warmly. "Now come on, shall I take you in ? I'll give you a couple of minutes together then I'll be back to take you both in to your families and you can be married, ok ?" Nathan grinned at her, now he was seriously over wrought and excited to see Alex. "Ok," he nodded, "take me in."

Natalie knocked sharply on the thick wooden door and immediately swung it wide without waiting for a reply. Nathan stepped across the threshold into a bright, high ceilinged room with tall thin rectangular windows and red leather chairs pushed up against the gold silk wall panels. It too had a Murano glass chandelier, ornate cornicing in gold leaf and cherubs painted in sections all over the ceiling. Nathan came to a halt in the middle of the room. He wasn't quite sure where he was for a second, the blood pumped so hard in his ears but then he heard a gasp and looked up. Alex stood before him, stunned and frozen to the spot. Nathan caught his breath too, he'd known Alex would look good but now, here in front of him, he thought he'd pass out, cry or throw up. Maybe all three.

This was nothing to how Alex was feeling. He'd turned as Natalie had opened the door and ushered in an excited but terrified looking Nathan, and then it felt like something had whacked him hard in the chest. He'd never seen him look like this before. In his wildest dreams he couldn't have designed a finer looking man. He couldn't move for a second, his jaw dropped open. Nathan did his best coy blush and slipped his hands into his pockets. It did nothing to dim the impact upon Alex who slowly shook his head.

He closed his mouth and stepped toward him. Nathan's heart beat faster the closer he got. When they were barely a foot apart Alex reached for his hand. Nathan looked down at it, amazed to feel the fingers that enclosed his clammy and shaking a little. He looked up into his face. "You, are so fucking beautiful," Alex breathed and looked him up and down again. Nathan laughed with pleasure, quivering at the look he gave him. "You don't look so bad yourself," he breathed back. Alex just shook his head and looked him up and down once more before gazing into his eyes.

"Christ Nathan, I am the luckiest man alive, the luckiest." He shook his head in disbelief and clutched Nathan into his arms, tight up against his body. "I just can't believe I've got you," he gasped savagely against his shoulder, gripping him with all his might. It made Nathan groan to be held like this. He wanted to fall on the floor and make love to Alex immediately. "I want you so much, so badly," croaked Alex, mimicking his own thoughts. Nathan choked out a half sob, "me too, oh God me too," he clutched back just as hard and could feel Alex's heart ramming against his insides as if it would crash through his ribs any second with longing.

Alex let out a half sob and then pulled away tilting his head back. He pushed a knuckle to the corner of one eye and shook himself before smoothing down his jacket and adjusting his tie. He watched as Nathan did the same. No damage, they both looked as incredible as before. When Nathan finished smoothing his sleeves and adjusting his tie he glanced up at Alex and felt his breath shudder out of him. It was hard not to cry with Alex dressed like this. His light pewter suit, cut without a waistcoat, sculpted close to his enviable body hung on him as if he were gliding down a Milan catwalk. It was impeccably made, Italian, and he too wore a white shirt underneath with a lighter grey silk tie, flecked with pale blue.

"I don't have the words when I look at you like this," Nathan managed. "Me either," said Alex, reaching up to thumb his cheek with shaking fingers. Just then Natalie knocked on the door. She walked in immediately again and smiled at them, nervous, holding hands and obviously utterly blown away by one another. "You both look gorgeous," she beamed. They laughed nervously and looked into each other's eyes. Alex squeezed Nathan's fingers for luck.

"Ready ?" Natalie gestured toward the open door. They eyed each other with total awe and nodded. "Ready," said Alex softly. "Ready," breathed Nathan as they followed her, walking hand in hand from the room, barely moments away from being together forever.

Natalie put both hands on the round handles of the double doors and pushed. They swung open with a soft swish. Alex tightened his grip on Nathan's hand and they walked inside. The celebrant smiled warmly at them from behind her table at the far end of the room. She stood in front of the high arched windows in between the long bookcases which flanked each wall. Two rows of chairs had been arranged parallel to each book case. Both families stood and turned in the rows as she beckoned to their sons. Alison and Caitlin let out audible sobs and the fathers had to clear their throats repeatedly at the sight of them. As the boys moved between them, hand in hand, tears slid down everyone's cheeks. When they stopped in front of the celebrant she made a gesture to the families to sit down.

"Welcome Nathan and Alex, welcome," she smiled kindly and asked them to turn and face one another holding both hands. " I think I'm shaking all over," said Nathan more loudly than he'd meant to and went red immediately. Both families laughed which broke the tension a little. "Hey," frowned Alex, "where are Ollie and Simon and all that lot ?" Nathan shrugged, "you said you wanted this to be more intimate, so it is." Alex gulped and shook his head again. His eyes moistening instantly. "Oh Nate," he whispered as more sniffing and throat clearing filled the room.

The celebrant stepped forward, speaking across the boys joined hands and said,"As this is a civil partnership, the legal part is accomplished as soon as Nathan and Alex have both signed the register. However, in our discussions they wanted to make it more of a wedding day and a celebration of their love, so before we come to the signing I know that they have something to say to each other." She touched them both gently on the shoulder and stood back.

Nathan looked nervously at Alex and drew out a dark blue laminated card from his inside pocket, to his astonishment he saw his name printed in white curly writing on the back. Nathan's hands shook very badly, he had never liked public speaking and now his parents were about to hear all the intimate things he thought about Alex, for a moment he wondered if he shouldn't say them, then he felt Alex close both hands around his, and looking up into his exquisite eyes, he knew that he wanted everyone to know how he felt about this boy. He inhaled deeply.

"Alex, when we met at school all those years ago, we were friends, not so much close friends, just members of the same class, nice to each other if our paths crossed but they didn't very often. Then we started to grow up and typically you excelled at everything even more than usual," Alex snorted and shook his head. Nathan continued, "I always had the support of my family, that I know, but I didn't feel like you, I didn't feel invincible, and I envied you that. It's always shone from you, that confidence and 100 per cent belief that you can simply 'do' things. It's awesome." He looked up, Alex's eyes were getting very shiny. "Three terms ago I came back from the holidays and I realised that not once had I thought about any of the bikini clad girls on my trip to Australia. They just didn't figure in my thoughts at all. It was right at this moment of realisation as I sat in Mr Stone's first English class of the term that you walked back in and my eyes nearly fell out of my head." Everyone laughed.

"That lesson I couldn't concentrate at all. In fact for the next three weeks I barely ate, slept or spoke until that fateful day when I couldn't hide my feelings any more and suddenly we were talking. Of course nothing happened until another three weeks after that when you came to climb up the trellis into my room that night," both families gasped and the mothers turned open mouthed toward each other. Alex laughed and glanced quickly at them but his attention was on Nathan. His heart thrummed listening to him.

"Carry on," he breathed, "I like this story," Nathan caught his breath at the look in his eyes, that night was clearly unforgettable to them both. He looked back at his card. "After that night, the things we said to each other, the feelings we finally admitted, my life changed forever." He slid the card back inside his pocket and held both of Alex's hands, looking deeply into his eyes he said, " because I never knew I would find the man of my dreams at this age and I never dreamed that he would be so beautiful on the outside and breathtakingly, and seemingly impossibly, so much more on the inside." Alex's eyes spilled over.

"I have never met a more wonderful person than you Alex and the fact that you want to be with me blows me away every single day. I promise that I will treasure you for as long as we both live and and be true and faithful to only you for every single day of my life. I love you more than anything else in the world. Thank you for marrying me today."

There was a stunned silence broken only by a few sobs. Alex's face streamed with tears. He took the celebrants offered tissues with a small laugh and wiped his face then he shook his head and pulled Nathan into his arms. They held each other as sobs erupted from behind them and their bodies shook with laughter and emotion. As they pulled apart Alex kissed Nathan's lips gently and leant his forehead against him. They turned their faces together to look at their families and laughed out loud at the melee of tissue boxes being handed around and everyone frantically dabbing at their eyes. They giggled, both still over wrought but loving it and pulled apart to right themselves and continue.

It took a couple of minutes and a few sips of water before Alex could look Nathan in the eyes again without his watering. He shook his head and blew out a deep shaky breath before he too reached into his pocket and drew out a card. His was neatly typed onto a tan coloured piece of parchment which would afterward roll up and tie together with a length of cream ribbon. Nathan loved the detail and smiled as Alex started to speak. He began once but only a voice quavering croak came out to everyone's amusement so he shook himself and started again.

"Nathan, through all my years so far, through all my ups and downs, achievements and failures, I have had my parents and sister beside me. No words can describe how much confidence they have given me, suffice to say, without their love and help I would never have collected so many sporting accolades, joined so many clubs and projects nor had so many wonderful experiences. I have led a very fortunate and happy life and I always believed I would meet someone special but then you came along. When I fell in love with you it hit me so hard I literally lost my breath."

He glanced up into Nathan's face before continuing, "we were friends for a long time, not bosom buddies but class friends and then a year ago I started to notice you. I watched you at break times as you slipped away from the others to draw under a tree. I watched you in English totally let yourself go when a story took you and how you always had to let go of the pen and shake the pain out of your hand from writing too fast." Nathan's parents chuckled and nodded in the background, he certainly knew their son. Alex continued, "but most of all what I saw is how good you are," he slipped the card back into his pocket and took hold of Nathan's hands, "and you don't know it." He breathed.

"You are kinder than most people could ever hope to be, you are so generous by nature but so self critical that you don't even notice. In a room full of a hundred people you would give away a hundred personal possessions without a seconds thought if you really believed those people would feel comforted by them. I have never met a kinder man." His voice shook and Nathan's eyes threatened to over flow. "I didn't know a person like you could exist," he said softly then looked down at their joined hands. "The fact that you are the most beautiful boy in the world too just cracks my heart open at the thought that you are mine...," he pushed the fingers of one hand up against his eyes as his voice cracked. Tears splashed from Nathan's eyes onto their linked fingers. Alex let out a sob, coughed and cuffed at his eyes. He tilted his head back and took the offered tissues once more. "Sorry," he laughed self consciously at Nathan who shook his head with a grin and swiped at his own tears.

Alex looked determined and joined hands with him again. He looked Nathan deeply in the eyes, "I promise that I will never cheat or lie to you and I will spend the rest of my life in your arms thanking God that you said yes to me. I love you with all my heart and soul." He just about got the words out before another sob escaped him. They both looked at each other, shaking their heads grinning. "I love you," husked Nathan. "Me too," Alex breathed as they grabbed hold of one another and buried their faces in each others shoulders.

The room was awash with tears. "Oh for goodness sake !" Growled David as he took another proffered Kleenex and squashed it up into his reddened eyes. He coughed and looked at his wife who had her compact out and was pressing a whole tissue over first one eye and then the other. She laughed when she saw his expression. "Can you pass those please, thanks," croaked Jess as her mother passed her a very depleted box of boots tissues. "Thank goodness we brought two !" Caitlin said in a raspy teary voice as she took the kleenex back from Jack who shrugged, about to deny that he was crying until his sister looked at him and started to laugh.

"Shut up !" He pouted and looked away as his lips turned up at the corners. "I had something in my eye." Jas burst out laughing. Nathan and Alex pulled apart and looked over at her. Seeing everyone blubbing they laughed heartily and kissed one another gently on the mouth.

"Look what we've done to everybody," Nathan beamed. Alex's heart skipped a beat looking at his handsome face, "I'm glad we've had that affect on them," he breathed, thumbing Nathan's cheek. "Not just on them," Nathan smiled shyly back at him. Alex pulled him close and really kissed him. When they pulled away he said, "I will never let you go, and I will never hurt you." "And I will always love you from the bottom of my heart," said Nathan. They kissed again and held each other tight, never wanting this day to be over, it really was the best day of their lives.

Chapter Twenty One.

After the signing of the register, the celebrant pronounced them a couple in the eyes of the law and being a member of the clergy, she took the rings and blessed them over a bowl of consecrated water from the church font. As she passed them to the boys, each took the others finger and slid the rings back on. They stayed holding each others hands, looking down at them in awe and wonder. Slowly Alex raised his face to Nathan's. "We've done it," he whispered.

Nathan shook his head, "I can't quite believe it," he breathed. "I love you," said Alex and pulled him close. The kiss he gave him made both fathers look away after a minute. "My God !" Squeaked Jess at Jack and Jas from behind her hands. They were all grinning but it seemed so private and never ending. At last they pulled apart, "bugger me," said a panting Nathan, "I think I need a lie down now." The room erupted into laughter and the boys turned to face their families, their hands joined, they threw them into the air instinctively. "We're married !"

Both families jumped to their feet and ran to embrace them. After much hugging and laughing Alex poked his cheeks, "God these hurt now !" He grinned. Caitlin hugged him again, "you're married my darling, well done !" Alex beamed at her. "Sorry about that kiss !" He said, going a little red in the face but beaming still. "It's your wedding my love, you can have twenty more like it for all I care ! Do what you like." "Right," said Alex, his face lighting up, "where's my new husband, I've lost him already."

He peered over and between the families and caught Nathan's eye as he spoke to his Dad. David saw the look and beckoned to him. "Mum, Nathan's dad's waving me over, I'll be back in a sec." "Alright darling," she smiled and walked over to her husband deep in conversation with Jess and Alison.

As Alex strode across the room it made Nathan's heart crash against his ribs again, he couldn't believe he'd just married him. "Hi," he said with a huge grin as Alex reached him and immediately interlaced their fingers once more. David squeezed Alex's shoulder and smiled at him. "I just wanted to say congratulations boys, and thank you for looking after Nathan so well, he really is incredibly happy with you Alex." He held out a hand, " Welcome to the family." Alex shook his hand and grinned at Nathan's teary eyes. "You do realise we're gonna be like this all bloody day don't you !" "Like what ?" David frowned and then looked at his son and rolled his eyes, "not more water works !" Nathan laughed and nudged the tears away before they could fall. His dad put an arm around his shoulders and squeezed, "I'm only teasing son, if you can't get emotional on your wedding day then when can you eh ?" "Thanks Dad," said Nathan quietly and looked at his father with such love and appreciation that it nearly set him off too. "Oh God, don't look at me like that ! You'll have me sobbing in the aisles all over again !"

Nathan laughed. Alex's smile practically reached his ears. To see his beloved so happy and so loved by his family made his heart swell with joy. He slid an arm around Nathan's waist as David excused himself for a moment and disappeared out of the room. Nathan glanced at his watch, "an hour until we mingle with our guests in the orangery and two before food's served, blimey, I'm so hungry !" He moaned. Alex squeezed his waist and gazed into his eyes. "But happy my love ?" "More than you could possibly imagine," he replied and got a soft kiss in return that sent a thrill up his spine. "I'm going to do that all over your body tonight," Alex breathed against his ear, just as David returned with two caterers from the orangery bearing a tray of champagne flutes and another of canapes.

With a glass of champagne and about sixteen canapes a piece inside each of them, the families lolled about in the morning room chatting and laughing until it was time to wander down to the Orangery and meet their guests. Time slipped by so fast with Nathan and Alex loving every minute of it. Sam turned up an hour before everyone else to fulfil his role as photographer. He got some fantastic family group shots outside the front of the building as well as the boys on their own and took one of them holding a pen above the register, grinning with delight. Then he took them both on a 'posing' walk around the back of the mansion and had them sitting and standing in various parts of the garden too. He left them to get set up in the orangery so that he could take a grand entrance shot of them as they walked into the reception, so they wandered slowly back to their families, amazed that it was really happening and beyond happy.

"I can't get my head around the fact that we've just done this." Said Alex, slipping his arm around Nathan's waist as they walked around the side of the building. He looked at Nathan's face and saw him grin hugely and shake his head. "I know, it seems incredible doesn't it." They slowed right down, Nathan's arm, also around Alex, squeezed him gently. "Oh Al, is it really happening to us, this is really now ?" He breathed. Alex turned to face him, wrapping his arms around his back. "Yes," he said, serious for a moment but smiling at him, "and it will forever remain the best day of my life." He pulled Nathan into his body and kissed him deeply. When they parted and looked into each other's eyes, Nathan felt so strong, it was a strength he had never felt before. Because of today he knew he could do anything and that he would never be truly afraid to try new things ever again. He felt invincible.

The rest of the day was magical and passed in a blur of euphoria, walking into the reception holding hands with Alex was one of the most amazing moments of Nathan's life. His cheeks truly hurt as they made their way to the head table among their cheering, grinning loved friends and family. His heart raced with adrenaline when Alex leant over and kissed him as they took their seats, making everyone cheer again. Then there were brief but wonderful speeches from both fathers as well as Sam and Ollie which had everyone howling with laughter and reaching for the tissues in equal measure.

Alex's thigh never detached itself from touching his under the table for the whole meal, and every time Nathan dropped a hand Alex reached for it and sent his heart rate soaring once more. There were messages from family in Australia and Canada, an incredible gift from their class who'd all clubbed together and bought them a Tiffany champagne bucket which came wrapped in the signature pale blue and white packaging. Paul had been picked to present it to the boys and Alex stood up to thank everyone, his voice wavering noticeably with emotion and threatening to set the whole room off, but he and Nathan were truly touched.

They danced and danced all night, the smiles never leaving their faces and sooner than anyone wanted, the time came to go home. Everyone filed out of the reception and down the steps toward the wedding car. Alex had been in charge of that task and it took Nathan a double take to realise what he'd done. It was a dark blue Bentley. "What the...!" He stared from the top of the steps as the last of the guests flowed down them to the gravel and 'oohed,' as they stood beside it. "Shaggy dark blue carpets....?" Nathan whispered. "Ahuh," Alex grinned.

"But Al we can't afford....," Alex shook his head, "it's ok Nate, I know someone and this is a freebie to wish us a happy future." Nathan's jaw dropped open, "Who the hell do you know ?" Alex grinned and slid an arm around his waist, "Uncle Francis. The thing is he's had a movie car hire company for years. They've got four hundred cars over here and 500 out in L.A. Just about every car you see in the movies," - he shrugged, "one of Uncle Fs." Nathan's face was a picture. He stared at the car and shook his head. "Toss, toss, toss....!" Started chanting the crowd all of a sudden. Nathan frowned, "toss ?" Alex laughed, "oh yes, sorry, that's my other surprise," he smiled as his father passed him the flowers from the middle of their table.

"Oh no," Nathan reddened and laughed as Alex passed them to him, "I feel silly.....!" "Come on, it's tradition !" Alex grinned and joined him in holding on to the stems of the bouquet as they turned their backs on the guests who cheered joyously. After a loud '3,2,1' from the crowd, the boys hiked them high into the air. It took a while for the flowers to spin back to earth as Alex had such a strong arm. There was an almighty whoop as Jess, Jasmine and their friends dived to catch them but then uproarious laughter filled the air as the bouquet scrum broke and a dishevelled looking Jack emerged grasping a rather knocked about bunch of flowers. Nathan laughed so hard he had to hold his ribs. Jack scratched his head and looked at the flowers with a mystified expression. "Well that's just bloody typical isn't it !" He shrugged.

Nathan's dad stepped out from behind the boys and clapped his son gently on the shoulder. "Do you mind if I say a quick word son ?" Nathan shook his head. David stepped forward and shushed the guests. "I know the boys didn't want long speeches today, and you've already heard from me once so I'll keep this brief. I just wanted to thank you all from the bottom of my heart for coming and for making this, their wedding day, so special. It's been a truly wonderful celebration, a day that I'm sure they will never forget. I'll finish by asking you to join me in giving three cheers for them both. Hip hip...," everyone hoorayed.

Then Alex stepped forward. He smiled at all their friends and loved ones and his eyes threatened to overspill again. It had been the most amazing experience of his life and to know that everyone had come to share it with he and Nathan blew him away. He gulped at their sea of faces and smiled as he pressed his hands to his heart. "To everyone now standing before us, Nate and I would like to say a big thank you. I know that we've both had the best day of our lives and to have you all here to share in it with us makes it all the more incredible. Thank you so much for coming and I'll leave it there or I might start to blub again. You all mean so much to us that I might not stop !" He beamed back at Nathan, reached over to take his hand and got a kiss in thanks. Everyone cheered again and the boys made their way down the steps into the car. Once inside they could still hear all their guest s clapping and cheering. The Bentley turned away from them and started to head down the drive, their friends from school pretended to be paparazzi and sprinted after them with out stretched phones flashing constantly. Alex laughed and waved. Nathan did too but quickly stopped and said, "what the hell's that noise ?"

"Baked bean tins," said their driver casually. "What ?" They both frowned. "Tied on the back," he answered again. "I believe your brothers and sisters have been collecting them for a few weeks. There's eleven tied to the back, some ribbon too. There were twelve but someone stood on one so there we go." Alex looked at Nathan as they both collapsed with laughter. "Oh my God my cheeks hurt !" Nathan pushed at them with his fingers and then yawned mightily.

"Tired my love ?" Alex asked softly, brushing back his fringe. "Yes," croaked Nathan and leant his head against his shoulder. "That's a shame," Alex whispered. "Not too tired...," said Nathan quickly, his voice muffled against his jacket. Alex felt a thrill run through him and wrapped an arm around him, squeezing him in an unmistakable way. "Oh Nate," he whispered against his hair. Nathan's heart thrummed with anticipation. "How far away from the flat are we ?" He asked, raising his head to meet Alex's eyes.

"Ten minutes, maybe fifteen tops," Alex whispered. "Good," Nathan closed his eyes as Alex covered his lips with his mouth and began to kiss him with pent up longing. "Christ you'd better stop that for a minute," he panted as they pulled away. "I know," Alex thumbed his cheek, "I just can't bloody wait though." "Me neither," Nathan husked and pressed his face against his shoulder again.

Alex cuddled him close. Ten minutes seemed so long in their state and they were silent, almost holding their breaths until the car came to a stop outside the flat. Nathan looked up at the building, his stomach leapt with nerves all of a sudden. Then they were on the pavement, keys in hand and waving the driver off with profuse thanks. Alex turned his eyes back to Nathan's, glad to see the same mix of emotion in them as his own, nerves, breathlessness but most of all, the passionate need to be naked and alone with each other instantly. He reached for his hand and they ran upstairs. They didn't stop running until inside the flat. No curtains were closed, so moonlight flooded every room. They dropped their clothes where they stood and ran to the bedroom, gliding immediately under the duvet and reaching out for each other. Nathan thought his heart would burst with longing in those brief seconds until their skins touched and his head flung back.

It was like an electric shock, always like this with Alex, as soon as his warm taut skin brushed his own, it ignited such a passion in Nathan and tonight it burned through him like wildfire. He groaned aloud as Alex folded him into his embrace, clutching him up against his body and moaning in ecstasy. "Oh Nath, Nath," he groaned, finding his mouth and pressing his tongue inside. He clasped at Nathan's round firm bottom with his hands, squeezing and pulling his body in close, every part touching. "Oh my God," Nathan panted and squirmed against him. Nothing mattered but this, being up against his lover, feeling his hardness thrust against his belly and groin.

Moaning such guttural throaty noises, Nathan's head spun as Alex found his mouth again and curled his arms all the way around him, rolling him over in his embrace until Nathan lay on top of him. Every touch nearly sent Nathan over the edge. He gasped down at Alex's foggy eyed expression, "if we do anything else at all I'm gonna cum immediately," he said through ragged breaths. Alex nodded and stroked his face, "me too," he panted. They rolled over again and somehow Nathan found himself straddling Alex's body. They gazed at each other, both knowing what the other longed for. Nathan licked his palm all over, his eyes never leaving Alex's. He wrapped his hand around him and felt Alex almost explode beneath him. "Not yet," he whispered and positioned himself to slide slowly onto him.

There wasn't time to say anything else. Alex groaned and with one big grunt, exploded inside him. He gasped for air as he thrust his hips upward and clamped his hands down on Nathan's thighs when he made to move. "Stay there," he pleaded. Nathan, so breathless and close himself rotated his hips. It just made Alex harder. "Fuck !" He gasped, locked his arms around Nathan's body and rolled him underneath, still together. Nathan closed his eyes and pressed his head back into the pillows, he didn't care about anything but the feeling of Alex pumping into him. "Oh Christ, oh Christ," he panted. Alex reached for his rigid cock and curled his fingers around it, but as soon as he began to move his hand, Nathan let out a contorted scream and came like never before. He clutched at Alex's forearm with his hand, feeling the cold metal on his wedding ring rub against him. His head swam with dizzying mind blowing pleasure as Alex tensed and exploded again, gasping and thrusting at him, burying his head against the skin of his shoulder. Nathan wrapped his arms around him and kissed his temple then lay back in the bed to recover as they gasped together, sweaty, sated and amazed.

At last Alex raised himself up on his arms and looked down at Nathan. He blinked slowly as his eyes took in every inch of him, admiring his every contour. He cupped his palm to his cheek. Nathan put his hand to Alex's chest, enjoying the feel of his heart beating through his warm flesh. Alex bent low and kissed him gently on the lips. "How are you my love ?" He whispered as he drew away again, smiling down at him.

Nathan beamed his killer watt smile. "I feel the best !" He whispered back. Alex grinned and stroked his face. He manoeuvred to lie beside him and patted the duvet close about his body. Nathan wriggled around to face him as they lay their arms across one another, looking into each others eyes in the moonlit darkness, he sighed happily. Alex's eyes searched his face, "I love you very much," he whispered. Nathan beamed with pleasure and blinked his lovely long eye lashes. "You do ?" Alex nodded as his cheeks hunched up into a great big grin again, "I really do," he breathed. He found Nathan's left hand and joined their fingers. He deliberately jiggled the wedding band on his ring finger and loved how it made his eyes sparkle and a little laugh escape him. "I love holding your hand, and I loved putting this on you today too," he jiggled the ring again. Nathan blushed and laughed at the enormous tingle of pleasure that went up his spine.

"I loved putting yours on you," he replied, searching suddenly for Alex's other hand under the duvet. They shuffled around until they could easily put both hands palm to palm.

"And palm to palm is holy palmer's kiss," whispered Nathan. "What ?" Alex sounded confused. "It's from Romeo and Juliet, when they're being a bit coy with each other though clearly in love. They hold hands like this and she says, "let lips do what palms do." Alex raised his eyebrows, "does she now ? Well if it's good enough for Shakespeare, then it's good enough for us. Come here my love," he husked with sudden longing in his eyes once more as he reached out and pulled Nathan back into his arms. "I will never, never get tired of doing this," he whispered, thumbing his cheek and covering his mouth with gentle kisses.

In the morning, Nathan woke up squinting against the daylight. His slight groan woke Alex who took one look at his scrunched up eyes and jumped out of bed to shut the curtains. He slid back under the duvet with a grin and slipped both arms around Nathan's warm ribs. They both sighed and snuggled up against each other. "God that feels good," Nathan croaked with sleep. Alex chuckled softly. "It does doesn't it." He kissed the top of his head. "But it's too early yet my love, go back to sleep." "Ok," husked Nathan and murmured softly against Alex's chest as he drifted off into a deep peaceful slumber.

The next time he woke, Nathan still felt tired, but more awake. He sat up against the headboard and wondered where Alex was as he rubbed his eyes and yawned getting his bearings. He yawned again and tucked the duvet around his hips, crossing his arms across his bare chest. He heard footsteps and then the door pushed open and Alex came in bearing a tray with coffee, toast and orange juice. Nathan grinned to see him and loved the proud look on his face as he brought the tray to the bed and set it down in the middle. He climbed in carefully, he was wearing a t-shirt and pj bottoms, he nodded at Nathan, "Do you want some clothes ?"

Nathan shook his head and drew the crumpled duvet up his chest as far as it would go. "No, this, you and a coffee will do me," he smiled. Alex beamed at him and leant over to kiss his mouth, "morning beautiful." Nathan beamed back at him and took hold of his left hand, fingering the wedding band for a moment. He blushed with pleasure as he looked at it and smiled back up at Alex's thrilled expression. "I know, it's wonderful that we've done it isn't it ?" Alex breathed.

"I can't quite believe it isn't all a dream yet !" Nathan grinned with shining eyes. "It isn't a dream, it's really us," Alex replied, handing him a plate of toast, buttered and jammed, just as he liked it. "I know," Nathan took a bite and watched Alex pouring out coffee. "We're going on honeymoon today !" He gasped excitedly. Alex chuckled softly and took hold of his hand again as they both bit into their toast.

"If you'd told me six months ago that I'd be here, married today and living in my first home, about to go on honeymoon, I wouldn't have believed you but it's all true and I've never been so happy in my life Nate," Alex declared. Nathan beamed with joy. He laid his head back against the bed as he looked at him. With their hands joined, sunshine filling the room and food in his belly, he too had never known such happiness. "I've asked before, and I'll ask it again Al, what did I do to get this lucky ?"

Alex picked up a glass of orange juice and handed it to him before glancing at the big clock that ticked away silently above the bedroom door, a wedding present from Nathan's parents. They had hours yet until they had to head to the airport. He sipped his coffee and looked into Nathan's eyes. "What did you do to get so lucky ?" His face looked so content as he answered, "you just wanted it Nate, wanted it and deserved it and you were born into a wonderful family of generous loving people. How I got so lucky on the other hand is a different matter entirely," he shrugged, making Nathan laugh, "but maybe after a life time of loving you I'll be able to find the answer to that one. Maybe, just maybe."

Twenty years later:

A light breeze ruffled Alex's hair as he trod carefully across the rocky surface and slid in behind Nathan, wrapping both arms around his body and both legs on either side of his. The ground was warm underneath him having absorbed a lot of the suns rays. He turned his face up toward the heat and held Nathan close to his chest. It sent a thrill up his spine when Nathan pressed his cheek against his heart and groaned sleepily. He lay both arms on top of Alex's and squeezed gently. Alex closed his eyes and let out a shuddering breath.

"God Nate, I love it when you do that." Nathan chuckled softly, "and that," Alex breathed into his hair before kissing his head. They were silent for a moment and then both opened their eyes to look out across the Veld. From their mountainous view point it was simply stunning, copper red ground and shimmering heat stretched before them to the horizon. "Wow," whispered Alex, sliding his sunglasses back across his eyes. "Ditto," murmured Nathan doing the same.

Alex rubbed his thumb on Nathan's forearm, "your skin still feels so soft you know, even after all this time." "Well duh ! I'm 38 not 98 thanks !" Nathan laughed. Alex grinned behind him. "Yeah I know, you still look fucking hot actually." Nathan giggled, it rumbled against Alex's chest, then he sat up and shifted round to face him. Alex leant in and kissed him, cupping his cheek with his palm. "Your face is really warm love, don't get burnt," he frowned.

Nathan's face split into his killer watt smile, "you'll always worry about me won't you," he grinned, picking up Alex's hand and interlacing their fingers. "Always," smiled Alex, sliding his hand through Nathan's hair. They sat, holding hands, jeaned, tanned and happy, just looking at each other in the warmth. Alex looked Nathan up and down, he was still such a fine looking guy. Lean, athletic, a few grey hairs coming through but not many. He sat beaming at Alex in rugged scuffed jeans with pale thigh panels and a summer lumberjack shirt in lavender, white, dark pink and turquoise checks. It looked incredible on him and showed off his tanned torso, unbuttoned at the neck. Every time Alex looked at him dressed like that he wanted to lick him at the base of the throat. He grinned at the thought.

"What are you smiling about now ?" Nathan asked with an eyebrow raise. "Oh, nothing," shrugged Alex. "Yeah that'll be the day," Nathan laughed.

Alex lay back across the sun warmed rocky ground. Nathan crawled across him on his hands and knees, sinking his body down to lie tucked up beside him, nestling in the crook of his arm with the other hand stretched out across his chest. Alex held it, rubbing his skin softly. It felt lovely and Nathan shut his eyes. He could stay like this for a long time. Eventually Alex sighed, "you know what Nath, my life with you has been so amazing, I couldn't have asked for anything better." Nathan raised his head, "what do you mean 'has been,' are you going somewhere ?" "No," Alex chuckled.

Nathan lay his head back down against him and murmured softly again, it really was heavenly cuddling together in the sun. "But would you like 'us' to ?" Alex suddenly asked. "Would I like us to what ?" Nathan propped himself up onto his elbow and Alex turned to face him doing the same. "Would you like us to go somewhere ?" Nathan frowned, "but we are Al, we're here in South Africa for our anniversary, look, little clue, heat, lovely scenery....see, not home !" Alex laughed at his description, gently shoving his shoulder. "Yes very funny, I know we're on holiday but I mean how about we move. How about we move to another country ?" Nathan lifted up his shades and squinted at him, "you're serious aren't you ?" Alex nodded and sat up, clapping his hands together to brush some grit off.

Nathan joined him and started to feel a little tingle run through him, he loved it when Alex had an idea. "Go on," he encouraged. "Ok, well look at our lives right now. We have the house," "I know, I still can't believe your mum and dad let us live there," Nathan interrupted. "Well yes but it's not rent free is it, we did take over the mortgage." "Even so," shrugged Nathan, it's a pretty amazing deal they gave us." Alex nodded, "I know but it does make sense for them to move somewhere smaller and they're so happy in our flat, Mum did always secretly covet that bathroom." Nathan's lip turned up at the corner at he cut in again, "yeah, even if she did paint it 'mint green,' ugh !" Alex laughed and took his hands, "shush, I'm trying to tell you my plan dopey !" "Ok, ok," Nathan grinned and zipped his mouth shut. Alex continued.

"We have the house. Mum and dad live in our flat which they are buying off us. We have the mortgage to finish paying, it's got five years left to go then its done. However, we have the cafe too and it's going SO well lately Nate, you know that." Nathan nodded.

"So why don't we do this, sell the cafe, rent out the house, buy up a going concern abroad and run 'Nate's Place,' out there !" Nathan rubbed a finger across his lips in thought and then smiled at him, "so do this all again, just somewhere new and maybe hot ?" Alex nodded excitedly, "definitely hot !" He beamed. Nathan looked excited too, "ok, I'm liking the sound of this, but where Al ?"

Alex pushed his sunglasses into his hair and squinted directly into Nathan's eyes, "Australia." He said. Nathan stared at him. "Christ !" He whispered. Alex looked anxious, his heart thumped in his chest. Nathan rubbed his chin and thought as he squinted off into the distance for a little while. Alex looked down at his hands, almost holding his breath as he waited. "Alright," said Nathan eventually, "let's do it."

Alex's eyes shot up to his, "really ? You really want to do it ?" Nathan nodded with a grin, "I'll go anywhere with you Alex, you know that, and it's a good plan." "Oh my God, thank you, thank you my darling," Alex launched himself at Nathan, clutching him with both arms making him laugh out loud and pushing him gently back across the warm ground. He gazed into his eyes and sank his hips down to meet Nathan's. It made Nathan rasp out a shuddering breath.

"God your body," he groaned as Alex's lips touched his. When Alex pulled away and looked down at him, thumbing his cheek and sending shivers of pleasure running all over him, Nathan reached up and caressed him softly too. "I love you so much Al," he whispered. Alex picked up his hand and kissed the palm, "it can't be as much as I love you Nate, it just can't," he breathed. "Thank you for saying yes." Nathan smiled up at him, "I'd go anywhere with you my love, I mean that." Alex grinned and caressed him still. "Just one more thing though, I think we should call it 'Nate's Diner.' 'Nate's Place,' sounds a bit old fashioned now, what do you think ?"

Nathan exhaled slowly, thoughtfully. "That's great Al but what about you, isn't it time we put your name in it too ?" Alex shook his head, "I don't need that, I have you as my husband every day and that's all that matters." Nathan smiled up at him, "thanks," he said shyly as his cheeks tinged with red. It made Alex's heart turn over with joy, he would never tire of seeing that flush come to his cheeks.

"I've asked it before Nate, and I'll ask it again, how come I got to have you all to myself. How did I get so lucky ?" Nathan laughed under him, it reverberated up through Alex making his body react. He bent and kissed him once more and pulled away to stroke his warm cheeks. "Twenty years ago I remember waking up together in our flat for the first time and I said maybe in a lifetime of loving you I'd be able to answer that, do you remember ?"

Nathan nodded gently, thrilled at the memory, "how could I forget. And have you found the answer now ?" He breathed. Alex moved his shades carefully back into his hair and gazed down into his beautiful eyes. "Well I'm only part way through my lifetime of loving you Nate, how about I let you know at the end ?" He whispered softly. "Suits me," breathed Nathan happily, curling his arms around his back as their lips met.

The delicious sun warmed their skins and a light breeze ruffled their hair as Alex kissed him on and on, groaning with pleasure at the love of his life encased safely in his arms.

THE END.